Burning Embers

An Alexis Parker novel

G.K. Parks

Copyright © 2020 G.K. Parks

A Modus Operandi imprint

All rights reserved.

ISBN:
ISBN-13: 978-1-942710-19-6

For my mom and dad

BOOKS IN THE LIV DEMARCO SERIES:

Dangerous Stakes
Operation Stakeout
Unforeseen Danger
Deadly Dealings

BOOKS IN THE ALEXIS PARKER SERIES:

Outcomes and Perspective
Likely Suspects
The Warhol Incident
Mimicry of Banshees
Suspicion of Murder
Racing Through Darkness
Camels and Corpses
Lack of Jurisdiction
Dying for a Fix
Intended Target
Muffled Echoes
Crisis of Conscience
Misplaced Trust
Whitewashed Lies
On Tilt
Purview of Flashbulbs
The Long Game
Burning Embers
Thick Fog

BOOKS IN THE JULIAN MERCER SERIES:

Condemned
Betrayal
Subversion
Reparation
Retaliation

ONE

I leaned over the railing and watched the lights flash across the stage below. Normally, live music and crowded clubs weren't my scene, but this was a special occasion. Detective Nick O'Connell and his wife Jen swayed gently to the beat a few feet away. I had never seen Nick so enamored. The detective caught my eye and leaned closer, shouting over the music, "Jen wants to get closer for the encore. We'll meet you out front when the concert ends."

"Have fun," I shouted back, nodding in case he couldn't hear me.

James Martin wrapped his arms tighter around my waist and brushed his lips against my ear. "Do you think they're having a good time?"

I turned to face him. "I think so. This was really nice of you."

He smirked. "Well, I'm a nice guy, and since their anniversary was last week, I thought we should take them someplace special. Jenny said they danced to this song at their wedding." He nodded at the stage. "Of course, it wasn't a cover. And they had a DJ, but," he shrugged, "close enough."

My forehead crinkled. "How do you know that? Are you stalking them? Did you steal their wedding video?"

Martin laughed. "It's because I pay attention. Jen told us this last month when we went out to dinner. She used it as an excuse to wheedle details out of Nick. She wanted to know what he planned for their anniversary."

"I must have missed it." I hadn't been in the right frame of mind to pay attention to most things. I was just surprised Martin had. I ran my hands through his dark brown hair, smoothing down some of the wayward locks. Now that Nick and Jen left, the balcony was empty. We were alone. I stood on my tiptoes and kissed him.

"It's been a rough two months, Alex." Martin pulled me close and hugged me. "But we'll be okay."

"Yeah." At least, I didn't have to pretend to give a shit about the band anymore. Martin was uncharacteristically quiet, so I knew something was on his mind. "What are you thinking?"

"At first, I was thinking I want what they have." He pointed to the spot Nick and Jen found near the stage, and I watched them dance. Knowing Nick, he was probably thinking about pickpockets and drug dealers. That's what I would be thinking about. "But then I realized, we already have it and more." Martin nuzzled my neck.

"I love you."

"I know." He smiled. "And you're all I need."

"You're just saying that because I have better taste in music than they do."

"That's debatable." He nudged me with his shoulder. "Come on, let's go."

"You don't want to wait 'til the end?"

He gave me a knowing look. "You've been itching to escape since the moment we arrived. I thought the private balcony would help, but you're obviously not comfortable here. We'll meet them outside."

Martin led the way down the steps and out a side exit. He nodded to the bouncer on the way out. I wasn't sure how he'd gotten us the VIP treatment, but being a CEO meant Martin had plenty of contacts and his job and wealth afforded him a lot of perks, which he was always willing to share.

The cool night breeze eased the pounding in my head,

and I inhaled deeply, relieved to be away from the recycled indoor air. Even though the club no longer allowed smoking, the years of cigarette smoke continued to linger in the walls and furniture. I removed the earplugs, watching as Martin did the same. For a man who loved to blast rock music, he surprised me by taking steps to safeguard his hearing.

Even with the earplugs out, everything still sounded muted. Half a dozen food trucks lined the streets near the club. They knew they'd make a killing off the drunks searching for sustenance after the concert and the few of us who remained sober but were now starving. Not that I was speaking personally.

Martin clicked a few buttons on his phone and looked up. The glossy black of his town car stood out against the bulky, light colored trucks lining the streets. "Why don't you grab a table before the club empties? I'll get the champagne from the car."

"Martin, you're talking about Nick and Jen. They'd be happy with beer from a can."

"Jen would prefer champagne."

"Fine, but when Nick kicks your ass for flirting with his wife, don't expect me to intervene."

"Do you think I'm flirting with her?"

"Yeah, but I'm used to it. You're always so damn charming. You flirt with everyone. I saw you making eyes at the bouncer. You just can't help yourself." I jerked my head toward the car. "Go get the champagne. I'll be waiting." He turned, and I called to him, "If you're lucky, I'll let you charm the pants off me when we get home."

He turned back around, a devilish glint reflecting in his green irises. "Maybe we should ditch the O'Connells. They don't need us chaperoning their date."

"I thought you said you were a nice guy." I walked backward toward the picnic tables set up in the vacant lot at the side of the club, never taking my eyes off him.

"I am, unless you'd prefer a bad boy tonight."

I rolled my eyes, but I couldn't wipe the smile off my face. For once, things felt normal. I hadn't seen normal in so long, I barely remembered what it looked like. But it looked damn good. "I just want you, handsome."

Pleased, Martin grinned and jogged to the car. I turned around before I tripped over my own feet and headed for the closest picnic table. Two dozen round, plastic-coated tables were crammed together, blocked on three sides by the tour bus, an equipment van, and one industrious food truck which partially blocked the street exit.

Taking a seat, I read the sign on the truck, *Easton's Eats*. It didn't tell me anything about the cuisine, but I assumed the man inside the truck was Easton. He wiped his brow with his forearm as he completed the prep work. He finished chopping what might have been onions. From this distance and angle, I couldn't be sure, and then he went to the back door, cracked it open, and glanced out. He looked nervous. Maybe he was afraid of getting ticketed or having to move once the band was ready to leave.

Martin slid into the seat beside me and placed the champagne bucket on the table. "What's wrong?"

"Nothing."

He followed my gaze to the truck. "Do you know who that is?"

"Some guy named Easton."

"Chef Easton," Martin corrected. "He's supposed to be incredible. He's in the running for a Michelin star."

"The food truck guy?"

Martin squinted at the truck. "That's him."

I gave Martin a suspicious look. "Did you plan this?"

He held up his palms. "I swear I had no idea. I just checked the food truck app, but there's no mention of him. It must be one of those secret pop-ups chefs do sometimes when they want to experiment with the menu or gain a new following." Martin glanced at the tour bus. "Maybe the band hired him. I should find out if he caters."

Before Martin could cross the lot, the club doors opened, breaking the serenity. The rumble of the crowd grew louder as more and more people filed out. Lines started forming at the other trucks, and the surrounding tables quickly filled with our fellow concert-goers. Martin dropped back into his chair, waving to Nick and Jen, who pushed their way through the crowd. The line grew in front of Easton's Eats, snaking around the clustered tables. Even from this distance, I felt the anxiety radiating off the chef. Something wasn't right.

"James, Alexis, thank you so much," Jen gushed. She brushed the damp tendrils of hair out of her face and reached back to redo her ponytail. "That was a blast. That's the best gift anyone has ever given us."

"You're welcome," Martin said. "We're glad you had fun."

"You never told me you danced, Nick. What was that? Salsa? Mambo?" My gaze darted from Nick's face back to the chef. Maybe I was projecting my anxiety onto the man.

"You're always such a buster, Parker," Nick muttered, but I recognized his playful tone instantly. "Don't be jealous of my moves." O'Connell put an arm around his wife. "Seriously, though, thanks. This brought back a lot of memories." He kissed his wife and eyed the champagne. "Not to sound ungrateful, but don't you think that's a little cheesy?"

"Nick," Jen elbowed him, "be nice."

"I tried to tell Martin you'd be happy with beer from a can, but he wouldn't listen," I said.

"I do prefer longnecks, but a can's fine too." Nick winced as Jen dug her nails into his arm.

"We can't take these two anywhere," Jen said to Martin. "Just ignore him. This is lovely, but you shouldn't have gone to this much trouble."

"It's nothing, really." Martin chuckled. "Plus, assuming we're eating something Chef Easton prepared, the champagne will be the perfect accompaniment, unless you have your heart set on a beer. Then I'll grab you a beer, Nick."

"Nah, man. This is great. I was just giving Alex a hard time."

"Yeah, someone ought to." Martin squeezed my side, and I gave him a sideways look, knowing the wordplay running through his mind without him having to say it. "Are you guys game for some of Easton's Eats?"

"I've heard great things about him," Jen said. "How about James and I get the food while the two of you hold our table?" She leaned over and kissed her husband. "If people try to steal our chairs, you can threaten to arrest them."

"Okay."

Martin zeroed in on me. "What would you like?"

"Surprise me."

Our conversation from earlier returned to his mind. "I intend to."

Nick watched Martin and Jen get in line while I stared at the chef. He was busy filling orders, but he kept sneaking glances out the back door. The hair at the back of my neck prickled, and I tore my eyes away from him and studied the crowd. They were clueless. Even the drunks didn't appear belligerent. The concert had mellowed them. A few were even singing quietly or humming. I wasn't used to being around such happy people; it freaked me out.

"What is it?" Nick asked.

"I don't know. I'm getting a weird vibe."

"Me too."

His words increased my anxiety tenfold, and I turned to check the street. The picnic tables left us out in the open and completely exposed. Threats could come from anywhere.

I scanned the row of food trucks. Each had a line, but those crowds seemed just as docile as this one. Maybe I was losing it. But Nick felt it too, and even if my private investigator instincts were on the fritz from recent disuse, Nick's cop instincts should be spot-on.

"I think it's our chef." I jerked my chin at the food truck parked in front of us. "He's nervous."

"You're right. I'll go around the side and see what he's looking at through the back door. Stay here and guard our table." He walked away before I had a chance to protest.

I kept my focus on Nick as my hand drifted to my purse and slipped inside. Dammit, my gun was in the car. Club security wouldn't allow me inside with it, and since I didn't possess federal agent credentials anymore, they wouldn't make an exception. At least O'Connell had his off-duty piece with him.

He returned a moment later. "I don't know. I didn't see

anyone suspicious nearby, but it's too crowded to tell. Maybe we should wait and see how it plays out."

"With your wife and Martin here?" I didn't like the possibilities going through my mind.

O'Connell glanced back at the bouncers who were now keeping tabs on the growing line of fans congregating near the rear exit. Between club security and the band's personal bodyguards, the chance of a legitimate threat decreased substantially, but more people meant more chances for violence to break out. One person with a gun or knife could cause a lot of damage in a short amount of time.

"I don't like it either." He reached for his phone. "I'll ask dispatch to send some units to work crowd control. If someone is planning something, that should make him think twice."

I studied the crowd, the cars on the street, and the other food trucks. The only person exhibiting suspicious behavior was Chef Easton. "Why is he so nervous? Do you think he's planning an attack? He could have anything inside that truck." Thoughts of exploding food carts went through my mind. That happened during the first case Nick and I worked together. It's how we met.

"Maybe he's not used to working such a large crowd on his own. Didn't Martin say he's a legit chef? Like poofy hat, white jacket wearing chef?"

"So?"

"They usually have staff and helpers." Nick fell silent. Neither of us believed that was it, but before we could continue our paranoid musings, Jen and Martin returned with our food. "Hey, hun, this looks great. Any problems ordering?"

"None. You wanted the cricket burrito, right? I thought you pointed to it when you went to read the menu at the side of the truck."

"Hell no." Her teasing demanded Nick's full attention, and he carefully unwrapped the fanciest burrito I had ever seen and checked the contents. "Was that a joke?"

Jen giggled and dug her fork into her plate of scallopini. "We've been married ten years, and you actually believe I'd feed you crickets?"

"I wouldn't put it past you, woman, especially if you read a medical study saying crickets are healthy."

"They are healthy," I said, my eyes roaming the area, "and good for the planet. Eat up."

Martin put the tray down and studied me. "Alex, what is it? What's wrong?" He knew me better than anyone and could read my body language like a children's book.

"I don't know."

He took a seat and scooted closer. "Talk to me."

"It's nothing." I shook my head and reached for a fork. "What are we eating?"

"Vegan ceviche." Martin didn't believe it was nothing.

"No crickets?" I asked, watching as the crowd lessened.

Martin grinned. "Relax, Nick. Crickets weren't on the menu. Jenny's just pulling your leg."

Jen gave Martin an annoyed look. "You're no fun."

"Good." Nick rolled up his fancy burrito, which probably wasn't actually a burrito, and took a bite. A patrol car went down the street, and he gave me a pointed look. He surveyed the crowd. I kept my focus on the chef, but the car had no effect.

As the crowd dwindled, and the band slipped out of the club and into their tour bus, the area cleared. A few uniformed officers arrived to check on the few who remained and made sure none of the drunks drove home. No shots were fired, and they didn't find anyone suspicious enough to hassle.

Three of the food trucks pulled away, and I watched Easton fill a few sacks with food and hand them to a tall man with an earpiece. Based on the tight black t-shirt and crewcut, he had to be security. He took the bags and entered the bus. One of the cops placed an order, dropped by our table to say hello to O'Connell, and went on his way.

"What was that about?" Jen asked, suspicious of her husband. "Did you call for backup?"

"My fault," I interjected. "Something just doesn't feel right. It's probably anxiety."

Jen offered a tight smile. "I didn't want to ask. How are you holding up? After everything that happened, it's normal to be anxious."

"I'm okay, I guess." As another truck pulled away, I spotted a camera lens pointed out the window of a silver sedan. "Nick, check out my four o'clock."

Nick looked over my right shoulder. "Fuck." He turned to his wife, but before he could say anything, Martin caught on to the situation.

"We'll go wait in my car," Martin said. His eyes found mine. "Be careful." He glanced at O'Connell; their unspoken agreement was so loud it was practically audible.

After grabbing my gun out of the car, I took up a position beside Nick. "Parker, stay behind me," O'Connell ordered as we crept down the block and crossed the street, coming up behind the shutterbug. O'Connell tapped on the window with his badge. "Police. Roll down your window, and let me see your hands."

Instead, the driver hit the gas. Nick jumped back as the car rolled forward, gaining speed. I tried to make out the license plate, but the light above the plate had burned out. Whether intentionally or accidentally, I didn't know. The smell of burning rubber and screeching tires caught everyone's attention, and I watched Chef Easton dive for cover inside the food truck.

While O'Connell called in a description of the car, I returned to the food truck and knocked on the window. The chef cowered next to the grill, hugging his knees to his chest. He looked up at me. "We're closed."

"I'm not here for dinner. Although, the ceviche was excellent." I gave him a friendly, reassuring smile. "Is everything okay?"

He gulped and climbed to his knees, peering out the window before standing up. "Okay's not the word I'd use."

O'Connell joined us and badged the chef. "What's going on?"

Easton glanced around. "Not much, officer. Someone just threatened to kill me."

TWO

"O'Connell, come on." I let out a frustrated huff. "There has to be something you can do."

"Like what?" Nick glanced back at Easton, who busied himself cleaning the grill. "He won't give me any details. He said he filed a police report but no one took him seriously. He hasn't committed any crimes, as far as I'm aware. So what do you want me to do? I can't force him to speak to me."

"Fine." I glanced at Martin's waiting town car. Another otherwise perfectly normal evening had been ruined. "What about the car and driver?"

"Did you get a plate?"

"No."

"Neither did I, but dispatch has a description. If a patrol unit spots it, they'll have cause to pull it over, given the busted lights in the back. I'm just not holding my breath." He jerked his chin at Easton. "Maybe you can get him to confide in you." Nick clapped me on the shoulder. "Thanks for the lovely evening. Next date night, let's stay in."

"Tell that to Martin and Jen." But after tonight, I had a feeling Jen wouldn't pester us to go on any more double dates, and Martin would gladly stay locked at home with me.

I watched Jen climb out of the car and give Martin a friendly peck on the cheek. She waved to me, and I waved back. Surprisingly, she didn't look upset. Nick shook hands with Martin, cocked his head to the side, and offered an encouraging smile before taking his wife's hand and leading her to their parked car. After they drove away, I turned my attention back to Chef Easton.

"I'm closing up for the night," Easton said. "Thanks for your concern, but I'm taking care of this matter."

"You should talk to the cops. They can help."

"I tried that, and they didn't do a damn thing. I'm not wasting my time again. I have too much to do as it is." He wiped the counter. "Why do you care so much?"

"Hazard of the job." I slid one of my Cross Security business cards through the pick-up window. "In case you change your mind or want to explore an alternative solution, give me a call."

He picked it up and snickered. "Wow. I'm impressed."

Confused, I waited for him to elaborate, but he lowered the shutter. I trudged back to the car and slid into the back seat beside Martin. "I'm sorry."

"You don't need to apologize. Shit happens. A lot." Martin told his driver to take us home. Once the car was in motion, he put up the privacy screen.

"Yeah, to me. Shit happens to me. To us. I look for trouble."

Martin laughed bitterly. "Yeah, you do. And when you don't, it looks for you. So what's the deal?"

"I don't know. Easton said he received a death threat."

"From the guy in the car?"

"I don't know. We didn't exactly get a chance to question him, but given the way he peeled out, I assume he must have something to do with it."

"What are the police doing?"

"Whatever they can. So nothing. Nick said he'd look into the matter tomorrow, but I don't think he'll find much. Easton said he reported the threat, but the police didn't take him seriously. At this point, he just wants to be left alone."

"What about the car?"

"We didn't get the plate."

"Do you think we were in danger tonight?"

"It's possible."

"I hate this." He stared at the partition in front of us. He couldn't even look at me. "What if the asshole in the car was there for you?"

"Martin, c'mon, that's just paranoia talking."

"No, Alex," he turned to face me, "I'm serious. People have been determined to hurt you since the moment we met. Why would tonight be any different? What if he was watching you? What if he had a gun or planned to abduct you?"

"Haven't we been there done that?"

He ignored me. "I didn't even realize anything was wrong until I came back to the table and saw the look on your face. God." He shook his head. "I used every connection I had to go through tactical training with the police department's elite unit just to prove to you I could take care of myself, and I didn't learn a damn thing."

"So you can't take care of yourself?"

Martin sighed. "You know what I mean. I should be more cognizant of potential threats, the way you and Nick are."

"You're not a cop, Martin. You didn't grow up on the streets. You grew up in a world where people are decent and civilized, where business meetings are conducted in a boardroom and end with a handshake. When things take a turn for the worse, you face a fleet of process servers and legal battles, not violent and dangerous individuals. You have no reason to notice these things or assume the worst."

"Don't I?" His eyes met mine. "You're not the only one with scars. Do you want to compare gunshot wounds? I think we're tied." He stared out the window and exhaled, fogging the glass in the process. "I'm sorry. I shouldn't have said that. I'm not mad at you. I'm just annoyed at myself. I should have noticed something was wrong. I should have done something." He rubbed his forehead and exhaled again.

"What would you have done?"

"For starters, eaten at a different food truck."

"The food wasn't so bad. Plus, the look on Nick's face when Jen told him it was crickets, that was priceless."

Martin chuckled, but it seemed forced. "That was pretty funny."

"Was Jen angry Nick and I spoiled her evening?"

"No. She's used to it. She's been married to a cop for years. At some point, it must get easier."

"It doesn't sound like you agree."

"We're not married, Alex. How would I know? And let's not forget, you aren't a cop."

"Now you sound like my boss. Lucien Cross tends to point that out quite frequently, too. It's probably why he hasn't handed me a case in over a month. The bastard hates cops and won't have anything to do with them. He wants to punish me for bringing my last three cases to the attention of law enforcement. It's no wonder he can't stand me. He and Chef Easton would get along great."

Martin stared out the window. "I don't think that's the reason Cross hasn't assigned you any new cases." Martin exhaled again and drew a smiley face on the fogged glass. "I might have misread the situation at the food truck, but I know we're headed into deadly waters with this conversation." He nudged me and pointed at the smiley face, making sure I noticed it. "No more shoptalk. I know exactly how to salvage our night." He lifted my hand to his lips and kissed my knuckles. "Didn't you say something earlier about how charming I am?"

I snorted, remembering why I thought Martin had a mood swing disorder.

*   *   *

"Alex." Martin shook me awake. "Hey, beautiful, open your eyes. You have to get dressed."

"What?" I squinted against the harsh overhead lights and cringed when another shrill beep sounded. "What is that noise?"

"Fire alarm." Martin tugged on his jeans.

"Is the building on fire?" I blinked, wishing we could

turn off the wailing siren. My brain was fuzzy from sleep. *Think, Parker, think.*

"I don't think so. I don't smell smoke, but I doubt they'd have a drill at this time of night. I'll find out." He left the bedroom and went to the intercom at our front door.

I dressed in the first thing I found, slipped on my sneakers, and grabbed my jacket. Martin and I almost collided in the doorway. He grabbed my shoulders, and I knew he hadn't slept a wink all night. He was too calm and far too awake.

"The concierge says there was a toaster oven fire on fourteen. It set off the alarms. The fire's out, but we have to evacuate until the fire department checks the building. You should probably grab whatever you need for work. We'll be locked out for a few hours, maybe longer."

"Okay." I rubbed my eyes and returned to the bedroom.

Opening the closet, I grabbed a handful of hangers. Almost everything I owned was inside this apartment. In the event it burned to the ground, I'd need enough work clothes to get me through the week. Martin, on the other hand, slipped his suit, tie, and shirt into a garment bag and grabbed his briefcase. Most of his belongings were at his house, so he didn't have much to worry about.

"Grab my gun out of the drawer," I said. "And don't forget the box of ammo. Fires. Bullets. Bad mix." He tucked them into the duffel bag and zipped it. I grabbed my car keys, and he locked the door behind us. "Hell of a night for this to happen," I mumbled, opening the door to the stairwell.

Twenty-one flights later, we reached the lobby. "Let me drive, Alex. You look tired." Martin took the keys from my hand, thanked the concierge for the heads up, and led the way to the parking garage across the street. "Your place or mine?"

"My apartment's closer to work."

"Yours it is." Martin turned the key in the ignition, checked the mirrors, and pulled out of the space.

The excitement from the abrupt wake-up didn't last long, and my eyelids drooped. I curled up on the seat and focused on Martin. "Were you asleep when the fire alarm sounded?"

"No."

"I thought you'd be exhausted. You wore me out. Sex for us is a competitive sport. We could compete in the Olympics."

"Did I score the gold?" Martin smiled appreciatively. "You definitely did."

"You would have, but your dismount was sloppy. The judges would hold that against you on a technicality."

"My hip cramped at the end, but I didn't think it affected my overall performance."

"I'm pleased to tell you it did not."

He glanced at me and winked. "Good." He drove one-handed, using his free hand to reach for mine.

I fought to keep my eyes open. By the time he parked outside my apartment building, I had fallen asleep. The sudden lack of motion woke me, and I looked around, confused and barely coherent.

We trudged up the six flights, and Martin unlocked the door. I dropped everything onto the couch in the living room and stubbed my toe on one of the moving boxes on my way to the bedroom. Shedding my clothes, I dropped onto the mattress and wrapped my arms around the pillow.

Martin followed suit and climbed into bed beside me. "Come here," he coaxed, and I traded the pillow for his chest. He traced random patterns on my back, but I was asleep before he even completed a figure eight.

When I awoke a few hours later, I was alone. My head pounded, and my body ached more than it had in the last two months. It had been a rough night.

Rolling over, I checked the time. I was supposed to be at work in forty minutes. Oh well, Cross would have to get over it if I missed the morning meeting. There was no reason I needed to be there. He hadn't assigned me a case or asked me to meet with any new clients since the incident. And that wasn't about to change anytime soon.

Reluctantly, I got out of bed and went in search of Martin. He spent almost every morning working out, so I expected to find him on my treadmill or doing pushups or crunches in the living room. Instead, he sat on the steps of my fire escape with the phone pressed to his ear.

He left the window open, so I heard a few snippets from his side of the conversation. "Do you think it'll help?" Martin rubbed a hand through his hair, something he often did when he was nervous or frustrated. "No, I don't want to come in. We tried that before. Isn't there anything else?"

Work? I wondered.

"No, Doc, I have a conference coming up. I'll be out of town for the next week and a half."

Doc? I swallowed. Who was he talking to?

"A vacation. Yeah. It might. We'll see." Martin rubbed his eyes. "I'll let you know, but I'm not putting her through that. This is my problem."

"Martin?" I called, pretending I wasn't eavesdropping. "Where are you?"

"I have to go. Thanks for taking my call. I'll see you when I get back." Martin hung up the phone and came inside, finding me in the living room. "Good morning, gorgeous." He pulled me close for a kiss. "I hope I didn't wake you."

"You didn't. The alarm did. What's going on?" I nodded at his phone.

"Nothing important. I had a question that needed answering." He noticed the time. "We should get ready. I asked Marcal to pick me up here. Do you want to ride to work together?"

"I guess. I don't know." I took his face in my hands and forced him to look at me. "Is everything okay?"

"Minus our unexpected, middle of the night relocation, everything is great." He pressed his lips to my forehead. "I need to shower and shave, unless you want to go first. Or you could join me."

"Anything to conserve water." I forced myself not to dwell on the dark circles and bags beneath his eyes.

THREE

My eyes started to close, so I blinked several times and tapped my cheeks. *Stay awake, Parker.* Reaching for my coffee cup, I took a sip and eyed the clock on my computer screen. It was almost eleven, and I'd already completed several dozen criminal background checks. Since I missed the morning meeting, my boss assigned me the most tedious task imaginable.

As soon as I finished this stack, I'd break for an early lunch and try to squeeze in a quick nap. It's not like I had anything more pressing to do, and after last night, I was exhausted. Although, fire alarm or not, most nights I barely slept. Napping at work had become the norm, and one I was sure Cross would frown upon, if he knew about it.

For a private investigator at one of the city's most prestigious security firms, life should be exciting. I shouldn't have the luxury of napping on the job, but since Lucien Cross refused to assign me any new cases and since I didn't currently have any clients on the side, I was stuck performing background checks and other humdrum tasks. I shouldn't complain. Life was safer this way, but a part of me, the part that missed being a federal agent, wanted to do something to make a difference.

Investigations weren't always about saving lives or

stopping criminals, but most of them were. And these background checks would probably ruin lives rather than protect them, but on the bright side, as long as I finished on time, it didn't matter how many naps I took in between. Maybe that was a good thing.

I finished the last check, made a few notations on the form, forwarded the documents to our client, and sent a copy to Cross. Before I could close the window, my boss uploaded a new spreadsheet to my dropbox. Great, more background checks.

Rolling my eyes, I highlighted the first name and started on the new list. Lunch and a nap would have to wait. I was in the midst of grumbling to myself when someone knocked on my open office door.

"Hey, Alex, do you have a minute?"

I didn't even bother to look up. "It depends. What do you want, Renner?"

Bennett Renner leaned against the doorjamb and scanned the hallway. "We need to talk about last night."

I spun away from the screen and sat up straight. "What about last night?"

"Are you working a case? You and Detective O'Connell?"

The silver sedan, I should have recognized it. It was part of the fleet of company cars. I drove one just like it. "You were the asshole who sped away."

Renner glanced into the hallway again and lowered his voice. "Guilty."

"What the fuck were you doing there?"

"The same as you, I'd imagine."

"I doubt that very much." I pointed to the chair in front of my desk. "Close the door and sit down. You have some explaining to do." I waited for him to take a seat before I asked, "What were you doing outside the club last night?"

"What were you doing?" he countered.

"Bennett," I warned, "you knocked on my door. So spill. What's going on? Who did you have under surveillance last night?" If he was watching me or anyone I cared about, there would be hell to pay.

"Easton Lango, same as you."

"Not the same as me."

"No? Then how did you just happen upon him? It took me an entire freaking day to track down Easton's location, and you expect me to believe you just stumbled upon it accidentally and with Detective O'Connell in tow?"

I squeezed the bridge of my nose. "Start at the beginning. Why are you following Easton Lango?" I closed the criminal database and searched for Easton Lango on the Cross Security network, but the chef's name didn't pop up. "Easton isn't a Cross Security client, so why are you tailing him? Did one of our clients hire you to spy on him?"

"Not lately." Renner gave me his best dead-eye stare, hoping I'd crack under the pressure and confess. But since I had no clue what was going on, we might end up stuck in a stare-off all day. So much for my nap. After what felt like an eternity, Renner said, "You really don't know what's going on? O'Connell didn't ask you to take the case?"

"No," I said, exasperated. "Enlighten me or get out."

"Lucien doesn't know about any of this, and I intend to keep it that way. You aren't the only one who takes the occasional side job."

That got my attention. I stopped what I was doing and looked up at the former police detective. "Are you sure you should trust me with this information? Cross Security is crawling with rats." I just didn't know if I was looking at one of them.

"I trust you. You've never given me any reason not to." Renner attempted a friendly smile and leaned closer. "I need you to keep this to yourself. One of my buddies on the force sent Chef Easton my way. He thought I might be able to help the guy out since the PD didn't find anything to go on. Easton and I exchanged a few phone calls earlier in the week, but I don't know much about the situation. He's convinced someone's trying to kill him. His restaurant burned to the ground a few months back. The arson investigators ruled it an accident. Fire, police, even the insurance investigators concluded it was bad wiring. No one was at fault, and Easton was cut a check. But last week, Easton went back to the precinct, pestering the police to do something. My buddy, Jake Voletek, caught this guy's case, but the PD can't do much. It's not an open case, and without any evidence to back Easton's claims, the department won't waste resources investigating. Voletek thought maybe there was something I could do."

"Why the secrecy? Why can't you tell Cross?"

"It's complicated."

I knew our boss hated working with the police, but this was ridiculous. "It's my understanding Chef Easton's in the running for a Michelin star. That would make him a freaking rock star in the culinary world. Isn't that precisely the type of client Lucien salivates over?"

"Normally, it is, but Easton's ex-wife, Bridget Stockton, is on retainer. It'd be a conflict of interest to sign him as a client."

"Why?"

Renner looked sheepish. "She originally hired us to find out if he was cheating on her. Cross Security tailed Easton. I took several money shots, and she used them to get out of paying alimony."

"But that's over and done with, right? Is their divorce final?"

"It is, but Easton's ex-wife is a partner at Reeves, Almeada, and Stockton. She's one of the top defense attorneys in the state, and as you know, they contract us to perform investigations for a lot of their cases. Easton may be a big fish, but she's a fucking shark. Lucien would much rather have her on the hook than her ex."

"How long have they been divorced?"

"Over a year. I performed the work for her fifteen months ago, but Cross Security's done a lot of work for Reeves, Almeada, and Stockton before that and since."

"I didn't know any of this."

"You've been here for months. How do you not know this?"

I had met Mr. Almeada several times, and Cross had told me we had a barter system worked out between our firm and the law office. But I didn't realize what that meant. That's why he wanted distance from the police. If defense counsel feared we might share our investigations or findings with the PD, it would undermine their work product and research, potentially jeopardizing their cases and their clients. "You said you spoke to Easton a few times. Does he know where you work and that you cost him his alimony?"

"Yeah. He figured since we did such a great job for his ex, we must know our shit." Renner snickered.

"I gave him my card last night after you scared the bejesus out of him. Why did you drive off like a bat out of hell?"

"I thought O'Connell got wind of the case and asked you to look into it. After the shit that went down with you and Kellan, I didn't want you to think I was spying on you or interfering in your investigation."

"Idiot."

"Anyway," Renner ignored the dig, "that's actually why I came to see you. Easton called and wants to set up a meeting. Since Cross Security took the initiative to protect him last night, he thinks we're open to taking his case. He's on his way here."

"Are you sure Cross doesn't know about this?" The one thing I'd learned over the last few months was our boss knew a lot more than he should. He had eyes and ears everywhere, and he wouldn't approve of Renner's methods of finding new clients.

"He might, but he's choosing to ignore it. These situations arise occasionally. And since I know you and Lucien have an arrangement, you're the only person in the office I trust to handle this."

Cross and I did have an arrangement, the terms of which we were still hammering out, but suffice it to say, Cross knew I liked to moonlight. And he couldn't fire me for it. "What do I need to know about your client?"

"Despite our phone conversations, I don't know much. And technically, Easton's not my client yet. We don't have a contract. I promised to do some checking. That was it. He didn't even tell me where he'd be yesterday."

I stared at Bennett, wondering if this was a joke. "That's why you were spying on him?"

"It was part of my process." He held out the file he'd been holding. "This is what my pal in the police department sent over and my preliminary research."

Renner glanced at his watch. "I gotta run. Lucien gave me a new case this morning, and I'm supposed to meet the client for lunch. I can't be in two places at once, and since you and Easton already have a relationship, I could use the assist. C'mon, Parker, help a guy out. I'll owe you."

"You already owe me." But I was bored, and this had to be more interesting than performing an endless string of background checks. "I'll add it to your tab."

"Thanks. You're a lifesaver. I'll let reception know to send him straight to you."

Before I could say another word, Renner left my office. He moved quickly for a man with a limp. I doubted his injury was much of a detriment, but the police department thought it was, which is how he ended up in the private sector. Honestly, everyone at Cross Security was a broken toy, but some of us hid our scars on the inside.

"Let's see what we have here." I rubbed my palms together and splayed open the folder. The first thing I found were dated surveillance photos of Easton Lango in several compromising positions with a limber blonde. She couldn't have been more than twenty-two. For a moment, I wondered if she was even legal.

It was the old casework Renner performed for Easton's ex, Bridget Stockton. *Why do men always have affairs with blondes?* I wondered. Well, maybe it was true what they say, and this was why blondes had more fun. They just borrowed the guy and didn't have to deal with any of his drama. If I were smarter and had fewer moral guidelines, that philosophy might have solved some of my problems.

Putting the photos aside, I found the police report and Renner's current research. The victim, Easton Lango, didn't have a record or ties to any criminal organizations. He owned a small restaurant that burned down. He filed a claim with his insurance and received compensation. I scanned the arson investigator's report, but the fire department determined the fire was caused by bad wiring. Before I could figure out why Easton was convinced someone wanted to kill him, my phone rang.

I hit the speaker button. "Yes?"

"Ms. Parker, Mr. Renner's 11:30 is here. He's waiting in

conference room one."

"Thanks. I'm on my way."

I grabbed the file and a legal pad and went down the hall. Last night, Easton wore a bandana, but today his dark blue and silver highlights were on display for the world to see. *Chefs are artists,* I reminded myself, making a conscious effort not to stare.

Easton wore jeans and a tight black t-shirt, exposing veiny, muscular forearms. His hands were scarred. Compared to most of Cross Security's clientele, this guy stuck out like a sore thumb. For a moment, I wondered if Renner passed him off to me so he wouldn't have to admit to the chef's face he was the reason Easton was missing out on five-figure monthly alimony payments. Then again, I doubted Renner wanted to get into hot water with the boss. It was no secret I didn't have the same hang-ups as most of my coworkers when it came to job security. I changed jobs almost as often as people changed their socks.

"Mr. Lango?" I asked, entering the conference room.

His sharp brown eyes zeroed in on me, and he glanced into the empty hallway as I pulled the door closed. "I'm supposed to be meeting Bennett Renner, and you don't look much like a Bennett. You look more like an Alexis Parker." He fished my card out of his pocket and tossed it on the table.

"He got called away at the last minute. He asked me to speak to you. Is that a problem?"

"Are you his secretary?"

"No, although he offered me the job the first time we worked together." I closed the blinds and took a seat across from him. "I'm an investigator, just like Renner. But if you'd be more comfortable speaking to him, I'll have him call you later."

Easton leaned back in the chair, finding something about the situation amusing. "Nice to meet you, again." He extended his hand, and we shook. His calloused and scarred palm felt rough against my skin. "I'm Easton, but you already know that."

"How can I help you?" I settled back in the chair and clicked the pen.

"I don't know what Bennett's already told you."

"Why don't you start at the beginning?"

"My restaurant burned down three months ago." He reached into the leather jacket hanging on his chair and removed some pages from the inside pocket. He slid the report over to my side of the table and pointed to a highlighted paragraph. "They said it was an electrical fire. Do you believe that shit?"

"Sir," I began, but he interrupted.

"Easton." He softened the correction with a dazzling smile, showing a mouthful of perfectly straight, white teeth. Despite the circumstances, his first instinct was to flirt. I was surprised, given how gruff he'd been the previous night, but he'd been afraid. Today, he had nothing to fear, and Nick and Martin were nowhere in sight. I knew plenty of men like Easton. In fact, I was dating one of them. "Chef Easton, if you want to be formal, but it's entirely unnecessary."

"What makes you think the fire wasn't an accident?"

"I know my restaurant. I bought the building. It was mine. My blood, sweat, and tears went into that place. I spent a decade building a following and scraping enough capital together to open my own restaurant. I had countless inspections prior to buying. Everything was checked and rechecked. I wasn't taking any chances, and two months after it opened, it burned to the ground. This wasn't bad luck or an accident. Someone intentionally set that fire."

"Did you receive any threats?"

"Dozens."

I didn't expect that answer. "Did you notify the police?"

He flipped through the report. "Yeah, but they didn't take them seriously. Or they didn't take me seriously." The blue hair might have had something to do with it. He spun the paper around. "They didn't even bother to mention it in their report. See? Nothing. Nada."

"When did you receive the first threat?"

"A month before I quit my job at Bouillon, someone left a nasty note on my windshield. That was roughly six months ago, give or take."

"Do you still have it?"

"I should have kept it, but it pissed me off. I crumpled it up and tossed it away. I didn't think much about it. I figured it was just some prick who didn't like his meal." Easton rubbed a hand over his mouth and reached for the glass of water.

"What did the note say?"

"Just that I was a talentless hack who would fail once I went out on my own. I can't remember the exact wording, but I'm pretty sure it said my dreams would burn to the ground. After that, I got several ugly messages on social media. The police said they were harmless internet trolls, not quite to the level of criminal threat, and there was nothing they could do." Easton pressed his lips together. "I blocked them and deactivated some of my accounts. Most of it stopped after that, but a few people continued to send vicious messages."

"Did anyone trace the IP addresses?"

"I don't know. I doubt it. All I know is it was one thing after another until the fire." He searched my eyes. "Did you see something last night? You and that cop went after that guy in the car. Do you know who he was or what he wanted?"

"He wasn't there to hurt you."

"Are you sure?" Easton asked. "Last night, you seemed just as freaked out as I was. You must have noticed something. Did Bennett find something? Is that why he sent you to keep watch over me?"

"Actually, running into you last night was just a coincidence. I was out with some friends and thought we'd grab a bite."

"Yeah, okay," Easton said, unconvinced.

It was time I got us back on track. "Why were you so nervous last night?"

"First night jitters. That was the maiden voyage of Easton's Eats. I figure whoever burned down my restaurant will come for my truck next. I want to be proactive, but the police don't give a shit."

"Have you received any recent threats? Anything since the fire?"

"No, but I know he's out there, watching, waiting."

I was intimately familiar with that feeling. Most of the time, I tried to write it off as paranoia, but it rarely was. However, I didn't know if Easton's instincts were as finely tuned as mine. "Obviously, you've made enemies, Chef. Someone doesn't want to see you succeed, so tell me about these enemies. Who would threaten you and set a fire?"

He thought for several moments. "I don't know. Galen Strader. Asher York."

I scribbled down the names. "Who are they?"

"My rivals. Galen and I have been competing since culinary school, and Asher's just a prick. To be honest, it goes with the territory. We're rock stars. Have you ever watched any cooking shows where the chef is a real bastard?"

"I might have seen one or two."

"It's not an act. And I won't apologize for it. Our creations are meant to be perfection, so we hold the kitchen staff to the same insane standards the critics hold us to. Every dish we serve represents us. It has to be perfect."

I pushed the notepad closer to him. "In that case, I'll need a list of your employees and coworkers. And while you're at it, write down anyone who stood to profit from your restaurant's demise. Investors, competitors, silent partners."

"You think one of them did this?"

"I know a thing or two about working for a difficult boss, so it's possible."

"I'm a hard ass for a reason. My staff knows what to expect. I don't dish out anything they can't handle." He smiled again. "You appear to be a capable woman. I'm sure you've never had a case you couldn't handle."

Brushing off the compliment, I asked, "What happened to your staff? Was anyone hurt in the fire?" I slid the report away from him and skimmed the rest of the details.

"No one was hurt. No one was there."

"Where are they now?"

Easton's brow furrowed. "I don't actually know what most of them are doing now. I had a hell of a time dealing with the full-timers and the unemployment office, but after that, everyone went their separate ways. By now, I'm sure they've moved on to other kitchens. I lost Dante, my sous chef, to Asher." He finished writing down the names and shoved the pad toward me. "I want whoever's responsible to pay."

"What about your insurance?"

"It kept me from declaring bankruptcy, but I'm ruined, Alexis. May I call you Alexis?"

"I prefer Alex."

He nodded. "Without a kitchen, I'm no one. I'm Picasso without a paintbrush. The fire took everything. Whoever set it wanted to destroy me, and they succeeded. That's why I bought the food truck with the insurance money. No staff. No overhead. I just hope it'll be enough to allow me to rebuild from the ground up and get back on my feet."

"But you haven't received any more threats since the fire?"

"No." He frowned. "This is why the police won't do anything. They said there's nothing for them to do. But I don't want my truck to meet the same fate as my restaurant. I can't lose everything a second time. I can't go through that again. I want this bastard to pay."

I understood the anger. Life wasn't fair, and it didn't play by the rules. The police didn't open an investigation because none of the evidence suggested this was arson. More than likely, bad luck and terrible timing had claimed another victim.

Easton picked up the pen, again finding my eyes. "The police thought I was wigging out and weaving conspiracy theories. Do you believe me, or is this your way of humoring me? Because my time is precious. If you're not going to take this seriously, I'll find someone who will. Bennett's been wishy-washy since the get-go. I just hope you're not the same."

Honestly, I didn't know what to think, but Easton believed he was in danger. My gaze dropped to the burns on his hands. The professionals determined it wasn't arson, but maybe they got it wrong. "How did you get those? Were you at the restaurant when the fire broke out?"

He nodded and flipped his right hand over to show me the burn on his palm. "I just finished doing inventory and was in the office placing orders when I smelled smoke. When I grabbed the doorknob, it was already hot." He turned his hand back around. "The rest of these happened on the job." He pointed to a red scar across his knuckles. "Hot oil from the fryer." He turned his left hand over and pointed to some burned flesh on the inside of his wrist. "That's from being careless and reaching across the front burner." He pointed to several more marks, the result of various chopping accidents. "Cooking is a dangerous business."

"So is this." I gestured around the office. "But we follow our passions, right?"

"Something tells me I've come to the right place."

FOUR

After Easton Lango wrote down everything he could remember about the night of the fire, I told him I'd look into the matter but couldn't make any promises. At the moment, I wasn't even sure if this was my case or Renner's. He might take it back once he got his ducks in a row. However, faced with the option of working on a possible arson case or conducting another three dozen background checks, I opted for the arson case.

Two things didn't make sense. First, Easton said he smelled smoke, but the fire alarm never sounded. After last night, I knew the smoke detector should have notified him of the danger long before the building was ablaze. Second, regardless of what the investigators determined, Easton believed he was in danger. Unless he was paranoid or delusional, his claims warranted attention, especially given his history of threats and his quasi-celebrity status.

I'd just put in requests for copies of the arson and insurance investigators' original reports and scheduled a couple of interviews when the intercom buzzed. "Ms. Parker, you have a walk-in. I told him he needs to make an appointment, but he insists you have a standing lunch date."

"Send him in."

I wrote Asher York and Galen Strader on a sticky note and got up to close the blinds. The only windows in my office faced the hallway, and I didn't need any of my coworkers spying on me, especially Kellan from across the hall. The assistant led James Martin to my door, asked if we needed anything, and returned to her post at the front desk.

I pushed the door closed, and Martin backed me against it, his hands on my face and his lips against mine. His fingers tangled in my long brown hair. He must have forgotten my rule about no funny business in the workplace. He stopped to take a breath, and I slipped out of his grasp.

"God, I missed you," he said, his voice hoarse. That explained why he burst into my office like a newly released felon.

"It's only been five hours. How will you survive the tech conference's twelve-hour days?"

"I have no idea."

"Oh wait, it's being held inside a Vegas hotel. So we should assume gambling and strippers. And let's not forget legal prostitution, recreational marijuana use, and lots of stigma-free day-drinking." I winked at him. "You'll be fine, handsome."

Martin chuckled. "You really think that's what we'll be doing at the conference?" He stepped away, and I noticed the brown paper bag he dropped on the chair. He picked it up and carried it to the glass coffee table in front of the l-shaped sofa and unpacked our lunch.

"Yep." I took a seat beside him and reached for a container of leftover crab salad.

He handed me a fork and went to grab a glass of water from the cart in the corner. He peered at my notes. "What are you working on? Did you finally pester Cross into assigning you a case, or is this about the car that sped away last night?"

"The car, sort of. It's about Chef Easton."

Martin peered at the notes on my desk. "All of this is related to Chef Easton?"

"No. Cross has me running more background checks." I made a face. "Renner asked if I'd meet with one of his clients, who happens to be Chef Easton, but it might be a one and done. It turns out Renner was the asshole spying on us last night." I glanced at the clock, wondering when Bennett would be back from his lunch meeting.

"Is he the one you don't like?"

"No, that's Kellan. Renner used to be a cop. He knows O'Connell. Said he freaked and took off, but I don't know."

"Odd."

"Yeah." I speared some crab and popped it into my mouth. "I told Chef Easton I'd look into some things, but I don't know if there's even a case here." That reminded me I needed to call O'Connell, and I crossed to my desk and added that to the bottom of my sticky note. Until I determined how much I trusted Bennett, I would verify the details with Nick.

Martin rattled the ice cubes in his glass and took a sip. "You seemed sure last night."

"Things change."

"Like how you said we'd ride to work together and then you left before I finished shaving?" His green eyes bore into mine. "With the way you left so suddenly, I thought you might be working on something important. Or there was another fire."

"In a way, there was." I shook my head, not wanting to get into the details of Easton's case. "How is our apartment? Is it still standing?"

"It's fine. Whoever lives in 1408 got wasted last night, put some pizza bagels in the toaster over, and passed out. The sprinklers put out the fire in the apartment, and the fire department cleared the building. Marcal dropped by to check on things, and he moved a few of your packed boxes while he was at it."

"After our near miss, I'm not sure I want my things sitting in our apartment. What if the place burns down?" What was it about fires today? Sheesh.

"Are you reconsidering moving back in with me?" Martin asked. "Is that why you ran out this morning?"

"No, we're good. I just spoke to someone who lost

everything in a fire, and it freaked me out."

"I promise I'll do my best to keep our house from burning down. The apartment building I can't guarantee because way too many people live there. But your things should be safe at home with me. And I have a fire safe for anything you want to keep safe." He chuckled. "I guess that's why they call it a safe."

"You need sleep."

He shrugged. "Why'd you leave, sweetheart? What happened?"

"Nothing." I returned to my spot on the couch and popped a piece of crab into my mouth.

However, Martin knew me better than anyone. "Bullshit. Talk to me. Am I driving you crazy?"

I snorted, nearly launching the crab out of my nose. "No, I just thought you might like some privacy. I heard you on the phone this morning."

His forehead creased. "So?"

"You were talking to a doctor."

"Not a doctor, a therapist."

I put the container down, my appetite gone. "I didn't know you were seeing anyone regularly."

"Yeah, for about six weeks. It hasn't made much of a difference, but it's only been a few sessions. This morning, I had a question, and since it was early, he had time to talk." Martin put one knee on the couch so he could face me and ran his thumb against my cheek. "Don't worry about me. I'm okay."

I leaned into his palm. "You look tired. You didn't sleep again last night. How many nights has it been?"

"Two, maybe three." He toyed with a strand of my hair. "You're one to talk, Alex. We've practically been sleeping in shifts these last two months. We need a break. He thinks a vacation might help."

"When will you have time?" I asked. "You probably shouldn't even be here. You told me you needed the rest of the week to prep your presentations and speeches for the conference. That's why I didn't drop by the Martin Technologies building for lunch."

"It's okay. You don't always have to come to my office

for lunch. I can come to you." As if realizing something didn't make sense, he looked around the room. "Did you eat before I got here?"

"No."

"Is lunch on the way?"

"No."

"Does Lucien allow you to eat, or is he hoping you'll starve to death?"

"Shh. Don't say his name too many times. He's like *Beetlejuice.*"

"So what do you do on the days we don't meet for lunch?" Martin asked, suddenly intrigued by my routine. Until two months ago, we rarely met for lunch. We were both workaholics, but life kicked us in the teeth, again. Martin insisted our lunch dates allowed him to keep his priorities straight, but really, it eased his fears to see me during the day. And it broke up the monotony of performing background checks.

"Nap."

"You're serious?"

"Don't knock it 'til you try it. And I think maybe you should try it."

"Maybe I will, but first, I want to run something by you. Just keep an open mind."

Automatically, worst case scenarios ran through my head. I gulped and prepared for the worst.

"Do you think you could take a few more days off?" he asked.

"Probably. Why?"

"I thought we could use the time to squeeze in that vacation you asked about. You already agreed to come with me to the conference as a mini-getaway, but let's really give it a shot. Let's take a few days and go on a real vacation. I know Vegas isn't exactly Monaco, but my meetings will be finished Friday night. They have a brunch scheduled Saturday, and we can leave for the beach right after that. Marcal's offered to fly out and get my beach house prepped. What do you say?"

"That means I have to finish packing up my apartment this week. We have to get everything moved out by the end of the month, and if we're going to be away for an additional week, now's the only time I have to do it. I still have a lot of crap to go through." Thoughts of the phone call with his therapist played through my mind. "Hey, if you changed your mind, I don't have to move back into your house. The apartment we share is great, last night's events notwithstanding. Your house can stay yours."

"And your apartment will stay yours, and our apartment will be neutral ground." He shook his head. "That might have been the original plan, but we're not doing that. I already told you it's not my house. It's ours. You're my everything. In case you haven't noticed, I don't want any more barriers between us, but it's okay if you do. I can respect that. Regardless, you deserve a vacation. We'll take care of the packing this week, and I'll hire movers to handle whatever we don't finish. Plus, while I'm in stuffy meetings and conferences, you can gamble, see a show, hire a hooker, whatever makes you happy." His eyes met mine. "It's Vegas, baby."

"Do you have an arrangement with the hookers?"

"No, just the showgirls." He said it in jest, but given Martin's reputation, I suspected there might be some truth behind the joke. "C'mon, totally naked male strippers. You can even see the ones with the Australian accents. And the hotel always comps a few hundred in chips to get started in the casinos. It'll be fun. And then it'll be seven days of you and me and absolutely nothing but sun and sand."

"Stop twisting my arm," I teased.

"So yes to the vacation? And no changing your mind, like this morning with riding to work."

"Yeah, I'll go. Who else will keep you out of trouble?"

"Funny. I was going to ask you the same thing." He reached for his lunch and took another bite. "For the record, I was joking about the hookers."

"We'll see."

He put his lunch down and lunged for me, tickling my sides and making me squeal. Of course, it was at that moment I heard the knock followed by the familiar sound of my boss clearing his throat. Martin sat up, straightening his tie and smoothing the creases on his vest.

"James, I didn't know you were here," Lucien Cross said, striding into the room without invitation. "I didn't mean to interrupt."

"You're not." I took a sip of water. "Do you need something?"

Cross took a seat in the chair across from us. "I just had a question about the requests you made this morning, but we'll discuss that later. I don't want to intrude on your lunch." He zeroed in on Martin like a shark circling a seal. "I heard you were asked to open this year's tech conference. A lot of new technology is being introduced. Is Martin Technologies showcasing anything new?"

Seamlessly, Martin shifted into business mode. "We are, but it won't be revealed until the conference. We have to keep it hush-hush. We don't want any leaks. I'm hoping to attract a few new partners and form several mergers."

Hence, the prostitutes.

Lucien hid his scowl. "Anything to do with biotextiles? As I've said before, I'd love the opportunity to partner with your company. Biotextiles and tactical wear go hand in hand. Outfitting and protecting my people would just be the start. Think of the other applications. Sales. Private security." Lucien's eyes drifted to me. "Biotextiles are lighter, more durable, and have shown greater strength and resistance to bullets and other projectiles than most of the vests and armor we use today. It's a practical solution for most safety concerns. And it would be the perfect way to ensure my investigators stay safe in the field."

"The technology isn't there to mass produce on the scale your endeavor would require, and Martin Technologies shies away from projects with obvious military application. I'm sure you understand." Martin reached for his glass and took a final sip.

"Just think about it." This had been Lucien's personal mission, and it was the reason he hired me. He thought I'd be the perfect bridge to get him in Martin's good graces. However, things did not turn out the way Cross hoped, and now the three of us were stuck in limbo. But out of the three of us, I was the one who got screwed.

"Should something change, you'll be my first call."

Martin stood and shook hands with Lucien. "I need to get back. I'll see you later, Alex." He leaned down and kissed me quickly on the cheek before disappearing out the door.

Cross leaned back in the chair and stared at me. "Do you think you could convince him otherwise?"

"Even if I could, he doesn't have the means to mass produce the materials needed."

"Are you sure about that?"

I glared at Cross. "There's a line. I don't talk shop with Martin. His business is his business. It has nothing to do with me, and it sure as hell has nothing to do with you." I cleared off the table and tossed the garbage into the basket near my desk. "If that's the only reason I'm here, then let me go."

"You're under contract."

"Do you want me to quit? Is that why you've been giving me these tedious tasks which are nothing but busywork?"

"The background checks may not be glamorous, but they are important. They have to be performed. Our biggest clients are these businesses."

"An assistant could do the work. You don't need me for this. You didn't hire me to be a grinder. Honestly, I don't think you need me at all."

"You've proven your worth, Alex. And for the record, I'm not punishing you." Cross stood. "I'm protecting you. Two months ago, you were kidnapped and nearly beaten to death by a client I assigned you. That never should have happened."

"I guess I fucked up."

Cross winced. "You didn't fuck up. I did. And I want to make sure nothing like that ever happens again. But your relationship with the local PD makes things messier for me. Our clients don't want police involvement, and every case you've worked has involved the police. You're my newest investigator and possibly my brightest, but you're also the most dangerous to my business. We have to iron this out, together." He sighed. "I don't know what to do with you or how to handle this predicament. Any suggestions?"

It was now or never. "I don't know, but I do have a favor

to ask. I need another few days off, on top of the week I already asked for."

"Have you recovered? If you're still experiencing pain or lingering symptoms, the medical staff can get you in to see a specialist."

"I'm fine. I just need a break."

He gave me a skeptical look. "Okay. Fill out the paperwork and leave it with Justin. I'll make sure you get the time off." He went to the door, but I stopped him.

"Lucien, you said you had a question. What is it?" More than likely, Cross heard Martin was in the building and wanted to ambush him.

"I'll ask an assistant to handle it. Oh, and you should know, I'll be out of the office most of next week, too. When we both get back, we'll sit down with legal and renegotiate your contract. I don't like you going behind my back, and now you have Bennett Renner doing the same. This has to stop."

"I agree, but I have nothing to do with whatever issue you have with Renner. If he did something, he did it on his own."

Cross let out an audible harrumph and continued down the corridor. We were at a stalemate. We had been since the beginning, and as the days went by, it was getting worse. Additional pieces were being drawn into the game. First, Cross had gotten Kellan Dey, another of his investigators, to spy on me, and now he wanted to put Bennett Renner's head on the chopping block over the Easton Lango case. Cross was one paranoid prick or a major control freak. My money was on both.

FIVE

When Renner returned later that afternoon, he invited me back to his office. "How did it go?" he asked. "Did Easton talk to you? What did he say?"

"He said a lot, just not much we can use." I spread the file out on his cluttered desk. "He believes someone intentionally set the fire."

Renner flipped through my notes. "According to Detective Voletek, my police contact, Easton claims to have received several serious threats prior to the blaze. Did he mention anything about them? Does he have any idea who might want to harm him?"

"I should have taped the interview for you," I quipped.

"Why didn't you?"

"Maybe I forgot. Y'know, the same way you forgot to tell me thank you."

Renner bowed and rolled his hand like a court jester acknowledging the queen. "Thank you." His eyes twinkled. "How 'bout I make it up to you? I'll extend my original offer again. What do you say?"

"What offer?"

"To be my assistant. When we were searching for the missing girl, you proved you have all the makings of an excellent assistant. And despite your oversight not to record the interview today, I'm still willing to let you assist me, just as long as you remember how I take my coffee."

"Cream, sugar, and a side of arsenic, right?"

"I switched to cyanide this month, but that's close enough. When can you start?"

"Ask Cross. He's days away from giving me the ax. Actually," I met Bennett's eyes, "my head isn't the only one on the chopping block. Lucien knows about this case, and he blamed me for it. So thanks a lot."

"Shit." Renner sobered; the joking entirely forgotten. "I'm sorry. I'll talk to him and explain the situation. I don't want this to impact your position here. You didn't do anything wrong. I'll make sure Lucien knows that."

"Don't bother." Getting back to business, I flipped to the two names Easton gave me. "Easton thinks a rival chef is behind this since the arsonist targeted his restaurant and the threats only began after he announced he was leaving Bouillon. Do the names Asher York or Galen Strader mean anything to you?"

"They didn't pop up in my preliminary research. Did you check into them?"

"Just the basics. York has several DUIs, and Strader has a minor assault charge."

"How minor?"

"He threw a plate at one of his kitchen staff."

"Nice guy," Renner said. "So we know Strader has a temper, and York has a drinking problem. With colleagues like that, it's no wonder Easton thinks someone is out to get him. Of course, the threat could have come from an angry customer or a food critic."

"Or one of his staff or any of a million other possibilities, but Easton focused on these two men. So it's a start. I didn't get much out of him in terms of his personal life, so I don't know how many skeletons we might be dealing with. You'd know better than I would."

Renner thought for a moment. "Let's leave Easton's personal life out of it until we know more. We don't want to cause Lucien to have palpitations if it's not necessary."

"You're no fun."

Renner snickered. "Tell me more about the interview. How did Easton seem? What was his demeanor like?"

"Frankly, he was amazed I was willing to take him seriously. He didn't think I believed him."

"Do you?"

I shrugged. "Something doesn't feel right. I just can't put my finger on it." I picked up the notepad and flipped to the next page. "Easton couldn't provide any solid details on his previous threats. He trashed what little physical evidence there was, and he blocked and deleted the online harassment. He said he reported it to the police, but I'm not seeing any notations in the police report." I handed the notepad to Renner. "Those are his social media account handles. He's deactivated several. I didn't spot anything malicious on the accounts he still has, but I didn't look too hard. I didn't want to step on your toes."

Renner reached for the phone. "Since Cross is on to us, there's no reason to hide this any longer. I might as well ask the guys in IT to check it out. If there's something to find, they'll find it." He made the request and skimmed the rest of my notes. He stopped on the question I scrawled in the corner of the last page. "Want to elaborate?"

"Easton Lango was in the restaurant when it caught fire. I saw the burns on his hands. He could be the arsonist, or the fire might have been attempted murder. Until we know more, I don't think we should rule anything out."

"It could just be an unfortunate accident. The fire department said it was electrical, and the insurance investigator signed off on it. You know how insurance works. They'll come up with any reason to avoid cutting a check. Do you really think they reached the wrong conclusion?"

"No one's perfect, but it sounds like you've already made up your mind."

Renner skimmed the police report again. "Honestly, I don't know. When I was a cop, cases like this made my day. They closed themselves. Just walk the scene, sign the paperwork, and call it a night." He reread the statement Easton gave the police. "If he burned down his own restaurant, why would he want the PD to reopen the case?

He already has the insurance money."

"According to him, it wasn't enough."

Renner reached for the insurance information, but the contract had a lot of fine print. "I'll have someone from legal look at this. Maybe there's a clause or payment schedule we're missing." He dropped the pages onto his desk. "Even if there is some stipulation that will trigger a heftier payout, it's a risky move, asking the authorities to reopen an investigation. If the fire is deemed arson, the cops will hunt for the culprit, and eventually, the guilty party will get caught. I don't think Easton's an arsonist, but he might be an opportunist." Renner opened his desk drawer and pulled out a recent copy of the paper. The lifestyle section featured a spread on area chefs. Easton Lango was featured above the fold. "The fire and his known rivalry with other chefs makes for a juicy scandal."

"You think that's why he's pointing fingers at Strader and York? He wants to start a public feud?"

"Could be. I'd say Easton's restaurant didn't generate enough buzz, so after the fire, he saw the writing on the wall and figured making false allegations and funding an investigation was the best way to start over with a clean slate and over-hyped publicity for his next venture."

"The food truck?"

"Or whatever restaurant he opens or decides to work in. My sources say he's had several lucrative offers from area restaurants. The hotter the story gets, the more sought after he'll be."

And people thought I was cynical and jaded. "Then why did you agree to take the case?"

"I didn't. I only agreed to a consultation with a potential new client. Plus, I owed my buddy at the precinct a favor, and he called in his chit. This is what he wants."

"Why?" Renner's story didn't make much sense.

"Have you ever met Jake Voletek?"

I thought for a moment, but I didn't think we ever crossed paths. "His name doesn't ring any bells."

"He's a legacy, came from a whole family of cops. Father, grandfather, brothers, all cops. With his name, he could sit back, serve his twenty years, and collect his pension. No one would think anything of it, but that never sat right with him. He's a self-starter. Instead of just focusing on the homicides that cross his desk, he likes to take a proactive approach and get involved early on. Whenever he gets the chance, he hangs around the front desk, fielding complaints and filing reports for walk-ins. That's how he and Easton crossed paths." The disdain practically dripped from Renner's words. "I've told him it's gonna catch up to him, but he doesn't care. He's a fucking Voletek. He has bricks for brains."

"I thought you said you're buddies."

"We are. He's just an idiot and a total foodie. As far as he's concerned, Chef Easton is a star. So between the hero worship and hero complex, Voletek decided something needs to be done. It didn't hurt that Easton promised he'd privately cater dinner for anyone who looks into the matter, and my pal intends to cash in."

"Cops are exempt from accepting rewards."

"Yeah, but private eyes aren't." Renner grinned. "Don't worry about the logistics. That's my problem, but since you've been so helpful, I'll make sure you get a doggie bag."

"So you don't think an actual crime occurred? You're just pacifying Easton so your pal gets some Kobe beef?"

"I don't know yet," Renner sighed, "but you make it sound so tawdry."

I gave him a wide-eyed look. Cross Security was a far cry from my old job as a federal agent. The FBI had a code of ethics, just like the police department. But obviously, Cross Security's ethics were as questionable as Lucien's, and the time away from the PD made Renner forget the oaths he had taken. "You're unbelievable."

"No, I'm not. But in case you haven't noticed, our clients aren't always on the level. They have their own agendas. Plus, I don't know enough about the situation yet to make a judgment call. That's why we're looking into it. Because I don't know anything yet." On that point, we were in total agreement. "What I do know," Renner said sharply, "is you're failing to consider two things. First, I spent weeks spying on Easton Lango for his ex-wife. Not once has the man ever taken the moral high ground. Hell, even with a thirty-foot ladder, Easton would still have to look up to find the moral high ground. And second, if my years on the force taught me anything, it's to trust the experts. They don't think a crime happened, and until I find something to the contrary, it wouldn't be wise to assume their assessments are incorrect."

"Fine," I conceded on both points, "but you're forgetting one thing."

"What's that?"

"Last night, Easton Lango was absolutely terrified. He's convinced someone is out to get him."

"The spotlight always attracts a degree of crazy, but most of the time, crazy people aren't dangerous. They're just crazy. However, if one of these online trolls or," he flipped the page, "cowardly note leavers, started that fire, the police need to know about it. The last thing this city needs is a crazed firebug running amok."

"Even if it turns out the firebug is our client?"

"Even then," Renner said, "which goes against Cross Security's policies. I have to discuss this case with Cross before I investigate. That's why I wanted to meet with Easton. I wanted to make sure there was even a case before I bothered bringing it up to the boss. What do you think? Is there something here?"

I laughed. "I'm pretty sure we already established that."

"Maybe I was hoping you changed your mind."

"Doesn't it bother you getting paid to protect these questionable individuals?"

"It's hard to stomach at first. I suggest keeping some of the pink stuff in your desk drawer. It helps."

"I'm serious."

"So am I."

I didn't like that answer. SSA Mark Jablonsky, my former mentor, was right. This wasn't the place for me. Maybe the solution to the stalemate was to forfeit the game. I started over more times than I cared to count. I could do it again. "In that case, I'll leave you to it." I edged toward the door. I had already dug a deep enough hole for myself. My connection to Martin was the only thing ensuring my position at Cross Security. Without it, I'd already be DOA.

"Where the hell are you going?" Bennett jerked his chin at the empty chair. "Aren't you the least bit curious?" He held up the notepad. "You think Easton's an arsonist or a potential murder victim. Don't you want to find out which is true?"

"First, I don't think he's an arsonist. I think it's a possibility. And second, this is your case."

"Do you have something better to do?"

"Not really, but Lucien has to approve it." Which under any other circumstances would have been incentive enough for me to stick with it, but now I was having doubts about everything. Existential crisis, here I come. I'd already forced Cross to remove the non-compete clause and grant me autonomy in the cases I selected. But the boss loved to micromanage, and the cases he assigned or refused to assign me were our biggest dilemma. Angering him by working a forbidden case would not help me when we sat down at the negotiation table. "My position at Cross Security is already on shaky ground. Are you sure you want to join me on the edge of the cliff?"

Renner shook off my warning. "What if Lucien signs off on it? Are you in?"

"Yeah, but I doubt he'll okay this."

"I'll admit it's a gamble. On the one hand, if Easton's claims are on the level, the chef will be grateful for our help. And if Jake's right about Easton's talents, the chef will be a Michelin-starred superstar soon enough. That will make him a very desirable client for Cross Security, despite his ex-wife. Lucien will thank me for finding him and bringing him into the fold. And on the other hand, if Easton Lango is a criminal or raving lunatic, and we expose him, Bridget Stockton might just throw us a bone. Either way, it's a win for Cross. That sounds like a decent pitch, right? Do you think Lucien will go for it?"

"I don't know."

"Let's find out." Before I could say another word, Renner picked up the phone and dialed Cross's extension. After some groveling and a repeat of everything we just discussed, Renner convinced Cross to give us permission to pursue the case and use whatever resources were necessary, but Cross insisted on one condition. I take the lead.

"What makes you so special?" Renner asked.

"It's so Cross can insulate himself. I'm free to take clients on the side. If things go south, he'll say Easton Lango wasn't a Cross Security client. He'll say he was mine."

"We could drop him and recommend another firm take over. Maybe someone from Pierce and Sharpe Investigations."

"Pierce and Sharpe? Did you make that up?"

"No, haven't you seen the late night ads on the local channels? They have a jingle. It's really catchy."

"And their names are Pierce and Sharpe?"

"I'm pretty sure those aren't their real names, but obviously, they could use the work. It's your call since it's your ass on the line."

I couldn't believe Cross accepted Renner's proposal. The boss never gave in to my requests that easily. Cross was up to something. I just didn't know what it was.

"Are you in or out, Parker?"

Assisting on this case had to be better than conducting endless background checks and napping through lunch. "In."

"Then pull up a chair and let's get to work."

SIX

"Anything?" I asked.

Renner hit the speaker button and put down the receiver. The annoying hold music filled the air. "He's checking." Renner looked at his watch. "He's been checking for the last forty-five minutes. Maybe we should call the cops. He might have gotten locked in the freezer. He could be dying of frostbite."

"Hang up. We'll try again another day." I leaned back, my vertebrae popping from the sudden shift in position. "What about Easton's coworkers? Have you found anything on them?"

While Renner was on hold, he'd been searching for dirt on the kitchen staff at Bouillon. According to Easton, the threats began a month before he resigned as head chef, which meant there was a good chance the suspect worked at Bouillon.

"They're an angry bunch. You should see the shit they post on social media. Wow." Renner's eyes widened, and he shook his head. "Vitriolic bastards, each and every one of them."

"Underpaid, unappreciated, and overworked can do that to a person."

"I guess." Renner clicked a key, sending his computer display to the big screen against the wall. "Just look at this. No wonder Easton thinks someone burned down his building. He spent every day with vindictive psychos."

It was a free-for-all with the back and forth. Several messages contained explicit and creative death threats. Obviously, we didn't have an absence of suspects. "What prompted that?" I pointed to one gruesome threat in particular.

"From what I can tell, Bryan, the dishwasher, and Kasey had something hot and heavy going on until Kasey caught Bryan with Isla, the pastry chef, horizontal on the chef's desk."

"Okay, but who are these other six people?" I asked, counting the other handles that popped up in the conversation thread.

"Other members of the kitchen staff." Renner exhaled. "Damn, this is more intense than those soapy dramas my ex-wife used to make me watch. Do any of them have records?"

I'd been scouring the criminal databases. "Most of them, but no felony convictions that I've found. Let's see. Petty theft, public intoxication, disorderly conduct, simple assault, possession, vandalism," I read the last one again, "and discharging a firearm within city limits."

"That's a scary thought. Who's packing heat?"

"Kasey, the sous chef." I scanned the argument. Luckily, she'd only threatened to use the paring knife to slice open Bryan's stomach, remove his intestines, fill them with sausage meat and force them down his throat. She never mentioned wanting to shoot him, so that was a good sign. Maybe. "Did you find any mention of Easton, his restaurant, or his food truck?"

Renner highlighted the relevant threads related to Chef Easton. "It's no secret they despised working for a hard ass prick, but the weird thing is, after Easton quit, they missed him." He highlighted a particular conversation involving Isla, Kasey, Jamie, and Max. That conversation dated back to before Bryan's two-timing, and I was surprised to learn Isla and Kasey had been friends prior to sharing the dishwasher. "Apparently, Chef Strader is even worse."

"Galen Strader?"

Renner nodded. "Son of a bitch took over as head chef the day after Easton quit."

"That fucks up our motive."

"Maybe for Strader, but leaving Easton with no other options might be the only way to get him to return to Bouillon. One of the kitchen staff could be behind the fire and threats. Given all of their internet bitching, maybe they took it one step further and left the note on the car to dissuade him from leaving. But it didn't work, so they burned down his restaurant."

"Or they just like to bitch." I read one of the lines and chuckled. *Easton might have been an asshole, but he was our asshole. We knew what kind of shit to expect from him.* "Do you seriously think they burned down his restaurant because they wanted him back?"

"Hell if I know. These people are nuts." Renner rubbed his eyes. "No one took credit for starting the fire. Aside from a few comments which might be construed as Easton got what he deserved or speculation that he might come back to Bouillon and beg for his old job, there's nothing solid here. We need to keep digging. Arson's one of the hardest crimes to solve."

"So you think it's arson?"

"If I didn't, why did we just waste the last few hours picking our way through this steaming pile of shit?" At least we were finally on the same page. "The scary thing is most of the kitchen staff fit the profile."

"Since when do we work off profiles?" I asked.

"We don't, but it's something to keep in mind. Arsonists tend to be in their teens to mid-twenties, lack impulse control, are poorly paid laborers, obsessed with fire, and have had previous run-ins with the law. That sounds like every single one of Bouillon's staff. And the most common reasons for arson are revenge, vandalism, concealing another crime, and excitement with a possible sexual component. Based on what I've read, I'd say those are all possibilities."

When Bennett laid it out like that, I found it hard to

disagree. "Do you think Easton was sleeping with members of his staff?"

"He did when he was married. I think she was a waitress. She was too young to be anything else. She couldn't even drink. She was still in college, probably trying to pay her way through school." Renner shook his head. "Easton was a decade older and in a power position over her. It was sleazy."

"Was she the woman in the photos?"

"Yeah."

"Did you ever see him with any other women?"

"Just the one, but from what I know about Easton Lango, I wouldn't put it past him."

"Maybe she left the threats."

Renner shook his head. "The moment Bridget confronted him, Easton broke it off, and his mistress quit. I kept on him until the divorce was finalized, but I never saw the girl again. That was over a year ago. She doesn't fit the timeline. But it's possible he could have been screwing someone else he worked with. And even if he wasn't, none of these people are stable. Who knows what they might do if he pissed them off. Personally, I wouldn't turn my back on any of them, and the scariest part is they're responsible for preparing people's food." Renner cringed. "I might just stick to sandwiches and pre-packaged meals from here on out."

"You could always cook." Unfortunately, based on our findings, everyone was a suspect.

"Only if you want to see another kitchen burn down." Renner's words triggered a thought.

"What about the competition? If Easton's culinary skills are that impressive, every restauranteur and Michelin star wannabe would want to shut him down or worse."

"Why do I feel like this is only the tip of the iceberg?"

I pointed at the acerbic conversation threads on the big screen. "Even if the fire was due to faulty wiring, someone threatened Easton. We have to find out who." I reached for my notes. "We need to know who worked at Sizzle prior to the fire. If any of the kitchen staff, management, or waitstaff knew Easton before he opened Sizzle, they could just as easily be responsible for the threatening note and setting the fire."

"If they're anything like the staff at Bouillon, I wouldn't doubt it," Renner said. "Let's look into the vendors while we're at it." He removed the projected display from the big screen. "Cross Security doesn't have its own arson investigator on the payroll, so we hire experts when necessary." He pushed the phone to the edge of the desk. "Since I just spent the last forty-five minutes on hold with Bouillon's GM, it's your turn to make the calls. Ask an assistant to make an appointment with Dilbert Haskell. He's one of the best, and we've used him several times in the past. Hopefully, he'll be able to tell us more about the fire."

I picked up the receiver and made the request while Renner texted Easton for the information we needed. Hopefully, it would point us in the right direction. We had to narrow down the potential suspect list before we could move forward. Right now, Renner and I were spread too thin, even with Cross Security's vast resources.

"Haskell will get back to us tomorrow," I said, hanging up the phone after the assistant verified the appointment. "I must admit, this place has excellent turnaround."

"It's all in the name." Renner's gaze remained glued to his screen. "Can you check out Easton's online reviews? He said most of the threats came in on social media, so I'm guessing the asshole probably crucified him on a review site too."

I looked over Renner's shoulder, seeing a new list of names and companies. "Anything to avoid more background checks."

"Just remember that when you want a break from the insanity and hateful things people say while safely hidden behind a screen. I'm telling you, Parker, reading that shit will make your eyes bleed."

"We'll see."

I saved the criminal record searches to Easton's case file and switched gears. The hours flew by as I read hundreds of customer reviews, marking anyone who wrote something extreme on either end of the spectrum. One person's review bordered on pornographic and concluded with begging Easton to put another food baby inside of her. Perhaps one of his superfans feared he'd fail or didn't like the new direction the chef was taking his cuisine and threatened him in a misguided attempt to save him. I'd seen things like that before, which made limiting suspects that much harder.

After a thorough search of customer review sites, I switched to reading reviews from food critics and bloggers. Unlike the crazed fans and angry customers, these were written by professionals. For the most part, the critiques were bland in comparison. Even the more vicious reviews disguised their disgust with colorful analogies and SAT vocabulary words. But what I hadn't counted on was the comment section.

Food critics and bloggers each had their own following. We lived in an age of celebrity, where everyone had a brand and dedicated fans. I skimmed the comments, searching for anything related to Chef Easton, Bouillon, Easton's Eats, and Sizzle, Easton's burned down restaurant. But the mentions I found didn't relate to the fire or include any threats.

I worried a scathing review encouraged one of the critic's followers to commit an insane act. Had that been the case, I believed the follower would take credit for the crime to garner favor with the critic. But in case the arsonist was smart enough not to post publicly, I recorded the contact information for the food critics and bloggers and shut the computer. I needed a break. I glanced at Renner, who appeared to be in the midst of working on another case.

"What are you doing?" I asked.

"Sorry, Cross e-mailed me about our new client."

"Easton?"

"No, Leopold Zedula. My lunch meeting." Renner climbed out of his chair and stretched. "I need to run upstairs to check on something. Are you good here?"

"Yeah, fine."

"Thanks, Parker. I'll speak with Easton again to make sure we didn't miss anyone, but here's the workup on the list he sent over." Renner grabbed a stack of pages off the printer, handed them to me, and looked at the clock. "I should be back soon." He retrieved a few files from his middle drawer and left me in his office.

For the briefest moment, I thought about snooping. Hazard of the job, but I resisted. Bennett Renner wasn't the enemy, and if he was, finding out in the middle of a case wouldn't help us solve it any faster. Assuming, of course, this was actually a case and not the delusions of a paranoid chef.

Instead, I pulled out my cell phone and dialed O'Connell. I was convinced Cross had the office phones bugged, and I didn't want to speak to the police on his line if I could avoid it.

"What do you want, Parker?" Nick asked.

"Did you get a chance to look into Easton Lango's claims? I spoke to him this morning and saw a copy of the police report, but it doesn't tell me much." I shuffled through the pages until I found it at the bottom of the stack.

"It's been a busy day. Hang on, I'll see what I can pull up." The sound of O'Connell typing echoed in my ear. "Okay, so it looks like Lango filed several reports in the last four months. One for online stalking. One for the fire. Another for the fire. And one alleging death threats, though he didn't provide any proof or evidence."

"Does any of it track?"

O'Connell fell silent as he read the reports. "Lango didn't give us much to go on. He spoke to the desk sergeant, a few detectives, and the watch commander. It appears he's crying wolf, but based on the shutterbug in the car and the way he peeled out, I don't know. Unfortunately, patrols didn't spot the car, but that's no surprise."

"I found the car and driver, but it's not what we thought."

"Who was it?"

"Bennett Renner."

O'Connell let out a huff. "Son of a bitch almost ran over my foot. Why did he take off?"

"Supposedly, he was following protocol. Cross Security doesn't involve the police in an investigation unless absolutely necessary."

"Are you sure that's a Cross Security protocol? You never follow it."

"Hardy har. Is there anything else you can tell me?"

"I have a shit ton of cases to get through. Easton Lango doesn't want our help, and he's done nothing to help us help him. I'm inclined to agree with the rest of the police personnel who've looked into this matter. There isn't a case here."

"You're wrong."

"Okay, tell me what I'm missing. Do you have anything solid? A name? A lead? Evidence?"

"Not yet."

"When you get one of those things, let me know, but until then, I'm leaving it up to you."

"Now you sound like Renner."

"Ooh, low blow, Parker."

Unfortunately, the police didn't have enough to open an official investigation, which is what led Easton to Cross Security. And even though Cross didn't want to take this case either, Renner and I were too deep to stop now. I'd find proof. I wouldn't quit until I did. "I'll call you back after I check on a few things."

"You do that."

SEVEN

Ten minutes after Renner went upstairs to check on something, he was called away to Mr. Zedula's estate. And since Leopold Zedula was Cross approved, that took precedence. Hours passed, and I was left to plow through Easton Lango's past, present, and future by myself.

"I'm never doing you another favor." I glared at Renner's empty chair, placed the sticky note in the center of his computer screen, picked up the Easton Lango files, and returned to my office.

I caught the insurance investigator, Lou Hutton, just as he was calling it a day. Hutton remembered the scene. He'd seen dozens of similar fires over the course of his career. This one wasn't special. As far as he was concerned, it was a run-of-the-mill electrical fire. As part of his investigation, he checked the building codes and contacted the construction company and electricians who originally built the restaurant thirty years ago. According to Hutton, the new equipment overloaded the cheap wiring, causing the outlet to spark and the power cord to overheat. The fire spread and, eventually, took down the building.

I examined Hutton's photos, but I didn't know anything

about fires or arson, so I made a note to do more research. Easton said he had the building inspected several times. I'd have to get names and put in more legwork in the morning. I already had a meeting scheduled with the fire department's arson investigator for the following day. But patience was never one of my virtues, so I moved on to plan B.

Renner wasn't the only one who had friends in the police department, but I didn't know Sgt. Chambliss, the officer of record. O'Connell or one of my other pals in blue would have to make the introduction. I grabbed what I needed, checked my messages, and headed for the elevator. I didn't know where Renner went or when he'd be back, but it was getting late. Obviously, Cross intended to keep Renner so busy he couldn't work this case. I wondered what tasks the boss would have waiting for me in the morning.

I stopped at the front desk and smiled warmly at the assistant. "I need to fill out another personal leave request form."

"Short or long-term?"

"Short. I'll only be gone a few more days." Unless Cross has other plans for me.

She ran her pointer finger down the stack of baskets and handed me a sheet of paper. "You'll need this form. Mr. Cross has to approve all absences. After you fill that out, leave it with his assistant, Justin."

"Thanks." I tucked the form into the back of the folder and stepped into the elevator.

By the time I arrived at the precinct, it was late in the afternoon. Hopefully, shift change would work in my favor. The desk sergeant was busy dealing with nearly two dozen walk-ins. I glanced around at the assortment of people. The officers on duty had their hands full.

The desk sergeant recognized me and automatically called up to major crimes. Detective Nick O'Connell appeared at the bottom of the stairwell and squinted through the mess of people filing complaints. He pointed at me and crooked his finger.

"Parker," he said, "do I want to know why you're here? I

thought you said you would call."

"I'm looking for someone."

"You caught another missing persons case?"

"No. I'm looking for a cop. Sergeant Chambliss. Do you know him?"

O'Connell nodded slowly. "He's the watch commander. Does this have anything to do with the throng of visitors today?"

"No, and for the record, the mess in there isn't my fault." I gestured toward the front desk. "I didn't realize it was feeding time at the zoo."

"Lighten up, Parker. I'm just busting your balls. If you can't take my teasing, you have no business speaking to Chambliss. He'll eat you alive. What do you want with him anyway?"

I slid a copy of the crime scene report out of the folder and handed it to Nick. "Bennett Renner just found himself a new client, and he left me with the Easton Lango case. I'm trying to get the facts straight and figured I'd start at the top."

Nick scanned the page. "Why didn't Renner follow up with Chambliss? Did he do any work on the case before handing it off, besides attempting to run over my foot?"

"Actually, Renner doesn't know I'm here. He asked if I'd assist, and then Cross called him away."

"You're probably better off." O'Connell eyed the paperwork. "The investigation is closed. The fire was ruled accidental. What do you need Chambliss for?"

"I didn't realize you were his secretary."

"And I didn't realize you were Renner's," Nick retorted. "Be straight with me. That's how this works."

So I told O'Connell everything I knew about Easton Lango and the complaint he filed and the work I put in today. "Renner says Jake Voletek called and asked him to look into Easton's case."

O'Connell's eyebrows knit together. "Voletek? You're sure he said Voletek?"

"Yeah. Why?"

"That doesn't make any sense. Let's take a walk." O'Connell led the way up the steps. He opened the door to homicide, and I followed him inside. I didn't spot any familiar faces in the bullpen, but most of my cop buddies worked major crimes, not homicide. "Jake," O'Connell called, "I need to speak to you in private."

The scruffy detective on the phone held up his pointer finger, and O'Connell nodded before ducking into the break room. Bewildered, I followed Nick, who helped himself to a cup of coffee and popped open the pink pastry box. After selecting a donut with sprinkles, he shifted the box to face me.

"You're a walking, talking cliché, Detective." But that didn't stop me from grabbing the last chocolate crème and taking a bite. By the time Voletek joined us, O'Connell and I had devoured the evidence.

Detective Voletek smiled, giving me the once-over. "Hi, I'm Jake." He held out his hand and rubbed his thumb in a circle against my knuckles as we shook. "And you are?"

"Taken," O'Connell said.

I glared at Nick. I had no interest in the homicide detective, but it didn't hurt to flirt, particularly when I needed to convince someone to do something he didn't want to do. "Alex," I said.

"Alex, huh?" Voletek dropped my hand. "What can I do for you, Alex?"

Before I could answer, O'Connell asked, "Have you spoken to Easton Lango?"

Voletek's eyes darted to O'Connell's. "Why do you want to know?"

"I'll take that as a yes," O'Connell said.

"I don't care how you take it," Voletek replied. "Why do you care? Are things really that slow in major crimes that you got reassigned to the paperwork brigade?"

"I don't care who you speak to," O'Connell jerked his chin at me, "but she does. And she matters to me, so play nice."

"Does Jenny know that?" Voletek asked, the testosterone level increasing by the second.

"Of course, she does. Alex is one of her best friends. Got it?"

Voletek took a step back, nodding. "Yeah, Nick, I got it."

I didn't, but that was a conversation for another time. "Why are you asking about Chef Easton?" Voletek asked me.

"I work with Bennett Renner at Cross Security. He says you suggested Mr. Lango speak to us. I want to know why."

"It's simple. Chef Easton thinks someone wants to kill him. He asked to speak to a homicide detective about his case, and I volunteered." Voletek's gaze briefly flicked to O'Connell. "I'm sure you've been told the fire investigation is closed. They determined the cause was electrical. No signs of tampering or foul play, so without any evidence, there isn't much the police department can do. But from what Chef Easton told me, the fire might not even be the worst part. Someone's out to get him, and given the escalation, I wouldn't be surprised if the person responsible doesn't try something else in the future. That's why I suggested he seek outside help. Cross Security's the best in the business. If anyone can help him, it's you or, rather, your firm."

"Schmoozer," O'Connell muttered.

"You don't think Mr. Lango is full of shit?" I asked.

"No, ma'am."

I narrowed my eyes at Voletek, but I let the ma'am comment slide. "That wasn't Easton's take on it. Did Easton offer you a reward?"

"It's a catered dinner. Some reward," Voletek said.

"That explains it." O'Connell made a show of checking his watch. "I have to get back to work, Parker. I trust you can take it from here."

My eyes never left Voletek's face. "Yeah, Nick, I got this." After O'Connell stepped away, I said, "I don't care what Easton offered you." I lowered my voice. "It doesn't matter. What matters is if you actually believe there's a legitimate threat. Do you think someone intentionally set the fire?"

"That's what I told Chef Easton. I just can't prove it, and the evidence says otherwise."

"What about his previous threats? Did Easton tell you anything helpful?"

Without answering, Voletek turned and headed back

into the bullpen. I followed him past his desk and to a conference room. "Shut the door," he instructed as soon as I stepped inside. I kicked the door closed behind me. The detective pulled a rolling corkboard away from the back wall and flipped it around. "This is all I got out of him. I tried looking into it, but it's a bunch of dead ends. That's why I passed it off to Renner. I thought he might have other resources available. Y'know, less legal means of assessing potential threats."

I stood in front of the board and studied Easton Lango's sloppy handwriting. The detective had photocopied Easton's statement and dissected the various elements. Voletek highlighted a few key points, like the day, time, and place where the first threatening note was left. A string connected it to a photo taken outside Bouillon.

"How did you get this?" I flicked the photograph.

"Internet printout. I just wanted to see what the place looked like. That shot's from their website. I tried to get footage from the night in question, but without hard proof and no allegations of property damage, I couldn't convince the owner to turn over the security tapes. I think he's hiding something."

"Did you speak to any potential witnesses?"

"I spoke to some of Chef Easton's former coworkers, but no one remembers anything odd from that night or any night. Restaurants get all kinds, but no one stood out as angry or vengeful enough to leave a threat on the chef's car."

"You should see what they post online."

Voletek arched an eyebrow. "What?"

"Never mind. What about the general manager?"

"He was too busy for my questions and blew me off. He took my card and said he'd let me know if he remembered anything."

"He wouldn't talk to us either." I followed another string from the restaurant to a copy of the GM's driver's license photo. "Did you run a background check on Jensen Adler?"

"Nothing popped up." Voletek glanced at me. "Did you find something I missed?"

"No. Renner performed the checks, but he would have

mentioned if he found something. What about Bouillon's owner?"

"Which one?"

"What do you mean which one? We only know about one."

"Micah Maston was sole owner of Bouillon when Easton worked there, but after his departure, he sold most of the business to Chef Strader. From what I gather, Maston intends to retire, probably figures he'll sit back and collect dividends while Strader runs the show."

That was another strike against Galen Strader. The more I learned, the more I understood why Easton thought his culinary school rival was behind the threats. "Did Maston mention anything odd happening before Easton's departure? Maybe the restaurant received some threats when Easton was manning the kitchen?"

"I don't know. Maston didn't say much, but it's obvious Easton's departure left a bad taste in Maston's mouth. He said he washed his hands of Easton the moment the chef walked out the door. As far as he's concerned, Easton's replacement is better anyway."

"Shit."

"Yep. Strader's at the top of my list."

"Mine too. Easton said they've been rivals since culinary school."

"And since Bouillon received a scathing review in the paper after Easton left, that might have been enough for Strader to threaten Easton and sabotage his new restaurant. After all, it's not just Strader's reputation on the line. From what I hear, Galen Strader sunk everything he had into Bouillon. Most of Bouillon's patrons were loyal to Chef Easton, not the restaurant. Sizzle's success could have sunk Bouillon and bankrupted Strader."

"You're sure about that?" Speculation wasn't enough to get access to bank records.

"I'm just telling you what I heard."

"The fire happened while Easton was inside the restaurant. You really think Strader wants to kill him?"

"People kill for a lot of reasons, Alex. That's why I have a job. Plus, Strader has violent tendencies and anger issues."

"If that's the case, Strader might have threatened Easton online." We needed a peek at Strader's internet history.

"He didn't." Voletek made sure the door was closed and no one could hear us. "I had someone check his online footprint. The ugly messages and veiled threats Easton received didn't come from Strader, or if they did, Strader was careful enough to conceal his identity."

"Do you know who sent them?"

"No. The messages came from different IP addresses and accounts registered in foreign countries. Whoever sent them covered his tracks. I just know Strader never visited any of Easton's social media profiles with a device we can link back to him."

"Unless he got someone else to do it or he knows more about computers than we think."

"That is always a possibility. What does Renner think? Did Cross Security find anything I missed?"

"He doesn't know enough to speculate. We just started digging."

"I'm sorry he sent you to do his dirty work. Bennett promised me he'd handle this himself. I don't know why he involved you."

"It's better than the shit Cross wanted me to do," I mumbled under my breath. I examined the rest of the detective's notes. "Do you mind if I take these with me?"

"Actually, I do. I sent copies to Cross Security. Didn't you get them?"

"I did, just not your notes." This wasn't an open investigation. Hell, it wasn't any kind of investigation. Renner was right about one thing. Voletek had that ingrained desire to help people or possibly help himself to a reward. I didn't know the man well enough to judge. Maybe I'd ask O'Connell about it. They obviously had a history.

"I can have them copied and sent to you," Voletek offered.

"How about I just snap a few photos?" I held up my cell phone. "I can recreate whatever I need back at the office, and it won't inconvenience you. Plus, it'll save me time from having to do this research myself, and it'll get us one step closer to putting Chef Easton's mind at ease and this lunatic behind bars, assuming there is a lunatic."

"Go ahead."

When I was finished, Voletek escorted me downstairs and asked that someone from Cross Security keep him updated on the case. I told him this was Renner's case, and if he had any questions, he should contact his old pal. There was no reason to tell Voletek I was in charge. If he had a hero complex, like Renner said, he'd be all over my ass for progress reports, and I already had far too many men breathing down my neck.

Before I left the precinct, I detoured upstairs to major crimes, but O'Connell had left for the day. I spoke to the desk sergeant, but Chambliss' shift ended two hours ago. No wonder O'Connell didn't make the introduction when I first arrived. Maybe I'd let Renner handle that in the morning. I already had several meetings on the books, including a crash course in fire investigation. But that was tomorrow's problem. Right now, I had a dinner date with some moving boxes.

EIGHT

I stood in my bedroom, leafing through the papers I kept in my gun safe. I tossed my rental agreement on the bed. I wouldn't need that anymore. My hands stopped on a familiar creased and tear-stained envelope. My jaw clenched as I held the yellowing paper against my chest and closed my eyes.

My thoughts went to sitting on the floor, splitting takeout, and going over OIO case files with my late partner. After he was killed in the line of duty several years ago, my life had never been the same, but too much had happened since for me to hold on to this apartment as a tether to the past, to the person I used to be, or out of some misplaced or misguided sense of loyalty. It was finally time to leave this apartment and those events and others behind. Or so I told myself.

Truthfully, I didn't want that life anymore, not since I met Martin. I liked being a P.I. I just didn't know if I wanted to do it at Cross Security. Maybe now wasn't the right time to move with so many other big, life decisions looming in the not too distant future.

"Alex," Martin called, "the movers are here to take some of your things. Is that okay?"

"That's fine." I looked around my bedroom. The place

was a mess. "The living room's ready to go."

"Do you want them to take the TV now?"

I put the letter from Michael down. "Whatever."

Martin entered the bedroom, picked up the rental agreement, and checked the circled dates. "You don't have to do this. This is your apartment. If you want to keep it, you should. I don't want to pressure you into something you aren't sure about."

How did he always manage to read my mind? "I have to let it go, unless you're having second thoughts about letting me move back into your house."

"Our house. It's our house," he said firmly. "Like our apartment. And no, I'm not." He stared into my eyes through the reflection in the mirror. "It won't be like last time. I won't ask you to leave again. I promise."

"I know." But I couldn't shake the fear and heartbreak, reminders of the last time we intentionally tried living together. Granted, we lived together now in an apartment that was meant to be our weekend place, but it just happened. We didn't plan it. Most of the time, our plans failed. Maybe I was afraid this would be another one of those times.

"We tried being apart, and that didn't work for me."

"Me neither."

"For better or worse, things are different now," Martin said.

As usual, he was right. I'd just never tell him that. The dark circles beneath my eyes weren't new, but the ones beneath his were. I picked up an envelope from the edge of my dresser and handed it to him. "Here."

He took it and looked inside. "What's this? I'm not taking rent money from you."

"It's not rent. I want to pay you back, but it'll take some time. That's just the first installment."

He put the envelope down. "Is this why you decided to give up your apartment? If it is, I swear I'll tell the movers to turn around and put everything back where they found it. I don't want you to move in because of this. I don't want you to feel indebted to me."

"I do, but," I spun to face him, "that's not why I'm

moving in. I'm moving in because I love you and I want to. But this," I nodded at the envelope, "is something I have to do. Think of it as a side benefit. You get me and your money back. What more could a guy want?"

"Alex, no."

"You lost a quarter of a million dollars because of me."

Martin took a seat on the bed, suddenly exhausted. He held up the check. "I'm not taking your money. The ransom could have been millions, and I would have gladly paid it. I would do anything for you. Anything." He ran a hand through his hair, making the dark brown locks spike even higher.

"Then accept payment graciously, and don't argue with me about it."

He set his jaw, a sign of his stubbornness. "Should I tell the movers you changed your mind?"

"I haven't. Have you?"

He stood, pressed the check into my palm, and brushed his lips against my cheek. "No, and I never will." Before I could say anything, he returned to the living room and told the movers to take the TV. We didn't need an audience for our inevitable fight.

By the time I joined him, the only things left in the living room were my couch and coffee table. The rest of my furniture, my books, my computer, my files, and my movie collection were gone. Martin and I packed them before the movers arrived, and they were now on their way to Martin's house.

Martin offered to tackle the kitchen. Since cooking wasn't one of the skills I acquired while working for the OIO or as a private investigator, my cookware and appliances left a lot to be desired. But he wanted to salvage whatever he thought we could use.

"The coffeemaker's coming with me," I insisted. "And the large serving spoon."

"I have spoons."

"Good for you, but I like mine."

He faced me. "Alex, I'm barely holding it together. I don't want to fight about this. I don't want to think about the days I spent wondering if you were alive or dead, and I sure as hell don't want a weekly or monthly reminder of how close I came to losing you."

"You hate my spoon that much?"

He rolled his eyes. "You know what I'm talking about. Don't make me spell it out."

"Is that why you called the shrink this morning?"

"Dammit. Why does that bother you so much?"

"It doesn't." But it did, and Martin knew it. I turned away and stared out the fire escape. "I don't want to be the one who broke you. I need you to be okay because you're the glue that holds me together, but I know this is my fault. Do you want me to go back to therapy with you? We can talk through it together." Couples therapy didn't work well the first few times we tried it, but this wasn't about our relationship. This was about addressing trauma, and while I was perfectly content pretending I hadn't been abducted and almost buried alive, Martin didn't have the same coping mechanism in place. Now, whenever we were apart, he was anxious. And when we were together, he couldn't let me out of his sight, which was probably why he couldn't sleep. That and the nightmares.

"That's the last thing I need," he growled.

"Great, I did break you."

"You didn't break me, and I don't want to break you. I never want to make you relive that, and that's exactly what will happen if you come with me to see the shrink." He sighed. "If you must know, I called to ask about sleep aids."

"Did you get a prescription?"

"I don't want one. I just wanted to know what kinds of non-prescription options are available. Y'know, things like melatonin or herbal teas."

"What did he say?"

Martin ducked down and opened another cabinet. "You know doctors. They're a bunch of quacks." He pulled out a frying pan and examined the back. "But like I said, I don't need a constant reminder. So please, Alex, let the money go. It's something we'll fight about, and I rather fight about whose serving spoon is better because that's one argument that won't keep me up at night. And honestly, I could use some sleep." He peered over the counter and grinned.

"Plus, I already know the answer to that question."

I didn't know if the money was something I could let go, but I'd find another solution. Martin had a thing for exotic cars. Maybe in ten years, when I saved up enough, I'd buy him one. The thought that we'd even be together in ten years simultaneously frightened and comforted me. I always knew I was unstable, and yet, he was the one with a shrink on speed dial. We were a match made in heaven or the psych ward.

"Okay. I'm glad we're in agreement that my spoon's better." I blew out a breath. "From the way things look, I'll probably be out of work by next week, anyway. I should tighten my belt in preparation for the inevitable."

Martin put the pan down and came around the counter and wrapped his arms around me. "Is that because of this afternoon? Does Cross have an anti-hanky-panky policy?"

"Probably, but even if he doesn't, you know I do."

"Sorry, but I can't guarantee it won't happen again. I find you irresistible." He kissed my temple. "What's going on? You were late coming home tonight. Was that Cross's doing?"

"In a way. He made me primary on Renner's side case, so I was at the precinct doing research. But that's not the issue."

"What is?"

"After you left, Lucien asked me straight out if I could convince you to change your mind. He and I need to establish some ground rules now that I know his true motivation for hiring me. If we can't reach an agreement, it'd be best for me to move on."

"Maybe it'll do you some good to get away from the office for a few days," Martin said, but I could see the storm clouds hanging over his head. He despised Lucien Cross as much as I did. Maybe more. "It might help you gain some perspective or clarity, and I'm sure it'll make him realize what an asset you are. In the meantime, if there's anything I can do, name it, but I bet by the time you get back, Lucien will be groveling at your feet."

"Yeah, right. He wants you. He wants a partnership with Martin Technologies and thought hiring me was the best way to get to you, except he didn't realize we were dating. He just thought I liked to moonlight as your security."

"You did make an excellent bodyguard." Martin winked, hoping to cheer me up. "However, if you want to leave Cross in the dust, I have plenty of friends and business contacts I can call. Didn't Jablonsky offer to help you find another law enforcement job? The PD offered you a position with their counter-terrorism unit a while back. Don't be afraid to tell Lucien to kiss your ass. I'd be happy to do it for you."

"We'll see, but you know I like to fight my own battles."

"And everyone else's," Martin mumbled before returning to the kitchen.

I fell silent, watching as he examined my stainless steel cookware. He selected a few pieces to add to his collection, along with an enameled cast iron casserole dish Mark Jablonsky, my FBI mentor and Martin's best friend, had given me for the holidays three years ago.

"This is nice." Martin removed the cover. "It looks brand new. Do you ever use it?"

"No."

He chuckled. "Did Jabber give it to you?"

"How'd you know?"

"I gave him one exactly like it when he moved into his townhouse after his third divorce."

"It's probably the same one. You might as well take it back. Out of the three of us, you're the only one who knows what to do with it." I lifted the handle, remembering why I never used it. "It's damn heavy. Are you sure it isn't a weapon?"

"Do you always think tactically?"

"Force of habit."

"Should I be concerned why you're so adamant about holding on to the serving spoon? Does it shoot laser beams or something?"

"No, but that would make it a lot easier to get the ice cream out of the container."

"They make scoops for that."

I gave him a look, and he obediently dropped the spoon into the box.

Martin emptied a few more cabinets. "Don't forget to check online for events in Vegas. I know a guy who can get us tickets to just about anything. Let me know what you find, and I'll make the arrangements."

"We'll worry about that later. Right now, let's see how much packing we get done. I'm not leaving this up to strangers."

"We'll finish. I'll make sure of it." He emptied another cabinet. "Anything else you want to keep from the kitchen?"

"The microwave and I have some fond memories, but it makes a weird humming sound. I don't know. What do you think?"

"For someone who has zero photographs and very few knickknacks, you have an unnatural attachment to your microwave."

"It kept me fed on the days you didn't, but I guess I've traded up. We can donate it or leave it for the next tenant." I narrowed my eyes. "Where are my fridge magnets?"

"They're on the fridge in our apartment. Marcal grabbed them when he brought over the empty boxes this morning," Martin said. "You were already at work."

I took a seat at the island, glancing forlornly at the empty spot where my dining room table used to be. When we finished in the kitchen, I gave the growing donation pile the quick once-over but didn't see anything worth saving.

By now, most of the apartment had been emptied. Aside from the couch and coffee table, there was nothing left in the main room. The bathroom only had the most basic of toiletries, and my towels were too old and frayed to bother keeping.

"I'll pack up the bedroom tomorrow night, and the movers can get the rest of my furniture over the weekend." I spun in a circle, remembering the first time I ever set foot in this apartment. Considering everything that had happened over the last eight years, I knew there wasn't a chance in hell I'd get my security deposit back. A piece of carpeting was still missing from where I'd peeled it off the floor after O'Connell shot a psychopath intent on killing me. I should have moved then, but I didn't. Damn, my life was the plot of a bad action movie. "When's our flight?"

"Early Monday morning. We filed the flight plan with a seven a.m. takeoff time." Martin grabbed several boxes off the counter and followed me to the front door. "I can delay our departure a few hours if you don't finish packing."

I shook my head. "It's just the bedroom. How bad can it be?"

Martin chuckled. "Most of your clothes are already in our apartment, so I'm guessing the only things left to pack are the dozen shirts I've lost over the years. Any idea where they might be?"

"I plead the fifth." Before we made it out the front door, my phone rang. "Hang on a sec." It took a moment before I recognized the number on the display as Chef Easton's. Why was he calling?

"Hello?"

"Alex, I just called the police. I heard something. Someone's inside my house. I think they're still here," he whispered.

"Where are you?"

"In the pantry."

I heard a loud crash, and the line went dead. "Shit." I grabbed my car keys and made sure my gun was in my purse. "I have to go. It's an emergency." Before Martin could say a word, I dialed the office. I needed Easton's address. He said he called the cops. Hopefully, they'd get there before I did.

NINE

"Hello?" I called, pushing the door open with my foot. "Is anyone here?" I waited for a reply. When none came, I said, "I'm armed, and the police are on their way." Still nothing. "Easton? It's Alex."

Cautiously, I crept inside. Broken glass crunched beneath my feet, and I noticed the broken window. A brick lay on the floor with a note taped to it. I scanned the area for signs of danger before flipping the brick over with my foot.

*Die, asshol*e was scrawled on the note in red block letters. That would make handwriting analysis more difficult, but that was the least of the problem.

"Easton?" I bellowed.

I didn't hear anything. Where were the cops? I swept the living room and sitting room. For a renowned chef, Easton Lango lived in squalor. His couch looked like something he found on the side of the road. He had a TV mounted on the wall and a few tray tables to hold his lamps. Well, lamp. The other was broken and sideways beside a knocked over table.

Someone had been inside. I just didn't know if they were still here, and I had no idea where Easton was.

Swallowing, I aimed at the closet door before pulling it open. Several sets of chef whites hung inside. I pushed them out of the way, but the closet was empty.

I repeated the process in the bedroom and bathroom. I didn't find any other signs of a break-in or a blood trail. Hopefully, Easton had gotten away.

I entered the kitchen and flipped on the light, sweeping my gun back and forth and aiming at an apron that looked a little too lifelike. Exhaling, I noted the expensive cookware and appliances. Obviously, Easton only cared about the kitchen and not the rest of his house. If someone wanted to hurt him, this would be the place to strike, but nothing was damaged. The two thousand dollar blender and five hundred dollar mixer remained undisturbed.

None of this made any sense. I searched the entire house. Easton said he was hiding in the pantry, and it was the only place left to check. I ducked behind the counter and aimed at the pantry door.

"You're surrounded. We know you're in there. Throw out your weapons and come out with your hands up." Sure, it was just me, but there was safety in numbers. So it was me, myself, and I. "We won't ask again."

Nothing.

I edged closer to the pantry, the barrel of my gun leading the way. Thoughts of a shotgun blast ripping a hole through the thin wood door and my chest ran through my mind. I probably shouldn't have left my vest in the car. Oh well, too late now.

I yanked the door open. The walk-in pantry was dark, making it impossible to see any potential threats clearly. I reached for the pull cord on the overhead light, prepared to fire at the first sign of danger. The light came on, illuminating the packed shelves. No one was inside.

Taking an unsteady breath, I zeroed in on Easton's cell phone. Slipping on my leather gloves, I knelt down and picked up the dropped phone. The corner of the screen was cracked, but it didn't affect the functionality. Unfortunately, Easton password protected the device. I checked the rest of the pantry, noting several broken jars and dented cans. Maybe whoever threw the brick through the window found the chef hiding in the pantry and dragged him away.

Realizing the phone might be evidence, I put it down where I found it and stood up. I used my phone to photograph the scene and was mid-dial when thunderous footsteps sounded behind me. I took a step back and tugged on the cord, plunging the pantry into darkness. With all the shelves and foodstuffs, there wasn't much room to maneuver or hide. It was a good thing I was a decent shot and had the element of surprise.

The footsteps grew louder. Someone was in the kitchen. He was getting closer. And closer. Suddenly, a flashlight blinded me.

"Lower your weapon," he said.

I ignored the command, squinting against the harsh light. He stepped so close I could smell his aftershave. He reached out with the flashlight, the cold metal brushing against my arm. I jerked, swinging at the light and knocking his hand away.

"Take it easy. I'm not going to hurt you." He lowered the blinding beam of light and tugged on the cord. "Did Chef Easton call you, too? Where is he?"

I blinked, hoping to get rid of the red blobs impeding my vision. "Detective Voletek?"

He holstered his gun and waited for me to do the same. "Is there a particular reason you're hiding in the closet?"

"I wasn't hiding. Easton called and said someone was inside his house."

"I saw the brick." Voletek looked around. "Where is he?"

"I don't know. I searched the house but didn't find much." I pointed at the dropped cell phone. "We were disconnected. That's his phone."

"Shit." Voletek rubbed his mouth and crouched down, examining the damage. "Was it like this when you got here?"

"Yes."

"All right, I have to call this in."

"Easton said he called the cops."

"He called me."

"Shit," I muttered.

"I already said that." Voletek spoke to dispatch, giving them Easton's address.

While he was occupied, I wandered toward the back door. Easton Lango lived in a small cottage in the suburbs, but from what I gathered, this wasn't a safe neighborhood. A chain-link fence kept the tall, brown weeds from sprawling into the neighbor's yard. I checked the back door for signs of tampering, surprised to find it unlocked.

A set of deep tire tracks cut a path through the backyard. Perhaps the assailant abducted Easton and dragged him out the back and into a waiting getaway vehicle. I unholstered my gun and stepped outside. It had been dark for hours. No one was outside. I doubted the neighbors noticed anything, and if they did, they probably wouldn't tell us.

"Hey, Voletek, I might have something."

"Jake," he corrected, joining me on the cracked concrete slab that housed a rusty grill. "What is it?"

"The door was open, and we have tire tracks."

He didn't move from the spot on the patio. "I'll let the uniformed officers know. We're gonna need a crime scene unit down here." Anger flashed across his face. "Do you think this is an abduction?"

"It reads like one, but I hope not."

"Without a body, it doesn't look like a homicide." He glanced back into the kitchen. "It doesn't look like a robbery. Those kitchen gadgets would be worth a few grand. A thief would know that. He would have taken them."

"Did you read the brick?" I asked. The tire tracks didn't make sense, and I watched them disappear around the side of the house. What was on the other side of the house? "Why leave the threat if you're here to kidnap the target?"

"Maybe they didn't have a plan."

"Or Easton escaped." I took a step off the patio just as the sound of sirens filled the air. "Looks like your backup has arrived."

"All right. Let me brief them. Stay here."

Based on the width and depth of the tracks, I suspected they must have been made by a large vehicle. Perhaps

Easton used the backyard to park his food truck. He was far too paranoid to leave it unattended all night. But I doubted the neighborhood was zoned for this, just like it wasn't zoned for the drug den down the street, so he'd probably want to keep the truck hidden.

I followed the tracks around the side, unsure what I would find. Parked behind a shed to obstruct the view from the street was Easton's Eats. A dusty blue tarp had been thrown over the top to further hide it from view. Obviously, Easton didn't want to get ticketed or risk having the vehicle towed. He cared a lot about that truck. If someone wanted to hurt him, this would be the perfect place to do it.

Slowly, I crept toward the rear door. The shutter covered the order window, and the tarp blocked the windshield. There was no way to see inside. Tugging on the rear door handle, I found it unlocked. I turned on the small flashlight attached to my keychain and held it beneath my gun, sweeping the beam of light from left to right.

When I didn't see anyone inside, I climbed into the pitch black truck and searched for a light switch. That's when I heard a rustling sound. Someone else was inside.

I spun toward the sound. The beam of light caught a rush of movement right before the gun was knocked from my hand. I didn't have time to process or recover before the object struck again. This time, it missed, but I felt the whoosh of air blow my hair back as it passed inches from my face. A guttural scream followed, and as my eyes adjusted, I ducked, narrowly escaping the swing of the aluminum bat. It banged against the window, breaking it and showering me in pieces of glass. The attacker swung again, but I grabbed the end of the bat in both hands and tugged, my palms stinging from the impact.

He yanked hard, and I let go, sending him sprawling into the corner of the truck. I scooped up my gun and flashlight and pointed them at the assailant. "Don't shoot. Please," he begged.

"Easton?"

Dazed, Easton rubbed the back of his head. "Alex?" He hit a switch, and the interior lights came on. "I thought you were the asshole with the brick." He put the bat on the counter, grabbed a towel, and wiped the sweat from his brow. "Did I hurt you?"

I rubbed my hand, relieved his second swing missed or else he might be cleaning brain matter off the counter instead of just the broken window. "I'll live. Are you okay? What's going on? I thought something happened to you. I thought you were abducted."

"I'm fine. A bit freaked, but otherwise good. Thanks for showing up when you did. I thought they came back. I thought they found me."

"Who?"

He looked uncertainly at my gun. "Have you been inside my house?"

"Uh-huh."

"Then you know."

I blinked, wondering if one of us had sustained a head injury. "You're not making much sense. Spell it out for me. Who are they? What did they do?"

"Did you find anyone inside?"

"No." I tucked my gun away, realizing the sight of it was making him nervous. "Did you hit anyone else with the bat besides me?"

He shook his head. "I'm sorry. I'll get you some ice and tell you what happened."

"You can tell us what happened," Voletek said, appearing at the rear door. He reached for the radio. "Cancel the all points. I found Easton Lango. Be advised, we're coming inside."

Easton led the way out of the truck. Two cruisers remained parked in front of Easton's house, but by now, they killed the lights and sirens. The house diagonal from Easton had their porch lights on, and I thought I saw someone peek out through the blinds. *Nosy neighbors*, I assumed, reminding myself to speak with them later.

"What's going on, Chef?" Voletek asked as we entered the kitchen and Easton took a seat at the table. "Do you know who did this?"

Easton shook his head. "No idea. I was in the living room, planning out the menu when I heard noise outside."

"What kind of noise?" Voletek asked.

"The rumble of an engine and a radio with the bass turned all the way up. I thought the neighbors were having another of their parties." The way Easton said parties meant he knew they were dealing drugs. "This block has a lot of traffic. People in and out at all hours of the day and night. I only moved here so I could save up enough to start my own restaurant." A dark cloud settled over Easton, and he scowled. "Anyway, I didn't give it much thought until that brick came crashing through my window. That's when I grabbed the bat and called you."

"Why didn't you tell me this on the phone?" Voletek asked.

"Most of the cops I've talked to have had more important things to do. I figured you'd just think it was vandalism and not bother to show up."

"Is that why you didn't call 911?" Voletek asked.

"Yeah." Easton glanced at the uniformed officer taking notes from the counter. "After I called you, I realized the car was still out there."

"Can you describe it?"

"It was a classic muscle car, black or maybe dark blue. It looked like a Mustang, sixty-something, I'd guess. It had been tricked out. Undercarriage lights, spinners, and that sick stereo."

"What color were the lights?" I asked.

"Neon green."

"Have you ever seen that car before?" Voletek asked. Again, Easton shrugged. I didn't think the chef paid much attention to anything that wasn't related to cooking. "What about the driver? What did he look like? Have you ever seen him before?"

"I don't know. It was too dark to see."

"But you're sure the brick came from the car?" Voletek asked. Easton nodded, and Voletek told the uniformed officer to radio in the intel. Obviously, we traded one BOLO for another.

"How long was he out there?" I asked.

"I don't know. He just sat there, like he was waiting for something or someone. I checked the rest of the house and figured I'd wait for help to arrive. I thought about bashing in his windshield with the bat, but I didn't know if he had a gun." Easton stared at the table, reddening with embarrassment. "I should have done something."

"You did the right thing," Voletek said. "In situations like this, it's best to let the police handle it. When citizens take matters into their own hands, things gets messy. He might have said you assaulted him. It's best to think before you act."

"Yeah." Easton didn't sound convinced.

"When we spoke, you said someone was inside the house," I said. "Why don't you tell us about that?"

"I was hiding in the pantry, waiting for help to arrive. That's when I heard him come inside. Or I thought I did. I don't know." Easton ran a shaking hand through his multi-colored hair.

"Relax," Voletek said. "You're okay."

Easton got up from the table and circled the kitchen. "I thought I heard him in here, but when I opened the pantry door, the kitchen was empty."

"Was the back door open?" I asked.

Easton blinked. "Um..."

Voletek glanced at me. Witnesses and victims often forgot details in the heat of the moment. "It's okay. Take your time."

"The door was closed, but it might have been unlocked. I can't remember. I heard rustling out back and feared the bastard intended to sabotage my truck. The car out front and the brick might have been distractions. I don't know how I got outside. All I know is that I ran out back to check on my truck, and that's when I saw him."

"Saw who?" Voletek asked.

"I don't fucking know." Easton went to the fridge. He ripped open the door before slamming it shut. Then, as if remembering a forgotten promise, he grabbed the towel from the hook and opened the freezer. He wrapped some ice in the towel and dropped it on the counter in front of me. "He wore a watch cap. He might have had a mask. I don't know. I couldn't see much. But he was messing with the tarp. I surprised him, and he took off. He got into the car and drove off before I could stop him. That's when I went inside the food truck. I figured I'd stay out there to guard it."

"Instead, you surprised me," I said.

The wheels turned in Voletek's head. "Did you get the plate?"

Easton sighed. "No."

"Did you see anyone when you got here, Alex?"

"No."

"What time was that?" Voletek asked.

"I don't know." I looked at the clock. "Less than ten minutes before you arrived."

"Okay. Hang tight. Let me see what I can do." Voletek strode out of the kitchen, leaving us with an officer who was poking around in the pantry.

"Why didn't you call Bennett Renner?" I asked.

Easton let out a huff. "I did. He promised he'd get here as soon as he could. I guess I'm not his top priority." He exhaled and attempted a smile. "I guess I'm yours."

"Maybe," I admitted, "but don't tell my boyfriend."

TEN

After assigning a patrol to sit outside Easton's house, Voletek pulled me to the side. "I spoke to the neighbors. No one remembers seeing any cars that fit Easton's description."

"You think they'd talk to you?" I glanced pointedly at his badge. "This doesn't seem to be the most cop friendly neighborhood."

"You're right, but I have a weird feeling about this. You saw the damage inside. What caused it?"

"I'm guessing the Louisville slugger."

"Those are traditionally wood, not aluminum."

"Do I look like I care?"

Voletek laughed. "So we're in agreement the damage in the pantry is from Easton trashing his own place?"

"Probably, unless we're dealing with several unsubs. What did forensics say? Did they find any prints?"

"A few partials and some smudges, but nothing appears recent. I'd say they probably belong to whatever houseguests Easton has had in the past month or so. We only found one set of prints on the note, and when we ran them through the scanner, they matched Easton Lango. The lab will verify it, but we have no reason to doubt the findings. This bastard is clever. He wore gloves and didn't leave any evidence behind."

A silver sedan pulled up behind Voletek's SUV, and Bennett Renner got out of the car. "Hey," he waved, glancing around, "is Easton okay?"

"Shaken up, but fine," I said. "And for the record, I didn't call the cops. Make sure Cross knows that."

"Will do." Renner saw Easton watching us from the front door and waved. "Why the boarded up window?"

"Someone threw a brick through it," I said.

"Yeah, someone," Voletek muttered. "I'll see what forensics turns up on the letter and the handwriting, but I don't think we're missing anything. The car's probably our best bet. A custom job like that should be easy enough to find."

"Do you have a starting place in mind?"

"Maybe." Voletek eyed me, and I knew we had the same thought. We wanted to know what Galen Strader drove.

Renner gave the two of us a strange look. "What's going on, Jake? Is there something I should know?" He glanced at me. "Do the two of you know each other? You seem awfully close."

"We just met today." I faced Voletek. "Does this mean the police are opening a new investigation?"

"I'll see what I can do, but the brass hates being wrong. Easton's right. They might write it off as vandalism or a teenage prank since nothing was stolen and no one was hurt. I'll do what I can. These threats are real, and if we don't identify the party responsible, he'll escalate."

"Someone needs to catch me up to speed," Renner said.

"I will," I promised.

"We took the tarp into evidence. Maybe we'll find something on it. I should head over to the precinct and see if I can locate the car." Voletek reached for his phone and sent a text message.

"Keep us looped in," Renner said.

"Since we didn't find prints inside the house, I'm sure you won't find any outside either. The guy probably wore gloves," I surmised.

"I'll look anyway." Voletek narrowed his eyes at Renner, his brow furrowing. He saw something I didn't, and he didn't like it. "The patrol unit will sit on Easton until we know more. It'll give the chef a brief reprieve. Hopefully, he can rest easy. I'll let you know what I find."

"Let us know when you're pulling the protection detail," Renner said.

Voletek nodded and got into his car.

I watched him drive away. "Where were you? Easton's your client. This is your case. Just because Cross wants to cover his ass and lists me as primary, that doesn't mean you can drop the ball."

"I'm sorry. I got held up."

"I don't care. When a client calls and says someone has broken into his house, you haul ass."

Renner grabbed my shoulders. "I know, Parker, but I got held up. Literally. Held at gunpoint, held up." He released me and rubbed his jaw. His knuckles were battered. That must have been what Voletek noticed.

"Are you okay?"

"Yeah, but I was dealing with that when Easton called. I told him to call you. He said he already called the cops, but I knew you'd show up. What did I miss?" After I caught Renner up to speed, he whistled. "Sounds like the chef nearly bashed your skull in. Obviously, he's not making this up. The fire must have been arson."

"Or a terribly timed coincidence." Which I didn't believe. I glanced back at the house. Easton hadn't moved from the front door. This was the second time I'd seen the chef freak out. Last night and tonight. I hated to think what tomorrow would bring.

Renner led the way up the path to the house. "Jake's a good guy, and he's a good cop. But it gets him in hot water with the brass when he fails to fall in line. Sergeant Chambliss said there was no case, and the investigation is closed. Now it's open again, and if I know the PD, they'll want to close it as soon as possible. They won't like that Jake's poking around."

"He's just doing his job."

"Which is why he always lands on his feet." Renner shook hands with Easton and followed the chef into the house. After asking how our client was, Renner rubbed his palms together. "Let's see what the police missed."

While Bennett went over the details with Easton for what felt like the fourth time, I grabbed the large Maglite from my trunk and checked the sidewalk, street, and every inch of Easton's yard for clues. The police officers watched, calling out unhelpful suggestions when I was close enough to their car to hear them. *Thanks, guys.* At times, I understood why Cross despised the PD.

Aside from some litter, I didn't find anything. Nothing indicated a vehicle had idled in front of the house or that the occupant sent the brick through Easton Lango's front window. I stood at the curb and stared at the house. There was a good fifteen feet between the house and the curb. Assuming the average weight of a brick and the height of the window, I wondered how hard it would be to throw it through the window from inside the car. Honestly, I didn't think it was possible.

I returned to the house, shutting and locking the door behind me. "When the man you encountered escaped, did he get behind the wheel?"

Easton thought for a moment. "No." He paled, making the dark blue pop in stark contrast to his skin tone. "There's two of them."

"That'd be my guess."

Renner looked up from his seat on the couch. "You searched the house before the police arrived, right?"

"I didn't search it. I cleared it."

Renner thought for a moment. "Did you contaminate the scene?"

"I don't think so." Aside from stepping on the broken glass, pushing the clothes around in the closet, and picking up Easton's phone, which I returned to its previous position, I didn't think I disturbed anything. Renner climbed off the couch. From the way he moved, I could tell he was hurt. "What are you thinking?"

"How'd you get inside?" Renner asked.

"The front door was open." The realization hit me. "Shit."

"I know it was locked," Easton said. "That was the first thing I did after the window broke. I made sure the door was locked. Then I picked up the brick, read the note, dropped it, grabbed my bat, and called Voletek and you guys. You know the rest."

"Do you have a security system?" I asked.

"You're joking, right?" That would have been too easy.

"Alex, you and Easton go around the house and see if anything's missing. Since patrol's already been through here, we won't know how much damage they've done, but let's hope it wasn't too much. I'll grab some gear out of the car." Renner didn't leave any room for debate.

When Easton and I completed the walkthrough of his house, finding nothing stolen or disturbed besides the pantry items and the broken lamp, we found Renner scanning the living room for radio frequencies. I arched an eyebrow, but Renner put a finger to his lips to keep me from asking the question. If the intruder planted a bug, we didn't want to tip him off that we were on to him.

"So, Chef, I saw that spread in the paper. The critics speculate you're in the running for a Michelin star."

"Was." Easton's expression soured. "You have to have a restaurant worthy of making a special trip to even qualify, and I have no restaurant. Food trucks don't count."

"I've been meaning to ask you," I grabbed a piece of paper and scribbled down what Renner was doing before Easton could ask the obvious question, "why were you parked outside the club the other night?"

"The band's manager contacted me. They put in a special request for private catering, but since I already planned on announcing the official food truck launch at the end of the month, I figured I could use the dry run. In case it flopped, no one would officially know, and I could change the name before any more damage was done to my reputation."

"From the looks of it, I thought it went pretty well. The food was magnificent." I glanced at Renner, who nodded, encouraging me to continue the conversation as he moved into the bedroom.

"It could have gone smoother. I have to perfect my prep and make sure the stations are organized." Easton winced. "Shit. The broken window."

"Don't worry about it. That's the least of your problems," I said.

Easton picked up his phone from the counter and added a reminder. After that, he picked up one of his notebooks and modified his ingredient and recipe list. Obviously, focusing on work would serve as an outlet for him to relax after the crazy night he had.

Renner finished his sweep of the rest of the house and entered the kitchen. The device let out a beep, and Renner moved closer to the sink. Based on the display, we knew a signal was being broadcast. But from where? I got up from the table and helped Renner search.

"Wow," I said, finding a tiny camera hooked to the side of the fridge. It was practically indistinguishable from Easton's magnets, which was why the police missed it.

Renner followed the cord as it wrapped around the fridge coil and hooked to a battery pack and signal booster. He disconnected it. "You're right, Chef. You had an intruder."

Easton looked up from his notepad, squinting at the camera. His gaze darted from Renner to me. "Who would do something like this?"

"You tell us." Renner put the camera in a bag and took off his gloves. "It was focused here. What's significant about this spot?"

"That's where I cook. I test out recipes and work on techniques."

"A competitor, maybe." As far as I could tell, that was the only benefit of placing the camera there.

"Whoever it is went to a lot of trouble." Renner checked the back door. "Let me scan your truck. Someone might have bugged that too. And I want to get some mechanics to look at it before you take it anywhere."

"I'll give you a hand," I offered. "Easton, are you okay in here?"

He glared at the side of the fridge. "Fine."

"Okay. We'll be right outside if you need us." I followed Renner out the door. "What do you think? Do you think someone sabotaged the truck?"

"After the fire at Sizzle, I wouldn't doubt it. Clearly, our client isn't crying wolf. I want to put the house under surveillance in case these assholes return. They know we found the camera. I just don't know if they're crazy enough to try again."

"What do you think they wanted?"

"If Easton's right, they want the secret to making the perfect tart."

I would have laughed at the absurdity if it wasn't true. Everything read like sabotage and unhealthy competition. Another chef in the running for stardom would have plenty of motivation to burn down Easton's restaurant, sabotage his food truck, and steal his secret recipes. Galen Strader remained at the top of my suspect list with Asher York as a close second, along with countless other unnamed culinary geniuses – *evil* culinary geniuses.

After checking the truck and finding nothing amiss, we went back inside. Easton scribbled furiously in his notebook as he paced back and forth. I glanced over his shoulder, wondering why the intruder didn't steal the book, but I found it was written in an indecipherable shorthand. I couldn't make heads or tails out of the doodles, but they meant something to the chef. Easton stopped writing and looked at me.

"Now what?"

"Tomorrow morning, mechanics will check your truck, and we'll find someone to replace the window," Renner promised. "I want to outfit your house with surveillance equipment, but until that's done, I'd like to stick around, if that's okay with you."

"I'd appreciate it." Easton dropped into a chair. "What about the camera and the latest death threat?"

"We'll have Cross Security analyze the camera. Hopefully, that will lead to the intruder. The police have the note, so until they finish with it, there's nothing we can do about it." Renner turned to me. "Why don't you take this back to the office and get started tracking the buyer? See if the techs can trace the signal. If Jake calls, let me know what he says."

"Roger." I scooped up the bag from the table.

"You can meet us back here tomorrow morning, after

your morning meeting with Cross." Renner kept a straight-face, but his eyes shone with amusement.

"I hate you," I said and headed for the door.

ELEVEN

"Hey, Alex. I haven't seen you working this late in a while. Burning the midnight oil?" Gus from building security asked.

"It looks that way." I held up the evidence bag. "The techs won't be happy to see me."

"You're making them work for their overtime."

"I doubt anyone at Cross Security gets overtime."

The guard laughed. "Have a good night."

"You too."

After dropping off the camera, I went to my office to get some work done. The names of potential suspects stared up at me from the list I made earlier. Pushing it aside, I dug into Galen Strader. Even though Voletek said he'd follow up on the car, I was confident I could get the information faster. It wouldn't take long to link the car to Strader and call it a night, except Strader didn't own a car. That put a chink in my plan.

However, I was nearly certain whoever threw the brick through Easton's window had at least one accomplice. I picked up the list of names and checked vehicle records, but nothing popped up. I wondered if Easton's description was accurate. He didn't strike me as a car guy. The neon green lights might have been the only part he got right. After all, with that fancy dye job, I had no doubt he knew his colors better than he knew his cars.

Since I couldn't track the car, maybe I could track the lights. Several auto body shops specialized in customizations. Unfortunately, at this time of night they were closed. That would just be another thing I had to look into in the morning.

Unsure where to go from here, I paced in front of my desk and forced my mind to go back to the beginning. Renner told me last night it took him a long time to track down Easton Lango. And Renner was a professional dick. Locating people was in his wheelhouse. Since receiving the online threats, Easton had been much more secretive about his whereabouts and location, only posting things related to cooking or inconsequential details. He stopped checking in at the locations he visited and posting pictures from venues and clubs. The slew of photographs with him and various young, attractive women stopped around the same time he left Bouillon, but that hadn't been enough to deter the arsonist from striking.

Since Easton recently moved, most internet searches of public records still displayed his old address. Cross Security pulled the address from the DMV, but normal people didn't have access or wouldn't think to do that. So how did the brick-thrower find Easton?

Another thought crossed my mind. Perhaps one of Easton's old coworkers knew where he lived. I scanned the list of suspects again. The easiest way to mark off names was to check alibis. Since I couldn't come up with a better idea, I went to Bouillon.

By the time I arrived, the restaurant had locked their doors for the night. I tried knocking, but no one came to the door. Instead, I went around the back. The cars parked behind the restaurant belonged to the staff. I checked each vehicle, but I didn't find any stray bricks or classic muscle cars.

"Hey, what are you doing?" a scrawny guy with a deep voice asked from the open doorway that led into the restaurant. He kicked the doorstop beneath the heavy metal door and stepped outside, hauling a bag of garbage twice his size out to the dumpster. I recognized him from his social media posts as Bryan the two-timing dishwasher.

"Just the man I wanted to see." Confusing him with my enchanting smile, I added, "Oh come on, Bryan, we met at that club. Don't you remember me?"

"No, I don't."

"Are you serious? We had a wild night." I approached him, holding the smile. "You were amazing. And that thing you did," I let my eyes momentarily roll back, "exquisite."

Bryan grinned. "Oh yeah?" Just as I suspected, he was a horndog.

"Yeah." By now, I was close enough to peer into the kitchen. A few exhausted and disheveled cooks sat at the stainless steel counter, eating whatever dinner they made for themselves now that the kitchen was closed. They passed a bottle of wine around. "It looks like you guys had a rough night."

"It's like this every night."

"Do they do that every night?" I pointed to Max, one of the prep cooks, who was now glugging the remainder of the wine directly from the bottle.

Bryan grabbed my wrist and pulled me away from the door before anyone could see me. "You shouldn't have come here."

"But you told me where you worked. I thought you wanted me to surprise you."

Bryan grinned, dropped the trash bag, and pushed me up against the wall. "I have a surprise for you. Why don't you meet me back at my place?"

"I don't know. Watching them is making me hungry." I placed my palm against his chest and shoved. "Do you guys eat like that every night? I guess I picked the wrong profession."

"It depends. Usually, we eat before the restaurant opens. Chef Strader prepares the family meal before shift starts to test out the day's specials, but we eat whatever's left from the day's prep after hours. Sometimes, the kitchen runs out of food, so we just clean up. It depends how busy we are. Chef Strader's stingy with the ingredients. He doesn't believe in wasting food."

"Smart man," I said, doing my best to peer around the corner and see inside.

"He's a cheap bastard."

"I take it you don't care for your new boss."

Bryan's brows knit together. "Didn't I tell you that the other night?"

I bumped playfully against his arm. "You told me a lot of things and showed me even more."

His lids lowered, and his eyes traveled up and down my body. "Stephanie, right? Sorry, it took me a minute. I'm terrible with names, but I'd never forget a face like yours," he said, even though he wasn't looking at my face.

I didn't want to know how many people this guy slept with in a given month, but knowing what I did, I definitely didn't want him near my food. Perhaps that's why he washed dishes.

"I'm sorry I couldn't get you a reservation. I begged the maître d', but Bouillon's booked for the rest of the month. Maybe I can swing something for the following month. Just remind me later. After I clock out, I'm free the rest of the night. Let's go somewhere."

"I can't tonight." At least I figured out how he was scoring so much tail. "So there's no way you can sneak me onto the guest list?" I pushed out my bottom lip in a pout.

"Sorry. It was easier to score last minute reservations when Easton was here. He always kept a few tables empty for unexpected guests." Bryan's expression soured. "But Easton's gone now. And from the looks of it, he won't be back." He stepped away from the door, dragging the bag of garbage behind him.

That comment piqued my interest, and I followed him to the dumpster. "Why not?"

"Didn't I tell you? Chef Strader runs this place. He even bought a share of the business. It's his now. And everyone has to do what he says. He's changed a lot of the rules. He checks everything. Cyndi can't pencil in names without the chef noticing."

"He sounds like a tyrant." I had a million more questions, and since Bryan thought I was someone else, he might answer them, thinking this was some kind of foodie foreplay. "What does he think about you taking a break?" I turned up the flirtation.

"He'd kill me."

"Isn't that a violation of labor laws?"

"Sure, tell that to the union. Oh wait, we don't have one."

It was no secret restaurant workers were among the least unionized in the country, which probably explained the poor wages and terrible work conditions some of them faced. But that wasn't my battle. Although, it did encourage me to tip well. "Is Chef Strader here? I'd love to have a word with him."

Bryan blanched. "You can't. In fact, you need to get out of here. I'll call you, okay?"

I fought to hold back my laugh. "Is the chef here?"

"Well, no..."

"No? Then why can't you take a break? You could sneak me into the kitchen and dazzle me with whatever your friends are eating. It looks delicious."

"C'mon, you gotta go." He grabbed my arm and tried to pull me away from the building.

"I won't say anything. You could tell them I'm your sister or your cousin." I batted my eyelashes. "Your kissing cousin."

For a moment, he actually considered it before shaking off the thought, probably remembering Kasey's threat to disembowel him and feed him his own intestines. "We'll do it another night when things aren't quite so hectic. Chef has some days off scheduled in a few weeks. I'll call you, and you can drop by then. But tonight, he had an emergency and left in such a hurry we've been scrambling." He rubbed my arm. "You understand, right?"

"What kind of emergency?"

"Dunno. He didn't say."

"Who's in charge now?"

"He left Kasey to run the kitchen. Now, please go. I have to get back to work."

"Kasey, your ex? Is that why you're rushing me to leave?"

"No." He rubbed his face. "I don't know. I have work to do, and I can't leave until it's finished. Do you want to meet up later?"

"I told you I can't. Why don't you get someone to cover for you?"

"No."

"Why not? Is anyone else missing tonight?" I hated asking questions in such a circuitous fashion, but I didn't want any of the kitchen staff to get suspicious and tip off Strader that we were on to him.

"Seriously, babe, what's with all the questions?"

"I'm just curious." I turned my attention to the cars in the parking lot. "Hey, do you know who has the neon green undercarriage lights?"

His brow furrowed. "Lights?"

"I'm just curious."

"I have a cure for that." He leaned in for a kiss, and I put my hand over his face and pushed him away. "Don't be like that."

"You have no idea who I am."

"Of course, I do, Stephanie. We met at the club. You were into the kinky stuff."

I rolled my eyes. "Just answer the question, and I'll go."

"I don't know anything about green lights."

"And no one else took off early tonight?"

"No, everyone's here. And they're gonna wonder where I am if I don't get my ass back inside."

I nodded and took a step back, wiping my hand on my pants. "The next time you see me, I suggest you pretend you don't know who I am."

He gave me a funny look. "All right, we can play it that way if you want." He glanced back inside, probably to make sure Isla and Kasey weren't close by. "Thanks for being cool about the situation." The sarcasm wasn't lost on me.

"I'm the coolest." I stepped away.

After copying down every plate in the parking lot, I returned to the office. Based on vehicle registrations, it appeared Easton's former kitchen staff was present and accounted for. This was getting me nowhere. I dialed Voletek. My call went to voicemail, and I hung up.

Strader's early departure from the restaurant was suspicious as hell, but to be thorough, I checked into Asher York and Dante Bisset, the sous chef York wooed away from Easton after the fire at Sizzle. Bisset drove a cheap compact, and York owned an electric car. Neither of those would have the horsepower necessary to make the rumblings Easton heard, but in case he was mistaken due to the booming stereo, I left messages with their auto insurance companies. If Bisset or York tricked out their cars, they should have reported the modifications. But in case they didn't, I'd have to track down their vehicles and check them out or convince Renner to do it.

As of this moment, my money was on Chef Strader. Every piece of circumstantial evidence pointed to him, and he had motive. In a last ditch effort to find solid proof, I researched his car club. Given the number of speeding tickets, I knew he must use the service often.

Fast Lanes leased the sportiest and flashiest cars in the city, from new exotic imports to mint classics. If a sixty-something Mustang had been outside Easton's house, it might have come from Strader's car club. I tried phoning, but they kept normal business hours, unlike the rest of us. I perused their website, checking out photos and details. I found several classic Mustangs, but I didn't find any mention of more modern street racing modifications. I'd ask in the morning, but to save time, I e-mailed a request for additional information about any of their vehicles that fit the description of the one Easton claimed was outside his house. The sooner we identified the source of the threat, the sooner we'd close the case.

Then I opened the intraoffice communication window and sent a request upstairs for additional information on Galen Strader. Upstairs would do the workup and get it to me in the morning. It was one of the benefits of working for Cross Security.

Whoever broke into Easton Lango's house wanted to ruin him and possibly sabotage his latest endeavor – Easton's Eats. My gut said it was a rival chef or possibly even a critic. I scanned some of the scathing reviews Easton had received over the years. Several critics had accused him of being a fraud. Maybe the surveillance camera was meant to expose him. If they caught Easton unwrapping a breakfast pastry or preparing a frozen dinner, they could post it online and destroy whatever was left of his career and reputation. Or they could have placed the camera there to steal whatever new recipes he concocted. Easton said he used his personal kitchen to test new techniques and create new dishes. I hated to think what would have happened if Renner hadn't swept for bugs. The footage might have been worth its weight in gold to one of Easton's competitors or detractors.

I made a few final notes, updated my to-do list for tomorrow, which at this point would more accurately be described as my things-to-do-later-today list, and turned off my computer. In the last twenty-four hours, I had dealt with enough surprises to last me a month. Hopefully, things would remain quiet from here on out. I was no longer accustomed to the craziness, and on very little sleep, I had no desire to deal with any more crises.

At least the drive home was uneventful. When I stepped into the lobby of our apartment building, the night manager greeted me. "Good evening, Ms. Parker."

"Quiet night?" I asked.

"Let's hope so."

A new notice on the wall caught my eye, and I took a step closer. Behind the desk was an updated fire safety inspection certificate. "Any code violations I should know about?"

"No, we follow all health and safety standards. The building is up to date on fire codes. But since the fire department had to inspect the building last night, they went ahead and checked the fire alarms, extinguishers, and reviewed our evacuation plans."

"How often do they do that?"

"Once every three years."

Realizing they must have done the same for Chef Easton's restaurant, I understood why the chef was convinced the fire had been arson. After tonight, it was obvious someone had it out for him. Still, the fire might have just been bad luck or bad wiring, but I didn't believe that.

"You ever bribe a building inspector?" I asked.

The night manager stared at me, unsure if I was joking or serious. Eventually, he said, "No, ma'am."

"Me neither, but it happens." I studied the certificate hanging above the previous one. The forms were nearly identical with just a few minor administrative changes. By law, they had to be displayed for the public, but Easton might have had copies elsewhere. Honestly, I didn't know what I was thinking or even if I was thinking. This probably had nothing to do with the break-in or the camera hidden in his kitchen, but a string of unrelated incidents was rarely unrelated. That's why the cops were convinced Easton sabotaged himself. "A fire is just a fire unless it's arson."

The night manager appeared bewildered. "Ms. Parker, is there something I can help you with? I can call Mr. Martin. He's upstairs."

Shaking away the tangle of thoughts, I stepped away from the desk. "No, I'm okay. I'm sorry to have bothered you. Lack of sleep and all."

"It's okay. Good night."

"Night."

After getting out of the elevator, I glanced up at the smoke detectors and sprinklers. The red, glass encased box halfway down the corridor looked freshly dusted and shined. The firefighters were no slouches when it came to checking the building. *Stop it*, I tried to silence the voice in my head. Now that I was home, I couldn't get thoughts of the case out of my mind. How badly did someone want to hurt Chef Easton? Did they want to scare him, or did they want to kill him? Was Galen Strader a murderer in the making?

Pondering this, I entered the apartment and found Martin in the living room, working on his presentation. He looked up when I came in.

"Is everything okay?" he asked.

"Yep."

His brow furrowed. "You have that look. The one that says you're on to something."

"I don't know. I have a lot to do tomorrow. Someone

broke into Easton's house. The police are investigating, but Renner's staying with the chef to keep an eye out."

"Did anyone get hurt?"

"No, but Easton will have to replace a couple of windows. Renner's banged up, but that had nothing to do with the chef's case." Actually, I had no idea what happened, but it was none of my business.

"Is this your case?"

"Mine and Renner's."

He nodded, holding back the words on the tip of his tongue. "And our vacation? Is that on the back burner?"

"No, unless you need to reschedule."

He visibly relaxed. "Nope. We're all good here."

"Okay." I looked at the clock. It was already after one. "I have an early morning. From the looks of it, so do you. Do you think we'll actually get some sleep tonight?"

Martin cocked his head to the side and went back to reviewing his presentation.

"I can stay up with you," I offered, unsure of Martin's emotional barometer.

"No, you need to sleep. You have to be sharp for work. I'll come to bed in a few minutes. I just need to nail this down tonight, so I can go over it with Luc in the morning." He nodded to the boxes piled in the corner. "I brought your stuff back here. Marcal will take it to our house tomorrow. Hopefully, the apartment building won't catch fire between now and then."

"Bite your tongue."

I fell asleep before Martin came to bed, but the sound of him groaning woke me. I blinked and squinted at the clock. 4:43. Well, some sleep was better than none.

"Martin." I ran my hand gently over his ribs and across his stomach, tracing the indentions outlining his abdominals. A thin layer of sweat coated his skin. "It's okay, handsome. I'm here." His nightmares tore at my heart, and I hated to think what mine must do to him. I'd been plagued by nightmares since before we met, but these sleep disturbances were a recent occurrence for him. And I knew I was the cause of them.

He quieted, and I hoped he didn't fully awaken. He

hadn't gotten a peaceful night's rest in weeks, and it was starting to show. I retracted my hand, but he shifted, grabbing hold and lacing his fingers with mine. He took a few unsteady breaths, lengthening and slowing each inhale and exhale in an attempt to force his body to relax and his mind to calm.

"You're okay. Everything's okay," I whispered.

"I know." He squeezed my hand. "It's not your fault."

"How do you always know what I'm thinking?"

"I must be a mind reader." He opened his eyes and stared up at the ceiling. Any minute, he'd get out of bed either to work out or shower, depending on if the recent burst of adrenaline was enough to overpower the exhaustion.

"Is that why you're going to Vegas? You're hoping to headline your own show? What's your stage name? The Marvelous Martin? The Mystifying Martin?"

"Martin the Magnificent."

"That was my next guess."

He chuckled. "I know. I read your mind."

I let out a displeased growl and made a face. It was too early for the banter.

"That's not nice, unless you meant it literally. I'm okay with literally. Actually, I'm in favor of literally." He smirked and tapped my temple. "Remember, I can hear your thoughts." He looked at me and winked. "Fine. You can be on top. After all, I can't think of a better way to chase away the bad dreams."

"You're not as funny as you think you are."

"No? Then why am I getting my own show in Vegas?"

"You aren't. That's only in your dreams."

"My presentation notes say otherwise." Martin rolled onto his side so he could face me. He was the only person I knew who could wake from a nightmare and still have a pleasant disposition. Or he'd learned in the last two months there was a good chance he'd get lucky since these late night exchanges often led to cuddling and kissing which led to more than kissing. "I'm glad you're coming with me."

"Am I?"

It took a moment for his sleep-deprived brain to catch the double entendre. "That sounds like a challenge."

"Do you ever think maybe this is the reason for your nightmares?" I asked as he nuzzled my neck. "Maybe this is triggering a Pavlovian response. Perhaps we shouldn't reward bad behavior."

"Nightmares aren't behavior, Alex. The way I see it, making love is like an ice cream cone to distract from a scraped knee. It's a sweet escape from the terrifying thoughts." He stopped kissing my neck and met my eyes. "Now you're wondering if you should be offended."

I punched his shoulder playfully. "Stop reading my mind."

He settled over me. "Fine, I'll ask the shrink about your Pavlovian theory the next time I talk to him. Will that make you happy?"

"What did I just say? Get out of my head, Martin."

He laughed. "Fine, but only if I get my ice cream and you take back what you said about my Vegas show. I was hoping you'd be my lovely assistant."

"You're insane and insatiable."

"That's why we're the perfect match." He adopted an announcer voice. "Martin the Magnificent and the Alluring Alexis will amaze you with their mind boggling chemistry and acrobatic sexcapades."

I shoved him onto his back, my hair brushing against his face. "Shut up."

"Make me."

TWELVE

Lucien Cross slid a blue folder across the conference table. Unsure what I'd find, I opened it while he droned on about implementing proper measures to ensure our safety and our clients' safety. A part of me wondered if Cross' speech had anything to do with Renner's mishap yesterday. Perhaps I'd ask Renner about it later.

"All right. No more mistakes, people. Take precautions. We're a security and investigation firm. Don't forget, we employ dozens of security personnel. You need muscle or protection, take a team with you. Is that clear?"

A chorus of affirmatives filled the already cramped conference room. I'd heard similar speeches while working at the OIO, but the energy didn't feel right. This felt more like a locker room speech by a coach after an abysmal practice.

"Dismissed." Cross leaned back. The chair squeaked as it bounced beneath him. I closed the folder and looked up, finding Lucien staring at me. "I approved your vacation days."

"Thanks."

He picked up a pen and tapped it on the table, chuckling to himself. "Y'know, three months ago, I would have assumed you asked for the time off so you could go with

James to the conference and scope out the security and brief a detail."

"You would have been wrong."

Lucien nodded, the pen tapping a slow rhythm. "That doesn't happen often." He sat up straight, the chair letting out another ear-splitting shriek. "Tell me you don't give a shit about his security. That you have nothing to do with it."

Even the two shots of espresso in my cappuccino weren't enough to prepare me for this conversation, so I avoided it. "Renner wanted me to update you on the Easton Lango situation."

"Go on." After Cross was up to speed, he rocked back in the chair again, cringing at the shrill squeak. He pulled his phone from his pocket and pressed a button. "Justin, have someone from maintenance oil the chairs in the conference room." He disconnected, clearly finding this to be a more immediate concern than my case. He put the phone on the table. "So once again, you've found yourself in the midst of a police investigation."

"Just the break-in. The police don't care about the rest of Easton's allegations."

"Now it's a break-in." Lucien worked his jaw. "I take it you read the report." His gaze flicked to the folder. "We'll know by the end of the day who bugged Easton Lango's house."

"Great."

"Not great. I want to know what you intend to do with that information."

"It depends."

"On what?" Lucien found the conversation intriguing, like a game of chess, but I sensed he was leading me into a trap.

"Our client's wishes take top priority. We'll see what he wants to do."

"But it's a police matter. You'd be withholding valuable information in an active investigation. That could be construed as obstruction of justice."

"Does it matter?"

"Fuck, Parker, everything matters. But you already

know that. You're just giving me the answer you think I want to hear. How about you try that again? And this time, I'd like the truth."

Rage boiled to the surface, probably for no other reason than lack of sleep. "Listen, I'm not some goody two shoes. I've done this private sector thing before. Hell, I did it behind Jablonsky's back when I worked at the OIO. I get that not everything is black and white. I am so fucking sick and tired of you treating me like a snitch, especially when you're the one who tasked Kellan Dey to tattle on me." We discussed this before. More times than I wanted to think about, but I hadn't gotten past it. As the days went on, it festered, fueling my annoyance and rage with Cross and this job. Truthfully, I didn't trust any of them, not even Renner. "What are you so afraid of, Lucien? What do you think's going to happen if I ask the police to step in and make an arrest?"

"Worst case, you'll take this firm down, along with whoever's after your client." My boss cleared his throat, but otherwise remained unfazed by my outburst. "Bridget Stockton is a formidable woman. She's educated, brilliant, and invincible. She knows enough about police procedure and law to do whatever she wants and remain untouchable. It's also possible she's angry and vengeful that some blue-haired asshole who couldn't get his shit together for the first five years of their marriage stepped out on her with a waitress he met at work while she was slaving away to make a life for them."

I made the conscious effort to keep my jaw from dropping. I never fathomed Bridget Stockton, Easton's ex-wife, would still hold a grudge. As far as everyone was concerned, she took Easton to the cleaners with their divorce settlement. She was successful. He wasn't. Doing something insane, like tossing a brick through his window or potentially setting his restaurant ablaze, could cost her everything. And smart women normally thought about the consequences of their actions before doing something criminal. That's why most offenders were men. Like my friend Kate used to say, it was a biological deficit on account of the stupid stick.

"You believe Bridget Stockton's involved?" I asked.

"I'll save you some time. Fast Lanes doesn't have any tricked out or modified cars in their inventory. They would never bastardize a piece of machinery like that."

"What does that have to do with Easton's ex?"

"Bridget drives a steel grey '67 Shelby. I don't know if it has undercarriage lights, but I thought you should know." Cross studied the expression on my face. "Don't look surprised. We both know ex-lovers make prime suspects." He stood up. "Do what you have to, but if the techs trace the camera back to Bridget or a party she or her firm have been known to use, I'll need you to tread carefully. Cross Security is vast, but I'm not a fool. There are very few entities with the ability to bury me, and Reeves, Almeada, and Stockton might be one of them."

"Yes, sir." I collected my belongings and strode to the door.

"Alex," his commanding voice had grown softer, less harsh, "I've apologized for the deception and the things you've endured since coming to work here. I am not your enemy. It's important you understand that and believe it."

I didn't bother to turn around. "How can I?"

"You choose to."

*   *   *

"How is it you look worse than I do?" Renner let me inside. "Did you stay at the office all night?"

"No, but I did some digging." I went into the kitchen and splayed the folders out on the counter. "Where's Easton?"

"He's in the shower."

"Okay." It was easier to discuss matters without the client present. "We haven't gotten anything back on the bug yet, but Lucien thinks Bridget Stockton might be involved."

"That's what I was afraid of." Renner poured a cup of coffee from the French press and took a sip. "Did he order us to stand down?"

"Not yet. She drives a dark-colored '67 Shelby. After I

leave here, I'll see if it has any modifications, but I don't think she fits the profile. You know her, right? What do you think?"

"She's a shark. She hates Easton. There's no question about that. The last thing she'd ever want is for him to be successful. I just don't know if she'd go to the extremes." Renner took an uneasy breath, rubbed his collarbone, and rotated his shoulder. "But even if she wouldn't do it herself, she's a defense attorney. She knows people who might do it for her."

"You think she would risk everything just to fuck with her ex?"

A cynical chuckle sounded from behind me. "You must be talking about Bridget." Easton grabbed two mugs out of the cupboard, filled them, and handed me one. "She's a lot of things, but this isn't her style. She would set my hair on fire before she'd burn down my restaurant."

"You're sure?" I asked.

"Absolutely."

I glanced at Renner who took a sip. It seemed the three of us were in agreement about Bridget Stockton, but one of her unscrupulous clients could have done her a favor. "She drives a '67 Shelby. Is it possible that's the car you saw last night?"

"No, I would have recognized her car. We used to drive around in that thing all the time." He went to the cabinet and found a bottle of whiskey and poured some into his mug. "We had some great memories in that car. I'd know it anywhere. Plus, she'd never consider picking up a brick. She'd be afraid of breaking a nail and ruining her manicure." The tiniest bit of loathing crept into his voice, and he took a sip. "Maybe I fucked around, but that was only after she fucked us up. She put her career above everything else, especially me. Even when we were together, her mind was on work and climbing the corporate ladder. She didn't care about my career when we were together, and she doesn't give enough of a shit now to do something like this. The only reason she would want me to fade into the background is so the reasons for our divorce never come to light."

"She's afraid you'd make her look bad," Renner said.

"Or worse, she'd look like a victim." Easton took a big gulp, probably burning his mouth on the hot coffee.

"I'm glad to hear you're not bitter or resentful," I said.

Easton snorted and took another sip. "Give me a break. After the things that bitch did, I can be resentful. I never did anything to hurt her."

Renner and I exchanged a look. We had photographic proof to the contrary.

Sensing this, Easton amended his statement. "I never flaunted my affair in her face." He looked at Renner. "She asked you for proof. She wanted to see who I was with and what I was doing. I didn't parade it in front of her. I never set out to hurt her."

"Did she do that to you?" I asked.

Easton drained the mug and put it in the sink. He stared out the window. "A few weeks after I landed my dream job at Bouillon, she makes a reservation and nearly gets me fired by goading me into a knockdown, drag-out fight. Then the day after our divorce was finalized, she comes back to Bouillon with some guy, probably a male model she hired. They couldn't keep their hands off each other. She wanted me to know she won."

This changed things. "She tried to sabotage your career before. What makes you think she's not responsible for doing it again?" I asked.

"It's not her." Easton leaned against the counter. "I'm sure of it."

"Why, man?" Renner asked. "I know what it's like to have a crazy ex-wife. I wouldn't put anything past mine."

"I haven't seen Bridget since the day after our divorce. She's moved on." I heard the sadness in his voice. Despite everything, a part of him still loved her. "She wouldn't waste her time. She showed up at Bouillon in an attempt to force me to show my true colors. She thinks I'm a no-good loser or the devil. Either way, she's convinced I'll destroy myself. She wouldn't get any satisfaction out of my failure if she had to orchestrate it."

"That's messed up," Renner mumbled.

"That's Bridget." Easton looked at me. "Does this mean

you didn't have any luck identifying who planted the bug?"

"We should know tonight."

Normally, Cross Security techs were better at tracking signals and IP addresses, and I wondered if Lucien intentionally delayed them from getting me the intel. Dammit, I shouldn't even think like this.

Renner turned and glanced at the time. "Have you heard from Jake?"

"Not today," I said.

"Let me give him a call. Maybe the PD has something for us."

While he spoke on the phone, I told Easton about my trip to Bouillon and asked about his former colleagues. He didn't recall any of them driving muscle cars, but that could have changed in the last few months. However, he found it strange Strader left work in the middle of a shift.

"I guess he figures he can do whatever he wants since we're no longer vying for the position of head chef." Easton rolled his eyes. "But the Galen I know wouldn't walk out of the kitchen without having a damn good reason. You think he paid me a visit last night?"

"I shouldn't speculate."

Easton let out a string of expletives and slammed his palm on the countertop. "Son of a bitch."

"Hey, now," Renner returned to the kitchen, "don't jump to conclusions. Detective Voletek's on the way. Hopefully, he'll be able to shed some light on this matter."

"Whatever." Easton stormed out of the room. A moment later, the bathroom door slammed.

Renner poured another cup of coffee and grabbed a carton of cream from the fridge. "You need to be careful," he warned. "Easton Lango is a loaded gun. You don't want to point him in the wrong direction."

"I wasn't pointing him anywhere. I asked a question."

"Same difference." Renner took a seat and reviewed my notes while we waited for Voletek to arrive. After I left last night, Renner asked Easton about the employees and crew from Sizzle and had Cross Security put together profiles. We'd have to follow-up, but at least it was a start.

The doorbell rang, and Renner and I met the detective

at the front door. "Come outside," Voletek said. "There's been a break in the case."

THIRTEEN

"I found the car." Voletek pointed at the screen. The MDT, or mobile data terminal, displayed footage from the city's camera system.

"The lights aren't green," I said.

"Just wait a minute." When the car slowed and eventually came to a stop, the undercarriage lights changed colors. When the car accelerated, the lights beneath the car changed again. "Each color represents a different gear. When the car isn't in motion, they remain green."

"Did you ID the driver?" I asked,

"Not yet. We couldn't make out the plates. It looks like he sprayed them or used a plastic cover to prevent the cameras from reading the numbers. However, this is where my genius comes into play."

"And your modesty," Renner said.

"Don't be jealous, Ben." Voletek nudged Renner, eliciting a groan from my fellow P.I. "There are only three area shops that specialize in these particular lights. This morning, we subpoenaed their records. Uniforms are combing through them now. Once we get a match, we'll know who paid Easton a visit." Voletek glanced at me. "If you wouldn't mind, maybe you could speak to the nosy neighbor across the street and get some corroboration for when I make an arrest."

"You're a cocky bastard, aren't you?" I teased.

"I'm not finished yet," Voletek said. "The brick and note were a bust, but we found duck fat on the tarp."

"Duck fat?" It was a common ingredient in many gourmet dishes. "It could have come from Easton."

"Sure," Voletek agreed, "but it preserved a perfect fingerprint."

"Way to bury the lead, Detective." I waited for Voletek to elaborate.

Renner shook his head. "The print's not in the system. If it was, Jake would have led with it."

"Yeah, well, I don't see either of you making any progress." Voletek's gaze shifted from Renner to me. "Unless you're holding out on me. I thought we were in this together."

I stepped out of the police cruiser. "I should see if the neighbors are feeling chatty." I left it up to Renner to update Jake. It was his case. His friend. His decision. However, even though the print didn't give us an ID, it did rule out a lot of suspects. Basically, the entire kitchen staff at Bouillon was in the clear with one obvious exception, though with Strader's record, his prints should be in the system. So he couldn't have left the print on the tarp. Things were getting more complicated by the second. Who paid Easton a visit last night?

Not surprisingly, the neighbors wouldn't talk to me either. They probably saw how chummy I was with the police, figured I was one of them, and not so politely slammed the door in my face. "Thanks for your help," I bellowed, unsure if they could hear me through the thick wood door.

My gaze lingered on the drug den down the street. Five cars were parked out front, and four tough guys lounged on the porch. With the police car out front and Voletek's unmarked cruiser in Easton's driveway, I didn't think canvassing the neighborhood would hurt. Backup was too close for anyone to try something.

I continued down the block and stopped in front of the

house. Three of the men eyed me suspiciously. The fourth might have been asleep or blasted.

"Good morning."

No one spoke, but one of them scratched his junk.

"Did you guys happen to notice anything strange last night?"

Again, utter silence.

I held my fist beneath my mouth and tapped on it with my other hand. "Is this thing on?"

One of them snorted before looking away. "What do you want?"

"There was a break-in last night."

"We don't know nothing 'bout it."

"No, of course you don't. But the police are investigating, and they're going to hang around and make a nuisance of themselves until they find some evidence. The sooner they solve the case, the sooner they'll get out of the neighborhood, and the sooner you can get back to business."

"Whatever," the one with the itchy crotch said. "We don't talk to cops."

"It's a good thing I'm not a cop."

The one to his left snickered. "Who are you?"

"I'm a private investigator."

"You don't look like a dick." Obviously, Itchy Crotch was the leader of the pack.

"Thanks, but I can't say the same about you."

The other two cackled, and the one who might have been asleep gave them a slit-eyed death glare.

"You wanna say that again, bitch?" Itchy Crotch got out of the chair and took a step off the porch. I could see the bulge of a gun tucked beneath his shirt. Regardless, I knew he wouldn't shoot me in broad daylight in front of a police cruiser.

"Come here," I crooked my finger, "I want to tell you something."

He ambled down the cracked and stained walkway until he towered in front of me. "What?"

"Unless you want twenty-four hour surveillance outside your house and every single one of your friends to get pulled over and searched before and after they leave, I suggest you tell me what you know. Otherwise, no one's going to come here to party. Understand?"

"Don't threaten me."

"I'm not threatening you. I'm warning you what the police are planning. I just spoke to a detective, and he said they're going to have units ready to roll in on your visitors tonight. I wanted to give you the heads up."

"Why?"

"Because they think you're involved. But I don't. If someone got a little too wasted and threw a brick through a window, just say so. It'll save us both a lot of trouble."

"That's not what happened." Itchy Crotch leaned closer, probably so his friends wouldn't hear him. "Some car we've never seen before drove up. It had plenty of horses and was flashy as fuck. Two guys got out. One went around the back. The other grabbed something out of the trunk. Next thing I know, the front door's open, and the car's burning rubber."

"Did you get a plate or a description of the men?"

"Nope, but they ain't part of my crew, and they ain't none of my friends. You feel me?"

"Yeah, I feel you."

"Good." He slapped my ass and spoke loudly. "Now get goin' unless you want to see what my dick does." I'm guessing whatever it did would explain the constant need to scratch.

I turned and headed back to Easton's house while listening to the whistles and catcalls from the peanut gallery. The last part was about posturing and saving face with his pals. Itchy Crotch didn't want to be deemed a snitch by cooperating, but he wasn't an idiot. He knew the damage a constant police presence would have on his business, and he was cautious enough to buy into my lies. Unfortunately, what he said didn't help much.

Voletek waited for me beside the car. "Do you have a death wish?"

"You asked me to speak to the neighbors. You didn't specify which neighbors."

"Did you get anything useful?"

"Two men in a muscle car surrounded Easton's house. One threw the brick and probably breached the front door. The other went around back, presumably to do something to the food truck."

"Why didn't you tell me about the camera in the kitchen?"

"It's Renner's case. It's his decision."

"You should have called as soon as you found it."

"Sorry."

Voletek considered my apology. "Bennett Renner said you used to be an FBI agent. How'd you end up with Cross Security?"

"Look, Detective, I don't know you, and you don't know me. But now's not the time for a heart to heart. Did Bennett tell you Cross Security's suspicious about Easton's ex-wife?"

"He did, but he doesn't buy it."

"I'm glad you're up to speed." I palmed my keys, watching as the window repair van and the home security van pulled to a stop in front of the house. Renner introduced Easton to the men and instructed the team where to get started. "Are you sticking around, Bennett?"

"At least until everything's installed. I'm waiting on my car guy to check out the truck."

"Do you think the bastards from last night sabotaged it?" Easton asked, joining us in the driveway.

"We want to make sure they didn't," Renner said.

"What should I do?" Easton asked.

"Nothing to do. We just need you to hang tight a little longer." Renner glanced at Voletek, who agreed.

Easton rubbed his forehead. "Fine. I have to contact my vendors. Let me know if you need me."

"What are you going to do?" Renner asked me.

"I have meetings with various arson investigators, and I might drop by Reeves, Almeada, and Stockton for a consult."

"Parker," Renner warned, "I thought you didn't want to ruffle Lucien's feathers."

"No ruffling, just a quick trip. Honestly, I don't think Bridget Stockton has anything to do with this, but I want to make sure." I turned to Voletek. "Can you send a photo of the car to Cross Security? I need to print a hard copy."

"Once we sort through the auto body shops' records, I'm sure we'll get details on the lights. There's no reason for you to stick your neck out," Voletek said. "I got this."

"That's not what you said a few days ago," Renner mumbled.

"I'm glad you got this," I said, "but I'd still like a copy of the footage or at least a still of the muscle car. Y'know, something to commemorate working our first case together. I'm nostalgic like that."

Voletek glanced from Renner to me. "Fine."

I smiled sweetly. "Thanks, Jake, but if you really want to do me a favor, you'll question Chef Strader and find out where he went last night. His prints are in the system, but two men came here last night. And since Strader left Bouillon in the middle of a shift for some unknown emergency, he's still my prime suspect." Even though I couldn't link the car to Easton's rival, my gut said Strader was involved. We just had to prove it.

"I'm way ahead of you. We have an appointment at noon. I'll tell you what I learn on one condition."

"What's that?" I asked.

"The two of you," he pointed to Renner and me, "will share your findings with me."

"No problem," Renner said.

FOURTEEN

"Ms. Parker?" Lou Hutton stepped into the opening between two partitions. "You wanted to speak to me about a claim I paid."

"Yes, sir." I glanced around. For an insurance firm, I expected nicer offices, not particle board cubicles.

He grabbed a folding chair from where it leaned against an actual wall. "Step into my office, and please excuse the mess."

I entered the office, not surprised to find press-wood furniture and cheap equipment. Most insurance companies made money hand over fist, but if the décor was any indication, this one must issue payouts like lollipops at the bank. Perhaps I should consider switching, like all those commercials insisted. A half-eaten submarine sandwich and an open bag of chips sat on the desk next to a can of diet cola with a pink reusable straw.

Lou came up behind me, opened the chair, and plopped it down before brushing crumbs from his desk and taking a seat. "I've never gotten a complaint about a payout before. This is new territory for me."

"It's not a complaint, just some basic questions." A rotting apple core caught my attention, and I crinkled my nose at the odor it produced. Covering my disgust with a fake sneeze, I decided it'd be best to breathe through my mouth. "Do you remember the fire at Sizzle?"

"Sizzle," he wiped his greasy palms on his pants and blew the crumbs off the keyboard, "that's a terrible name for a place that burned down."

"I don't think Mr. Lango expected that to happen when he named it."

Lou looked up at me. "No, of course not. We don't think this was arson."

"Why not?"

He appeared even more distressed by that question than the possibility he accidently implied Easton intended the restaurant to burn to the ground. "What do you mean?"

"Just what I said. How did you determine it wasn't arson?"

"It was electrical."

"You're positive?"

"Um...yeah?"

"Is that a question or your answer?"

He sputtered. "Ms. Parker, we reviewed the reports we received from the police and fire department. I walked through the scene with the arson investigator. He showed me the source of the fire and the burn patterns on the walls. It wasn't arson."

"If it had been, would Easton Lango be entitled to a larger payout?"

"If he set his own restaurant on fire, he wouldn't get a dime."

"What if someone else set his restaurant on fire?"

Lou chuckled uneasily, as if I were making a joke. "Assuming the resulting investigation concluded a third party was acting on his own volition, Mr. Lango would eventually receive whatever his policy covered, which is what he received from us after we made our final assessment."

Legal hadn't found any hidden clauses or alternate pay schedules, but I figured it didn't hurt to ask. "Why didn't you hire an arson expert to assess the situation?"

"We don't employ anyone with those qualifications full

time, and hiring an expert in that particular field is costly and time consuming. Since the fire wasn't suspicious according to the fire department's arson investigator and the police officers who worked the scene, we performed a final assessment and wrote it off."

"Great." Ready to leave, I stood. "Thanks for your time."

"Wait a sec." His eyes darted to the opening between the cubicles. "Why does Cross Security think it was arson?"

"We don't, but our client does."

Lou nodded, as if that made perfect sense. "Ah." Then his brow furrowed. "Why would Mr. Lango insist on that? Is he confessing to the crime?"

I blinked, wondering if the fermented apple fumes and mold had affected his brain. "He believes an unknown third party set the fire."

"Oh, that makes more sense." He leaned forward and lowered his voice. "Do you think that's true?"

"I guess we'll find out." I nodded at him. "Thank you for your time. I'll let you know if I have any other questions."

He extended his hand, so I faked another sneeze. And he retracted his hand. Turning on my heel, I walked through the opening in the partitions and out of his office. I didn't want to be rude, but the last thing I wanted was a greasy handshake. I had to get to my next interview, and shaking hands with one of the city's bravest with secondhand potato chip grease wouldn't endear me to him.

* * *

Lt. Ted Payne wore the dress shirt and insignia of the city's fire department proudly. His shirt was crisp with pin-straight pleats lined up perfectly with the pleats in his slacks. His desk was neatly organized, despite the towers of files covering the top. He stood, leaning forward and offering me his hand.

"Detective Parker?"

"Just Alex," I said. "I work private investigations. We don't get titles."

He smiled, his eyes crinkling at the corners. It was the only indication of his age, aside from some slight greying at his temples. I guessed he was probably around forty. He was Lou Hutton's polar opposite. "You have a question about an investigation?"

"The fire at Sizzle."

Payne's eyebrows knit together. "When did it happen?" I gave him the exact date and address. He read the tabs on the stack of folders. "Is this an open investigation? I'm not seeing it here."

"No, sir, your office already concluded it was electrical."

"Oh. Okay. Come with me." He led the way out of the office and down the hall to the records room. He opened the door to a small room jam-packed with filing cabinets. After locating the proper drawer, he removed a thick file and put it down on a desk beside a computer. "That was one hell of a fire."

He showed me the photographs. The structural damage led to a partial collapse. Ash, dust, and rubble covered everything in a thick, chalky layer of charcoal. I flipped through the images, recalling scenes of explosions, but I never worked a fire investigation. The OIO didn't deal with those sorts of issues.

"See this?" Payne flipped back to the last photo I looked at and pointed at a charred outlet. "We see these a lot in electrical fires. Appliances require a lot of energy, and given the building's age, the wiring installed probably wasn't meant to withstand the amperes of a modern-day commercial kitchen."

"Shouldn't the inspection have flagged this?" I asked. "Easton Lango had the building inspected several times. It passed all the necessary checks and met the required standards."

"The city's standards are decent, but they could be better. Most fires occur inside inspected buildings." He saw the look on my face. "Scary, I know, but that's why we give lessons on fire safety and what to do in the event of a fire."

"Stop, drop, and roll."

"Among other things. Baking soda is a good fire retardant for small fires."

"Great. I'll buy some on my way home."

His forehead crinkled, unsure if I was being serious or

flippant. "Anyway, based on the burning and scorch marks, we know this was the point of origin. The fire started here, at this outlet. The sparks probably ignited a towel and traveled." He pointed to a large scorch mark against a different wall. "That's from a flare-up, most likely from cooking grease. These other flare-ups were probably from pantry items stored in polypropylene bags, liquor bottles, or oil containers. It's hard to say for certain. We found remnants of all three at the scene." He pointed to downed metal shelving on the floor. "Each is commonly found in commercial kitchens and restaurants."

"Mind dumbing that down for me? Polypropylene bags?"

"Polypropylene bags are petroleum based, and if the contents are heavy in carbs and fats, like cheese puffs or potato chips, you basically have a cocktail for disaster once ignited. Here's a tip. If you're ever camping and can't find kindling, use potato chips. They'll burn for a few minutes which is usually long enough to get a fire going."

"I thought you were in the business of putting out fires, not starting them," I teased.

He laughed. "I have to know how they start in order to prevent them."

That reminded me of the PSA commercials when I was a kid with the bear in the woods, but I kept my mouth shut. "Okay, so the fire started at the outlet and spread throughout the kitchen."

Payne nodded. "If it had been extinguished immediately, it might have been contained to this area, but unfortunately, it spread into the dining room."

"Shouldn't that have taken time to burn and spread?"

"The kitchen went up quick." He pointed to more photos of the destruction. "There should be a fire barrier between the kitchen and the rest of the restaurant, which is why we think it spread through the walls, possibly the ceiling. Once it hit the dining room, it would have taken longer to burn. The furniture and décor have to be flame retardant, but fire is unpredictable. Anything can happen. Maybe the front door or an open window attracted the flames and fed the blaze."

"How long did it take firefighters to respond?" I pointed at the collapsed front wall. "I would have thought the building could have been saved. Is damage like this typical?"

"They arrived within the normal estimated window. It's not their fault. It's an old building. Unfortunately, we see this a lot. The contractors might have cut corners and skimped. Until something like this happens, we have no way of knowing how put together a building really is."

"Lovely."

"Isn't it?" Payne said with an equal amount of sarcasm. He narrowed his eyes at the photographs, pointing out water and smoke damage before reaching for a magnifying glass to study a piece of the crumbled wall. He flipped past the photos to the report at the end and reread the findings. "The drywall acted like tinder paper. It's why the front wall came down."

"Is that normal?"

Bewildered, Payne said, "Not at all."

"Is the building still there?"

"What's left of it. The city didn't demolish it. The remaining structure is stable. Basically, the dining room is what collapsed, but the interior walls are strong enough to support the rest of the building and what little remains of the roof. After venting, chunks of it crashed through the burning building."

"Was anyone hurt?"

"No incident reports were filed. The responding firefighters weren't injured." He checked the page a second time to make sure the details were correct and offered me an encouraging smile, despite the terrifying images. "We're trained for this, ma'am. Fires are dangerous, but we do our best to minimize risk." He continued scanning the page. "Easton Lango called 911 and reported the fire. According to this, he was treated for burns to his hand."

The horrific images had derailed my train of thought. "How did you determine he wasn't responsible?"

The lieutenant gave me an odd look. "Isn't Easton Lango your client?"

"He is, and for the record, he did not start the fire. But

given the destructive nature of the blaze and the burns on his hands, I just thought he might be a suspect."

"Most fires aren't crimes. People make mistakes. My prime suspects are unattended burning candles, questionable extension cords, inappropriately stored flammable materials," he gestured at the photos, "electrical outlets, and unexpected sparks, not people."

I nodded and flipped back through the photographs. I had no idea how fires behaved, but this one was terrible. Even Lt. Payne admitted this was a bad one, which spread inexplicably fast and ate through drywall faster than a mouse with a chunk of cheese. "What about the oddities?"

Payne smiled patiently. "That's why my office investigated the scene. Things like this shouldn't happen, but it looks like a poor layout and shoddy materials. Luckily, the fire spread in this direction." He pushed the photos aside and pointed to a blueprint-like sketch. "When I spoke to Mr. Lango about it, he said he escaped out the back."

"Is that odd?"

"No." He sensed my confusion. "I'll tell you what. Why don't I take you to see it firsthand? Would you like that?"

"I would."

He looked at his watch. "I have some time now, if it's convenient for you."

"That sounds great. Do you mind if I have an expert meet us there?"

The lieutenant ducked his head, attempting to conceal the unexpected bark of laughter with a cough. "I guess I'm not particularly impressive. Is it the shirt? Or maybe the tie?" He looked up, a twinkle in his eyes, and gestured at his tie clip. "It's my fire engine tie tack, isn't it? I knew no one would take me seriously with a fire engine tie tack."

"It's not you. I just don't know what I'm looking at and might need someone to decipher it for me."

"That's fine. Why don't I give you a ride and you can call your guy on the way? After we walk the scene, if you have any more questions, I'll answer them on the ride back."

"Sure, thanks for being so obliging. The police department hasn't been nearly as friendly." They were also accustomed to me asking for favors. Aside from the occasional odd jam, I normally didn't pester the fire department. Hopefully, that wasn't about to change.

He neatly folded the file and tucked it under his arm as he led the way out of the room and back to his office. He grabbed his hat and keys. Once we were inside the bright red SUV, he handed me the file. "Look through that and tell me if any other questions come to mind."

"Actually, there's something I haven't been able to figure out."

"What's that?"

"Why didn't the fire alarm go off?"

FIFTEEN

My question stumped Lt. Payne. He glanced at me before returning his attention to the road. "Dead batteries in the smoke detector?"

"The place was inspected prior to the fire. The batteries were checked. According to Easton, the alarm wasn't beeping or acting up. So why didn't it go off?"

"Did we test it?" He jerked his chin at the file. "There should be a note in there. It's one of the first things we check."

I searched the file but didn't find any form or notation concerning the smoke detector. "I don't see one."

"That's weird. The truck company that put out the fire should have checked the fire prevention system. I'll contact their chief when I get back to the office. They might have forgotten to forward the paperwork to us. It happens sometimes. You saw the twin peaks on my desk. We have a lot of open investigations. Sometimes, things get misfiled in the jumble."

Or rubberstamped. However, I didn't mention my theory or add my two cents.

"Now that you bring it up, I'm wondering why the sprinkler system in the dining room didn't slow the fire's progression or put it out. That's why restaurants are required to have a fire barrier between the kitchen and the rest of the restaurant and why the dining room has to have sprinklers. Kitchen fires are common, so these measures are meant to protect diners. The sprinklers should have saved the front of the building. Unless," Payne rubbed his mouth, "I don't know."

"What are you thinking?"

"The fire most likely jumped rooms through the walls or ceiling. It's the damn drywall. It shouldn't have burned that fast or that easily. Sure, the paper burns, but gypsum doesn't."

"Are you still convinced this wasn't arson?"

"I'm not saying anything until I personally walk the scene. That file doesn't answer a lot of questions. Who signed off on the final report?"

I flipped to the page and read the signature at the bottom. "You did."

I watched him out of the corner of my eye. I could tell he was beating himself up for signing without paying attention. Perhaps if I had a mountain of paperwork to contend with on a daily basis, I might do the same. I suspected SSA Jablonsky had done that a time or two at the OIO. Good leaders trusted their people, but we were all human. And humans had bad days and made mistakes.

"You should know, Easton Lango received several death threats prior to the fire, and he's still receiving them." I watched Payne, curious to see his reaction.

The lieutenant shook his head, as if trying to shake off the guilt and blame he felt. "Under the circumstances, I think it's a good thing we're checking out the building. Depending on what I find, I'll consider reopening the investigation. None of this makes sense. Maybe there's an explanation, a misfiled report or lost paperwork, but if that's not the case, I fear you might be right."

We parked in the vacant lot beside a hunter green 4x4. A balding man sat inside, texting on his phone. At the sound of our doors closing, he looked up.

"Hey, Dil," Payne said, clapping the balding man on the shoulder as soon as he stepped out of the car. "You might have your work cut out for you. Ms. Parker's been telling me some pretty disturbing things about the owner of this place. The BFI might have gotten it wrong."

"Ted, Ted, Ted," Dilbert Haskell, the arson expert, made a tsking noise and shook his head, "I see the Bureau of Fire Investigation can't function without me." He poked at Payne's tie clip. "You haven't changed one bit. I can't believe you're still holding on to that stupid thing."

"I can't get rid of it," Payne said. "A mean old bastard gave it to me and told me it was my lucky charm."

"And you were dumb enough to believe me when I said it." Dil turned to face me. "You must be Alexis. Cross Security's certainly classed itself up since the last time we crossed paths. Nice to meet'cha." He extended his hand. "By the way, let me apologize now for whatever this guy might have said about me." He jerked his thumb at Payne.

"She didn't tell me you were the expert," Payne said. The worry returned and creased his features.

"Shit, son. I know that look." Dil rubbed his jaw. "What'd you step in?"

"We're about to find out." Payne led the way into the roped off building, ignoring the neon yellow flyer warning trespassers it was unsafe to enter.

Dil gestured for me to go ahead, so I followed Lt. Payne into the destroyed building. Broken and burned furniture littered the floors. Dil came up behind me, letting the beam of his flashlight bounce off the blackened floor and what remained of the other three walls. Payne knelt on the ground near the front corner of the building, sifting through the rubble.

"I don't get it," he said. He held up a chunk of the wall. "The gypsum didn't burn. Well, it burned but to the level we'd expect given the blaze."

"So why did the wall come down?" I asked.

"The fire," Dil said unhelpfully.

"No shit," Payne parroted my thoughts. "But how often do kitchen fires take down a commercial structure?"

Haskell bagged a small piece of rubble. "I'll have the lab analyze this for accelerant or defects." The arson consultant nodded at me. Obviously, he took his job seriously. After all, Cross Security only hired the best. "I'll look around and see what else I find. You sent me a copy of the report from your client, but I'll get the full report from my former colleagues at the BFI." He glanced at Payne, who was examining the walls. "You'll send it over, right, Teddy?"

"Yeah, once I piece it back together. Ms. Parker pointed out a couple of discrepancies." Payne ran his hand against the wall and rubbed the soot between his fingertips.

"What is it?" I asked.

"It looks like the sprinklers activated." He indicated the smoke and water damage. "Although, it's hard to say for certain."

The dining room was completely destroyed. Between the fire and the methods used to extinguish the blaze, nothing was salvageable. The few chairs and booths that remained intact were covered in layers of soot. The wood had warped and buckled from the heat and water damage. I had no idea how anyone could make heads or tails out of what happened inside. I was out of my depth. No wonder there were so few arson investigators. It looked like chaos, a scene out of a Hieronymus Bosch painting.

Payne pulled a handkerchief from his pocket and wiped his hands on it. "Let's start in the kitchen. It'll make more sense to follow the path the fire took."

"Sure."

By now, Haskell had already wandered deeper into the restaurant. When we entered the kitchen, we found the consultant examining the outlet. "There's no doubt this is where the fire started," he said. He indicated the scorch marks around the outlet and wall. Kneeling down, he found a thick, frayed, and burned cord. "This is your culprit."

Payne flipped through the photos in the file, verifying that's what the fire investigation had noted. "Looks like we're in agreement about the cause."

Haskell smirked. "That's because I taught you right."

I gave Payne a quizzical look.

Haskell watched the exchange. "Teddy was my protégé. Before I retired, I worked at the BFI for fifteen years. He came up through the ranks under my command."

"Ah, I see." Although, it was common for private sector consultants and experts to have learned the ropes while collecting government paychecks, I couldn't help but wonder if that would bias Haskell's findings since Lt. Payne was his prized pupil.

"Don't worry," Payne said, "he gets a kick out of pointing out the BFI's shortcomings. He doesn't think we function well without him. If we missed something, he'll find it because he wants to rub our noses in it."

"How else are you gonna learn?" Haskell asked.

Payne scowled and turned away. Until now, they'd been exceptionally buddy-buddy, but I could see the digs were weighing on the lieutenant, probably since he figured they missed something and Haskell would find it.

"I don't see a smoke detector," Payne said. "Truck must have taken it to test."

That's when I surveyed the kitchen. Even though the fire started here, the kitchen didn't look nearly as bad as the dining room, probably since most of the hard, metal surfaces didn't burn in the blaze. The stove and appliances still resembled charcoaled versions of what they used to be. The one thing I did notice was a lot of broken glass due to the extreme heat.

The fire spread in two directions from the outlet. One path went down the wall and across the floor while the other went up the wall and across the counter, leaving burnt ash where the flare-ups occurred.

"Cooking oil," Haskell said, shoving a lopsided and broken shelf out of the way to expose deep burns across the wall, floor, and shelving. "It really set in and cooked here. These burned longer and harder." He indicated the bubbled and pocked tiles. "If this had been liquor, the burns would be focused on the surface, not down beneath the grout and tile." He pried one up, exposing the damage beneath. "Since it's so close to the rest of the restaurant, the fire could have traveled through the vent," he kicked a grate near the floor, "and jumped the barrier."

"Could someone have used common kitchen items as accelerant?" I asked.

Haskell nodded. "That's entirely possible. I'll collect

samples but what you're asking would be impossible to prove. We'd have no way of knowing if someone spread the fire intentionally or if it spread naturally due to the location of the flammable materials."

"Unless we find scorch marks or a burn trail," Payne said. He brushed the rubble away with his foot. "I don't see a clear path on the floor." He moved to the remaining countertop and brushed away some dirt. "What do you make of this, Dil?"

Haskell leaned over Payne's shoulder and looked at the charred trail that ran up the side of the counter and across the top. "I'm gonna grab my camera from the car and take some photos." Without another word, he ducked through the opening.

"Does this mean something?" I asked.

"I don't know. It could have been a spill on the counter. Kitchen fires are difficult to evaluate." Payne followed the trail where it ended at the sink. From there, the fire took to the walls, before leaping back down and licking the counter on the other side before migrating across the three foot expanse to the shelving. "Honestly, there isn't enough scorching to indicate accelerant. It looks like bad luck. I'll know more once I locate the reports on the smoke detector and fire prevention system."

I nodded, aware of the familiar twitch at the back of my brain. This was intentional. No chef of Easton's caliber would leave a messy kitchen. And since the staff had gone home for the night, the place would have been pristine. The only possible reason the kitchen would be messy would be if Easton was working on a recipe. While I had clients who lied in the past, I didn't think Easton would make us go to this much trouble if he was to blame for the fire. Someone wanted to sabotage and potentially kill him. I just wondered if they had snuck inside his kitchen to do it.

Since Easton said he had been in the back office when the fire broke out, I went down the narrow hallway, past the walk-in freezer, and to the office. The hallway had significant amounts of smoke and water damage, and I could see the burn marks on the walls. No wonder the doorknob was hot when he touched it. Luckily, the blaze hadn't moved past the office door, and Easton managed to get out without being cooked alive.

The thought made my skin crawl. It would be a sick and poetic way for a chef to die. I shook it off as I entered the office. Aside from a thick layer of soot, the office appeared relatively undamaged. The filing cabinets were empty, as were the desk drawers. Easton must have salvaged as many things as he could.

I examined the door, growing queasy at the crunchy brown-red smudge on the handle that had probably been the skin of Easton's palm. Burning alive would be a terrible way to die, possibly the worst. And it was something I didn't want to think about.

I left the office and continued down the narrow corridor to the back door. From here, the building looked fine. No one would ever know it had been the scene of a horrific fire. It was strange how different things could look based on perspective alone.

By the time I returned to the kitchen, I understood why the fire investigators, police, and insurance wrote this off as an electrical fire. It would be too difficult to prove it wasn't. But Easton Lango knew it wasn't, and the death threat told me he was right. Now I just had to determine who would do something like this.

"Ready to go?" Lt. Payne asked.

Dil Haskell was on the phone with his office, requesting his techs come by to photograph the restaurant and collect additional samples. He hung up and smiled encouragingly at me. "I should have the results in forty-eight hours. I'll forward my report to Cross Security as soon as I reach a conclusion. If you want to discuss my findings further or have any other questions, call me."

"Thanks, Mr. Haskell," I said. "Bennett Renner or I will be in touch."

He nodded, clapped Payne on the shoulder, leaving a sooty handprint on the otherwise pristine dress shirt, and climbed into his truck.

Payne wiped at his shoulder, only making the stain worse. "I don't think there's enough here to prove the fire was arson. The blaze was triggered by an electrical fire.

Depending on what I find in the reports, that will determine how we proceed. You must have a million questions for me."

"Just one. How much skill is needed to make an intentional fire look accidental?"

"You're still convinced it's arson?"

"I'm convinced someone wants my client ruined, and this is how he did it."

SIXTEEN

"What did he say?" Renner asked.

"Officially, it's not arson. The cause of the fire checks out. It was electrical, but I can tell Lt. Payne has doubts."

"What about Haskell? What does he think?"

"Hell if I know. He exchanged some friendly jabs with the arson investigator, took some photos, and collected samples. He said he'd get the results back to us in forty-eight hours."

"That means he thinks there's something to find. Haskell's on board."

"Yeah, but from a legal standpoint, I doubt we have enough to convince the police to open an investigation."

"Have you spoken to Jake yet?" Renner asked.

"No." Renner was the first person I called when I left Lt. Payne's office. I peered out my windshield as I slowly circled the parking garage for Bridget Stockton's car or any car that might fit the description. "Has he called you? Did he identify the car or owner yet?"

"Not that I've heard," Renner said. "I'm not liking this. Voletek begged me for a favor last week, but now he's tromping all over our case. What did he need us for?"

I ignored the rhetorical question. "Are you still at

Easton's house?"

"No, I'm at the office. The food truck wasn't tampered with, but we found a tracker planted on the bumper of Easton's Eats. The tech department is in the process of tracing it. Once I get a location, I'll pay the masked bastard a visit."

"Maybe you should call Voletek."

I knew from his tone he thought the idea was ludicrous. "What are you doing?"

"It's best if I don't tell you."

"All right, but be careful. Lucien will shit himself if something else happens to you on his watch."

"I'm not his responsibility."

"You'd be surprised."

Just as we disconnected, I found the grey muscle car parked in a corner space. I double-parked behind it and got out of my car. I didn't know cars that well, but I knew the resale value on this one might be enough for Easton to open another restaurant. Maybe he maxed out his insurance, but a civil suit against a convicted or even suspected arsonist might win him enough to relaunch Sizzle.

Filing the possibility away that this could be an elaborate ploy, I crouched down on the ground, but I couldn't see beneath the car. After grabbing my flashlight, I slid between the Shelby and the car beside it and laid flat on my back. Staring up at the underside of the car, I shined my light beneath it to check for any modifications. I couldn't imagine someone would ruin a classic by tricking it out with some cheap undercarriage lights.

"What the hell are you doing?" a sharp female voice asked. I heard the telltale clicking of high heels on the pavement, and I slowly slid out from beneath the car. The car was a bust, and now I was busted. "Security's on the way. Who are you?"

"Ms. Stockton?" I recognized her photo from Cross Security's files, but I hoped to leave my employer out of it if I could.

"Who are you?" she repeated. "What are you doing to my car?"

"She a beauty." I stood up. "I'm guessing she's also a gas guzzler."

Her hand slipped into her purse, and she pulled out a small, black object. With the flick of her wrist, she extended the metal baton. "Answer the question."

I held up my palms. "Someone threw a brick through your ex-husband's window last night. Witnesses said they saw a muscle car leaving the area."

"Is he okay?"

That wasn't the question I expected. "He's freaked out."

She held the baton menacingly. "Did he say I did it?"

"No." I took a step closer. "I mean you no harm. I just wanted to make sure you weren't responsible. And you're not."

She blinked a few times. "You should have made an appointment to speak to me. Since you're here, you must know where I work."

"I do." Apprehensively, I eyed the baton. "I didn't want to bother you. I assumed you wouldn't want to waste your valuable time on matters that no longer concern you."

She flicked the baton closed but held it in her palm. "You haven't shown me a badge, so I'm guessing you're not a cop. Did he hire you?"

"Yes."

"What's your name?"

"Alex."

"No last name, Alex?"

"Nope."

She glanced to the side, eyeing the company car. "Cross Security." She chuckled. "The cat's out of the bag. You might as well tell me your last name. And while you're at it, you can tell me what's going on with Easton."

"Parker."

"Okay, Ms. Parker, you have ninety seconds to tell me what's going on before I have security detain you until the police arrive. I'm sure they won't be able to hold you for long, but it'll be interesting to see what happens when someone from my firm doesn't come to your rescue."

"Mr. Almeada will be pleased to hear that. I'm sure he's tired of saving my ass by now."

"Eighty-five seconds."

"Easton's being threatened and harassed. It started out harmless enough, just notes and anonymous internet trolls, but he thinks someone burned his restaurant down. Last night, someone broke into his house." Normally, I wouldn't blab to the first person who threatened me, but I wanted to see her reaction. If she was behind this, I expected smug satisfaction or an outright denial.

But the lady doth not protest too much or at all. She took a breath. "Did you question his harem of dumb sluts? One of them probably has an angry boyfriend."

"You're probably right."

"You're lying."

"I'm not on the stand, counselor. I didn't swear an oath. But I would like to ask you a question."

"Go ahead."

Slowly, I pulled out my phone and flipped to a shot of the car caught on the traffic cam footage. I held the device out to her. "Do you know anyone who drives a car like this?"

She studied the photo carefully. "I don't." And I believed her.

"Would you tell me if you did?"

"Probably." She met my eyes. "For you to be here, you're either exceptionally stupid or Easton's facing a serious threat. I've known Lucien Cross for years. He doesn't hire stupid. So that must mean someone's gunning for Easton. And you thought it was me."

"No, but I had to make sure it wasn't."

"Nine times out of ten, it's the aggrieved spouse, ex-spouse." She waved off the security guard who, by now, was closing in on our position. "This is the exception, not the rule." She went around the side and unlocked her door. "I might hate him, but I don't want to see him dead." She blew out a slow breath, internally fighting with herself over something. "Tell Lucien to pull out all the stops. I'll cover whatever expenses Easton can't."

"You're serious?"

She shot a warning look at me. "Don't look a gift horse in the mouth. If it turns out you aren't who you said, security has your plates. We will track you down." She slammed the door and revved the engine, impatiently waiting for me to move my car.

That didn't go as I expected. I climbed behind the wheel and left the parking garage. For a woman who hated her ex-husband, she had an odd way of showing it. Before returning to the office, I detoured to Fast Lanes, the exotic car club. I doubted a place like this would let Alexis Parker, P.I. wander the premises. And I knew they would never let Alexis Parker, soon to be unemployed, within sneezing distance of any of their vehicles. But they might welcome James Martin's girlfriend with open arms, assuming she was in the market for a fancy anniversary gift.

While one of the salesmen dithered on about the benefits of a yearly membership, I walked around the showroom, barely batting an eye at the exotic cars. The man must have thought I was a snob. Though, the dirt on the back of my jacket should have obliterated that notion. He must not have noticed.

I interrupted him in the middle of explaining the complimentary delivery and pick-up service. "Do you have anything edgier?" I asked. Cross told me he checked with Fast Lanes, and they didn't have any modified cars, but I had trust issues.

"Edgier?"

"You know, something fast and furious."

"Have you seen the Viper? We also have some classics, but they're checked out at the moment. Here's our inventory. We add new cars every year. I hear Mr. Martin has his own collection."

"Only new cars. I thought he'd enjoy taking some older models out for a spin." I took the offered tablet and swiped through the pages. "Do you have anything with illegal street mods?"

"Like racing cars?"

"Something like that."

"What exactly are you looking for?"

"I don't know." I handed back the tablet, not finding anything that fit. "Something flashy. Color-changing lights, a killer stereo, something fun to play with for a night or two. Something different from what he already has waiting in the garage."

The salesman gave me the unintentional once-over, probably thinking we were in the market for a third to invite into our bedroom rather than a new car. "We have hip, fun, and new. We also have classics. Exotics. American muscle. I'm sure we can find him something to fit whatever mood he's in or cater to whatever flavor he's looking to sample for a night or two."

"I don't know." I stared at the nearest car. "After a while, they all look the same, don't they?"

"We have more than just cars. We have other performance vehicles too. SUVs, trucks, both new and classic."

"He's really just a car guy."

A few Wall Street types were browsing, and the salesman must have realized they were more likely to join the car club than I was. "Here, take my card. Peruse our website and talk it over with Mr. Martin. I'll be glad to assist whenever you come to a decision and figure out which car you'd like to check out."

"Thanks." I took his card and tucked it in my pocket.

This wasn't an effective way to conduct an investigation. I already had a suspect and a damn good one at that. However, since Detective Voletek claimed he had a handle on Chef Strader, I thought it was important to explore other avenues. Now, I was rethinking that decision and regretting wasting most of my day. I needed to get back to the office and work the fire angle until the techs upstairs gave us something on the camera and the tracker.

When I entered Cross Security, I spotted Renner in an empty conference room. I ducked my head inside and made sure he was alone. "Hey, depending on how the rest of the day goes, I think we should put Chef Strader under surveillance."

Renner nodded, distracted by whatever was on the table in front of him. I peered over his shoulder. This had nothing to do with our case.

"Sorry, I'm about to meet with Mr. Zedula's head of security. I want to get some facts straight first. Can we talk about this later?"

"Sure." I studied the photographs of various velvet drawers containing what appeared to be diamonds. "Are you working a jewelry heist?"

"Don't worry about this." He practically shooed me away. "We have enough on our plate with Easton's case."

"Where are we on the camera and tracker?"

"Last I heard, the techs were working on determining the MAC address of the receiver. I don't know if they cracked it yet."

"I'll check," I said. "Stop by my office when you're done here."

"Will do."

SEVENTEEN

As usual, the tech department did not disappoint. They had the MAC address and were working on getting the IP of the device synced to receive the transmissions from the tracker. I didn't even think it was possible, but the techs were nothing short of miracle workers. They even found the store where the hidden camera and tracker were purchased, though gaining access to store records without a warrant would be entirely illegal, and assuming the case would result in an arrest, we were being cautious. We didn't want to screw with a police investigation, even though Lucien despised the cops. I suspected it was because he didn't want to waste time playing by the rules, not that I could fault him for that.

The nervous energy coursed through me. We would have answers by the end of the night. I knew it. I felt it. This might have been the simplest and shortest investigation I had worked since coming to Cross Security. I wouldn't mind more cases like this.

Resisting the urge to call Detective Voletek with the good news, knowing an act of hubris such as that would certainly jinx the investigation and my sudden unexpected good fortune, I went back to my original intended task. I had to find out more about the fire and who set it.

Dilbert Haskell hadn't e-mailed me his findings yet. I checked my watch. Forty-six hours to go, but still, it didn't hurt to look. I blew out a breath, rolled my neck, and began researching how to set a fire and make it look like arson.

Since I already knew the steps someone must have taken, I didn't know exactly what I expected to find. The cord had been tampered with which ignited the fire. Some type of accelerant, probably cooking oil, had been spread across the counter. The other suspicious spots Haskell and Payne pointed out had probably been the result of more carefully plotted and intentionally placed commonly found flammable kitchen substances.

Of course, this was all basic science. Anything to feed the fire would result in the fire spreading. Whoever it was didn't waste time on the back hallway, which could mean several things. I bit my thumbnail, hating the gnawing thought in the back of my mind. Easton was inside the restaurant when the fire broke out. If he set it himself, he would have needed to make sure he had an escape route. He wouldn't have torched the back hallway.

"Stop it, Parker," I grumbled. My client was not an arsonist. The tiniest bit of doubt wormed its way through my mind, but my gut said he wasn't. So he wasn't. It was that simple. It had to be.

Sighing, I reached for the phone. "Hey, Easton, I have some questions about Sizzle."

"Shoot," he said.

"Are you absolutely certain the fire alarm didn't sound?"

"I didn't hear anything."

"What about the sprinkler system? Do you remember if the sprinklers turned on?"

"I don't know."

I forced the curse down my throat. The back hallway didn't have a sprinkler system. It wasn't required. Just the dining area had been outfitted. "Did you take anything with you when you escaped the fire?"

"After I realized what was happening, I grabbed my laptop and my notebooks."

"What about the rest of the stuff from your office?"

He didn't answer immediately, so I opened the insurance investigator's report. It cataloged the items in the restaurant. "I went back for my files a few days later. The place was destroyed."

"I saw."

"You went there?"

"I just got back."

He let out an uneasy breath. "It's devastating. And to think, I spent weeks picking out the perfect tile and tablecloths, just so it could crumble." He cursed. "I want the fucking bastard responsible. Are you close to figuring out who did this?"

I pulled up building permits and blueprints from the city database. "We're getting there. Did you have the front of the restaurant remodeled?"

"Yeah, before I moved in. It used to have booths lining the front with windows at each table, like you'd expect from a diner. So I tore out the windows and rebuilt the front wall."

That might have explained why it collapsed when the rest of the building didn't. I read the work orders and shot an e-mail upstairs, requesting a profile on the contractors Easton hired. "Anything else I should know?"

"Like what?"

"Who had unfettered access to your kitchen?"

"My staff."

"And the night of the fire, do you remember who worked that day? Did anyone hang around later than usual? Did anything odd happen?"

"I've gone over this a hundred times with the cops, with Renner, with anyone who will listen."

"Go over it again. With me."

His story never changed. Every investigator made notes. The police checked alibis. No one from Sizzle worked late. No one hung around after hours. They all went home at least three hours before the fire started. Easton was alone. It was the middle of the night. The restaurant was locked up tight. The firefighters broke down the front door when they arrived because it was locked.

"You're sure the back door was locked too?"

"I know it was. I fumbled to get the door open."

"Okay," new thought, "who had keys?"

"Just me and my sous chef, Dante Bisset."

The light bulb clicked on. "The same sous chef who went to work for Asher York after the fire?"

"Yes, but the police said they spoke to him. He had an alibi. After that, they dismissed my claim completely."

"Have you spoken to Mr. Bisset recently?"

Easton's shrug could practically be heard through the phone. "We grabbed a drink last month. I asked him to meet me. I wanted to see how he was getting along with Asher and whether he'd consider coming back to me if Easton's Eats ever got off the ground." So someone else knew about Easton's latest venture.

"All right. Let me do some research. I'll call you back when I have something for you."

"Sure."

I ignored his dejected tone and put the receiver down. My fingers flew over the keys, typing Dante Bisset. Not surprisingly, he had studied cooking at Le Cordon Bleu. He graduated three years ago and worked in several famous kitchens before landing at Sizzle.

Bisset had no criminal record. Though he did amass a decent-sized debt, but those expenses were due to school and his chosen profession. He had loans to pay back, which meant he couldn't afford to remain unemployed. Even if he was loyal to Easton, which I had no way of knowing, he couldn't wait months to collect his next paycheck. Asher York used that to his advantage and swooped in before the burning embers had gone out to claim his new sous chef. However, since Bisset's debts remained, I didn't think someone paid him to start the fire. But since he was supposedly the only other member of Easton's staff with a key, I couldn't write him off without digging deeper.

I had a hunch. A quick social media search proved it was more than that. Dante Bisset was photographed driving a dark silver 1970 Pontiac GTO. "Motherfucker." I scribbled down his home address, but given the time, he'd probably be at work. I needed to get a look at the car. I needed to see if it had color-changing lights. Grabbing my jacket, I raced for the door.

"Whoa, where's the fire?" Renner asked as I skidded to a halt in front of him.

"Bad choice of words."

"Regardless, what did you find?"

"The car, I think."

Automatically, he checked to make sure his weapon was on his hip. "All right, let's go."

"I thought you were busy."

"That can wait. This can't." He eyed me. "Did the techs get back to you?"

"Not yet."

"Well, hot damn, Parker. You mean to tell me you found the car all by yourself? If you keep this up, I'll have to promote you from assistant to executive assistant."

"Bite me, Renner."

He pushed the button for the elevator. "Careful what you wish for."

We arrived at Delicious, Asher York's restaurant, at the start of the dinner rush. People waiting to be seated were already congregating around the bar. The bartenders hurried to fill orders while the hostesses seated guests. In the blink of an eye, the newly vacant stools vanished, consumed by the growing mass.

The restaurant was wedged in with buildings on both sides, so we strode down the block until we found an opening. Behind the building was the kitchen entrance and several no parking signs which three people ignored. I recognized York's electric car from my research. Beside it was a refrigerated delivery truck.

"Wine's here," Renner said, pointing to the logo. "If this is a bust, we can break in and drink away our sorrows."

"Now you want to hijack the wine distributor?"

"We could expense it to Cross."

"Deal." From here, I couldn't see behind the truck, so I followed a path around, my hand automatically rested on the butt of my nine millimeter. Call it a bad habit, but I was tired of being caught off guard. "That's it," I said, withdrawing my hand from inside my jacket.

Renner snapped a few photographs. The underbody

system was obvious, even from this angle. "I'll ask Easton if he recognizes it."

I stared at the spinners, wondering the point of the fancy and otherwise ridiculous custom hubcaps. Honestly, looking at the bastardized version of a classic, I understood why Fast Lanes kept their cars in original mint condition. This version no longer resembled what one would expect from a GTO, but it did make my job a lot easier.

"Congratulations, Alex. You found the car."

"Should we call Voletek?"

Renner peered into the front seat. "I don't see any bricks or masks. Nothing damning in sight." He went around to check the plates. After slipping on a pair of leather gloves, Renner touched the license plate. "Jake was right. There's a plastic cover over the rear plate. What about the front?"

I knelt down to get a better look. "Yep."

"All right. I'll let Jake know what's going on. In the meantime, let's make sure Mr. GTO doesn't take off without permission. Hang here for a sec."

While I waited, I visually inspected Asher York's car, but I didn't find anything suspicious. The rear door to Delicious was locked, key and code required. I surveyed the building, but I didn't spot any surveillance cameras nearby. Obviously, chefs didn't take security seriously enough. It was an epidemic. They needed to add a class on restaurant security in addition to restaurant safety as part of the culinary school curriculum.

The rumble of an engine drew my attention, and I hunkered down beside the delivery truck. Realizing it was Renner, I stood up, hoping he didn't notice I had been hiding. He parked the car behind the GTO, practically touching his nose to the muscle car's bumper.

"Okay, now that that's done, let's get some dinner."

"Are you insane?"

"We came all the way here, and we haven't even spoken to our suspect yet. We might as well eat, so we'll have an excuse to converse with him. The dining room wouldn't be the place for a chef, even a sous chef, to make a scene."

"They'll never give us a table."

"I bet you twenty bucks you're wrong."

"You're on."

We went around the building and in through the front door. If anything, the crowd had doubled in the last few minutes. The bar was so packed people were waiting in lines, two and three deep, just to get close enough to shout their order to the bartender. This would be the easiest twenty bucks I ever made.

"When I was moving the car, I called Jake and gave him a heads up."

"Is he on his way?"

Renner nodded. "I should ask for a table for three. Jake would hate to miss out on a gourmet meal."

I looked at Renner. The man must be delusional. "How hard did you get hit yesterday?"

"Trust me."

"I hate it when people say that."

While we waited in line to get to the hostess stand, I scoped out our surroundings. There was nothing particularly special about this place. It was just another expensive restaurant with a dress code. I glanced down, making sure I was dressed appropriately. Cross Security didn't exactly have a dress code, though Cross made sure his investigators knew to dress professionally. Most days, I wore my old OIO attire – black blazer, white shirt, dress pants. However, I upgraded my shoes to something more stylish.

"Do you have a reservation?" the hostess asked.

Renner offered a charming smile. "Actually, I don't, but I bet my friend you'd make an exception."

The hostess's expression soured, and she opened her mouth to protest, but Renner leaned in and whispered something to her that I couldn't hear. When he stepped back, she painted a polite, determined smile on her face and scanned the chart in front of her.

"Give me five minutes." She relinquished her stand to another hostess and disappeared into the dining room.

"What did you say to her?" I asked, amazed. The only time I'd seen magic like that was when it was performed by Martin the Magnificent.

"The less you know, the better," Renner said, a

mischievous glint in his eye.

EIGHTEEN

Renner pointed his fork at me, a piece of steak hanging from the tines. "You sure you don't want a bite?" I shook my head, and he popped the morsel into his mouth. "He doesn't know we're on to him, yet. You don't have to worry about being poisoned."

"I'm not."

He cut another slice of steak. "I don't know what they did to the steak, but it melts in my mouth like butter."

I picked at the crudité platter we'd received as an appetizer, compliments of the chef. "I'm guessing whatever it was involved the use of actual butter."

Renner laughed, nearly choking in the process. "Probably." He wiped his mouth and returned his napkin to his lap.

With the constant crowd and turnover, I had no doubt Dante Bisset was slaving away in the kitchen, along with the rest of Chef York's staff. Could Asher York be involved? Easton only gave us two names to consider, but from what I'd dug up, York appeared clean. Spotless, even. Strader had been my prime suspect until the car led us to Bisset, but since Bisset worked for York, maybe we were dealing with a ménage à trois.

Renner pointed with his fork. "Hey, is that Bisset?"

I caught a glimpse inside the kitchen as the door swung open and a server carried out two steaming plates. "Yeah."

"At least we know he's here." Renner finished his steak and looked at his watch. "What is taking Jake so long? He heard we were having dinner. He should have come running."

"Maybe he's solving a case," I said pointedly.

"So are we, and we're doing it while eating dinner. Therefore, we win."

The server returned, a haughty expression on his face. Obviously, he didn't approve of my lack of order, but past experience told me things would not go smoothly once we confronted Bisset. And I didn't want to deal with a confrontation on a full stomach.

"Anything else I can get you?" the server asked.

Renner grinned. "Dessert." He watched a cart roll past with baked Alaska and some fruit tartlets. "I like to end my meal with something sweet." He winked at me.

The server rambled off the list of desserts, and Renner took a painfully long time to decide, asking about the ingredients of each. I recognized it for what it was, a delay tactic, but the server probably just thought he had another indecisive and annoying guest to deal with. As if to put the man out of his misery, Renner received a text in the middle of his food-centric version of twenty questions.

Diners at another table caught the waiter's eye, and he politely excused himself while Renner read the message. "Jake's outside. I should get him something to eat." Renner tucked his phone away. "Do you think I can get an order to go? This place isn't exactly McDonald's."

Despite whatever criminal activity the sous chef committed, the server was innocent. Yet, he had become collateral damage, forced to endure our inquisitive wrath. "Probably, if you ask nicely."

"Do you think they'll wrap it in a foil swan?"

"It depends on what you order. Why is that important?"

He chuckled, shaking his head. "It isn't, but what self-respecting cop orders food that comes disguised as a swan?"

"So you're just busting his balls?"

"Pretty much."

"Okay, Bennett, what's the deal with the two of you?" I settled back in my seat, keeping an eye on the kitchen in case our suspect tried to sneak out.

"When I got hurt on the job and was laid up for six months, I ended up in a dark place. My wife left. I couldn't walk. I couldn't work. I couldn't do much of anything except sit around and feel sorry for myself. It was pathetic." Despite the words, he grinned, as if the story was comical instead of sad. "Every day, Jake dropped by after shift. He'd tell me about his day, which pissed me off, so instead, he started picking up dinner. And he'd tell me a story about everything he brought."

"Like the lamb came from Australia and was named Daisy?"

"Oh, he gave me grief like that too." Renner narrowed his eyes. "I need to stop affiliating with smartasses."

"I'm not a smartass. I'm hilarious." And if I wasn't careful, I'd turn into Martin.

"Jake probably said the same thing. You're both wrong. Anyway, somewhere along the line, I figured out he was actually serious about this stuff and not just making shit up to keep me from downing an entire bottle of pills."

I wasn't sure if Renner was serious about that last part or if he was taking dramatic license, but I could see it going either way. So I kept my smartass comments to myself.

"Eventually, I got back on my feet, collected some money from the city on account of my injury, and paid Jake back with a restaurant crawl. So anytime a food-related case pops up, he calls me."

"How cute. You two have a thing." And that thing dragged me into the middle of an arson investigation.

"Shut it, Parker." But I saw the playful look in his eye. "Needless to say, in order to avoid remarks like that, I make sure Jake's the joke."

"Aren't you sweet?"

He winked. "You bet."

The waiter returned and suffered through another round of questions before Renner ordered the Swedish meatballs to go, just so they'd be wrapped in a foil swan. Then he ordered a slice of baked Alaska, and since I couldn't let him suffer alone, I asked for two forks. Then I placed an order for a mini chocolate strawberry lava cake to go.

"Jake doesn't need dessert," Renner insisted.

"It's not for him."

"Ooh, someone's got a sweet tooth. No wonder you only ate veggies for dinner."

I kicked Renner under the table. At least now we had sampled enough items that our request to speak to the sous chef wouldn't seem abnormal. It wasn't uncommon for VIP guests to ask to speak to the chef or extend their compliments, but not many people asked to speak to the sous chef. However, I greased the server's palm with a large enough tip that he didn't think twice about it.

"As you can see, we're very busy, but I'll make sure he stops by your table before we bring out your to-go order." The server slipped the cash into his pocket, cleared away Renner's empty plate, and refilled our water glasses.

A few minutes later, a flaming dessert was placed on the table. Renner waited for the fire to go out and dug in. After he made sure it was safe and not poisoned, I tasted it. It wasn't bad. Idly, I wondered how the restaurant would fare after its sous chef was arrested.

"Madam, Monsieur." Dante Bisset stood before us. His chef whites had a few stains and splatters, and he looked tired and overworked. He shifted his weight from one foot to the other, antsy to get back to the kitchen. "You requested to speak to me. Is there something wrong with your dinner?"

"Quite the opposite." Renner dialed up the friendly factor. "It was delicious. I guess that's how this place got its name."

Bisset bowed his head as he took half a step back. "Merci."

"However, my companion and I do have one question for you." Renner put down his fork and pushed his chair back. He sensed it just like I did. Dante looked the type. I licked the whipped cream off my fork and put it down before placing my napkin on the table next to it. "Were you here last night?"

"No, I'm sorry." Bisset's brow scrunched. "Did you have a poor dining experience yesterday?"

"It wasn't the dining that was the problem. It was more of a window issue."

"Window? You didn't like where you were seated?" Bisset looked to me for an explanation.

The server had taken the knives off the table, and the forks were out of the chef's reach. So I said, "You shouldn't drive such a recognizable car when you commit a crime."

Bisset gulped. A fresh layer of perspiration erupted on his already sweaty brow. His eyes shifted back and forth. "I do not know what you mean. I have work to do." Bisset turned to walk away.

"Did you throw the brick?" Renner asked, and Bisset turned back around. The guilty expression on his face was plain as day. "Or did you leave the GPS on the truck? We found it and the camera."

"I do not know what you are talking about," the chef insisted. "Are you police?"

"No, we're private investigators," I said. "Chef Easton hired us."

The blood drained from Bisset's face. "Please leave." He gestured to someone standing near the hostess station. Restaurants didn't usually have security or bouncers, but Bisset probably figured a few of the busboys would run us off.

"Is that our cue to scram?" Renner mused as the two busboys approached us, but my eyes never left Bisset. He grabbed a jacket off the coatrack near the kitchen and put it on over his chef whites. "Gentlemen," Renner nodded to them just as the waiter pushed past the escaping chef with the foil swan and a box with my cake, "we're not here to cause trouble. We'll just get our food, pay our bill, and be on our way." He raised his voice so the nearby diners would hear him. "I'm just glad I don't work with someone who leaves death threats on people's doorsteps." Several people gave us strange looks, but Dante had already disappeared into the sanctuary of the kitchen. "I'm not sure

I want someone like that preparing my meals."

The waiter paled, utterly aghast. I conveyed my apologies and asked about Dante's whereabouts, but he didn't work the previous night. That was all the waiter knew. While Renner dug through his wallet, I watched the door to the kitchen swing open again. Bisset was gone. I reached for my phone, but Renner stopped me.

"Dante's car's blocked in, and Jake's waiting out back. You don't have to call him. He'll call us."

Instead, I heard dishes crash inside the kitchen, followed by a surprised yelp. The swinging door burst open, attracting the attention of several nearby diners. Bisset spotted us, still at the table, and stepped backward, knocking into another server who dropped several full plates to the floor.

"See, looks like he's back already." Renner nodded in the sous chef's direction. "Right about now, he's probably realizing he's trapped."

I didn't wait for Renner to tell me Jake would handle it. Dante Bisset knew he was caught. The desperation reflected in his eyes, and I feared what he might do. There was a good chance he burned down Sizzle and attempted to kill Easton in the process. I didn't want to know what he'd do in a room full of people now that he was cornered. This would be the perfect time to announce I was a federal agent or Renner was a cop and clear the restaurant, but that wasn't an option. We'd hung up our official credentials a long time ago. Instead, I darted around the crowded tables and burst into the kitchen, surprised when Renner didn't follow me. After eating that much steak and dessert, he probably couldn't move.

Bisset shoved one of the dishwashers aside, hoping to find another route out of the kitchen and away from me. Asher York screamed at him from his place in front of the counter, still focused on preparing the dish in front of him instead of realizing what was going on around him. If Bisset set this kitchen on fire, I doubted York would even notice. He'd burn along with his restaurant. Maybe Bisset hoped Easton was that dedicated. From what I knew of Easton Lango, it was entirely possible.

"Get out of the kitchen," I said, dismissing a few prep cooks as I moved past. I didn't draw my weapon. I didn't want Bisset to panic more than he already was. Panicked people acted irrationally, so the first thing I needed to do was get the sous chef to relax.

"Who are you?" York bellowed. "What authority do you have to tell my kitchen staff what to do?"

For a millisecond, I wanted to say I was with the health department and Delicious was shut down. That would get his attention, but I resisted. "I'm Alexis Parker. I'm a private investigator." I maintained the calm authoritarian tone when I spoke. "I need to speak to Mr. Bisset."

"He's busy. Whatever it is you want to ask, it can wait." York finished plating the meal and looked up, noticing a half empty kitchen and a floor covered in shattered dishes and dropped meals. "Get the fuck out of my kitchen."

Bisset edged even farther away, backing himself into the corner beside the walk-in freezer. He threw off the outer jacket he put on over his chef whites and fumbled to unbutton the chef's jacket, finding the thick material restrictive and suffocating. Asher York glanced back at him and then me.

"Dante, what's going on? Why are you undressing?" he asked. "Who is this woman?"

"I don't know. She thinks I'm someone else. She's confused."

"Maybe you're right." I held my palms up so he could see I meant him no harm. "I just need you to answer a few questions. Where were you last night?"

"Umm," Bisset stammered, blinking rapidly and practically shaking.

"You called in sick," York said. "What did you do?"

Bisset didn't answer. He looked like he might be in shock.

"Did you set the fire?" I asked, my eyes on Bisset. Slowly, I slipped my hand inside my jacket. The electricity in the air made my skin prickle. Instinct said things were about to go from bad to worse, though I wasn't sure why I thought that.

"What fire?" York asked.

"The one that destroyed Sizzle." I watched Bisset fidget. With his beady eyes, he reminded me of a mouse caught in a trap. Suddenly, his eyes grew wide, and he turned to run, knocking into the side of the freezer and nearly bouncing off from the force.

A knife flew through the air, and I spun in the direction from which it came and drew my weapon. "Everyone out now," I barked at the few remaining kitchen staff and aimed at York, who had picked up another sharp utensil. Rage covered his face. I'd rarely seen that kind of animosity and unbridled fury. "Drop the knife, Chef."

He ignored me, spittle flying from his lips as he screamed, "You set the fire? Are you planning to burn down my restaurant too?" He took a step closer, and I sidestepped around the counter, putting myself between the chef and his protégé. "Is that what you do? You get pissed and angry because you're a pathetic cook, so you destroy greatness?"

"Whoa, take it easy," I said. "The police have this place surrounded. Let's not do anything crazy." In the periphery, I spotted Renner taking up a position against the swinging kitchen door. Thankfully, his full stomach didn't take him out of the game.

York ignored me, his focus entirely on Bisset. "Answer me. Is that why you begged me to hire you? You want to destroy me too? Is this how you plan to make head chef? By eliminating the competition? You pathetic fuck." He strode forward, raising the knife. He didn't even notice I was blocking his path. Every cell in his body was concentrated on Dante Bisset. One more step, and I'd shoot him in the knee.

But Renner came up behind York, grabbing his right shoulder and twisting his left hand behind his back. Renner shoved the chef against the waist-high prep station, knocking the knife from his hand and slamming his face against the shiny stainless steel.

Bisset used the distraction to bolt. He pushed past me and ran for the swinging door. I raced after him. The sous chef collided with a table, his feet tangling in the tablecloth. He stumbled, tripping over the trailing white sheet.

"Bisset, stop," I bellowed. "There's nowhere to go."

He scrambled to pull himself off the floor. A young man got too close, and Bisset grabbed the boy's hand and spun himself around the kid, holding a steak knife against his captive's ribs. "I didn't hurt anyone," Bisset said. "And now, because of you, that psycho wants to kill me."

"All right," I held up my palms, "I'm sorry. You said you didn't hurt anyone, so I don't think it would be wise to start now. Let the kid go."

Bisset's breath came in shallow, rapid gasps. His eyes were mere pinpricks. The rumble of the crowded restaurant turned into a muffled quiet as everyone held their collective breaths. Then the stampede started. Those close to the front door ran out. A few pulled out their cell phones, though I didn't see a single one of them dial 911.

"You don't want to hurt him," I said.

Bisset released the kid, turned, and froze in place. The crackle of the stun gun buzzed, and Bisset dropped to the floor. Voletek looked around, holding up his badge. "Police," he announced. He patted down Bisset and cuffed him.

"Renner might need your help," I said.

"Watch him." Voletek headed toward the kitchen just as Renner hauled Asher York out in cuffs. "You got him?"

"Yep." Renner pushed York down into one of the empty chairs at a now empty table.

Voletek reached for his radio. Backup was on its way. "Sorry, everyone, the kitchen's closed." Voletek gave me a look. "I thought Cross Security was known for their subtlety."

"That costs extra," I said.

NINETEEN

"Go through it again," Detective Voletek said. He reached for his mug and took a sip.

"We've been over this three times." Asher York was tired of repeating himself, but his attorney didn't seem to mind. The man probably made $200 an hour. For him, time was money, literally. "I don't have anything else to say."

"Just one more time, please." Voletek flipped back to the first page of notes. "I can't quite wrap my head around this."

"That's because you're a fucking idiot," York mumbled.

Voletek pretended not to notice, but his back stiffened. "When did you first realize there was trouble?"

"When that woman burst into my kitchen and told everyone to clear out."

"Not before?"

"No."

"See, this is all your fault," Renner mumbled beside me. We had 'accidentally' wandered into the observation room while Voletek conducted the interview. "You're the reason York attempted to murder his sous chef."

"Shh." I put my finger to my lips.

According to York, he didn't notice anything amiss until

I showed up. That's when he realized Dante Bisset's strange behavior, and after hearing the questions I asked Bisset, York insisted he feared for his safety and the safety of everyone else inside Delicious and attempted to neutralize the threat. Until I made those accusations, York had no idea Bisset was dangerous or had been up to no good.

"Obviously, my client was acting in self-defense," the attorney said. "You have no reason to hold him."

Voletek glanced at the attorney. "That's not what the witnesses are saying. Until this gets sorted out, Mr. York will remain in custody."

York launched into another protest. "You can't do this. I didn't do anything. That psychopath is who you should be arresting, not me."

"Mr. Bisset is also under arrest. Any details you can provide concerning Bisset's whereabouts last night would be invaluable. Maybe we can make a deal." Voletek waited.

"He sure takes the long way around." I wondered why Voletek didn't dangle the carrot in front of York sooner. The man was a chef; he could probably take that carrot and turn it into a nice soup or something. Voletek just needed to give him the opportunity.

"That's Jake for you," Renner said. "He's by the book when it counts."

"Then what's the deal with the reward Easton offered and the bad blood between Voletek and Nick O'Connell?"

"I said when it counts." Renner glanced behind us to make sure we remained alone. He wouldn't risk getting his buddy in blue in trouble over some harmless gossip. "One," he ticked the points off on his fingers, "Jake's a foodie. We've established this. He wants that dinner, and he can't see what harm it'll do. He also knows that I'd be happy to invite him to join me, so it's no longer a bribe or reward. It's dinner with a friend. That's why he dropped this in my lap. Two, he's a good guy. He wants to do the right thing. He only passes me cases when he's sure there's something to be done that he can't do himself because of red-tape and regulations. It wouldn't matter if Easton was paying us in peanuts, Voletek would still have asked for my help. Three, he and O'Connell were in the same class at the academy. They used to be tight until Jake tried to pick up Jenny. That's when their friendship ended."

"Nick's wife?"

"She wasn't Nick's wife at the time. They just started dating, and Nick brought her to the bar across from the precinct. According to what I heard, Nick went to get a beer, and while he was gone, Jake did what he always does with badge bunnies."

"Jen's not a badge bunny."

"Jake didn't know that. And after he found out, he didn't exactly back off either. He figured it wasn't serious between Nick and Jen. It's always the same old story with Jake. He never knows when to quit, whether it's a case or a girl."

I turned my attention back to the window, unsure what I thought of Detective Voletek. As a show of solidarity and respect for O'Connell and his wife, I disliked Voletek on principle. But I didn't think he was a bad guy. I didn't think he was a bad cop either. However, after what I just heard, I knew he was a dog.

"I don't know anything." York raised his bound hands as if he wanted to choke Voletek. "I would tell you if I knew. Hell, if I had any idea Dante was some crazy psychopath, I never would have invited him into my kitchen."

"Did he approach you for a job?" Voletek asked.

"Yes." York lowered his hands, deflating as he exhaled. "He has exemplary credentials and amazing skills. His classical training makes him an asset. But I don't want someone unstable working in my kitchen. Tell him he's fired."

Voletek collected the paperwork and went out the door, nodding at the officer to move Asher York back into a holding cell. The chef shot a few final frantic questions to his attorney before being ushered out of the room. I didn't care what he said; if I hadn't stopped him, he probably would have killed or maimed Bisset. York was volatile, unbalanced, and obsessed. Bisset wasn't the only psycho in Delicious' kitchen. Based on York's history of DUIs, I didn't think the reason his hands shook while in the interrogation room had anything to do with nerves. He needed a drink. If he wasn't released soon, things would only get worse.

"What are you doing in here?" Voletek asked.

Renner grinned. "I told you this wasn't the break room, Alex."

"Out." Voletek pointed at the door, and we stepped outside. "Did you provide your statements in writing?"

"Yes, sir," I said.

"We handed them to the sergeant. We were told we're free to go," Renner said, "but we couldn't just walk out without saying goodbye."

Voletek glanced around the empty corridor. "I'll show you where the break room is," he said. Once we were inside with the door closed, Voletek blew out a breath. "I take it you heard what York said."

"We might have caught a word or two," I replied.

Voletek rubbed a hand over his mouth. "Okay, so after you left Easton's this morning, I spoke to Strader. He said he felt ill and had to leave work, but he doesn't have an alibi. No doctor's note. No trip to the pharmacy. Nothing. Since he has a record for assault, his prints are in the system, so we know he didn't leave the print in the duck fat."

"What about Bisset? As far as I know, until a few hours ago, he never had any run-ins with the police," I said.

"He didn't, but he was printed when we processed him. We'll know soon enough if he left the print on the tarp. What happened with the bug you found planted in Easton's kitchen?" Voletek rummaged in the fridge for the crushed swan, which Renner grabbed, along with my cake before we followed Voletek back to the station.

Renner pulled out his phone and held it out to the detective. "This message came in when you were busy making York sound like a broken record."

Voletek scanned the intel. "You're sure about this?"

"Cross Security knows what they're doing." Renner had shown me the message, which is why I was itching to take another crack at Bisset. "The camera and GPS tracker are synced to a single device. The IP links to Galen Strader's home address."

"You think they're working together?" Voletek emptied the contents of the foil onto a plate and popped it in the microwave.

"I do," Renner said.

"We do," I affirmed. "I spoke to Easton. He didn't sound surprised. Chefs of their caliber travel in small circles. It's a close-knit community."

"Close-knit? It's an incestuous, rage-filled clusterfuck of crazy," Renner said.

The microwave beeped, and Voletek took out the steaming dish. He grabbed a fork and put the plate down before taking a seat at the table. He seemed more interested in the food than in our speculation. He speared a meatball, covered in a thick, creamy sauce, and blew on it, waiting for it to cool while the sauce dribbled onto the plate. When it was cool enough to eat, he popped it into his mouth, closed his eyes, and savored the morsel.

"The first bite's always the best." Voletek opened his eyes and wiped his mouth. He skewered another piece and held it in the air, waiting for it to cool. "As soon as I spotted the car outside Delicious, I knew we were on the right track. And after what transpired inside the restaurant with the chef losing his shit and the sous chef nearly taking a hostage, I thought it best to have the vehicle impounded. A preliminary search didn't yield any damning evidence. I sent a few uniforms into Easton's neighborhood. They'll flash around some photos and see if anyone remembers anything."

"They won't," I said.

Voletek bit into the second meatball and chewed thoughtfully. "I still have to try. Once the system updates with Bisset's information, we'll know if his prints are a match. Until then, everything hinges on what he has to say, unless either of you has an ace up your sleeve. You tracked the camera, which you neglected to tell me about, and helped the PD get details on the GPS tracker. Any idea where they were purchased?"

Renner nodded. "They came from the big box store on the west end. The buyer paid cash, but from the security footage I've seen, I'm sure it's Strader. He was alone. No sign of Bisset or the car."

"That's gonna make this a lot more difficult." Voletek rolled the last piece around on the plate. "I was hoping you had leverage, something to make him flip on Strader."

"Why don't you arrest Strader?" I asked. "You have him for trespassing and illegally recording Easton, not to mention the B&E."

Voletek finished eating and washed the plate in the sink. "Uniforms will pick up Strader as soon as Cross Security sends us the evidence they've collected. In the meantime, I have to get Bisset to tell me what the two of them were doing at Easton's house."

"We already know what they were doing," Renner said.

"Do we?" Voletek arched an eyebrow. "What were they doing? Nothing was stolen. We have property damage, but Easton wasn't hurt. I need the evidence you collected, and I'll see what I can get to stick."

Renner went to make a call, and Voletek cleaned up the mess he made. He grabbed a bottle of water from the fridge and offered me one.

"No, thanks."

He poked at the container holding my cake. "Don't forget to take this with you when you leave. If it stays here too long, one of the vultures out there is sure to eat it." He shut the fridge and turned with a grin. "Or I might eat it."

"Is that the going price for convincing you to let me sit in on Bisset's interrogation?"

"I'm sorry. I can't do that."

O'Connell let me a time or two, but I didn't think mentioning it would help my case. "You know, I have served as a police consultant in the past."

"Yes, but now you're with Cross Security. The department didn't approve you for a consulting gig. My hands are tied." He moved closer, stopping just a few inches from me. "Why don't you tell me what you think I should ask Bisset?"

"Ask him why he set the fire."

"You're sure he's guilty?"

I wasn't, but I knew the fire was no accident. "Fine, then ask where he got the car. I ran the records. The GTO isn't registered to him. So where'd he get it?"

"It's his aunt's." Voletek consulted the notepad in his pocket. "She lives in an assisted-living place. She doesn't drive much anymore. He gave her his subcompact and took her car. Officers checked. She verified they traded vehicles a while ago. The GTO was too much for her to handle."

"Does she know what he did to her car?"

"She said he customized it."

"It sounds like they're close." I narrowed my eyes at his notepad, trying to read upside down. "What did you say her name is?"

"I didn't." He closed the notepad. "Didn't you promise to share your intel with me? You and Renner have been keeping me out of the loop."

"You've done the same thing. You never called to tell us how the conversation with Strader went."

"Fine. Stay here and watch me interview Bisset or don't. That's up to you, but I don't want you speaking to Violet Arnaud at Shady Groves. Do you understand?"

I smiled. "Absolutely."

He returned my grin. "Good." When I didn't immediately retreat, he realized I wanted to see what Bisset had to say. "You spoke to the arson investigators earlier, right?"

"Yes, but I haven't heard back from them yet. I don't have anything conclusive."

"I doubt you ever will." Voletek led the way out of the break room and toward the interrogation rooms. "I performed my due diligence. We don't have proof. Everything says it was electrical."

"Dante Bisset had a key and access to Sizzle's kitchen. To top it off, Asher York believed he did it. That's why he assaulted Bisset and threatened to kill him. There has to be a reason York jumped to those conclusions so easily."

"All right. I'll try to work with that. Stay here." He gestured inside the adjoining observation room. "Let me do my job. If you're struck with an epiphany, tap on the glass."

"Hey, Jake," I said, forcing him to stop in the doorway, "check his hands for burns. Lt. Payne said it's common for those who set fires to get burned in the process."

"Cars, burns, anything else?"

"Check his pockets for red markers like the one used to scrawl the threatening note."

"Officers didn't find any weapons on him when he went through booking, but maybe they missed a few spare bricks," he said sarcastically.

"You never know."

Voletek rolled his eyes and sauntered into the interrogation room. Hopefully, he'd take a different approach with Bisset, or we'd be here all night.

TWENTY

Like most men under arrest, Dante Bisset insisted he was innocent. He claimed he didn't throw the brick or plant the tracker or camera at Easton's house. When confronted with nearby traffic cam footage, Bisset denied it was his car. Though the work order Voletek dug up from the auto body shop said otherwise.

"That is your signature, right?" Voletek spun the receipt around. "These four numbers match the credit card in your wallet."

"I had some work done, so what?" Bisset's chef jacket hung unbuttoned over a heather grey t-shirt that showed perspiration stains. He was nervous.

"Not many people get color-changing lights installed because they stick out, especially when committing a crime."

"What proof do you have? My client already told you that isn't his car," the public defender said. Unlike York, Bisset couldn't afford fancy lawyers. However, by the luck of the draw, Bisset had gotten one of the best public defenders around. Voletek better be on his toes.

"If it's not your car, why did you pay for the underbody

work?" Voletek answered the public defender's question with one of his own.

Bisset looked to his attorney for approval before he spoke. "I had the work done as a surprise for the car's owner."

"Your aunt owns the car, right? Violet Arnaud? Her name's on the registration."

"Yeah, so?"

"Your aunt is eighty and lives in an assisted-living facility. Why would she want undercarriage lights?"

Bisset believed he'd come up with the perfect excuse. "To help her see at night."

"You've got to be kidding me," Voletek mumbled.

The attorney hid his chuckle. He knew it was bullshit, but he had a job to do. "Move on, Detective. The question's been asked and answered."

"We're not in court." Voletek reminded him. "So you're telling me that dear old auntie drove to your former boss's house and launched a brick through his front window with a death threat taped to it? Should I have her brought to the station to answer these questions instead?"

"No." Bisset glared at the detective.

"Well, someone has to answer for this. Easton Lango saw the car parked outside his house last night. He can identify it. That description led us to you, and when we picked you up at Delicious, the GTO was in your reserved space. We didn't spot your car, the subcompact that's registered in your name, anywhere. As far as I know, your aunt wasn't inside the restaurant, so what's going on, Mr. Bisset? Who drove the GTO last night? Why was it parked at your place of employment in your designated spot today, if you didn't drive it?"

"I drive it sometimes."

"That's not what your aunt said." Voletek flipped to a signed statement officers had gotten from Bisset's aunt. "She said you graciously switched vehicles with her."

"Circumstantial. Perhaps, my client forgot." The attorney gave Voletek a look. "What other evidence do you have?"

"We have the gifts your client left behind."

"Gifts?" The attorney frowned. "You mean the brick and camera? They were dusted for prints. You have nothing. The handwriting on the note isn't conclusive. Your case is flimsy, and you know it."

"Perhaps." Voletek turned his attention back to Bisset. "Do you cook with duck fat?"

"Yes." Bisset sensed it was a trap, but he couldn't figure out the harm in answering.

Voletek removed a photo from the file and put it on the table. "We found a print on the inside of the tarp Easton used to cover his food truck. CSU speculates the person who planted the tracker on the bumper must have removed his gloves after leaving the device. According to Easton, he caught the culprit messing with the tarp when he confronted him outside."

"You're saying my client left a print?" the attorney asked, but the question was pointless. Bisset paled, his hair becoming increasingly wet and shiny as he mopped sweat from his brow. For someone who couldn't handle a little heat, I wondered how he survived all day in the kitchen. "You fingerprinted my client. Is it a match? Or are you wasting our time with the theatrics, Detective?"

"I'm waiting for the results to come back. Once they do, you know what will happen. It's in your client's best interest to cooperate now."

"I doubt that," the attorney said. "You're fishing, hoping to bully a confession out of my client. I won't let that happen."

Voletek ignored the public defender and stared at Bisset with the full intensity of a seasoned homicide detective. "You know what we'll find. We also know you had an accomplice. Uniformed officers are picking him up now."

"Galen?" Bisset squeaked, clapping a hand over his mouth the moment he realized his mistake.

Voletek gave the attorney a smug look. "Advise your client to tell me what he knows."

Though overworked and underpaid, the public defender saw a lot of these cases. He instructed Bisset to remain silent until Voletek provided proof of the man's involvement. Right now, everything the police had was circumstantial. However, when the lab results came back, there was no doubt the print found on the tarp matched Dante Bisset.

"I need a few moments to confer with my client," the attorney said.

Voletek grabbed the file and pushed away from the table. "Take your time. I have another interview to conduct. Maybe he'll be more accommodating."

I stood in the hallway outside the observation room. The mic and camera were off, ensuring Bisset's rights weren't violated. Voletek nodded to the cop who had brought him the fingerprint analysis.

"He's waiting in three, Jake," the cop said.

"Thanks." Voletek glanced down the hallway but made no move for the door. Instead, he took to leaning against the wall across from me. "It looks like Bisset and Strader paid Easton a visit last night."

"Told you so."

"Actually, I might have told you. I need to check the board. Initially, when I looked into the fire, I ran through the usual suspects, but I don't recall Bisset and Strader crossing paths." Before I could open my mouth with a suggestion, Voletek held up a hand. "I know. Close-knit community." He led the way down the hall and back to the squad room. After asking a few of his colleagues to check for a connection between the two men, Voletek ducked into the conference room and flipped the board around. He stared at the photo array and notations, tracing a red line from Sizzle to Bisset to Delicious. He backtracked to Bisset, scanning the man's bio.

"Well?"

"I don't have anything written down. Did you find anything?" Voletek asked.

"If I did, I wouldn't have wasted time asking what you found. There is an easier way to do this, Detective. You could call Easton and ask."

"Or I'll just ask Galen Strader." Voletek strode out of the room and down the hallway.

I practically had to run to keep up with him. He entered the third interrogation room and shut the door just as I caught up to him. Bastard.

"He's slimy," Renner said, sneaking up behind me.

I clutched my chest dramatically. "You're lucky we're in a police station, or I might have shot you."

He ignored me. "Chef Strader's slimy. Amir remotely hacked into Strader's computer. Strader has dozens of video files of his staff preparing meals."

"Isn't that illegal?"

"It is if they didn't know they were being filmed. However, I'm sure he told them about the security cameras inside Bouillon. Every video came from the restaurant's kitchen. I think he steals their techniques and ideas. He has notes attached to the video files with cooking instructions, ingredients, temperature, things like that. I bet it's why he bought into Bouillon. He wanted access to the security cameras."

"Maybe he wants to make sure they are following his instructions. Chefs are anal assholes."

"Isn't that redundant?"

I snickered. "It's suspicious, but it's not enough. Did Amir find anything else? What about videos taken from inside Easton's kitchen?"

"Just one. It had been deleted. He tried to recover it, but without direct access to the computer, he could only view the thumbnail screenshot." Renner held out his phone so I could see the screen grab Amir forwarded him. "The most watched video files feature his sous chef, Kasey. He watched those dozens of times. Strader's a creep. Perhaps he's also a creeper."

"Maybe he has a thing for her," I suggested.

Renner's shoulders lifted an inch.

"It could be a fetish or his version of foreplay." I thought for a moment. "Any videos of the dishwasher and the prep cook horizontal on Strader's desk?"

"Now who has a fetish?"

I glared at Renner. "Just answer the question."

"No, at least I don't think so. Amir didn't mention finding anything like that. As far as I know, all the videos on his computer relate to the kitchen and cooking. No porn. No cat videos. Nothing."

"It's his work computer. He kept it clean." I wondered what else he might have on the device. "Did you find any business records? P&Ls for Bouillon? Strader owns most of the restaurant, he must have documents and spreadsheets related to that."

"Amir got as much as he could, but Strader must have turned off the device. Amir lost the connection. That's the problem with a remote hack. There's no way of knowing what we might be missing without checking the actual device."

My thoughts went to the amorphous cloud and other backup systems. It was possible we could only view what had been synced rather than the rest of the files. At least, that's what Lawson, my favorite FBI tech genius, had taught me over the years. Though, Cross Security didn't seem to function within the previously established framework. The rules didn't apply to them. I was surprised Lucien hadn't figured out how to circumvent the law of gravity yet. That would probably be the next thing he did.

"Strader's stealing their recipes or using their ideas to improve on his own. That's probably why he set up the camera next to Easton's kitchen counter," Renner said.

"All right, let's run this by Easton and see what he thinks." In the meantime, the police would get a warrant and confiscate Strader's computer. Perhaps when Easton survived the fire and set off on his next venture, Strader realized it'd be easier to sabotage Easton by stealing from him instead of destroying him. But that didn't explain the death threat. There was more going on here. I just didn't know what it was.

TWENTY-ONE

"Thanks for meeting us," I said, gesturing to the threadbare sofa in homicide's break room. Easton took a seat on the couch, glancing out the door into the bullpen. "Did Detective Voletek have any more questions?"

"No, he told me to stay out of sight. If he needs anything else, he'll meet us in here. I don't think he wants his buddies to know he's working on my case," Easton said cynically.

"It's not that." Okay, it might have been that, but it was in Easton's best interest to remain out of sight since Bisset and Strader were only a few hundred feet away. Or else he might end up with more than just a brick through his window. "Did Renner catch you up to speed?"

Easton ran a hand through his brightly colored hair. "You think Galen Strader is behind this and Dante Bisset is helping him." Easton stared at the poster on the wall. "Did Dante set the fire? He had keys to my kitchen, to Sizzle."

"I don't know yet, but I will find out."

Renner stepped into the room and pulled the door closed. "We're working on determining the cause of the fire. We should have something definitive by Monday." He had a mug book in his hands, except when he opened it, it wasn't a mug book. It was an array of muscle cars taken from various angles. Mixed in with those photos were shots of Bisset's car. He took a seat beside Easton. "Do any of these look familiar?"

Easton flipped through the pages, stopping on Bisset's car. He stared at the three photos, one of the side, one of the front, and one of the back. "That's the car from last night."

"Have you ever seen it before last night?" Renner asked.

"No, I don't think so." He stared at Renner, as if hoping to determine the proper answer by reading my colleague's facial expression. "I don't know. Maybe."

"It's yes or no," I said. "It doesn't matter either way. The only thing that matters is you're certain it's the same car you saw outside your house last night."

Easton nodded, the blue hair bobbing up and down like a muppet on a kid's show. "I'm sure."

"I'll tell Jake." Renner closed the book and stepped into the hallway, leaving me with the more complicated task.

Easton watched him disappear down the hallway. "That's not the only reason you asked me to come down here. You said on the phone this has something to do with Bouillon."

"Tell me about the security cameras in the kitchen."

"There weren't any. At least, none that I recall."

"Strader must have had them installed after he took over."

"He did this, didn't he?"

"It looks like it. We linked the hidden camera we found inside your house and the GPS tracker on your food truck to Galen Strader's computer. We discovered several videos stored on his computer taken from inside Bouillon after you left. It establishes a pattern of behavior."

"Do you think he planted cameras inside Sizzle too?"

That was something I hadn't considered. "How would he have gotten access? Did you ever invite him into your kitchen?"

Easton's features pinched together. "I did. He dropped by to offer his congratulations, which was a thinly veiled attempt to spy on me. Like you said, pattern of behavior."

"Go on. Did you leave him alone in your kitchen? When was this?"

"It was opening week, so roughly two months before the fire. And no, I would never leave a rival in my kitchen. He might switch out the salt for the sugar or set the place on fire. But still, maybe he tucked a camera away somewhere when I wasn't looking. After last night, I wouldn't put anything past him. Did you find more footage or a destroyed camera inside Sizzle?"

"No, but we can't rule anything out. Hopefully, the police will come up with some answers."

Easton scoffed. "Forgive me, but I'm having trouble believing that." I understood his skepticism and hesitation, but Voletek was our best chance of getting to the truth, at least legally. "Did Galen rent that car?" Easton asked.

"No."

"You're sure? I heard he has a membership to a fancy car club."

"The car's registered to Dante's aunt." I filled Easton in on the details. "He's denying his involvement and said he was nowhere near your house last night and has no clue what we're talking about, but the car and registration say otherwise."

"Do you think he'll confess?"

"People do crazy things. Speaking of," I told Easton what happened at Delicious.

"Asher's always been a crazy fucker. I wouldn't doubt his involvement. Maybe the assault and accusations were meant to throw you off the scent. Maybe he and Dante staged the fire, and since you took Dante down, Asher wanted to make sure to discredit his little kitchen bitch before Dante ratted him out." Easton's eyes narrowed. "But that doesn't explain Galen Strader's involvement. There's no way in hell Asher York and Galen Strader would ever work together. Sure, they both want to see me ruined, but they'd never combine forces."

I rubbed my eyes. That sounded like paranoia or the ramblings of a criminal mastermind. "We'll get this sorted. But first, can you tell me how Dante Bisset and Galen Strader connect to one another?"

Easton chewed on his bottom lip while he considered the question. "Have you checked Dante's job history? Maybe they worked in the same restaurant before Galen hit it big."

"They didn't. At least, not that we can tell."

"Dante studied at Le Cordon Bleu. Strader and I went to the Culinary Institute. We graduated years before Dante. Um," Easton squeezed his eyes closed, grimacing, "Dante graduated three years ago. By then, Strader had already established himself. Maybe he taught a class as one of their master chefs or a guest lecturer. If not, they could have crossed paths at one of the big events like the gala. A lot of first-class chefs get called to work those things. Dante might have been apprenticing for another chef at the time and was asked to help out."

"Or maybe they shop at the same grocery store," I suggested.

"Maybe." Easton offered a contrite smile. "Guess I wasn't much help. Detective Voletek didn't like the answers I gave him either."

"It's not you. It's this mess, but we'll figure it out. I promise." I jerked my chin at the door. "Since Voletek hasn't come back with any other questions, you can take off."

"Great." Easton rubbed his hands on his jeans and grabbed his leather jacket from the hook behind the door. "At least the police escort saved me a few bucks and the hassle of finding a parking space. I didn't realize that was the conciliation prize for a busted window."

"It's better than the conciliation prize for screwing up an investigation."

"What do you get for that?"

"You don't want to know."

The charming, flirtatious smile transformed his face from one of anxiety and annoyance to something that would make a choir boy blush. "I'm not worried, Alex. I trust you know what you're doing. If you need me for anything else, you have my number. Don't hesitate. I'll be up working on improving my menu, so don't worry about disturbing me. Drop by if you want a taste. I would say my door's always open, but I hope it's not."

"Stay safe." The conversation reminded me I needed to make a call.

After telling Martin I would be working late and we had to postpone packing my apartment, I hung up and nearly collided with Voletek. Renner was half a step behind him and bumped into Jake's back when the detective stopped short. We were just one accident away from turning into the *Three Stooges*.

"Amir dropped off the evidence Cross Security collected. Unlike Bisset, Strader's talking," Renner said.

"Wonders never cease. Is he under arrest?" I asked.

Jake nodded. "I've questioned both he and Bisset several times. Initially, Strader didn't ask for counsel, which I found surprising."

"Ego," Renner muttered.

"Be that as it may," the detective continued, "Strader claims the camera and tracker were meant to be a prank. He hoped to catch Easton doing something embarrassing and humiliate him. Strader said they do things like this to each other all the time. That they started this tradition back at the CIA."

"CIA?" I asked.

"Culinary Institute of America." The corners of Voletek's eyes crinkled. "You don't think either of these jokers is spy material, do you?"

"It's mostly intelligence gathering," I said.

"But they lack intelligence." Renner pushed past us, intent on grabbing a cup of the sludge the precinct masqueraded around as coffee.

"All right, so throwing a brick through a person's window is now considered a harmless prank. You should tell someone about that. They'll need to update the penal code."

"That's actually where things get interesting. Strader says he didn't throw the brick through the window. He's blaming Bisset." Deciding coffee sounded good, Voletek filled a mug and held it out, but I shook my head. He took a sip and put the cup down. "So I spoke to Bisset again and told him what Strader had to say. Right now, they are both conferring with counsel. Once they have a few minutes to stew, I suspect they'll turn on each other."

"Counsel?" I asked.

"After I confronted Strader about the property damage, criminal trespass, and death threats, he realized this was serious shit and lawyered up."

"I warned you not to do that," Renner said.

"Yeah, yeah." Voletek waved off the comment, but I knew the detective wanted Strader to ask for an attorney. A legal expert would drive home the ramifications of Strader's actions and the jeopardy he might be facing. The pressure might be enough to get him to talk, or he'd clam up. One or the other. "I offered a deal to whoever talks first." Voletek glanced at his watch. "I'm saying twenty minutes. Do you want the over or under?"

I chuckled. "And to think, I haven't even left for Vegas yet."

It took a lot longer than twenty minutes, but by the end of the night, Galen Strader and Dante Bisset had sung like larks or jailbirds. The alleged hazing and fraternity pranks Strader played on Easton were supposedly harmless, but they were meant to intimidate and throw the chef off his game. Strader said he left the original threatening note on Easton's windshield when the news broke that the chef was leaving his position at Bouillon to start his own restaurant. At the time, Strader was working as a private chef, and loathed the idea of his culinary school rival setting out on his own, though Strader quickly changed his tune when he was offered Easton's old job and scraped together enough capital to buy into Bouillon.

According to Strader, he and Easton could finally duke it out fairly since they both had restaurants of their own. Bisset admitted to terrorizing Easton the previous night, and he even copped to some of the hateful and threatening social media comments and posts, but he wouldn't admit to throwing the brick through Easton's window. He said Strader did it, and Strader denied it. However, they both admitted to being at Easton's last night, but neither was willing to confess to setting the fire at Sizzle.

"Let's divide and conquer. Maybe when faced with the

evidence you've obtained," Voletek glanced from Renner to me, "they'll open up." Renner and another detective entered one interrogation room, and Voletek opened the door to the second one. "I'll get him primed. When you see an opening, jump in."

After a recap and update, Voletek asked Galen Strader about the fire at Sizzle.

"I told you I don't know anything about the fire at Sizzle. It's a kitchen. Shit happens. Burners get left on. Towels and aprons get tossed on the counter. If you turn your back for one second, who knows what might happen. I didn't set the fire. If anything, I wanted Sizzle to last longer than it did. How else could I prove I was the superior chef?" Strader asked.

Voletek rubbed his eyes, the first sign of fatigue he'd shown since this circus began. "Why were you spying on Easton and his food truck?"

Strader rolled his eyes, as though the answer should be obvious. "Food trucks are the hot new craze. Brick and mortar restaurants are going mobile by launching their own trucks, and trucks are turning into restaurants. I wanted to know what Easton planned."

"Is Bouillon launching its own truck?" I asked.

"In the spring," Strader said. "It takes time to get permits and licenses. And that doesn't even take into account finding a serviceable truck. I thought...well...I..."

"You wanted to see what Easton was doing so you could copy him," Voletek said.

"No, improve on his failures." Strader glared at us. "I didn't hurt anyone. I didn't steal anything. I didn't do anything wrong."

"You threatened him. You trespassed. You violated his privacy. You spied on him." Voletek ticked off points on his fingers until Strader's attorney stopped him.

"My client has been nonviolent. He's cooperated. He rode to Easton's house with the real criminal." The attorney turned the notepad around. "Galen is prepared to testify against Dante Bisset should this matter go to court. These alleged crimes you're accusing my client of are fairly innocent. No harm was actually done. The camera didn't record anything before it was discovered." The attorney wanted the felony charges lowered to misdemeanors. The DA and judge always had final say, but the police came up with the initial charges, and the lawyer wanted Voletek to recommend misdemeanor offenses that could be pled down to fines and community service instead of serving hard time.

"I still don't get it," I said. "How did you and Dante Bisset cross paths? What kind of conversation could the two of you possibly have had before setting out for Easton's house? How long have you been conspiring together?" I got to ask those questions because I wasn't a cop or acting in any official capacity. Voletek wanted to appear appeasing to Strader and his plight, but I didn't have the same hang-ups. My loyalty was to my client, though Strader had no obligation to answer my questions. However, like most people caught in a jam, he thought talking would somehow get him out of it instead of digging himself deeper into the hole.

"We aren't conspiring. We're friends, or we were until Dante turned out to be a psycho." Strader slammed his fist on the table. "Dante and I met when I visited Sizzle. He was Easton's sous chef. Honestly, Easton treated him like shit. Easton treats everyone in his kitchen like shit, and if you don't believe me, ask my staff. They'll tell you firsthand how terrible it was working for an egomaniac like Easton Lango."

Have you looked in the mirror? "Go on."

"Dante and I kept in touch while he worked at Sizzle."

"You wanted an inside man to tell you what Easton was doing," Voletek said.

Strader didn't even have the decency to look ashamed. "Yeah, so? That's not a crime. I can be friends with whoever I want, and friends talk about work. Big fucking deal."

"What caused the bad blood between Dante and Easton?" Voletek asked.

"I don't know exactly. I assume it's the way Easton treated him. Dante never told me why he hates the guy, but we kept in touch, even after Sizzle burned down. After the accident, Dante went to work at Delicious, and we've stayed in touch since."

"You're using him to spy on Asher York," I said.

The attorney gave me a sharp look, but before he could warn Strader not to answer, the chef said, "It's not a crime to talk shop with a friend. Dante and I are friends, or we were until Dante flipped out last night. He threw the brick through the window while I was planting the camera."

"How'd you get into Easton's house to plant the camera?" Voletek asked.

"Easton left the back door open. I went in through the back and put the camera inside the magnet on his fridge. While I was inside, I heard the window shatter, and Dante stomped through the house. I didn't know he was going to break-in or destroy anything. We didn't discuss that. We just wanted to pay our old pal a visit."

I opened my mouth to say something else, but Voletek grabbed my elbow. "We'll have to ask Mr. Bisset about this. We'll be right back."

Once we were outside the interrogation room, I spun to face Voletek. "The timeline doesn't make sense. Easton said the window broke first. That's when he called for help and hid in the pantry. He would have seen Strader if he was already inside the house."

"I know."

"Then what the hell are you going to do about it?"

"My job."

TWENTY-TWO

Unlike Chef Strader, Dante Bisset wasn't cool and collected. The second interview I watched him give was only marginally better than the first. Bisset was sweating profusely. He was freaked out, just like he had been when Asher York threw knives at him.

"Easton said he met with Dante last month for drinks. Why would Dante agree if he hates Easton?" I asked as the three of us stared through the two-way glass while Bisset's hands were cuffed behind his back.

"I don't know." Voletek glanced at the clock. "But he finally admitted to driving to Easton's and throwing the brick through the window. He even said he wanted to sabotage Easton and Sizzle."

"But why?"

"C'mon, Parker, it's obvious." Renner fiddled with his phone, scrolling through some text messages before tucking the device into his pocket. "Chefs be crazy."

"Like bitches be crazy?" My death stare did nothing to deter Renner from continuing his explanation.

"We've seen it with Asher York, who flipped out in the midst of his kitchen on nothing but speculation and conjecture, and with the way Strader behaved in regards to Easton. Since Bisset's still an up and comer, he has even more to prove, hence crazier." The phone beeped, and Renner fished it out, shot off a response, and dropped it into his jacket pocket. "Even our client isn't that stable. He tried to brain you with a baseball bat because you entered his food truck."

"He's scared," I said.

Voletek agreed. "He is, but the men in custody have admitted to making threats, breaking in to Easton's house, attempting to sabotage Easton and his food truck, and placing the camera and tracker. The only thing they deny is setting the fire. I wouldn't put it past any of them to have done it, even Asher York, who by all accounts seems to be uninvolved, but it is possible the fire was an accident. The experts insisted it was, and coupled with what we now know about the men terrorizing Easton, it's possible Easton jumped to conclusions given the stress he was under at the time."

"The stress might have been a contributing factor. Maybe Easton didn't notice the warning signs of an electrical fire. Maybe he failed to notice the circuit breaker kept tripping, a weird smell, like something burning, charring or sparking around the outlet, or the power cord was damaged. It happens. People make mistakes, and if they are tired and stressed, they're more likely to make even more mistakes," Renner insisted, but I didn't buy it. It was too easy. His explanation felt wrong.

Voletek studied my expression. "Look, Alex, now that we have two confessions, the PD has grounds to obtain multiple search warrants. We will search everywhere imaginable and everything. If there's something to find, we will. But this is over. In the meantime, tell your client to file a couple of TROs ASAP. It's the weekend. Strader, Bisset, and York will be held until the arraignment on Monday, so there's nothing for Easton to worry about. He's safe. No one's going to hurt him. I promise you that."

"What about when Monday rolls around?" I asked.

"These chuckleheads won't go near him again." There was no point arguing with Voletek's conviction. "I will stay on top of things until we know exactly what happened."

Renner's phone beeped again.

"Who is that?" I asked, taking my frustration out on Renner, who wasn't as invested in protecting our client as I was. And it was his damn case.

"Lucien." Renner met Voletek's eyes. "Are you pulling the protection detail, Jake?"

Voletek nodded. "We can't justify keeping them around."

"Okay. I'll drop by Easton's and fill him in on our progress and next steps. If he wants added protection, I'll have a team from Cross Security keep an eye on him." Renner nudged me with his shoulder. "You should go home. It's late, and I'm guessing you have a lava cake to deliver. I'll make sure Easton's okay. Jake's got this. I got this. And we won't know more until the arson investigator gets back to you. Plus, don't you have to get ready for your vacation?"

"How do you know about that?" I asked.

Renner cocked an eyebrow, wondering if I sustained a head injury. "You told me. Plus, Lucien announced you'd be out for the next two weeks, so the rest of us would have to make do without you." The phone beeped again. "Parker, you can do as much digging as you like. No one's gonna stop you, but the case is practically closed. Take the win." The phone beeped again. "Jesus," Renner sighed dramatically, "I heard you the first ten times." He clapped Voletek on the shoulder. "I gotta go. Keep me apprised."

"Will do."

"I mean it this time," Renner warned before striding down the hallway.

"Doesn't this seem too easy?" I asked. "Why did they confess to everything but the fire?"

"First off, Strader didn't have a choice. You caught him red-handed, so he did what any normal human being would do and threw his accomplice under the bus. Second, they're smart. They listened to their lawyers. No one got hurt. In the grand scheme of things, the crimes they confessed to are minor, and they cast enough aspersions to potentially confuse a jury. They have no reason to confess to the fire."

"Do you think they set it?"

"Perhaps, but you've seen the reports. It looks accidental, and with the insurance payout and the arson investigator's notes, it'd be impossible to prove otherwise without a rock solid confession. However, Easton could pursue a civil suit. Since you want to stay on the case, you should suggest that to him."

This wasn't about money. It was about justice. "Easton won't be made whole until he knows who to blame."

"I am truly sorry about that," Voletek said, the sincerity undeniable, "but at least he can rest easy knowing we caught the guys. He isn't crazy. Everyone else in the food service industry might be, but he isn't."

"Yeah, we'll see."

On the drive home, I couldn't figure out what was bothering me about the case. Maybe some of Easton's paranoia had rubbed off on me, but in my heart, I knew what the problem was. We still didn't know who set the fire, and that was the only thing he really wanted me to figure out. Sure, he wanted to feel safe and he wanted the harassment to stop, but losing Sizzle destroyed him. He had to rebuild figuratively and literally. Having a real answer was the only way he'd be able to move on. I needed to keep digging.

I unlocked our apartment door, glancing down at the box in my hand. Though Renner and I ate dinner at Delicious, I wondered if giving Martin the dessert was a good idea. It could be tainted. "Damn, I'm losing it."

"What?" Martin looked up from the coffee table where his presentation notes were currently scattered. For a moment, he looked cross, then his features softened and his eyes warmed. He smiled, put down the notecards, and met me in the doorway. After kissing me, he eyed the box in my hand. "I'm not used to you working late. Thanks for calling."

I winced at the slight bitterness to his tone. "I called."

"I know. Thank you."

"I brought you dessert to make up for it." I held out the box.

"Just put it in the fridge." He went back to the couch. "What are you working on?"

"Chef Easton's case. The police made a few arrests. Detective Voletek thought it'd be prudent for Renner and me to hang around in case he had any questions since we handed over the evidence we collected."

Martin nodded, busying himself with clicking through his presentation slides, but from the speed at which the screens flew by, I knew he wasn't reviewing them. "Are you going to say it?"

"Say what?"

"You have to cancel our trip. You're too busy. You can't come with me."

"I'm not. The case is closed."

"Really?" He looked up. His eyes stopping on the pile of folders tucked beneath my arm. "What are those files for?"

"Martin, stop." I put everything down on the counter and took a seat beside him. "I hate it when you get like this. What the hell's your problem?" I closed the cover on his computer. For a moment, I feared he might lash out. Shutting him off from his work was, in essence, the same as taking catnip away from a feral cat, but Martin just sunk into the cushions. He didn't care, which scared me more than the harsh words and fiery stare I expected.

"I'm sorry. I'm just tired, so damn tired. I'm not used to you working late or being gone at night. Not anymore. And now," he gestured at the files I left in the kitchen, "the cycle's starting over again. We haven't even recovered from the last trip around and now..."

I took his face in my hands, but he pulled my hands away, threading his fingers in between mine. "Nothing's changed. We're leaving Monday. I just want to make sure everything about this case is explained away."

"You can never let anything go. That's why I love you. Hell, that's why we're together. I've always been worried you might not make it back, but now," he pressed my palm against his chest, "that fear gives me palpitations. We'll be okay. I just thought I'd have more time to process and regain my footing. I'll cope." He saw something in my eyes that brought a smile to his lips. "You've got that look. You're on to something. And you're excited about a case for the first time in months. All that matters to me is that you're okay. And you are."

"Martin," I began, but he shook his head.

"No, it's okay. Tell me about your case. I want to hear about it."

"You're right. I can't let things go. I can't let you go." My eyes teased him. "And I sure as hell can't let you go to Vegas unsupervised, so it's case closed."

"Bullshit. The only thing that gets you this excited, besides me, is when you're working on something. So what is it?"

"Are you sure?" Normally, topics like this were off limits because I didn't want to freak him out, but I knew he'd be more freaked out not knowing. So I told him everything. "In the event someone from Fast Lanes calls, pretend you don't know me. The salesman probably thinks we're swingers."

"Like I'd ever trade you out for the night or share you with someone else." Martin lifted my hands to his lips and kissed my knuckles before releasing me. "Just do me one favor."

"Anything."

He smirked, and I wondered what ridiculous thing he was about to ask. "The next time you go shopping for a third, you bring me with you."

"There won't be a next time."

"You say that now, but who knows what you'll decide next week when I'm stuck in conferences all day and you're lonely and bored."

I gave him a playful shove. "I doubt I'd get that lonely."

"Who am I kidding? You'll probably spend the week rereading the police reports. We both know you have no idea what to do when a case closes itself in two days. Have you ever worked an investigation that resolved this quickly?"

"A few with Mark when I was still at the OIO, but they were usually minor."

"Isn't this?"

While I pondered that question, Martin went back to work. Even though tomorrow was Saturday, he had to go into the office for half a day to finalize everything before the convention. And despite my insistence he gets some sleep, he wouldn't budge. The tension radiated off of him, and I knew not all of it was related to projection numbers. Even though we'd been together for a long time, he hated my job, and he hated how depressed and restless I got when I wasn't working. There was no simple solution, but he'd grown to accept my work, risks and all. However, his recent string of nightmares probably indicated some degree of shell shock and meant his subconscious wasn't nearly as enlightened and onboard as the rest of his psyche.

So while Martin worked on his presentation, I dug into the reports on Sizzle and continued researching arson. An hour later, I pulled the cake out of the fridge and grabbed a fork. Martin joined me at the counter, deciding he also needed a break and wanted to see what could be so good to warrant the little sighs and moans escaping my lips. The cake might not have made up for canceling our plans, but it came damn close.

"You should go to bed," he said, wiping some strawberry filling from the corner of my mouth. "I'll be in soon."

"I'll wait up with you. The more of this I finish reviewing, the less I'll have to contemplate." I watched him lick the strawberry off his thumb. "This won't ruin our beach trip. You have my word. No work once we leave for the beach, agreed?"

"Deal." He pushed the last bite of cake closer to me, and once I scooped it up, he tossed the container and went back to the coffee table to finish working.

When the sugar crash hit, I rubbed the grit from my eyes. I noticed Martin had stretched out on the sofa. I had no idea how he could keep going. He'd been running on fumes for weeks.

Shifting gears, I searched news sites for information and speculation on the fire at Sizzle, but my focus was shot. Somewhere along the line, I ended up reading about other local fires, looking for hints and tips to determine if arson was the cause.

Martin let out a growl, like a wounded animal. It resonated deep in my gut, my instincts screaming danger. I grabbed my gun before I even had time to think about what I was doing.

My beloved was under attack. He thrashed against the sofa cushions, knocking a throw pillow off the couch before settling down. I swallowed, placing the nine millimeter back on the counter while I watched him. Fortunately, the nightmare ended without waking him, and he rolled onto his side. And to think, he spent years giving me shit about sleeping on couches.

Deciding to let him sleep, I went back to my research. Hours later, a buzzing caught my attention. It was morning.

I set the coffeemaker to brew, expecting to see Martin frantically collecting the scattered paperwork. Instead, he remained asleep on the couch. The buzzing stopped, and I checked my own phone to make sure it wasn't the cause of the interruption. Perhaps, now would be a good time to get some sleep. I hit the cancel button on the coffeepot when Martin's alarm chimed.

He jumped up, startled. Rolling to the left, he barely caught himself in time before falling off the couch. Confused, his gaze whipped back and forth. "Alex?"

"Morning," I said from my spot at the counter.

He turned off the alarm on his phone and sunk back onto the cushion. "You're up early."

"Try again."

He rubbed his eyes. "Don't tell me you've been up all night. Why didn't you go to bed?"

I shrugged.

His eyelids drooped, and he fought to hold them open. "Come here." He held out his arms and pulled me down against his chest. He was warm from sleep, and I nestled into the space between him and the backrest, my head on his shoulder and my left arm wrapped around him.

It didn't even take me five minutes to fall asleep, but the buzzing from his phone instantly woke me. "Turn that off."

He wrapped his arms around me, and we drifted back to sleep. I don't know how much longer we slept on the couch. But his phone rang and then mine. While he spoke to Luc Guillot, Martin Technologies' VP, he handed me my phone.

It was Chef Easton. "Someone tried to break in again last night."

TWENTY-THREE

"I don't understand." Easton toyed with a wayward strand of blue that kept falling in front of his eyes. "I know what I heard."

"You don't live in the quietest of neighborhoods." Renner rewound the footage and played it again. "We checked the video twice. No one was here. You're safe, Mr. Lango."

Easton slid the bar across the bottom of the screen, moving the footage forward to the alleged time he heard footsteps on his front porch, but no one was there. He glanced up at the Cross Security detail. A four-man team guarded the house. One was stationed inside the food truck, another in the house, and the other two covered the back and front. Combined with the automated security system, an intruder would have been spotted.

"I'll check for footprints," I said.

"I already did that," Renner said.

"It won't hurt to look again."

"Thanks." Easton continued to watch the footage. "Wait, look." He pointed to a shadow crossing in front of his house. "What's that?"

Renner checked the timestamp, switched to another

camera view, and pointed to the racoon scampering across Easton's front lawn. "You're right. A masked bandit was here last night."

Easton scowled, and I glared at Renner. "Come on," I tugged on his elbow, "help me check the perimeter."

We shut the door behind us, and Renner rolled his eyes. "He's paranoid, Parker. I don't blame him. He has every reason to be, but no one was here. Between the guards and the cameras, it's just not possible."

"I know, but in case Harry Houdini or the Invisible Man stopped by, we should check for tracks."

"It's a waste of time."

"Most things are."

Since it rained last night, the ground might have been soft enough to hold a few footprints, or an intruder might have left mud on the walkways. But aside from a few pawprints, courtesy of our furry bandit, there was nothing to find. I crouched down at the end of the driveway, checking the road and sidewalk for tracks, but there weren't any.

"You could always go talk to your friends at the end of the block," Renner said.

"Shut up, Bennett." Truthfully, I didn't expect to find anything, but I had to make sure. Easton couldn't afford for us to be wrong. Mistakes got people hurt or killed.

Renner held up his palms and took a step back. "Fine. Do what you want. But tell me something." He waited for me to stand up and face him before speaking again. "Why do you look like you're in worse shape than our client? This isn't a complicated case, Parker. Jake arrested the culprits last night. Are you working on something else? Or is there something going on I should know about? You can trust me. What can I do?"

"Nothing. I just don't want to drop the ball on this. Your focus has been split since the second you handed me this case. And since I'm leaving Monday, I want to make sure it's tied up in a nice neat bow. I don't like leaving a mess behind."

"Okay." But he didn't believe me. "Since our client listens to you better than he listens to me, why don't you go over the details of a TRO and the protections Cross Security can provide? I hear money's no longer an issue. Though, I never expected Easton's ex-wife to shell out the cash. Why do you think she'd do that?"

"A part of her loves him. And the part that hates him doesn't want him to hurt unless she's the one hurting him."

Renner snickered. "Are we sure she didn't set the fire?"

"No, but you heard Voletek. The fire was an accident."

For the first time today, Renner considered the possibility he was wrong. "I have an errand to run. I'll meet you back at the office. We'll go over the reports again, just to make sure we aren't missing a connection or key piece of evidence."

"Why the change of heart?"

"I have a vengeful ex-wife too."

* * *

"I found it," Lt. Payne said. He held out an evidence bag containing the smoke detector and a sheet of pink paper. "It was tested. Works perfectly."

I pressed the test button, wincing at the deafening chirp. The once white device was now covered in a layer of soot that left streaks inside the plastic bag. I read the label, making sure the case number and date corresponded to the paperwork. "Where was it?"

"The truck company still had it. When someone from my office picked up the files, they must have forgotten to grab it." He dropped into the chair across from where I sat. "It looks like your client was hit by a string of bad luck."

"What about the crumbled wall? Yesterday, you found that odd."

"I still do," Payne said. "After you left, I checked building permits. Easton Lango renovated the restaurant. The exterior wall was replaced and rebuilt. Preliminary tests show the materials the new contractors used didn't match the rest of the building materials. They weren't nearly as sturdy or heat resistant."

"Sabotage?"

"Probably just another example of a construction

company cutting costs. You won't believe how many structure fires we see because of subpar materials and workmanship."

"Maybe we could push for negligence or public endangerment." I scribbled it down in case Easton wanted to pursue civil damages.

"I don't know. It will depend on whether the project met the minimum safety regulations. Dil Haskell's conducting the testing. He'll be able to tell you more."

I pondered the obvious discrepancy. "Easton said he finished taking inventory and was in his office placing orders when the fire broke out. He smelled smoke, and the door handle was already hot. He never heard the fire alarm. Are you sure it sounded?"

"I'll be frank with you. There's no way to say for certain. The device is operational. The batteries were tested. You can read the report yourself. Are you sure your client is remembering things correctly? Maybe he was wearing noise canceling headphones, or he fell asleep. Or he just didn't hear it. Fires are loud. Most people don't realize it, but they are." Payne picked up the fire department's report. "EMS checked him when they arrived, and so did the police. He wasn't high or drunk, but he could have hit his head or the adrenaline dump dulled his senses. It happens. People shut down when they're afraid. I've seen victims go temporarily deaf or blind from shock."

I chewed on the inside of my lip. Easton Lango wasn't the calmest or most rational man in the world. I'd seen the full extent of his fight or flight, when he hid inside the food truck the first time we met and when he launched a premature attack after the break-in. I scanned the rest of the report. Sizzle had fire extinguishers in the kitchen and inside Easton's office. He would have attempted to smother the fire. "Sizzle was his baby. He would have done anything to save it." Trying to save his restaurant might explain the burn on his hand, but he had no reason to lie about it. "It doesn't make sense."

"I don't know what to tell you. Unless the police or Dil uncover something else, it looks like bad luck. Everything we looked at yesterday appears suspicious, but when taken with what we know, it can be explained." He jerked his chin at my stack of research. "You said Easton just finished taking inventory, right?"

"Yes."

"Did he put everything back, or is it possible he left some containers on the counter? We know the frayed wire ignited, which triggered the fire."

"You think Easton's carelessness caused his restaurant to burn down?"

"I think it was an accident, but I can't deny there was a human element involved. The fire wouldn't have spread the way it did or as quickly unless someone left out the right materials to cause the perfect storm." The corner of his mouth screwed up. "That's why it looks like arson. That might be the reason Easton insists someone set the fire. Deep down he knows it's his fault, but he wants to blame someone else. He needs to blame someone else."

I pushed away from the table. "You're probably right." At least about the blaming part.

"I've seen it far too often. An old lady leaves the stove on or puts a towel close to the oven to dry off, and the next thing you know, the apartment's on fire. She loses her cats or," he let out a frustrated, somber sigh, "a child or grandchild. Those are the worst. Once she finds out the cause, she always blames herself. It's heartbreaking that one stupid mistake can destroy everything."

"You're sure that's what happened here?"

"Like I said, I don't know. But I've worked enough of these scenes to believe that's the most feasible explanation."

"No spontaneous combustion or act of god?"

"Maybe that's what started the fire."

"So how can you tell when the old lady just made a mistake or when she intentionally wanted to off herself or her deadbeat son?" I asked. "As far as I can tell, intention is the only thing that separates arson from an unlucky mishap."

Payne snorted, slightly disconcerted by the question. "Who hurt you, Ms. Parker?"

"I do this for a living, and before that, I worked in law

enforcement."

"Local cop?"

"OIO agent."

"OIO?"

"Office of International Operations."

"Which deals with what? Terrorism, bombings, stuff like that?"

"Among other things."

"Well, this isn't like that. Most people make mistakes. Haven't you ever left the burner on after you took a pot off the stove? Or accidentally put something metal in the microwave?"

That's why Martin was in charge of the kitchen. "Sure."

"You weren't trying to burn down your apartment or kill yourself, right?"

"Depends on the day," I joked.

He frowned, not finding my comment amusing. Admittedly, it was morbid, especially for someone who didn't know me or understand my twisted sense of humor. "The point is you're not an arsonist or pyromaniac, as far as I know, just like the majority of people. Plus, I've never encountered an arsonist who called us to put out the fire while he remained at the scene. So either your boy is one brazen psychopath, or he's just another guy who made a mistake."

"Unless someone else was there."

"Or that." Payne stood. "It's up to the police to figure that out. I only deal with fires."

"Lucky you."

Payne cocked his head to the side, reading the printout at the top of my stack. "Are you gunning for my job, Ms. Parker?" He picked up the sheet and held it up. "Why are you researching other area fires? Is there something I should know?"

"I couldn't sleep last night."

"So this is light reading?"

"I'm trying to figure out what signals I should look for to determine if the case is arson." I shrugged. "Sorry, but I have a terrible time taking people at their word. I have to reach my own conclusions, but I lack the proper knowledge base."

"Which is why you should defer to the experts." He glanced around my posh office. "That's why Cross Security always defers to the experts."

"I'm new in case you couldn't tell."

"Oh, I can tell." He pulled the chair around the desk and sat beside me. "Since I'm not on duty, I'll give you a crash course. Will you be more apt to listen to what I have to say when it doesn't have to do specifically with your case?" The playful tone in his voice clued me in that he was teasing, but in case I missed it, he threw in a wink for good measure.

For the next forty minutes, Lt. Payne leafed through the articles I printed and explained why a warehouse fire was arson while a fire in the changing room of a department store wasn't. It was a fine line. The only thing that signified arson was the mens rea or intent. Otherwise a fire was a fire, regardless of the cause or source. It all came down to a person's intent.

"How do you know what a person's thinking? You said you only investigate the scene."

"How do you prove a crime occurred?"

"Collect evidence, speak to witnesses, question the suspect, and build a case."

"I do the same, but it all comes down to what I find at the scene. The key is determining whether the fire was accidental or deliberate." He held up a finger to keep me quiet before I could ask the obvious question. "Yes, I know. Sometimes, fires look deliberate but aren't. That's why we dig deeper. When we aren't sure, the police get involved."

"So if the old lady from your example intentionally set the fire but pretended to be senile or remorseful, how would you make the determination? Couldn't it go either way?"

"You think that's what happened at Sizzle?"

"I don't know, but someone else might have been in the kitchen."

"Are you sure you don't think your client's responsible?"

"He's not."

I noticed Renner lingering in my doorway. He was back

from running his errands, but unlike most of the men I worked with in the past, he didn't barge into the room. He waited just outside my office, intrigued to see where the conversation would lead.

"Since we didn't find a timer, the person had to set the fire and leave. Unless a witness saw this or the culprit comes forward, the evidence is inconclusive. Nothing inside Sizzle suggests this was planned or premeditated. Aside from setting a fire to conceal another crime, most intentional fires are planned. We normally find timers or accelerant or something to kick-start the blaze. The things that kick-started the blaze in Sizzle were items commonly kept in the kitchen. Maybe it's a crime of opportunity, but who set it? A ghost?"

"Or the Invisible Man." Easton might be crazy, but I wasn't too far behind.

TWENTY-FOUR

"It's all about motive and opportunity," Renner said. "That should be our focus."

"That's been our focus since the beginning."

"With the exception of our detour to investigate the break-in." Renner leaned over my desk. "May I?" I slid to the side, and he entered his log-in information and opened his e-mail. "All right, let's say Easton Lango isn't paranoid or hallucinating. I dug into his ex-wife, but Bridget Stockton was out of town when the fire occurred. I checked travel records and called the hotel where she stayed. She didn't do it."

"I told you that yesterday."

"You also told me it doesn't hurt to be thorough. Of course, this doesn't exonerate any of her criminal clients or their associates. Her financials don't appear suspicious. I had Amir check into her online activity. Aside from an exorbitant amount of online shopping, everything checks out."

"We've already checked into the staff at Bouillon, Easton's former Sizzle employees, and Asher York."

"Yeah, and the ones with alibis we struck from our suspect list, but there are other names worth exploring. We could go back over the food critics."

"It's also possible another chef might have a butcher knife to sharpen," I said, attempting to be clever. "But we're back to our previous problem. Whoever set the fire had to have access to the kitchen. The doors were locked. The staff had gone home for the night. No one was there."

"Like the ghost from last night? This is why no one believes the fire is a crime, not even Lt. Payne." Renner closed his e-mail since Amir hadn't sent anything useful.

"What do you think?"

In the last seventy-two hours, Renner had flip-flopped multiple times. "The jury's still out. The evidence is inconclusive, but we're getting paid."

"Is that why you've had a sudden change of heart?"

He licked his lips and eyed me. "It's your case, Alex. You aren't satisfied yet, so we'll keep digging. I heard what Lt. Payne said, and even though we haven't worked together that long, I know how you operate. You won't stop until you're sure."

I closed my eyes, my head throbbing from my own indecisiveness. Renner wanted to help, but I knew he didn't believe there was anything left for us to do. This had been his case, but since Cross put me in charge, Renner stepped down from steering the ship. Maybe he realized I'd do whatever I wanted anyway. No wonder I usually worked alone.

"We need to find out if someone else was inside Sizzle. Once we do, we'll know if this was arson." I grabbed my bag. "Easton's security cameras didn't catch much."

"But they were damaged in the fire."

"The restaurant's in a commercial area. There must be cameras nearby. Let's find out what they can show us."

Renner and I spent the afternoon scoping out the neighborhood and speaking to area businesses. Even though it was Saturday, most retail shops and eateries were open. Surprisingly, almost all of them accommodated our requests, but it was hard to find cameras with a good angle on Sizzle. And it was even harder to review footage from three months ago.

"Thanks anyway." I handed the store manager my card.

"In the event you or any of your employees happen to remember anything, please let me know."

"Will do. Is there anything else I can get for you today? Maybe lens cleaner to go with the shades?"

To gain compliance, Renner had purchased a pair of designer sunglasses. "I think I'm good." He peeled the UV sticker off the corner and put them on. When we exited the store, he glanced at me, my reflection staring back from the mirrored aviators. "Do I look like Maverick?"

"Only if Tom Cruise gained thirty pounds and grew several inches."

He glared, or at least I assumed he did since I couldn't see his eyes. "I spoke to Sgt. Chambliss yesterday when we were at the precinct. He didn't remember anything odd about the scene, but by the time he arrived, there wasn't much left to see. Between the fire and the water, most physical evidence was destroyed. Since the front wall came down, it'll be nearly impossible to determine if there was a break-in. He told me officers checked the back door. They didn't find any signs of forced entry. The lock didn't appear to be tampered with. I don't think it was picked."

That meant whoever set the fire had to have a key or made a copy of the key. While Renner drove us back to the office, I phoned Easton and asked if he kept a spare key hidden outside the restaurant, which he did not. Then I asked if he changed the locks when he moved in. He did. Nothing about this was simple.

"Who had a key?" I asked.

"Dante and me." It was the same thing he told me yesterday.

"That's it?"

"Yep." He sighed. "He must have done it. There's no other explanation."

At the moment, I was keen to agree. "I don't think he'll confess."

"Probably not." Easton went quiet for a time. "What about last night? You told me Dante was in custody, along with Galen and Asher. Who was prowling around my house?"

Scrunching my face together, I tried to come up with a

satisfactory explanation, but I couldn't think on my feet. And I was sitting down. That really said something. I blamed lack of sleep.

"You think I'm overreacting?" Easton sounded hurt.

"I need an honest answer, Chef. Who have you screwed lately? We know you stepped out on your ex-wife, but you haven't told us anything about your mistress. How many other flings have you had this year?"

"A few."

"Are you seeing anyone right now?"

"Not at the moment." His voice contained a smile. "Are you interested?"

"Only in solving your problems. Give me their names and numbers. We'll investigate discreetly. While you're at it, tell me about any other chefs or members of your cooking staff you might have pissed off. If someone's hoping to intimidate or harass you, it's probably personal."

Easton didn't respond, but my phone beeped. I pulled it away from my ear and looked at the screen. He sent a text with names and phone numbers. Most of the women didn't have last names. Some of them didn't even have real names. He just referred to them as ingredients or cooking adjectives. *Honey, Sugar, Sweets, Spicy, Saucy.*

Grumbling, I forwarded the list to Amir, hoping he'd be able to get us names and addresses from the phone numbers. "You were right."

"About what?" Renner asked.

"Easton Lango is no choir boy."

"Who'd he screw?"

"Apparently half the grocery store."

* * *

More dead ends. I stared at the crossed off names on my list and turned the page. No one remained. I clicked the list Amir left in my dropbox and scrolled down, double-checking to make sure I didn't miss anyone. *All right, that's enough*, I decided. I performed my due diligence. I even watched traffic cam footage from around the time of the alleged disturbance to see if I spotted any suspicious motor vehicles near Easton Lango's neighborhood. Besides the normal riffraff, no one stood out. The Cross Security protection detail even spoke to the nosy neighbor across the way. No one paid the chef's house a visit last night.

It was simple. Easton was scared. He had every reason to be. A brick sailed through his window with an attached death threat. That would make anyone edgy. I knew that from experience. After my apartment was broken into, I spent several nights sleeping with the lights on. Easton would recover. The police had the men responsible in custody.

But aspects of this case bothered me. Chef Strader suffered from peeping Tom syndrome or had a voyeuristic fetish, though I was certain it wasn't sexual in nature. He wanted to observe his competition and emulate or steal from them. What was the saying? Something about imitation being flattery.

I rolled my neck from side to side, working out the kink. We lived in a digital age. It would be easier and less obvious for Strader to stalk Easton online, but the threatening messages Bisset anonymously sent to Easton caused the chef to retreat from broadcasting his life and creations to the world. Maybe that's why Strader got creative and started stalking in person and bugging his competition's kitchen.

The other thing that didn't make sense was Dante Bisset's role. Bisset didn't have a record. He didn't have any documented psychological issues, at least none we knew about. Bisset was talented with a bright and promising future. Why would he risk it all over his old boss? Why would he pretend to be friendly with Easton when he clearly loathed the man?

"Bennett," I said, drawing him from his reverie, "you've spent a lot more time with Chef Easton than I have. He never mentioned Dante Bisset as a suspect. He said they grabbed a drink. That they were friends. He trusted his sous chef with a key to the kitchen. Do you think they had a falling out?"

"If they did, he never told me. Jake's gathering evidence. You should ask him."

"I guess I will." The call went to voicemail, and I left a long, rambling message filled with my theories and questions that needed answering. Hopefully, the police detective would get back to me. I wasn't confident he would, but perhaps that was the pessimism talking. "Easton believes it's arson," I repeated for what felt like the millionth time. At this point, I, too, was having doubts. Just because he believed it, that didn't necessarily make it true. Maybe Lt. Payne was right, and Easton feared he did this to himself and hoped we'd prove him wrong. That would explain why he'd been so adamant that the police reopen the investigation.

"Welcome to the dark side," Renner said. He climbed off my couch. "Are we ready to put this thing to bed, yet? You've looked. I've looked. Detective Voletek, several police officers, the fire department and arson investigators, and the insurance company have reached the same conclusions. There isn't enough evidence to prove the fire was intentional."

"Unless we're just not seeing it. Lt. Payne and Dil Haskell admitted the scene appears suspicious. A human element fed the fire and caused it to spread rapidly."

"Fine, I agree." Renner held up his palms. "But that doesn't mean Dante or someone else set the fire. It just means we don't know exactly what happened."

"Let's see what Dilbert Haskell comes up with before we throw in the towel."

"Just make sure you don't toss it on top of an open flame or we'll have another fire to investigate." Renner grinned, and I let out an annoyed harrumph.

Leaving the office, I drove to Shady Groves where Violet Arnaud lived, but an unmarked cruiser and a blue and white were parked in the visitor spaces. I recognized the cruiser as Voletek's. Since he didn't take my call earlier, I knew he didn't want to see me now. We weren't exactly best friends yet, so insinuating myself into his follow-up interview wouldn't be the most prudent course of action.

Instead, I shot him a text that read a little like a stalker-centric summer movie. *I know where you are. Ask Violet if Dante ever mentioned having a beef with Easton.*

Beef, funny, Voletek replied. *I'll check. Do you have anything for me?*

Listen to your voicemail.

I already did.

After typing out a snarky response, which I deleted before I got myself into trouble for my creative suggestions, I examined the car Dante traded for his aunt's. A few twists of a coat hanger and I was inside the car. Donning a pair of gloves, I checked the glove box and beneath the seats. Then I popped the trunk. I didn't find a damn thing.

With nothing left to do, I went home. Digging deeper into Bisset's history held appeal, but the police were in the midst of doing that. Stepping on their toes would not earn me any brownie points. Voletek made that much clear. Too bad he hadn't been just as forthright answering my questions.

When I stepped through my front door, the warm, inviting smell of Indian food wrapped itself around me. "Martin?" I called. Either he had gotten a jump on the packing, or a burglar had broken into my apartment and brought dinner with him. A muffled response originated from my bedroom, and I followed the sound. "What are you doing?"

Martin was standing inside my closet, which was no small feat since I didn't have a walk-in closet. A row of dresses, jackets, and worn jeans hung to his left while he searched the back corner for something. Finally, he backed out of the cramped space with a stack of heavy file boxes in his hands.

They teetered, and I ran to grab them before they toppled to the floor when he bumped against the closet door and dresser like a pinball. I'd forgotten how heavy they were, and I let out an oof as I lifted the top one from the stack.

"Hey, beautiful. The rest of your file boxes from the top shelf are by the door. We might as well add these to the stack," he glanced down to read my writing, "since they're labeled and everything."

"Where's the tape?" I asked, leaving the bedroom and noticing the boxes waiting near my doorway.

"On the counter." He put the two boxes beside mine, snaked his arm around my waist, and spun me toward him, kissing me on the mouth. "I also ordered dinner. I hope Indian's okay."

"You rarely let us order Indian takeout. You complain the smell lingers for days."

"It does, but that's the next tenant's problem, not ours." He released me and reached for the tape. After securing the lids on top to make sure nothing spilled out, he went into the kitchen. "I might have gone overboard with the ordering."

"I don't mind." I unloaded the bags. As usual, he ordered all of my favorites. "You're in a good mood." I went to grab a fork and stared at the empty drawer. The realization hit me like a gut punch. I shut the drawer. "Did you have a good day?"

"Pretty good. The presentation is ironed out. The board and I have worked out our goals for this year's tech conference, and we have a solid plan to reach each of our objectives. It's coming together nicely." He popped the lid off a container of naan and scooped some tandoori onto the piece. "Of course, it helps that I slept last night. Unfortunately," he pushed the container closer to me while he reached for the roti and butter chicken, "you didn't."

"We sleep in shifts, remember?"

"We should work on that."

"We should." I took a big piece of naan, filled my plate with butter chicken and dug in.

After dinner, Martin tucked the leftovers into the fridge while I went to pack the rest of my bedroom. My bottom dresser drawer held a collection of Martin's shirts. Three dress shirts, purple, pink, and blue, sat beside four of his t-shirts.

"I knew you had them," Martin said triumphantly. He folded each one neatly, running his hands over the dress shirts in the hopes of smoothing the creases. But they didn't budge. He set his jaw, his eyes narrowing. "I'll ask Rosemarie to press them."

"Don't bother. I like them wrinkled. They're softer this way." He gave me a confused look, and I laughed. "You're not getting them back. Think of it as a mercy borrow. It's for your own good. In the spring, someone might mistake you for an Easter egg and try to crack you open. I can't let that happen."

"A mercy borrow? Is that anything like a pity fuck?"

"Do you want to find out?" I jerked my chin at the bed playfully, but Martin saw the sadness in my eyes.

"What's wrong? Are you afraid I won't share my clothes? You know I think they look better on you than me, anyway."

"I was just thinking I'd like to spend one more night here." I ran my hand along the side of the comforter.

"We have a lot of memories in this place. Good and bad. Do you remember when we first got together? I practically lived here. How about we box up a few more things, drop your files and whatever else will fit inside the car at our apartment, pack an overnight bag, and spend the rest of the weekend here? We have enough Indian food to last until we leave for Vegas. And you obviously have plenty of my shirts to wear if you're running short on clothes. We can have one last hurrah in this place."

"That sounds nice, minus the last hurrah. That sounds way too ominous and final." Then again, everything right now felt ominous and final. Something told me I'd have regrets. I just didn't know what they'd be.

TWENTY-FIVE

I opened my front door and grabbed a couple of boxes and put them in the hallway. The constant smell of cooked cabbage and mildew would not be missed. Martin waited for me to close the door, lock the deadbolt, and pick up the boxes before we headed down the steps. The two boxes I carried looked like nothing compared to the five he had stacked so high he couldn't see in front of him. We just made it to the car when my phone rang.

"Parker," I answered, wincing when I saw the disturbed look in Martin's eyes. "Hello," I corrected.

"Hi, Ms. Parker. This is Dil Haskell. The lab tests have come back. I have the results right here."

"I didn't expect to hear from you so soon. You said forty-eight hours, but with the weekend, I thought it might take longer."

"When it's for Cross Security, we put a rush on it."

Of course, you do. "We appreciate the quick turnaround." I closed the trunk, slid behind the wheel of the company car, and put the call on speaker. Silently, Martin got in beside me, eyeing the device as if it were a snake preparing to strike. "What can you tell me about the fire?"

"I'd say we're looking at arson, but it'll be damn near impossible to prove." Dil coughed a few times, apologized for hacking in my ear, and laid out the facts. "I sent my team of investigators in to search the place. We checked everything, top to bottom. You remember the vent I found behind the shelving in the kitchen?"

"What about it?"

"They found grease inside. That's how the fire jumped the barrier."

"Okay." This was progress. Proof. "What kind of grease?"

"Based on the chemical composition, it appears to be lard. Not atypical for a restaurant."

"What else did you find?"

"Remnants of oil on the counters, which Ted pointed out. The floors in the dining room had some kind of coating. We found it tested in streaks, which we're used to seeing when people douse a room with gasoline or another liquid accelerant, but it wasn't gas. It didn't flash burn the way we'd expect. It was a slow, continuous burn, mostly around the baseboards and trim and on the wood paneling. That's why we didn't see strips of charring. That's why the fire did so much damage in such a short amount of time. It burned hot."

"How can you tell? The entire place is extra crispy. Everything's charred."

"That's the continuous burn part." Haskell coughed a couple more times. The wet hacks sounded unpleasant and downright painful.

"Are you okay, Mr. Haskell?"

"I'm okay, just got a nasty cough. I probably caught whatever's going around."

Martin gave me a curious look when I missed the turn for our apartment. "I need to make a brief stop at the office," I whispered. He nodded, sinking into the seat and rubbing a hand over his mouth as he continued to stare at my phone like it was the root of all evil.

"Huh?" Haskell asked.

"Nothing," I said, "so you were saying something about the streaks being odd."

"We found the suspicious coating mostly against the walls. We can only speculate what it might be. So far, we haven't found a match to the precise chemical compound."

"Do you have any idea what it is?"

"We're still testing other samples, but it appears to be some kind of sealant. Whatever they used thirty years ago to treat the wood and prevent mildew or mold might be why your client lost his restaurant. It caused the fire to burn even hotter. That's why so much of the furniture went up, even though restaurants are required to use non-flammable décor."

"That doesn't point to arson. That makes it sound like bad luck." Haskell said it was arson. Aside from the grease in the vent, he had yet to give me something to work with. "What else did you find?"

"The samples we took of the front wall are different from the rest of the building. They tell a different story. The front wall cooked until it crumbled. That shouldn't happen. The building materials were significantly different, so I did some digging into the contractor. His name has crossed my desk before. This isn't the first project he's completed that resulted in a devastating structure fire. My team checked the building permits and materials used. I even investigated the foreman, contractor, and the rest of their crew." Haskell didn't say anything else, but I could read between the lines.

"You think one of them is a firebug?"

"I think one fire's an accident. Two's a tragedy. And three makes this a crime. But good luck proving it. I'm just a fire-obsessed old man. I never found anything conclusive in my investigation of the construction company. It could be the city's standards are so lax every building is a ticking time bomb or a building inspector is on the take."

For a moment, the arson investigator reminded me of Mark Jablonsky, and from the way Martin's lips quirked in the corner, I knew he was thinking the same thing. I stifled my chuckle. Apparently, there was something to be said about that generation. Nine times out of ten they knew exactly what they were talking about, even though most people would think they were raving mad or going senile.

"How long have you been investigating the construction crew?" I asked.

"Off and on for almost a year, but we've never found anything concrete. Our claims have yet to stick. And no one's ever had a vested interest in us continuing pursuit. When taken individually, the fires just aren't suspicious enough, not even Sizzle's."

"So why did you tell me it's clearly arson? It sounds like the fire might have been thirty years in the making." I wondered if Haskell wanted to enlist me to fight on his behalf in the crusade against the construction company. He probably thought my client would be more than happy to lead the charge, but I wasn't a pawn to be used in their game.

"It wasn't. It was set intentionally and recently. The grease could only have gotten inside the vent sometime after Sizzle passed inspection."

"How do you know?" I looked at Martin, wondering if he was following along better than I was, but he appeared just as confused.

"Because ventilation and air flow are part of the inspection. The filters and vents have to be clean," Haskell proclaimed, as if I should have realized it sooner. "Someone put the lard in there and smeared it up and down the wall on both sides. That was intentional. There's no other way it could have gotten there. Though, some might argue otherwise. Here's my expert opinion, Ms. Parker. The grease in the vent signifies the fire was intentionally spread. Plain and simple, that means arson. Whoever did it probably wanted to set the dining room on fire. Whether or not they wanted it to completely destroy the building, I can't say for certain. A lot of additional factors played a contributing role in decimating the restaurant. Those might have been bad luck, but the grease wasn't."

"Did you find grease in the other vents or throughout the ventilation system?"

"Just trace amounts."

"Why haven't you taken this to the police or the fire department?"

"Cross Security hired me to investigate. It's up to you what you do with those findings."

"I'll need you to talk to the cops."

"You're forgetting one thing, Ms. Parker."

"Alex," I corrected, feeling at this stage in the game it was only fair. "What's that?"

"It's the vent leading out of the kitchen. Even with the exhaust fans and other required safety implementations, anything in constant contact with cooking fumes, smoke, et cetera that isn't cleaned regularly will end up with grease build-up. And no one ever thinks to clean the vents, unless it's the exhaust fan or the grate over the stove."

"Would grease from the stove make it to a vent near the floor?"

I could practically hear Haskell's shrug. "Conceivably, with enough time and meal prep, but Sizzle was only in operation for two months. It wasn't long enough for that kind of build-up. That's how I know it was intentional, but the authorities might still discount the possibility. Fires are tricky things."

"All right. Thanks." I bit my lip, my thoughts going in a million different directions. "Send me your files, and whatever details you can provide on the contractors and construction workers." That was one avenue I hadn't explored. "I'll find a way to prove it." I disconnected and stared out the windshield. Everyone else said it wasn't arson, but Haskell said it was. It would be a tough sell.

"You probably should have dropped me off at home," Martin mused. "It looks like you'll be working late again."

I tore my eyes away from the road and looked at him. "How are you feeling?"

His brow furrowed. "Fine?"

"Is that a question?" He let out a low grumble, and I got to the point. "I'm serious. With the exception of last night, you haven't been sleeping. This," I gestured to the phone before turning my gaze back to the brake lights in front of us, "stresses you out. Me coming home late stresses you out. I know you're all in, so I'm not going to play through our usual greatest hits."

"Thank god."

"And I do believe that we'll be okay. That you'll be okay. I know a little bit about what you're going through."

"I know. I saw the t-shirt in your drawer. *Been there, done that.* But for the record, I've never been just okay. I'm fucking amazing. Always have been, always will be."

I snickered. "Be that as it may, I need you to make a decision. You know about my case, about what I'm working on, all the things that I'm sure Lucien Cross would hate to know I've divulged to you since you're an uninvolved third party and all, but this isn't normally what we do. We're doing this whole open and honest communication bullshit your therapist harped upon."

"Our therapist," he corrected. "That was the one we went to see together."

"Yeah, whatever. They all say the same things."

He laughed. "That probably means it's something we need to work on."

"Which is why you know every damn thing about this case. So here's the million dollar question." I pulled into the garage and parked the company car in my reserved space. "Do you want to come upstairs with me while I make a few calls and get everything squared away? This way, I won't work too late, and we can return to our regularly scheduled program. Or would you prefer to take my car or call for a ride and go back to our apartment?"

His eyes sparkled. "That depends?"

"On what?"

"How does the million dollars work?"

Now I was confused. "What million dollars?"

"The million dollars you mentioned in regards to answering the question. Is there a right answer that wins a million dollars? Or do I pay you a million dollars?"

I gawked at him. "Martin, you slept. I didn't. Why are you asking me inane questions?"

He licked his lips, the playfulness draining from his features. "It's easier than the alternative. We both know that call fucked up our plans for the next two weeks."

TWENTY-SIX

Martin and I spent most of the night reviewing Haskell's report and running background checks on the construction company, Ames Bros. Construction, affectionately dubbed ABC. Those were the same initials I used to refer to Martin's attorneys. When everything was said and done, maybe the construction company would have to hire the law firm to get them out of this jam. But I didn't find anything damning in their records, and even Martin with his keen eye for business and finance didn't spot anything suspicious going on with the construction company or its workers. The contractors appeared to be on the up and up.

The next morning, I got up bright and early, intent on conquering the day. Since Dilbert Haskell was willing to bend over backward for Cross Security, I planned to take advantage of my security firm's prestige for once. He graciously agreed to meet me at Sizzle for another walkthrough, so I phoned Voletek and convinced him to join us.

"Bribing a cop is a crime," Voletek said, taking a cup of coffee from the carrier. "Good thing I don't consider consumable goods bribes."

"Isn't that what got Cross Security into this mess?" I retorted.

"Point taken." He popped the top and took a sip. "So what do we have here, Mr. Haskell?"

"Dil," the consultant corrected, already sifting through the rubble as he made his way inside the building. "Didn't Alex catch you up to speed?"

"She did, but I'd like to hear it from you."

As the men went over the same limited facts, I went around the back of the building to check out the rear exit again. Crouching down, I inspected the lock. The police were right; there were no signs of a break-in. I trudged back inside just as Voletek swabbed the interior of the vent, sealed it in a tube, and tucked it into his jacket. The detective looked up at me, the ah-ha evident.

"Lard," Voletek said.

"Yes, lard," Haskell replied. "That's what our lab tests show."

"I'll need you to forward me the results. The crime lab will run a test to verify, but this is a major breakthrough."

"Come again?" I ran a gloved finger over the countertop.

"That's olive oil," Haskell volunteered without me asking.

"It's not the same type of grease." Voletek stood up, offering a hand to Haskell who gratefully took it. "Chef Easton doesn't use lard in his restaurant."

"Are you sure?" I asked.

Voletek nodded. I knew chefs didn't have trading cards, but if they did, Voletek would have the entire collection and every single one of their stats memorized. Obviously, the second part was true, even without the trading cards. "Chef Strader, on the other hand, has several pastry recipes that rely heavily on lard. It's one of his key ingredients."

I tried to recall Easton's recipes, but I didn't remember anything that required flaky crusts. Pastry wasn't his passion or his forte. "What about Bisset? He studied in Paris. What do they use?"

"Depends on the region, but typically butter," Voletek said.

Still, that didn't prove anything. Anyone could go to the grocery store and buy lard, not just chefs and arsonists. "What did Strader tell you?" I asked.

Voletek grinned but refused to answer. "Dil, I need your help to build my case."

"Sure, whatever I can do for you, Detective." Haskell glanced at me, hoping his answer was acceptable.

"You can't just swoop in and steal my expert," I teased, squaring off against Voletek. "What do you know?"

"Dante mentioned lard yesterday when I questioned him after paying his aunt a visit. I didn't understand why he kept insisting the baking supplies he brought her had nothing to do with Easton, but I knew there was something to it."

"What did you find?" I asked.

Voletek showed me a photo he took of the items inside the woman's pantry. Among them was a half empty tub of lard. "Forensics dusted the containers and analyzed the contents, but we didn't find anything out of the ordinary. Prints matched her and Dante. Nothing indicated the items came from Easton or his kitchen, so the other cops were willing to write it off as Dante being paranoid that we wanted to pin theft to his laundry list of crimes. But I had an inkling there was more to it than that." Voletek stepped closer to me and lowered his voice, not wanting to share the intel with Haskell. "The lab can analyze the chemical composition, trace elements, fat percentage, things like that, and determine if the lard in the vent is a match to what's in Violet Arnaud's cupboard. If it's the same, we have our man."

"How long has the container been in Violet's cupboard?"

"According to Violet, her nephew brought over the baking supplies when he was in between jobs. It must have been a week or two after the fire. He told her he didn't need them anymore, and she took it as a sign he was depressed about losing his job. That's when they switched cars. She thought letting him drive around in her late husband's GTO would make him feel more manly. More in control of his life. Hell, she probably figured it'd get him laid and cheer him up."

"So you think Dante did this?"

"With Strader's help. Strader's the lard expert. I found the same size container and brand inside Bouillon that I found in Violet's pantry. That can't be a coincidence." Voletek stared at the vent and the charred wall. "Since Dante brought it over before he went to work for York, it might mean something."

"It means they'll go another round of pointing fingers at each other instead of taking the blame."

But Voletek was determined to get to the bottom of it. "Then I break the cycle. Dante said Strader's been slipping him money in exchange for intel, first on Easton, now on York. Maybe Strader paid him to set the fire or worse."

"So Dante Bisset doesn't actually hate Easton?"

"I didn't say that. I just think he's envious and wouldn't care if all of their restaurants burned to the ground, but since he's taking payoffs from Strader, it changes everything. Asher York knows something. I don't know what, but he does. If my assumptions are correct about the lard and its origins, maybe York will lead us in the right direction. He knows more about Strader and Bisset's interactions than he's let on. Once I tell him his sous chef was selling him out, he'll tell me everything I want to know."

"Yeah, okay," I took a step back and surveyed the destroyed kitchen again, "but we still don't know who set the fire. I doubt York knows, and since your prime suspects will either deny it or blame the other, you'll never get a jury to convict. I doubt you'll even convince the DA to pursue charges on the matter when they know how it'll play out."

"I didn't realize you were a prosecutor," Voletek said.

"I'm not."

"Then don't concern yourself with that. Leave that up to me," Voletek grinned at Haskell, "and my new best friend."

Haskell gave Voletek the same tour he'd given me, pointing out what he and his team of experts uncovered. I made some notes, examined the portion of the wall that had been cut to expose the interior and another portion of wall that had crumbled due to the fire and water damage. While Haskell was pointing out the unexpected demolition of the front wall, I spotted pieces of the front door poking up from the rubble.

The heat had partially melted the thinner portion of the

door handle, where it rested against the thick wood frame, but most of it remained intact. The firefighters had breached the door, splintering the frame and causing even more destruction. Based on the remnants, there would be no way to tell if the arsonist forced his way into the restaurant via the front door, but maybe the lock could tell us something.

"What did you find?" Voletek crossed to me and helped wrestle part of the door free from the debris. He eyed the blackened lock and handle.

"No signs of forced entry out back," I said.

"We can't say the same for this one." Voletek examined the charred, splintered edges. "I'm not even sure it was standing when the fire department arrived on scene. Do you recall the reports?"

I'd read them dozens of times. "It's my understanding they breached the door and the wall came down after they arrived. They couldn't save it. Lt. Payne said they responded within the normal estimated window, but their efforts weren't enough to save the building or stop the wall from crumbling."

"They busted it down," Haskell said. "It's protocol. They had to check for survivors." He brushed some soot off the surface. "I doubt there's anything left to recover."

"What if you remove the lock? The blaze might not have damaged the interior. It could be disassembled and examined for signs of tampering. Bump keys are notorious for destroying the internal mechanisms," I said. "The heat from the fire could have caused the metal to expand, making the door appear to be locked even if it wasn't."

"Good call." Voletek picked up the two-foot piece of door. "I'll have the boys from the crime lab come and collect this. Who knows, maybe we'll get lucky." He looked around what remained of the dining room. "The lard's the real kicker, but this could help. My money's on Strader. He's the lard king, but Dante helped him pull it off. I'm sure of it. If nothing else, Dante concealed Strader's crime. At best, he's an accomplice. At worst, he's our firebug." Voletek reached for his phone and made the call.

"What do you think?" I asked Haskell.

The consultant checked the standing walls one more time. "It sounds like the detective has this under control. This should help further your investigation, right?"

I nodded. "My client will be pleased. He wanted someone to prove the fire wasn't an accident, and I must admit, after speaking to Lt. Payne yesterday, I was having doubts."

"Teddy's a good guy. I trained him. He knows his shit, but he's got a lot on his plate. This job takes it out of you." Haskell rubbed his chest absently. "Like you said, Alex, grease is common in restaurants. No one would bat an eye at lard inside a kitchen, especially with an air vent that close to the supply shelf. If I still worked at the BFI, I doubt even I would have caught it, but now I have the time and staff needed to really dig in deep. It struck me oddly, and since it's my job to find inconsistencies, that's all I look for."

"I'm glad you do."

"I probably wouldn't have found them if you and Ted hadn't asked for my help." Haskell narrowed his eyes at the wall. "I still don't know why sealant would react the way it did to the fire, but we may never know."

"What about Ames Bros? You said you thought they could be involved."

"I know they're shady. Sound commercial construction work doesn't collapse because of a kitchen fire, especially an exterior wall. I'll keep digging. If they're putting lives in danger, someone needs to stop them."

After conducting hours of research last night, I didn't find any proof to Haskell's assertion, but gut instincts couldn't always be proven. Although, in this case, it appeared Easton Lango's had been, and no one believed him the first few times he said it either. "Talk to Lucien Cross. He might be able to open an investigation." I had no idea how far out on a limb my boss would go for one of his expert consultants, but it couldn't hurt to ask. "In the meantime, I'll keep my eyes open for anything strange."

"Thanks. You also might want to check into the inspection guidelines. If Ames Bros only met the minimums, that could explain this." He waved his hand at the rubble. "I've been telling the city they need to have more stringent fire regs, but they never listen to me. They might listen if it comes from someone else."

Voletek hung up and joined us just outside the roped off area. "CSU is on the way, but since the crime scene has been unprotected for months, any evidence we uncover might be contaminated and thus inadmissible. Still, it's best to make sure we're not missing anything. I just wish we thought to look sooner." The detective squinted at the burned out building. "Can you meet me down at the precinct, Mr. Haskell?"

"Absolutely."

"Okay," Voletek turned to me, "anything else you want to add?"

"Keep me looped in."

"Besides that." The corners of Voletek's lips twitched. He thought he had me figured out. Cocky bastard. I shook my head. "You did a good job, Alex. No wonder everyone sings your praises." I resisted the urge to roll my eyes. "I have to speak to Chef Easton again, but rest assured, I won't give up until I figure out exactly how that lard got inside his vent."

"Do you believe he's a suspect?" I wondered why Voletek wanted to question Easton again.

"As a rule of thumb, everyone's a suspect. But no, I don't think he's to blame, but maybe he'll remember Dante or someone else bringing odd ingredients into his kitchen. You never know."

"Fingers crossed."

Now to call Renner and give him the good news. Our involvement in the case had ended and just in time for my vacation. Martin would be ecstatic and relieved, and Easton would be pleased, as would Cross. At least, that's what I was counting on.

TWENTY-SEVEN

"Are you sure that's everything?" Martin asked. He offered a hand up and backed me against the bed until my calves bumped against the mattress. The movers had already taken the frame. Just the mattress, box spring, and bedding remained.

"Everything but what we need for the morning. Maybe it's stupid to stay here tonight. It would make more sense to box everything up now and go back to our place."

"Since when are we that practical?" He tried to toss me onto the bed, but I shifted my weight and wrapped my limbs around him, wrestling him onto the bed with me. "Damn, you're feisty today. You're like a playful kitten." He nipped my earlobe. "I didn't expect you to be in such a good mood."

Truthfully, I wasn't, but it was easier to pretend and let Martin distract me for the rest of the day. The packing was done. One box remained open, and in the morning, I'd throw my sheets and blankets into the box along with our clothes. Aside from a few pieces of furniture and half a dozen boxes, my apartment was empty. Tonight wasn't that different from the first night I spent in this place. I was about to embark on another journey; the unknown spread out before me.

After gorging ourselves on leftover takeout and enjoying one final hurrah, as Martin put it, I stared at the ceiling while memories of the last eight years played through my head. I spent more than half of my twenties in this apartment. This was my first home. I'd miss it. I worked a lot of cases under this roof, from federal investigations to private sector gigs. How many times did I have to spackle and repaint the living room wall because I'd hung up case notes and photos? Ten? Eleven? It might have been more than that.

My mind got derailed on that point, and my thoughts shifted to the fire at Sizzle. How many times had those walls been repainted or wallpapered over? The restaurant had changed hands a number of times in the last thirty years. Most restaurants flopped within two years, so it probably had gone through ten or twelve renditions before Easton Lango bought it. That was a lot of different coats of paint, wallpaper, and paneling. Could that have had anything to do with why the fire burned so hot in localized areas? Maybe it wasn't the sealant. Maybe it was the layers of chemicals and paper or some type of interaction among the different chemicals and cleaners.

Reaching for my phone, I typed myself a note and tried to go to sleep. We had to get up in two hours to catch our flight, but thoughts of other recent area fires kept me awake. What if it wasn't the construction crew who used substandard materials? What if it was one of the companies that provided the décor?

Martin rolled to face me. "Hey," he brushed a strand of hair away from my face, "are you all right?"

"Yeah, just thinking."

"It's not too late. You can change your mind."

"No, I want to come with you on your business trip."

He chuckled. "Not about that. About the apartment. You didn't renew your lease, but your landlord will give you another month to decide, if you want. If you're having second thoughts, it won't hurt to pay for another month, just to be sure."

"That's not necessary. It's fine. I'm fine."

He stared at me through the dim lighting. "Okay, if you're positive."

"I am."

He propped a few pillows against the wall and leaned back. For the next two hours, we reminisced. Martin said he'd miss this place as much as I did, though he spent a lot of time complaining about how tiny and cramped it was. I suppose nostalgia always gave things a lovely rose tint.

When the alarm blared, I got up, dressed, and finished packing. The best thing about not sleeping was avoiding that tired, dragging feeling first thing in the morning. With everything packed, I sat at the counter, staring at the spot where the coffeemaker used to be.

"Coffee will be waiting on the plane." Martin yawned.

"Did you sleep at all last night?" I'd been so consumed by my internal thoughts that I didn't notice what he'd been doing until he spoke to me.

"A little."

"I'm sorry."

He waved the thought away. "No worries. I'll sleep during the flight. I don't have anything official to handle until my lunch meeting, but I'd like to get some things done once we arrive. I could always take a nap if I need to. We'll see how it goes. At these conferences, I tend to play it by ear."

Marcal, Martin's valet, arrived to pick us up and take us to the airport. Marcal went over our itinerary and promised, after he dropped us off, that he'd return to my apartment and wait for the movers. By this afternoon, my apartment would be completely empty.

"Thanks," I said.

"Anytime, Ms. Parker." He smiled at me from the rearview mirror.

Martin asked about the beach house, and they went over instructions and an estimated timetable while I stared out the window at the buildings zooming by. In no time, we arrived at the airport, the wheels in my head spinning over nonsensical facts and random exhaustion-fueled musings. Marcal unloaded our luggage, wished us a safe trip, and promised to call if any problems arose.

Once we were airborne, Martin settled down on the sofa. Just one of the perks of private jets. He closed his eyes and within minutes fell asleep. Either he was appropriately exhausted after last night or getting out of the city erased the stress he'd been carrying with him for the last two months. I was safe and away from danger, and it appeared that's all he needed to believe in order to sleep.

My job was going to kill one of us. I always thought it'd be me, but after these last few weeks, I feared the stress might do him in first. He needed to relax. He needed to realize nothing had changed. It was always like this and probably always would be. Hopefully, the time away was exactly what he needed.

When we landed almost seven hours later, though with the time difference the clock said it was less than four hours later, Martin was raring to go. Frankly, I was surprised he didn't drop to the floor to do push-ups in the airport. By the time we got into the waiting town car, he was already on the phone with his associates.

I stared bleary-eyed out the tinted windows at the desert sun, fighting back a shudder. I didn't like the arid heat. However, by the time the car pulled up to the hotel, there wasn't much sky left to see among the skyscrapers and neon lights, though they didn't look quite so neon in the bright sunshine. I stepped out of the air-conditioned vehicle, the dry heat suffocating as it stole my breath. Martin tipped the driver who helped the hotel staff load our luggage onto a cart.

He spoke to the bellhops, who obediently trailed behind us. The hotel clerk handed us each a room key. I snickered at the PH written on the sleeve. Of course we had the penthouse. Martin didn't believe there was any other way to travel. Admittedly, he wasn't wrong.

"Thank you." Martin smiled graciously, dazzling the hotel clerk with his charm and sophistication, or at least that's how the manager appeared, though I suspected a fair amount of botox had probably frozen the man's face into the shape of utter adulation. It probably helped when dealing with irate guests or angry, newly broke, and drunk gamblers.

"Mr. Wingate left a message." The clerk handed Martin an envelope. "He's waiting for you in the private dining hall."

Martin tore open the envelope and skimmed the note. "Alex—"

"Go. I'll get us settled upstairs."

"Thanks, sweetheart." He pressed his lips to my temple. "Text if you go out or leave me a note in the room."

"Sure."

The clerk gave me a rundown of the casino, the restaurants and hours of operation, the locations for the indoor and outdoor pools, fitness center, and a few brochures detailing headliners performing here and at the sister establishments. I didn't care. I just wanted to get some sleep.

The bellhop took me upstairs, unloaded our bags, practically offering to unpack and turn down the bed. Did I tell him I was tired, or was he just astute? After tipping him well, I unzipped Martin's garment bags and hung his suits in the closet. Having fulfilled my duties as loving girlfriend, I sunk onto the bed. Now to sleep, except, as usual, my mind was racing.

"Stop it," I snarled. Reaching for my phone, I sent a message to Renner. Since it was Monday, the chefs would be arraigned and released until their next court date. I had to make sure Easton was safe.

Spoke to him earlier. Bridget helped him file a TRO. Cross Security will continue to keep an eye out.

I snorted at the response. The ex-wife wasn't as hands-off as she wanted me to believe. I wondered if she reached out to Easton or vice versa. It didn't matter. I wasn't cupid, and based on what I'd seen, they were better off apart.

After exchanging a few more texts concerning my revelation last night, Renner assured me he'd run it by Detective Voletek. *Aren't you on vacation?*

I glared at my phone and put it down, not dignifying the question with a response. It was my vacation. I could do whatever I wanted, except sleep. The case had me too wound up, so did the move. When we returned home, my life would be irrevocably different.

Oh god. My breath caught, and my heart rate skyrocketed. I'd been through enough panic attacks to know what this was. I also knew it was stupid. Nothing was different. Not really. I hardly ever used my apartment. I didn't need the extra expense. I didn't need the safety net. I was safe with Martin. He was my home.

Blowing out a few steady breaths, I dialed down the emotional turmoil to a more tolerable level. I needed to relax and stop thinking about everything. Turning on the TV, I flipped through the channels until I found a classic cartoon station. Nothing could distract like a moving picture box featuring a cat chasing a yellow bird. Eventually, I sprawled out on the bed and closed my eyes. Thoughts of fires were the furthest thing from my mind.

A few hours later, Martin let himself into the room. I rolled over, watching him dig through his bag. He pulled out a travel case and put on his fancy watch and Harvard business school ring. Even though Martin always appeared cool and charismatic in business settings, he was nervous but concealed it well. He'd never admit it, but he wanted to make sure his qualifications and success were obvious. He hid behind those trinkets to bolster his confidence and encourage others to be reassured by his words.

"Hey," I slurred, rubbing the sleep from my eyes, "if you don't get mugged, you'll be great."

"The word you're looking for is magnificent." He turned to the mirror and fixed his hair. When he stopped fussing over his appearance, he asked, "Have you been in the room all day?"

"It's my vacation. I'm sleeping in."

"Okay, but think about joining me later for dinner. I'd like to know one person in the audience isn't secretly hoping I flub my speech or plotting to steal my watch."

Climbing off the bed, I gave him a peck on the cheek. "Knock 'em dead. I'll help you hide the bodies afterward."

TWENTY-EIGHT

I didn't make it down to dinner. In fact, I didn't leave our hotel room for the first three days of our trip. Martin was so consumed by the conference I didn't think he noticed. At least, I hoped he didn't. Aside from a few trips upstairs to grab notes, change clothes, or see what I was up to, he was gone fourteen to sixteen hours each day. He was in his element, which meant I had to find other ways to entertain myself.

In the city of sin, that shouldn't have been hard, but instead of gambling or stuffing singles into bright orange g-strings, I did what I always do. I kept digging into the fire at Sizzle.

Despite Renner's proclamation that the case was closed, I knew there was more to it. Detective Voletek couldn't get a confession out of Galen Strader or Dante Bisset. They copped to everything but the fire. When confronted with the tub of lard, Bisset clammed up, unlike Strader who told the police he had given several ingredients, including the lard, to Bisset two weeks prior to the fire. When asked why he did it, Strader said he wanted to teach Bisset the fine art of pie crust making as a reward for some insider recipe information.

"Doesn't that strike you as strange? Bisset worked for a competitor," I said. "Why would Strader want to help further the sous chef's cooking skills?"

"Strader was grooming Bisset for a position at Bouillon. With Kasey pregnant, he'd need to find a replacement when she went out on maternity leave," Voletek replied.

"Kasey's pregnant?"

"Yes, it turns out it's the dishwasher's baby. She's five months along. She told Strader about it right around the same time Sizzle burned down."

"It points to motive."

"I think so," Voletek agreed. "Though Strader hasn't stated it directly, I believe he was helping Bisset hone his skills in the areas where Easton falls short in exchange for a quid pro quo."

"Like a copy of the kitchen key or burning down Sizzle?"

Voletek didn't answer.

"What about the front door? Was the lock tampered with?"

"Listen, Alex," his voice was soft, "you know I can't discuss an open investigation. These details are sensitive and crucial to proving my case. I doubt O'Connell or any other cop lays his cards on the table whenever you ask. No matter how nicely you ask."

"Sure, they do. That's why I'm one of the most sought after police consultants in the city. They know they can trust me."

Voletek politely stifled a laugh. "Unfortunately, Chef Easton hired you, not the department. I've told you what I can in the hopes you'd have some additional light to shed, but I can't give you more than that. I am sorry."

Hanging up, I wondered if Voletek clued in Renner. They were buddies, and Renner had been a cop. Voletek might not have the same qualms reading in a former brother-in-blue.

However, after speaking to Renner, I realized my colleague hadn't even bothered to ask. He was enthralled in Mr. Zedula's case and had picked up another two investigations in Lucien's absence. He didn't have time to worry about a closed case now that we proved the fire was intentional and the police were confident they'd find the perpetrator. Chef Easton paid us for our time and extended his thanks. Cases didn't get more closed than that, but I didn't care. I wanted to know who set the fire.

"Send me everything Cross Security has and tell the techs to send anything new they receive directly to me. Lucien said it was my case, so that makes it my problem. Have we gotten anything else from Mr. Haskell? The last time we spoke he told me he planned to approach Lucien about opening a new investigation."

"Look at you. Don't deny it, Parker. You're good for business."

"Yeah, yeah, good for me." I hung up and blew into my closed fist. I glanced around the hotel room. It was a little after ten a.m. I had the rest of the day ahead of me, and I was getting itchy.

Dilbert Haskell said there had been other similar fires, so I dug deeper. I called Lt. Payne and told him about Haskell's suspicions, though I kept Dil's name out of it. Swamped with cases, Payne didn't want to hear the fire at Sizzle was part of a pattern. From a legal standpoint, he was reluctant to say he'd been wrong and the fire had been intentional. He'd change his tune when and if the police had a solid case. Right now, he stuck to his story. Lard was a common kitchen ingredient that found its way inside the vent.

"Cooking oils and fats when heated splatter, and since they aren't particularly dense, water molecules and steam can carry particles through the air. If the vent was open and sucking in air, as the steam cooled, the fat and oil were deposited, leaving a coating that built up over time," Payne explained. "We've seen other fires in commercial and residential kitchens when fans and vents aren't cleaned."

"Aren't those usually in hoods?" I asked.

Payne didn't answer my question. Instead, he said, "Grease build-up isn't an abnormal contributing factor to kitchen fires. Though it's something that should be checked and cleaned monthly."

"All right. What about the dining room? The wood around the walls burned oddly. Could it have anything to do with the various layers of paint, paste, and décor?"

"Anything's possible. In my twenty years, I've seen some of the damnedest things start a fire, even a horse."

"A horse?"

"Don't ask. You wouldn't believe me if I told you."

Realizing Payne wouldn't be much help, I thanked him for his time and hung up. Since the fire department didn't keep records the way I hoped, I'd have to do my own research.

I spent the rest of the morning and part of the afternoon researching Sizzle's previous owners. Cross Security pulled city records and building permits, and we scoured the intel for any structural changes that might have occurred. In the 1990s, the dining room was expanded, a wall was knocked down, and the bathrooms were moved to their current location. No other major changes occurred until Easton tore down the exterior wall and rebuilt it.

It was harder to get access to cosmetic renovations. I reached out to the ten previous owners, getting into contact with four of them. Only two still had receipts from their business expenses.

After wasting several hours, I knew this was a dead end. It'd be impossible to figure out what type of paint, primer, and wallpaper had been on the walls. Realization hit me hard. It didn't matter. The items on the walls didn't cause the fire. Someone did. I just didn't know if the person who set the fire wanted to permanently shut down Sizzle, or if he just wanted to scare Easton Lango. That's why I had been so gung-ho to analyze the contributing factors. But since I didn't know why the fire burned so long and hot, our suspects probably didn't know either, unless the sealant was the cause and the arsonist put it there or knew it was there before proceeding with his plan.

That was the reason I'd been chasing this down. I wanted proof the sealant wasn't part of the plan to spread the fire, but I couldn't figure it out either way. I phoned Haskell's office and asked for the chemical breakdown and reports. They couldn't match the composition of the substance to any product on the market.

"What does that mean?" I asked the chemist.

"It could be proprietary." Which is why I looked into construction crews and why Haskell thought they might be responsible. "Or it's something a firebug concocted to feed the fire."

Those words sent a chill through me. After several more calls to Cross Security and the PD to check into our questionable chefs' computer files for details on the sealant, I called it quits. I did all I could, and I didn't know what else to do. I had to have faith Detective Voletek would handle this.

Between Dante Bisset and Galen Strader, there was plenty of means, motive, and opportunity to go around. I just wished I knew who was responsible. My gut said Strader pulled the strings and Bisset danced for Strader's cash and empty promises. Even my client, Easton, considered the matter closed. So I needed to let it go. This was my vacation. I should be doing something fun and touristy instead of staying up nights and spending my days researching a police matter and driving myself crazy.

On a whim, I filled the hot tub and settled in for a soak. After a few glasses of wine, I got out and dried off. The good thing about Vegas – day-drinking was encouraged. And since it was three in the afternoon, I really didn't have any other excuse. Properly sloshed and exhausted, I flopped onto the bed and resumed my new favorite pastime, watching cartoons and napping.

The door to the suite opened, and I lifted an eyelid. My head hurt from dehydration. I reached for a bottle of water and took a few sips. Based on the position of the sun, it was still early. Maybe four or five.

"Tell me you're watching porn," Martin said.

"No."

"Then that better be the gambling tutorials which play nonstop on the hotel screen."

"Nope."

He took off his watch and tie and hung his jacket in the closet. "A pay-per-view movie?" He picked up the stack of poker chips from where they sat on the dresser and counted them, but they hadn't been touched. "Or a premium channel?"

"You can look, but I didn't see anything worth watching." I dropped my head back to the pillow and closed my eyes. He kicked off his shoes, tugged his belt free, and climbed onto the bed. He wrapped his arms around me and kissed the nape of my neck.

"I'm sorry I've been so busy."

"It's okay. I've found other things to occupy my time."

"Like what? Male escorts?"

"Hot tub and wine. Though, now that you mention it, I did order a handsome, six foot stud with striking green eyes. Did you see him in the hallway? He might have gotten lost." I turned to face him. "Oh, wait. He's here."

Martin grinned, pleased with the compliment. "Have you even left the room since we arrived?"

"Why would I? It has everything I need, and the bellhops are friendly."

"You should go out. I hear the pool's amazing."

"We have our own pool on the balcony." Though I hadn't used that one either.

"The one downstairs is huge. It looks like an oasis. There's a nearby shopping mall and a garden." He reconsidered. "Never mind. You hate shopping and flowers."

"I love shopping. I hate bills. And I don't hate flowers. They hate me. Well, pollen hates me, but the damn flowers think they're funny carrying around all that pollen. They mock me, Martin. They mock me."

He reached for the empty bottle. "How much wine did you drink?"

"Not enough. You're killing my buzz."

He squeezed me tighter. A few minutes later, he laughed. "I used to watch this all the time as a kid. I love this show."

"See, cartoons are awesome."

He glanced around the room again. "Normally, only stoners say that. You know recreational pot is legal here. Should I be concerned with what the room charges will show?"

"I'm not high. I'm just tired and a little hungover." I reached for the water and finished the bottle before closing my eyes.

"Me too," he mumbled.

When I opened my eyes again, it was dark. I turned off the TV, which now showed infomercials. Martin remained asleep beside me, partially dressed in his business attire. He looked peaceful. He hadn't had any severe sleep disturbances since we arrived. He was probably too busy to think about anything except acquisitions, mergers, and expanding product lines. I couldn't recall his itinerary, but since he hadn't moved in the last twelve hours, I hoped he didn't miss anything important. If he had, I'm sure his phone would have rung off the hook.

A few minutes later, he opened his eyes. "Hey," he murmured, "are you watching me sleep? I thought you found that creepy."

"Only when you do it."

He ran a hand through his hair. "What time is it?"

"Almost five a.m."

He nodded, his eyes clouded as he considered the events he missed, the meetings, the dinners, the drinks. But he shook it off. "I can't believe I slept all night."

"You needed it. How do you feel?"

"Pretty good. A little R&R is just what the doctor ordered."

"Have the nightmares stopped?" I asked. He refused to meet my eyes. "We need to talk about them."

"No, I'm not putting you through that. You lived it, Alex. I don't want to make you relive it because I have trouble sleeping. That's not fair. I won't do that to you." I saw the question in his eyes. "How are you okay? How come this doesn't keep you up at night?"

"It does, but I'm used to it by now. Truthfully, I'm more worried about you than anything else. I think that's why my subconscious hasn't had much time to be afraid for me."

"Don't be."

"Easier said than done. Nothing happened to me. I got a little beat up, but I escaped. The killer's behind bars. I don't have to fear him, and neither do you. That's why I can sleep at night. Is that why you can't? Are you afraid he'll get out or come back?"

"That's not it."

"Tell me what is. In case you missed the memo, I am the only other person on this planet who understands exactly what you're going through. Talk to me. The only way to get rid of the demons is to confront them. I learned that the hard way."

He searched my eyes for answers. "Every night, I dream I'm losing you. That I lost you. It's always different. But the results are the same. You're gone."

I found myself laughing. It wasn't rational. Initially, Martin looked bewildered, but eventually, he joined in. Apparently, we were raving lunatics. "You don't think I'd understand that? I invented that. Hell, that's why we've broken up every single time we've broken up."

"I know." He wiped his eyes, sobering. This was about more than my most recent brush with death. He had the same insecurities I did when it came to moving back into his house. And that's when I realized his nightmares hadn't become as pronounced and obvious until I told him I wanted to move back in. "I don't want you to leave me again."

"You're afraid I will."

"Things happen. Things happen a lot to us. I understand now more than ever why you'd leave because of some misguided attempt to protect me. I also know we don't have the greatest track record."

"I won't leave and you won't kick me out."

"It's more complicated than that. Every time you go to work, I don't know if I'll ever see you again. It makes me crazy not knowing if you're safe. I need to know where you are and that you're okay."

"I promise I will always find my way back to you. It doesn't matter what the situation is. I won't give up. I'll come home. You know it's true. I've never let you down. Sure, it might have taken a bit longer when we were broken up or I was broken and bleeding, but I always came back. So I always will. You can count on it."

"Yeah?" But I could tell words weren't enough to ease his mind.

I nodded, and he crushed his lips against mine. When we broke for air, the thought which had been at my periphery the entire time came to the forefront. He wanted a commitment. That's the glue he needed to hold himself together. "Do you need more than just my word? Because we're in Vegas." My cheeks burned, and my heart pounded. In a few seconds, I wouldn't be able to breathe. "People come here to do all sorts of wild and crazy things. Gamble, drink, get married. Throw a rock and you'll hit a chapel."

"Are you proposing?"

I nodded, blinking against the spinning room. "We're moving in together. It's the same thing, right?"

"Alexis, I love you," he pressed a hand against my neck, "but I won't say yes when the concept panics you. Breathe. Just breathe. You're okay." I clutched his hand and forced long, slow breaths in and out. "I want you to tell me why that scares you so much. Is spending your life with me that scary?" He suspected whatever terrified me about committing to us was the same thing that now terrified him, but it wasn't. I knew it wasn't.

"We've been over this before."

"Humor me." He waited patiently for my heart rate to slow and my breathing to normalize.

"You're a man of your word. If we enter into a legally binding contract, you'll never leave me. I don't doubt that, but I'll never know if the reason we're together is because you actually love me or if you're staying out of a sense of obligation. My adopted parents stopped loving me when I proved to be a disappointment. I wasn't who they wanted. If they could, they would have sent me back and gotten another kid, a different kid who would have become a prima ballerina, who would have fulfilled their dreams, but they couldn't get that other kid because they were stuck with me. I don't want to wonder if you secretly resent me or hate me. I don't want you to be stuck with me. That's why I'm scared. Because I'll always wonder."

"You never have to worry about that with us." He pressed his lips to my forehead, but I shook it off. That was ancient history. It didn't matter. "Since you feel that way, why would you ask me to marry you?"

"It's what you need."

The light dawned in his eyes; he realized it was true. "We'll figure something out." His gaze fell on the crack in the drapes. "Right now, let's watch the sunrise and go for a swim. I'm free until lunch, and I will be damned if we don't have a little fun on this trip."

TWENTY-NINE

I put my book down and reached for the tube of sunscreen. The pool was crowded, even though it was the hottest part of the day. While I slathered on the sunscreen, I watched a group of girls toast to their upcoming friend's nuptials. Vegas wasn't just a destination for shotgun weddings. It was also the perfect place to host a bachelorette party. Damn, now that I said it out loud, I couldn't escape the idea.

Couples were everywhere. The pool was filled with them. Although, a few might have been hired. I couldn't tell. It was difficult to differentiate hookers from vacationers. Though prostitution was legal, I didn't think the hotel would want working girls and guys to pick up prospective clients at the pool. Now if they were hired before they came to the pool, that was a different story.

The oddly shaped pool curved around. One end was shallow, letting people walk into it as if they were walking into the ocean. Another area had steps. A partially separated area allowed patrons to swim up to the bar and order, and there were even tiled seats where a person could drink or even dine while never getting out of the water. I wondered how many tiny umbrellas were inside the filters.

Even though Martin had taken me out for a nice breakfast, I was getting hungry, but eating and swimming weren't a good mix. At least that's what I'd been told over and over again. Though the cluster of partying men and women didn't seem to get that memo. Drinking and swimming also seemed like a bad idea, but everyone was doing it. When did I get so old and boring?

Movement caught my eye, and I watched a man surface in front of the waterfall. His back was to me, which is why he stood out. His skin was covered in inky black. Wings spread over his back, the tips kissing the tops of his shoulders while intricate feathers ran down his side, snaking around to his front. A dark, shrouded figure stood out from the center of the man's back, sharply contrasted by the elaborate, feathery mass. An angel of death. The only unmarked skin on his back were the two indentions where his pelvic bone jutted out.

I stared at the tattoo, the way it rippled as he moved. I'd seen it before. I studied the man, sure I was mistaken. Plenty of people must have similar tattoos. The water slicked back his hair, making it appear darker than normal. Lucien Cross? No fucking way.

I blinked, convinced I was seeing things. I only glimpsed part of my boss's tattoo once. It couldn't be the same. It just couldn't.

The tattooed man dove into the water, surfacing again with a beautiful redhead in his arms. She wore a bright red bikini top, barely large enough to contain her ample bosom. She squealed, grabbing his shoulders and practically climbing up his body. Her right leg snaked around his hip, her toes hooking around the inside of his knee.

Like her partner, she also had exquisite ink. A full-color leopard ran up the length of her leg. The tip of its tail resting on top of her foot while the rest of it appeared to be climbing up her leg in a similar fashion to the way she was climbing up the man's body. The leopard's head rested just beneath the band of her bikini bottom; its mouth open as if it intended to pull the bottoms off of her. The browns and oranges stood out against her fair skin, attracting even more attention than her fiery hair and bikini. She wrapped her arms around the man's shoulders and held him tight. He returned the embrace, turning in the water as he kissed her.

I stopped staring before he noticed. Luckily, my dark sunglasses made it impossible to see what had caught my attention. But one question remained. Was that Lucien Cross? Though he moved like my boss, he definitely didn't act like my boss. I pushed the thought aside, unwilling to consider the myriad of other questions Cross's unexpected appearance would raise.

Getting up, I crossed to the tiki bar to get some water and a snack. Obviously, I'd spent way too long in the sun. I needed energy to recharge before I hallucinated anyone else. The only thing more frightening than the Lucien Cross lookalike would be Mark Jablonsky in a speedo. And now that I thought of it, I knew it'd be next up on my list of heat-induced hallucinations.

Taking a seat under the awning, I ordered some ice water, a virgin daiquiri, and a salad. While I watched the bartender blend my daiquiri, a few other people swam up to the other side of the bar. Luckily, I didn't recognize anyone.

While I waited for my salad, I drank my water, asked for another, and started on the daiquiri. The waiter had just put down my lunch when the tattooed man stepped up to the bar. He wore sunglasses and navy blue swim trunks. The ends of the wings covered the sides of his ribs, and another tattoo I couldn't quite make out painted the corner of his chest.

"Enjoying your stay, Alex?" he ran a hand through his wet hair, sending sprinkles of water behind him.

"What the hell are you doing here, Lucien? Did you track my phone?"

He laughed. "It's a small world and an even smaller city. I figured we would have run into each other days ago. Guess I was mistaken."

"Answer the question." I glanced behind him, locating the redhead partially hidden behind the billowing cloth of a private cabana.

"The tech conference is here. Where did you think I'd stay?"

"That doesn't explain why you're here. It only explains why I am."

He leaned closer. "James isn't the only fish in the sea. Since he's not willing to work with me, I'll find someone else who's interested in biotextiles." He slid the sunglasses down his nose, eyeing me over the lenses. "Did you actually think I flew across the country just to ruin your vacation? I do have better things to do with my time."

I doubted it, but I didn't say as much. I wasn't that conceited. Lucien ordered a few sampler platters, mudslides, and a bottle of champagne, giving the waiter his cabana number and signing the receipt with his room number. As expected, my boss was staying in another of the hotel's penthouses. No wonder I never left the room. My instincts must have known danger was lurking down the hall.

"Would you care to join us?" Cross asked.

"No, I'm on vacation."

"Funny, it doesn't seem that way with the requests and phone calls you've been making back and forth to the office. I was told the police are building a case against the person who burned down Easton Lango's restaurant. Hasn't my firm satisfactorily resolved his issue? He sent final payment, and Renner's moved on to other clients. Did billing get something wrong? Is there some sort of misunderstanding?"

"No misunderstanding. Why are you checking up on me?"

"Not you. The office. So what are you doing?"

I licked my lips. "I'm enjoying my vacation however I see fit. Is that a problem? Am I using too many company resources?"

With the dark glasses, I couldn't see his eyes. His posture grew rigid, and the tone of his voice dropped the sweltering temperature ten degrees. "You know I gave you unfettered access to Cross Security's resources, as I do with all of my staff. That being said, I want to know why you haven't written off Lango's case. Did the police ask you to investigate?"

"No." I speared a cucumber and jerked my chin at the cabana. Cross had a one track mind, so it shouldn't be too hard to derail him. "Is that your girlfriend?"

He chuckled, the ice in his veins melting as he leaned across the bar to grab some napkins. "I have my secrets, just like you. Enjoy the rest of your vacation, Alex."

"You too, boss." So much for salvaging my last two days in Vegas.

Lucien's appearance ruined my good mood. When I finished eating, I went upstairs. After a quick shower, I sprawled out on the sofa and finished reading my book. But the words on the page didn't compute. I didn't like Cross being so close, but he had a legitimate reason for being here, just like I did. It really was a small world.

My phone beeped, and I nearly jumped out of my skin. What did Cross want now? Reluctantly, I reached for my phone, but it wasn't from my boss or anyone working on Easton's case. It was Martin.

Are you upstairs?

Yes, I typed. He better not give me grief after my poolside encounter.

Need to run something by you in person. Up in a sec.

Dozens of butterflies took flight in my stomach, but I only had a couple of minutes to worry before the suite door flew open.

"Alex," Martin called, "I've been thinking about our discussion this morning. I have an idea."

"What?"

He smiled, the look on his face one of pure joy. "Let me take you to dinner. I made reservations. It'll be private and romantic, and we can talk about everything."

"You're not planning on proposing, are you?"

"No." But the smile didn't fade. "Marriage is off the table for now. I don't want you to worry or freak out. We'll discuss that when we're ready, and until then, I am going to spend every day making absolutely certain you know how much I love you. You do know that, right?"

"Damn, you're cheesy. This is why I never let you pick the movie. It'd be romantic comedies all the way."

My dig didn't deter him, nor did it lessen the sincerity in his voice. "Come on. You know how much I love compromises and negotiations. This is genius." The confident, charismatic playboy eked out in those words. "I'm brilliant."

"And modest. What's your idea?"

"You have to agree to dinner if you want to find out." He looked at his watch. "Shit, I have five minutes until my next meeting. Say yes."

"Yes."

He grasped my face in his hands and kissed me. "Meet me in the lobby at eight."

"Be careful," I called after him.

He spun, confusion etching his brow. "I know how to handle myself in a meeting."

"Not that. Lucien's here."

"I know. I spotted him a few days ago. What does he want? Is this about you or me?"

"It's about the tech conference. He's looking for another partner. Maybe more than one."

Arching a questioning eyebrow, Martin didn't have time to wait for further explanation. "Eight o'clock. Don't you dare stand me up. I know how to solve our problems."

He ran out of the suite, leaving me to ponder why he wasted the time to come upstairs just to tease me with a snippet of information. Was he trying to drive me crazy, or did he hope the build-up would get so blown out of proportion in my head that whatever crazy notion he had would seem reasonable? Knowing Martin, it could go either way.

THIRTY

"A commitment ceremony?" I nearly choked on the lamb.

"It's what we both want. You'll vow to love and cherish me."

"Don't I get to write my own vows?"

He ignored my question. "We belong together. You can't deny that. It's just a promise you're mine. That you will come home. That it's our home. Everything is ours. Our lives will merge. It's what I want. It's how I know you won't die in some basement or abandon me and go off to California for six months." The basement thing neither of us could predict, but we were both willing to pretend. Most days, we needed to pretend or we'd live inside a panic room and never sleep a wink.

"I wasn't in California that long."

"It felt like years." He remained giddy. "Plus, it's what you want. It's not legal. I can walk anytime. There's no obligation. No strings. No penalties."

"Didn't you just contradict yourself in the span of two seconds?"

He thought for a moment. "No."

"So I have strings, but you don't? Talk about a double standard."

"Sweetheart, listen," he grasped my free hand, and I put down my fork before my wild gesticulating hurt someone, "this morning you asked me to marry you because you sensed I needed commitment and certainty that you'd always be in my life. But despite that, for whatever the reason, the thought of us always being together scares the crap out of you."

"The alternative scares me too."

"I know. That's why we have nightmares."

I laughed, and he rubbed his thumb over my knuckles. It was a compromise, not a marriage. Though, wasn't marriage compromise? My head started to hurt, but I saw the determined, exuberant look in his eyes. He wanted this.

"I have stipulations."

He released my hand. "So do I." He pulled out a piece of paper from inside his jacket. "Are you prepared to present your list of demands? Or should I go first?"

It didn't take long to iron out the details. We weren't waiting to do this, or I'd back out. And we were doing it in private. If and when we told people, it'd be after we got back from vacation, not before. The only exception would be Marcal and his family, who had to fly out to prep Martin's beach house. Since they were getting the house ready for our arrival anyway, Martin asked him to get the ball rolling on the ceremony.

"Rings." He licked his lips. "We need rings."

"I don't know." The room spun.

"You don't have to wear it, but I want a ring. I want the world to know I'm taken. That I'm yours."

"Are you sure this will alleviate your nightmares? It might just give me some."

"No, but at five a.m. you suggested this might help. And you're the expert. You know what I'm going through." His words hit hard, and I remembered a particularly rough patch and wanting nothing more than the security of knowing he'd always be there. Now, he needed the same from me, and he was willing to settle for a half-assed, non-legally binding statement that in reality didn't mean a damn thing but would mean the world to him. At any point, either of us could walk away. There was nothing holding us together, but he realized that and still wanted to give it a try. Sleep deprivation made people desperate, but his eyes weren't bloodshot. They were lovesick. "If it's too much for you, we won't do it."

"I can handle it. Let's do it."

After dinner, Martin and I took a stroll and window shopped at various jewelry stores. Tomorrow, we'd come back and pick out our bands. They had an onsite jeweler and repair shop, so sizing and inscriptions shouldn't be a problem. After all, last minute weddings were a common occurrence here.

It didn't mean anything. I kept repeating this while Martin practically skipped down the street. We stopped at one of the exclusive clubs. Martin got bottle service, and we cozied up in the corner. I had a new plan. To spend the rest of the trip inebriated.

After the club, we toured a few casinos. Each one its own mini universe. Paris, New York, circuses, rock-and-roll, movie themes, tigers, illusionists, and roller coasters. Entertainment was around every corner. Worries could disappear in a place like this, unless you spent a good portion of your TV viewing time watching gruesome crime scenes spread across this cornucopia of glitz and neon lights. In which case, you might start wondering if the parked limo has a body in the trunk.

Eventually, we stumbled back to our hotel. Martin dragged me over to the blackjack table, and we played a few hands. He tossed a chip to the dealer as a tip and cashed us out. After a quick stop at the roulette and craps tables, where more drinks materialized out of thin air, we took the elevator up to our floor.

"You smell good." Martin buried his nose in my hair.

We didn't have the best track record when it came to being drunk in hotel hallways. If the doors didn't open soon, that might extend to hotel elevators too. Though, that brought back thoughts of crime scenes and bodies. I pushed him away and straightened, just as the doors opened.

Lucien stood on the other side. He'd showered and dressed since the pool. The black t-shirt clung to his frame. He looked weird out of the office, as if he might just be a normal guy. "I'm glad I caught you, Alex." He nodded at

Martin, who eyed him suspiciously. "I was on my way to the front desk to have them ring your room."

"Why didn't you call my cell?" I asked.

"Don't you think I tried that? No one's been able to get in touch with you for hours."

Fumbling, I searched inside my bag, but I had left my phone charging in our room. "What is it? What's wrong?"

Cross glanced uncertainly at Martin. "Earlier tonight, someone set Easton Lango's house on fire."

"What?" The news nearly floored me, and I stumbled out of the elevator, regretting every drink. "Is he okay?"

"Just some minor burns. The fire department arrived in time to put it out."

"What started it?"

"Someone threw a Molotov cocktail through the window we just replaced."

"Shit." My mind fractured in a million tiny pieces. "All right, what's our priority?" I frowned. Priority didn't sound right. I repeated it, but it still didn't sound right. I shook it off and stared at Cross for answers.

"According to Bennett, the police are investigating. The fire's out, but Easton needs a place to stay. Depending on what the police department decides to do," Cross scowled, "I'm prepared to put Easton up in a safe house until we're sure he's safe."

"What about the detail? Why didn't they intervene?"

Cross fought to keep his voice neutral. He was always on his best behavior when Martin was around. "They did. A vehicle drove by. It didn't stop. It barely slowed. It didn't have plates."

"No surprise. What about," I fought against the fog for names, "Strader, and... and the other one? And the guy with the knife?" Bisset and York, I thought a millisecond too late. "Do they have alibis?"

"I don't know. The office updated me, and I told Bennett to give me the details to pass along to you."

"I need more details."

Martin chuckled, an unfortunate snort escaping which made me giggle. Lucien remained stoic, waiting for me to pull it together. I gulped down some air and blinked several times.

"Sorry, sir," I muttered sheepishly.

"Sleep it off and call Bennett. He'll fill you in, but Alex, I want to know what we missed, what my people missed. I tried asking you about it today at the pool, but you didn't tell me. Let's meet in the morning and go over the facts so I'll know how to proceed."

"Okee-dokee." Even to my own drunk brain, I sounded like an idiot.

"Is eight o'clock too early?" Though posed as a question, it was not. "I'll meet you downstairs in the restaurant." He looked at Martin. "James, sorry to interrupt. Enjoy the rest of your night."

"That's doubtful," Martin muttered as Cross headed down the hall in the opposite direction.

I stared after Cross until Martin dragged me toward our room. He unlocked the door and went to the fridge while I kicked off my shoes and took a seat at the table. First things first, get sober. Then call Renner. Martin put two bottles down in front of me.

"Drink that," he said. "It'll help."

I popped the top on the coconut water and gulped down half of it. With the time difference, it was too late to make any calls. Martin finished what remained in the bottle and cracked open a water while I made a list of questions that needed answering. At the moment, they seemed brilliant, but my brain wasn't firing on all cylinders. In the morning, I might not feel the same way.

Martin unbuttoned his shirt and tossed it onto a chair. "I can't leave yet. I have meetings tomorrow and the brunch on Saturday. I'll call a car to take you to the airport. Do you want me to check flights, or do you want to wait until you speak to Lucien?"

I looked up, his words a slap to the face, though he didn't say them with malice. "I don't know."

He continued to undress, preparing for bed. "It's fine. Just another fire for you to put out, literally this time."

This was it. Right here. Everything came down to this moment. My years at the OIO and training at Quantico had taught me to run toward these fires. I always reported to crimes in progress or the literal and figurative fire. I responded to emergencies. My job was to catch the criminal and do what I could to save lives. Easton Lango needed help. His life was in danger. He hired Cross Security to protect him, and his case ended up dumped in my lap. But Cross Security existed for years without me. Its reputation and prestige had nothing to do with me. They could handle this in my absence. They didn't need me. Martin did. I saw it. Maybe it was the booze goggles, but I'd never seen anything more clearly than at this exact moment.

"I'll do what I can to assist from here, but I'm not going home. I made you a promise."

"Alex, it's fine." He pulled down the covers. "You have to go."

"No, I don't. Chef Easton will be fine. I'll talk to Renner and Detective Voletek and make sure of it. You don't see Lucien hopping on the first plane and heading home, and neither am I."

"Okay." Though it didn't sound like he believed me. "Sleep on it, and let me know in the morning if you've changed your mind."

I pushed away from the table, shedded most of my clothes, slipped into his discarded shirt, and turned off the light. Wrapping my arms around him, I didn't let go until he fell asleep.

THIRTY-ONE

"Coffee?" Cross asked, sliding the ceramic pot across the table.

I nodded, filling my mug. I'd been up most of the night. After Martin fell asleep and I sobered up, I called the office. With the three hour time difference, it didn't matter that it was five a.m. when I placed the call, it was eight at home, and Renner had already been at work for an hour. After the hospital treated Easton's burns, Renner brought him back to the office. At the moment, our client was asleep on the couch.

The protection detail Cross assigned to guard Easton's house didn't get a good look at the firebomber. The vehicle ran dark. They barely had time to notice the sound of the engine before the glass bottle crashed into the front window. The window only cracked, but enough of the burning liquid made its way inside, which set the curtains on fire.

Easton and the security team tried to put it out by suffocating the flames, but that didn't work. Thankfully, the fire department arrived in record time, saving Easton's house. The front porch took the most damage. The wood railings and shutters needed replacing, but other than that, there wasn't much that could be done for the scorch marks on the concrete path, aside from a few fresh coats of paint.

"Renner said Easton's safe for now." I took a sip, eyeing the tower of breakfast pastries and fruit in the center of the table. "What do we know so far?"

Cross waved down a server and ordered ham and eggs. Stress usually killed my appetite, but for some reason, I was famished, probably on account of last night's drinking. After ordering an omelet and hash browns, I reached for a blueberry muffin and waited for my boss to answer the question.

"I spoke to the police. They've had surveillance teams on Galen Strader and Dante Bisset since they were released from custody. Supposedly, their whereabouts can be accounted for last night, but if the police are correct in their assumptions about Strader and Bisset, it's possible one of them did this or paid someone else to firebomb Easton's house."

"What about Asher York?"

"At this time, his whereabouts are unknown."

"Is that what the police said?"

"That's what I said." His eyes narrowed. "I don't like being kept in the dark. I'm in the information gathering business, so when I have questions, I expect answers to be readily available. I also don't expect a case Cross Security wrote off as closed to come back and bite me in the ass, but that's exactly what happened yesterday. Care to explain why?"

"People make mistakes."

"Not my people. Not usually."

"It's a good thing Easton Lango isn't a Cross Security client."

"Let me start again. What have you been investigating?"

"The fire at Sizzle."

Cross's eyes went skyward. As usual, he found our interactions frustrating. "Specifically?"

"The fire at Sizzle," I repeated slower. "Mr. Haskell and his team looked into it for us. They found lard smeared inside a vent leading into the dining room. He believes that's how the blaze jumped the fire barrier. He also found chemical residue on the wood paneling and baseboards that contributed to roasting the place."

"What did the fire department say?"

"They're waiting for the police to build a case before changing their story. We went through Sizzle's inspection records and the truck company's report. The sprinklers and alarms were functioning. It just wasn't enough to put out the blaze," an idea raced across my brain, "just like Easton and the team couldn't put out the fire at his house."

"Do you think they mixed lard into the Molotov cocktail?" The server returned with our plates, and Cross picked up his knife and fork and cut his ham into precise, neat squares.

"Not lard." I put my muffin down, my empty stomach forgotten, and told Cross about the sealant, Haskell's suspicions, and my research into the matter.

"Since the sealant has a unique chemical composition, I'll send techs to collect samples from Sizzle and Lango's house. It's probably a long-shot, but if it's actually an unknown form of accelerant, we might be able to link the two fires to one person."

"That's what I was thinking." I reached for my fork and dug into the omelet. "But let's not lose sight of the actual problem."

"We still don't know who wants our client dead."

"Our client?" I choked.

"Bridget's footing the bill. She wants the best for her ex." Cross waved his fork in the air. "I don't understand it, but Easton Lango's now our client. Do you still want point? You're on vacation."

"I'll assist remotely, but you should give it to Renner."

"For once, we agree." The wheels in Cross's head turned. "I assume you and Bennett performed your due diligence. You checked into family, friends, and business associates."

I nodded, wondering if it was strange Bridget Stockton was willing to foot the bill. I ran the possibility that she might have been inadvertently to blame for the attack by Cross, who made a call. Most likely, that wasn't the case, but misplaced affections by a stalker or admirer could manifest in strange and dangerous ways. Bridget Stockton made a living saving dangerous people. Maybe one of them wanted to return the favor.

"You have yet to tell me why you kept digging into the fire. What am I missing? Bennett said the police had a solid foundation for their case and Easton Lango paid our fee. Bennett thought our work was done."

"So did I."

"Bullshit." He dropped his silverware. "Did you continue investigating because you questioned the PD's conviction or skills? Because that I can understand."

"No, I just..."

"What, Alex?" For once he didn't bark the question at me. A flicker of compassion lined his face. "What am I missing?"

"It doesn't make sense. Why does Dante Bisset hate Easton so much? Why would he help Strader? He doesn't work for him. What is going on?"

"The police said Strader paid Bisset and promised him a position at Bouillon as soon as one opens up. Doesn't that answer your question?"

"Sure, it makes sense when you're talking about spying on a guy and stealing his secret recipes, but burning down a restaurant is extreme. Strader wanted to benefit from Easton's talents. How can he do that when Easton doesn't have a restaurant? Plus, Easton and Bisset were friends. What changed? How could they go from one extreme to the other without Easton realizing it?"

"Strader made Bisset a better offer. It happens. We know they broke into Easton's house," Cross pointed out. "It gave Strader the best of both worlds. He didn't have to compete for business, and he could still steal Easton's recipes. Plus, it gave Bisset everything he ever wanted, less competition for when he breaks out on his own, extra cash, and a new opportunity on the horizon. That trumps friendship any day, and it gave Bisset a chance to get revenge on Easton for being an asshole boss. Isn't that something most people dream about?"

"I've never entertained ideas about setting your office on fire."

"I'm glad to hear that." Cross dabbed at his mouth. "You

must admit, Strader's plan is brilliant, and now with a second arson attempt, it leaves the door wide open for the possibility of third party involvement, clearing Strader and Bisset of the more serious charge, even though they are guilty."

I didn't buy it. "Strader and Bisset confessed to everything except setting the fire. We still don't have any proof, and neither do the police. There must be something to find somewhere. The tub of lard isn't enough."

"That's why you went back to Sizzle? To look for more evidence?"

"It didn't help."

"I wouldn't be too sure. The police found a tiny piece of thermoplastic inside the lock. One can only assume it was part of a plastic key that broke off. The fire melted and misshaped it, but we know where it came from."

"How are you always two steps ahead of me?" The vein at my temple pulsed. "I don't know anything about a piece of plastic in the lock. How the hell am I supposed to know where it came from?"

"Oh really? Why did you tell the cops to look inside the lock?"

"To check for damage." Suddenly, I understood the significance of Cross's words. "You think someone printed a copy of Sizzle's key?"

"Isn't that what you believe? When we traced the bug to Strader, we checked his other recent purchases. He owns a 3D printer. All Strader had to do was review security footage from Bouillon once he became head chef. It might be why he bought into the restaurant, or he got Bisset to show him his key to Sizzle. Either way, Strader could have easily gotten access and had the means."

"I must be a genius to think to look inside the lock."

Cross stared, exasperated. "You mean to tell me you didn't know about any of this before you told the police to check the lock? You and Renner had us comb through Strader's purchase history. You knew he had a 3D printer."

"Full disclosure, I never read those reports. Renner did. The reason I told Detective Voletek to check the lock was because it was the only place we didn't look. Voletek believed it was arson, but he needed proof someone entered the restaurant and intentionally set the fire. As far as we knew, Easton was the only person inside, but this changes everything." It also knocked Bisset off my suspect list for the arson. He wouldn't have needed to replicate the key in order to break in and set the fire. At most, he was an accomplice, unwitting or otherwise.

"You really didn't know about the key?"

"No."

Realizing this was the first time I heard the news, Cross chuckled. "This is why we don't share with the cops. They never share with us."

"How did you hear about it? Voletek didn't tell me, and Renner didn't mention anything."

"I have my ways." Cross glanced at the time. He had somewhere to be. "Since I told the police Strader owns a 3D printer, the PD is testing his plastic polymer to see if it's a match to the polymer found inside the lock."

"But Strader and Bisset have alibis for last night. Don't you think whoever burned down Sizzle also tried to burn down Easton's house? We've been looking at this all wrong. The chefs threatened Easton, but they didn't set the fires. That's why they won't confess. They didn't do it." The key, though appearing to point to Strader, actually exonerated him as far as I was concerned. He could have bartered with Bisset for access to an actual key. The lard might have been the arsonist's attempt to conceal the actual crime. I tried to explain that theory to Cross, but my boss shot me down.

"They threw a brick with an attached death threat through Easton's window. That's a fact. Don't get hung-up on their alibis. Those aren't difficult to come by. It's the detective's job to break them, and if he can't, we will. Strader did this. We just have to figure out how he pulled it off."

It sounded like Cross was ready to play by his own rules and color outside the lines. I picked up my fork and scooped up some hash browns. His theory didn't fit. Mine did. Strader and Bisset knew the police were watching. They were already in enough trouble after confessing to the property damage, breaking and entering, and vandalism. I watched those interviews. They might have obsessive tendencies when it came to cooking and competition, but launching a forward attack on Easton a week later was suicide. They were too narcissistic to be that self-destructive.

"You're wrong."

Cross finished his ham and eggs and grabbed an orange from the tower. He peeled it slowly. "Why? Explain it to me."

"It would be ridiculous. Strader and Bisset must know they'd be prime suspects. If anything happens to Easton, the police are automatically going to look into the men who confessed to breaking into his house and threatening him."

"That's why they improved their technique. No brick. No note. And the vehicle couldn't be identified. They learned from their mistakes. They tried to kill Easton once, and he shut down and hid. So they let it go, but now Easton is days away from the official launch of Easton's Eats. They can't wait for the heat to die down. They have to stop him from gaining even more popularity and prestige."

"Why didn't they set fire to his food truck?"

Cross leaned forward. "They don't know where it is." He scanned the vicinity for signs of eavesdroppers. "I had it moved to a secure lot after the break-in. Since they couldn't destroy another of Easton's restaurants, they tried to destroy him."

"I'm telling you the threats and the fire aren't related. They are separate incidents. That's why we missed it. Easton presented them together, and coincidences are rare."

"I thought you were taught they don't exist," Cross muttered bitterly.

"This is the exception, not the rule." I finished my omelet and tore off a piece of muffin. My thoughts went to the research I conducted and the research and claims Haskell and Payne had given me. "There's a pattern." I blinked, realizing I'd overlooked an obvious fact. Several other recent fires had similar characteristics. That's why Haskell believed a construction company was to blame. He thought the decimated buildings were a result of subpar materials or shoddy workmanship, but my digging didn't back up his theory. "Did Dilbert Haskell approach you about investigating other similar fires?"

"No." Cross tapped a slice of orange impatiently against his plate. He knew I was on to something or too stubborn to accept defeat.

"He probably didn't get the chance since you fled the state." I wondered if Haskell had swabbed other fires. The unidentified substance we believed to be sealant might have shown up at other fires, and we just didn't know about it. "We're dealing with a repeat offender. If I'm right, that substance we found coating the baseboards and paneling is part of his MO."

"A serial arsonist? Are you serious?"

"I am." Dialing the office, I requested Cross's lab experts visit the other locations from my research and check for the mystery substance. When I hung up, I couldn't decide if Cross was impressed or enraged.

Lucien signed the receipt for breakfast and dragged me into an empty meeting room just off the hotel lobby. "You realize what you're saying sounds crazy."

"Eh, it wouldn't be the first time."

THIRTY-TWO

It was Friday afternoon, and I was itching to return home. *No, Parker*, my internal voice scolded. Cross and I agreed to let Renner take point. Chef Easton's case was his until Cross assigned it to me. Renner could handle this, and unlike Cross, he'd listen to what I had to say.

Video conference calls weren't my preferred method of communication, but under the circumstances, I didn't have much say in the matter. The lab techs on the thirty-second floor had already collected samples from three different locations Haskell had given us. Two of them tested positive for traces of our unknown substance.

"It isn't sealant," the tech said from the bottom right corner of my screen. "We've determined the ingredients. Most are fairly common, but we'll see if we find anything strange when we check with local suppliers."

"Thanks." I shifted my gaze to Renner who had his head turned away while he furiously scribbled notes. "Bennett, what are you doing?"

"Wading through this shit." He held a photo up to the webcam. "That's the only image the security cameras caught from the firebombing last night. Our suspect is a white male based on his exposed wrist."

"That leaves a lot of possibilities." I leaned closer to the screen. "The security cameras didn't see anything else?"

"It was too dark."

"What about thermal or night vision? Cross uses the best and newest technology."

"The fire knocked out both. Though, we did glimpse the approaching vehicle. It didn't have any plates, and the driver remained shrouded. We can't ID him. Though we know he was driving some kind of sports utility vehicle. Since no one noticed it approaching, it must be dark. I'm guessing black or blue."

"It's a start."

"Not much of one." Renner glanced down at the screen, but the tech had hung up on us. "I shared our footage with Voletek. He figures the vehicle was stolen. We questioned Easton about it, but he didn't recognize it. The police are looking into Bouillon's staff again, but they don't have any real leads."

"Did Voletek tell you about the piece of plastic key he found inside the lock?"

"No, but Cross did. After last night, Jake promised he wouldn't leave me hanging again." Renner saw the disbelief on my face. "I trust him, Alex."

"He's kept us in the dark this entire time."

"Regardless, what I can't figure out is why a serial arsonist has set his sights on Chef Easton. We've run through Easton's background. He's aired all his dirty laundry. Our client has a checkered past and questionable ethics, but aside from Bridget, I don't see who he's hurt to warrant this type of retaliation. I've checked under every rock, no stone unturned, and all that. I can't figure out who wants him dead, unless I'm staring right at the guy and not seeing it."

I tried to think about the possibilities. Given everything that happened recently, it was next to impossible to separate Bisset and Strader's threats from the fire, but I swore to Cross they were unrelated. Though the timing royally fucked up that theory. "What about Asher York?"

"He's MIA. After he made bail, he vanished. No one at Delicious has seen him. He didn't even bother to call in."

Renner quirked an eyebrow. "It looks suspicious, but I don't like him for this. He attacked Bisset with a knife in front of a witness. Arson isn't beyond the scope of possibility, but York has a short fuse. I don't think he'd execute a sneak attack. I think he'd walk right up to Easton and light him on fire."

"Didn't Easton say Bridget would do the same thing?"

"Yeah, he did. Easton obviously has a knack for pissing people off."

York's sudden disappearance didn't help matters. "What do the police think about York?"

"They don't know what to think, but locating him is a priority."

"And Bisset's and Strader's alibis?"

"They check out. Bisset spent the night at his aunt's. Dozens of witnesses saw him calling out bingo numbers until almost midnight. Even if he snuck out afterward, he couldn't have made it from Shady Groves to Easton's house in time. And Strader was at Bouillon. Kasey, Isla, and Max were with him. On top of that, the security cameras from the kitchen show him working on a new recipe until three a.m. He's not our guy."

"He could have altered the footage and threatened his staff if they didn't cover for him."

"That's what Lucien thinks," Renner said.

Cross believed Strader's alibi was bullshit since the chef was a technology nut, but I didn't think his coworkers would lie for him. Sure, they probably worried about their job security, but from the social media posts Renner and I had read, I had a feeling they would have gotten a cheap thrill from putting the boss behind bars, even if it was just for one more night.

"That brings us back to the beginning." I put my head in my hands, peering out between my splayed fingers. "Who would want to burn down Chef Easton's restaurant and home?"

"Isn't it more about the fire than the target for serial arsonists?" Renner asked. I didn't know. My research and profile didn't elaborate because anyone could do anything for any reason. Serial arsonists didn't fit into a nice, neat mold. Neither did serial killers. "As far as we know, the fires never hurt anyone."

"We need to flesh out the rest of our firebug's victims. It's the only way we're going to track him down." Oh, god. How did this end up turning into a citywide manhunt? I cringed, my skin crawling. "How long do you think this has been going on without anyone noticing?"

"Assuming Dil's questionable cases all link to the same arsonist, at least," Renner flipped to the back of the stack, "five years."

"How many fires?"

"Seventeen, but there could be more. Or less. We won't know unless we find traces of that substance, and not all these sites still exist. Most have been demolished. Some have been rebuilt." He swallowed. "You realize what'll happen if we're wrong. Our reputation, our livelihood, it'll go up in a puff of smoke. We can't unring this bell, Parker." He stared at me from the screen. "Are you sure about this?"

"Yes. I'm just not sure why an arsonist fixated on Chef Easton." Another chilling thought shot through my mind. "Why would the arsonist suddenly change his MO?" It was the same question I asked Cross, but just like our boss, Renner didn't have an answer. "The cause of the suspicious fires was electrical. Am I remembering that correctly?"

"Yeah, the point of origin was always near an outlet, though the cause varied. Frayed cord. Defective appliance. Improper connection. Overheated wiring."

"And no one was ever hurt?"

"Nope."

"Give me the case numbers. I'll run everything by Lt. Payne and double-check with the police department and hospitals just to make sure, but we have a big problem, Bennett. Until now, our arsonist hasn't been violent, but he tried to barbeque Easton twice. I don't want to know what will happen if he tries again."

"Don't worry about that. Easton's safe. Lucien has several safe houses. We'll get round-the-clock guards. We'll maintain complete radio silence. No one will know where he is. He'll be safe until we get it figured out."

I hated being so far away. Renner needed my help, and I

made a promise to Easton. "I can catch a flight tomorrow."
Even though I swore I wouldn't do it, the words exited my
mouth without permission.

"I appreciate that, but you said you needed the time off.
I got this. Plus, Lucien will be back Sunday, and with
Bridget's money covering expenses, everyone's getting
involved. If you're wrong, we're all going down together."
Renner chuckled. "I would tell you to enjoy the rest of your
time off, but from the looks of you, I'm not sure you've
taken any time off. Go drop twenty bucks on red eighteen
for me, and I'll see you next week." Before I could say a
word, Renner disconnected.

I crumpled in the chair. Too many theories and ideas
crashed into one another, misfiring my synapses and
leaving me motionless while I tried to determine my next
course of action. I couldn't let this go. I had to help. No one
else could die because I screwed up. I couldn't go through
that again, but when the suite door opened and I saw the
tension radiating off Martin in waves that he did his best to
hide, I made my decision and prayed I wouldn't spend the
rest of my life regretting it.

* * *

The breeze picked up, and I tucked myself further into
Martin's open shirt. He ran his hand up and down my
back, the platinum band on his ring finger clinking against
the beading at the side of my bikini bottom. He tapped it
again. The sound unfamiliar, even though he hadn't taken
it off since the ceremony.

The event was a blur. I remembered the orange and
pinks in the sky, the gentle crash of the nearby waves, and
the promises we made. Mine to always find my way back
and his to spend every day making sure I knew he loved
me. We couldn't promise much, at least I couldn't. But it
felt like everything.

Martin hadn't had a detectable nightmare since. His
eyes were bright, his complexion healthy, and the dark
around his eyes and broken veins surrounding his irises
had disappeared. He was at peace or as close to it as a

person could get when picking me as his life partner.

Honestly, I didn't think it had anything to do with the words we exchanged at sunset outside Martin's beach house on Saturday night. He was at ease because he knew I chose him over a case, and I had never done that before. I didn't make that decision lightly. But things were different now.

He was my priority. We were my priority. In the course of our relationship, everything between us had changed. Recently, he proved his love and conviction. It was only fair I return the favor. At this point, neither of us had any doubts about the other. I just feared the timing couldn't be worse.

I shifted, adjusting my top. The stitching around the cups had been driving me crazy ever since we got out of the water. I had a feeling I'd gotten sand in my top. Most people got sand in their bottoms. I got it in my top.

Martin's other hand combed my wet hair out of the way, and his fingers went to the double-knot holding my bikini in place. He tugged on one of the strings, sinking a finger into the center of the knot and separating the two.

"Don't you dare," I warned, suddenly much more alert. "This isn't a topless beach."

Martin didn't let go of the strings. "You're right. It's a private beach. That means it's topless, nude, or whatever we want it to be."

I looked around, but Martin was right. There wasn't a soul in sight. Frankly, I suspected he owned the entire tiny island. When I asked him about it earlier, he didn't deny it. A one lane bridge connected the island to the mainland, which was easily within swimming distance, but we hadn't spent a lot of time away from the property. And no one else had ventured onto the private beach while we had been here.

"I'll take off my top if you do," Martin said.

The white linen shirt he wore was already splayed open around his chest. However, since I found the breeze cold against my damp skin, I had insinuated myself into his shirt. "No." I slipped my hands beneath his back to keep them warm. He squirmed, unprepared for the sudden assault of cold against his hot skin.

He reached for the remote and turned the heat up on the hearth. The simulated fire burned brighter, and warmer air surrounded us. It was late summer. It wasn't cold, but compared to the three digit temperatures we left in Vegas, anything below one hundred degrees felt chilly, especially since my swimsuit was still wet from our dip in the ocean.

"Better?"

"Much." I kissed his chest until I felt another tug at my top. "Do it, and I'm getting an annulment."

He laughed. "I'd like to see you try. There's nothing to annul. We're committed. You can't annul that."

"You should be committed."

He gave the knot a final tug, and the taut sides went limp. He slid his hand to the strap around my back, and I pressed my chest against his.

"I'm going to kill you."

"I'm helping." He grinned, undeterred by my anger. "You've adjusted the top a dozen times in the last twenty minutes. It's driving you crazy."

"It's not the only thing."

He undid the bottom tie and tugged on the fabric until I lifted up just enough for him to pull it free. "Plus, you don't want tan lines."

"Neither do you." I stared down at his hand resting against my arm. "You should take off the ring."

"Never." He pulled out my ponytail holder, ran both hands through my hair, and tied my hair back up before kissing me. "I love you." He reached between us, fishing for the chain around my neck. He held the two bound rings and heart-shaped charm in his palm. "See, that's what it says right here in case you ever forget."

"I won't, just like I won't forget you took off my top for the entire world to see."

Martin smirked, sitting up while I clung to his chest to keep myself covered. He slipped his shirt off and wrapped it around me. "Better?"

"You could have done that first."

"True, but it wouldn't have been as much fun."

THIRTY-THREE

Leaving Martin's beach house was hard. For those five days, we were untouchable. Life was perfect. At least, I pretended it was.

Renner sent daily e-mail updates. Easton was safe. The BFI and PD were reopening old cases. The chemical compound popped up at several other fires. We no longer referred to it as sealant. It was an oxidizing agent. Only trace amounts remained, but we knew it was custom made by the arsonist. If we could track the substance, we'd find him.

Chef York remained MIA. Strader and Bisset were under constant police surveillance, though Strader claimed it was harassment and threatened to sue the city. But, given the circumstances, the police didn't back down.

No additional attempts had been made on Easton's life since he remained in utter seclusion at one of Cross Security's safe houses. However, tomorrow, he planned a second soft launch of Easton's Eats. It would be his first public appearance since the fire at his house, and given the social media shoutouts and posts, people knew the food truck's second voyage would be happening tomorrow. The police and Cross Security would be on high alert. The fire department knew to standby. Maybe this would flush out the arsonist, but I had my doubts.

Martin's jet touched down, my fingers leaving permanent indentions in the armrest. The relaxed, vacation vibe of his beach house and our perfect romantic getaway already a distant memory. I'd been a ball of nerves since we packed last night. I hadn't slept. I couldn't eat. The familiar unsettling feeling had crept into my psyche, warning me of impending danger. I tried to write it off as pre-flight jitters, but I knew better.

"Can we stop by my apartment before we go home to make sure the movers didn't miss anything," I asked. I knew they didn't, but so much had changed. I needed a minute to say goodbye to my old life.

"You heard the lady," Martin said to Marcal who helped load our luggage into the trunk. Martin opened the back door and waited for me to get inside before shutting the door and going around to the other side. "I've been meaning to ask, what are we calling one another?"

I gave him a confused look. "Most of the things I call you aren't very nice to say in front of other people."

"Alex, I'm serious. Girlfriend doesn't fit anymore. And given our professions, partner has other connotations. Life partner just sounds—"

"Cringe-worthy?"

"Yeah." He licked his lips, his eyes darting to the glistening diamond hanging around my neck and the plain silver-colored band. "I'm not a fool. I know our little private beach ceremony didn't mean much to you, but it meant the world to me. I loved every second of it. I'm hoping this means you'll give me the chance to prove to you we can handle more. I do want to marry you one day. So," he fidgeted, "can we go with fiancée since you're wearing my ring?"

"You just want to see how far you can push me before I jump out of a moving vehicle."

"No, I ..."

"It's okay," I smiled, "but the first person who asks me when the wedding is might get shot."

He laughed uneasily, probably unsure if I was joking.

Marcal watched us from the rearview mirror; I saw the words form in his mind. Martin's valet was ballsy enough to ask. Though, my firearm was safely out of reach in the trunk. The laughter that followed calmed my nerves, temporarily erasing my fears of the days to come.

Giving in to the exhaustion and adrenaline crash, I sunk onto the back seat. My head rested against Martin's shoulder as we rode toward home. Technically, the apartment was no longer mine. It was after the first of the month, but since I'd had it for so long, the landlord gave me a two week grace period to move out. He probably just wanted to make sure I had plenty of time to pack my things and go. The only place I wanted to go more desperately than my apartment was the office, but it was late. Everyone would be at home or with Easton at the safe house, and I didn't know the location. Work would have to wait until the morning.

Martin's phone let out a nonstop string of beeps as soon as he flipped it off airplane mode. Obviously, one of us needed to get a jump on things. He sighed, clicking as he replied to messages. Our five day break from the real world meant we had to face the consequences. Fortunately, with work and Martin's sleep patterns back to normal, I'd have plenty of time to dedicate to Easton's case.

The car slowed, and I looked out the window. We were three blocks from my apartment building. Traffic inched forward, and when the city bus turned at the next intersection, I saw the flashing lights ahead. Three fire trucks and several ambulances were parked in front of my apartment. *Not my apartment*, my internal voice muttered. Police cars blocked off the street, and traffic cops in neon yellow vests armed with flashlights redirected traffic.

Without thinking, I opened the car door and stepped onto the sidewalk. I didn't see the smoke at first, but I smelled it. My legs moved on autopilot, slowly at first, and then faster. I ran toward my home, my apartment, watching in horror as two firefighters carried one of my neighbors out the front door.

"Alex," Martin yelled after me.

I looked up, seeing the smoke for the first time. The ladder extended up the side of the building, and I watched men in full turnout gear climb the rungs and enter through a window. Others remained on the ground and the stairs, helping people down the fire escape. A few moments later, they pulled someone out. I couldn't see who.

"Stay back," a cop said when I pushed against the barrier.

"What happened?"

"There's a fire."

"No shit. What caused it? What...when?"

"Do you live here?"

I nodded. "Sixth floor."

"Is anyone else at home?" the officer asked, one hand already on his radio.

"No. The apartment should be empty. I was moving out. I moved out." I gave him my apartment number, and he relayed the information to the fire chief standing behind him. "Is it arson?"

"Alex," Martin jogged up beside me, the flashing lights painting his skin in strange hues, "is everyone okay?" He looked at the cop. "Has anyone been hurt?"

"Sir, the fire department is doing the best they can. Do you live here?"

"No." Martin brushed the back of his hand against mine, letting me know he was here.

"Then I need you to move along." The cop zeroed in on me. "The fire department may have some more questions about your apartment and neighbors. Wait over here." He moved one side of the barrier back so I could slip through.

"Alex, I'm not leaving you," Martin said.

The cop gave him another glance. "Who are you?"

"James Martin, this is my fiancée, Alex. We just got back from vacation and wanted to make sure the movers didn't miss anything."

"All right, Mr. Martin," he jerked his chin at the opening, "you too."

I waited in the designated area, dialing as I bounced from foot to foot. This wasn't an accident. First, I called Lt. Payne. He didn't answer. Next, I called Renner. Again, nothing. My third call connected.

"Voletek," I said, my voice breathy as I watched a chunk of the roof collapse, "my apartment's on fire."

"What?"

I gave him the address. I didn't have any facts or details, but he needed to know. This was his case, or it had been before I flew across the country and pretended everything would be in one piece when I came home. Now, I didn't know whose case it was or what was going on.

"Ms. Parker? Mr. Martin?" A gentleman in turnout gear approached. Since he wasn't covered in soot, I didn't think he'd been inside, and from the insignia he wore, I figured he must be in charge. He earned the right not to run into a burning building unless the situation absolutely required it.

"Yes." I couldn't even manage a grim smile as I watched another stretcher get loaded into an ambulance. Was that Tara, the elderly woman who lived on the fifth floor directly beneath me? I peered around the man, catching a glimpse of charred flesh on her lower leg. The sudden stench of roasted human flesh twisted my stomach, and the horror made my knees buckle. Martin steadied me, and I tried not to heave, which turned out to be a losing battle. But on an empty stomach, nothing came out. I wiped my eyes with the back of my hand. "Sorry." I focused on the fire chief and told him everything about the case we were investigating.

"Hang on a sec." He clicked his radio. "Payne, meet me at the front." The chief looked back at me. "Are you okay, ma'am?"

"Don't ask me that. Ask them." I watched as a child was carried out of the building. From the radio chatter, it sounded like the building had been cleared. "The fire might be feeding off an oxidizing agent. It's taken down a lot of other buildings."

Lt. Ted Payne rounded the corner of one of the trucks, shocked to see me. "Ms. Parker?"

"Good, you two know one another. She's been talking about an arson case and oxidizing agents." The chief waited for Payne to corroborate or possibly elaborate. After listening to the best way to address the threat, the chief stepped away, barking orders to the men fighting the blaze. Now that they knew exactly what they were dealing with, they had more effective ways of extinguishing the fire.

"What are you doing here?" Payne asked. He glanced uncertainly at Martin but didn't inquire.

"I live here. Lived here."

"Shit, when we did an occupant check, I heard someone say Alexis Parker, I just thought it might be a different Alexis Parker."

"No, same one." A horrifying thought sprang to mind. "Martin, our apartment."

Martin looked uncertain to leave me, but I was much steadier now than I had been. "I'll make a few calls. I'll be right over there." He stepped away, edging closer to the barrier to give us some space.

"What's going on?" Payne asked. "I thought this was your apartment."

"It is. Was. I moved out two weeks ago." I thought about the recent fire in our apartment and the safety check the fire department performed. Was this bad luck, or did the arsonist target me? "What do we know about the fire?"

"Right now, nothing."

"What the hell are you doing here?"

"Me and my team have been reporting to every call in case it's related."

"Before I left, you didn't believe the fire at Sizzle was arson."

"I said we didn't have proof, and since that day, Dil's done nothing but twist my arm. When Lucien Cross stepped in and the police got involved, we gave everything a second look. We won't let this clever bastard trick us again. Even accidental fires are being assessed. We have to find this guy. I should have listened to you sooner. I'm sorry."

I watched another ambulance pull away. "What happens to my neighbors now?"

"Anyone injured will be treated. When they're released, they might stay with friends or family. If they have nowhere to go, we have a fund to help out. If it's not enough, churches, charities, and the Red Cross will step in and make sure the necessities are covered and everyone has a safe place to stay. After that, they'll either move back in or find a new place to live." Another chunk of the roof collapsed, sending a cloud of dust into the smoky air.

"Our apartment's okay," Martin said quietly. He looked around, the devastating scene leaving a guilty taste in his mouth.

"Call Lucien. Tell him what's going on," I said. "I'll speak to him as soon as I'm done here."

Payne interrupted. "Get out of here. There's nothing you can do. Sometimes, these firebugs hang around the scene. The police have been taking names. You might be able to help the PD identify suspects, assuming you have a list."

"But..." I stared at the burning building, my heart breaking.

More radio chatter sounded, and the chief tapped Payne on the shoulder. "The fire's almost out."

Payne nodded. "I'll be there in a second." He gave me an encouraging look. "Go do what you're good at. I'll do what I'm good at, and we'll meet first thing in the morning and share our findings."

"What are you going to do?"

"We have to make sure the building is structurally sound and perform a search and recovery. I'll find the point of origin, determine the cause, and see if our firebug had anything to do with this. Sometimes, fires are just fires."

But that didn't make them any less devastating. I trudged back behind the line, taking the phone Martin held out. "Lucien, what the hell's going on?"

"Look, if there's anything you need, just say the word."

I recognized so many faces huddled on the sidewalk. The man I smiled at when we bumped into each other on the stairs. The mother with the twins who always dropped her mail. The grumpy cat lady who hissed every time I was too loud in the corridors. I didn't know them by name, or even very well, but we shared a home. I had to do something to help them.

"I don't, but a lot of people around here do."

"Yeah, of course. I'll do what I can. I've already dispatched some lab techs and two security teams to your other apartment and a team to Martin's house."

"Thanks."

"We'll find this bastard, Alex."

"I don't doubt that." I blew out a breath, unsure where to go from here when there were so many things I needed to do. "Where's Renner? Is he okay?"

"He's with Chef Easton and a security team. They're safe. We have jammers in place, but if you need to speak to him, I can redirect your call to the landline at the safe house."

"No, that won't be necessary, but–"

"Trust me. I'll make sure he's safe and so is his place."

We disconnected, and I handed Martin the phone. While I had been speaking to Payne, Martin sent Marcal to the nearest store to get whatever he could find. Marcal arrived with the town car loaded with bottled water, protein bars, snacks, and whatever towels, blankets, and clothing they had.

While Martin and Marcal unloaded the car, letting my neighbors grab whatever they needed, the delivery guy from the nearby deli came to help. He had thermoses, cups, trays of sandwiches, and bowls of soup. It didn't matter this was a big city, we took care of our own. Most of my neighbors had already sought refuge inside the deli, and now that the owner and the delivery guys extended the invitation, more departed for the temporary shelter.

We left a few cases of water and sports drinks for the first responders. Two police officers followed behind the group, figuring questioning the residents in an enclosed, safe environment would help.

"Am I free to go?" I asked.

The cop I spoke to earlier nodded. "We have your name, number, and address. Since the fire department's done with you, you're free to go. I am sorry." He jerked his chin at the building.

"That's life." And it sucked.

THIRTY-FOUR

"The test came back positive on your apartment building, the one you share with James." Lucien cleared his throat, a sign he was uncomfortable.

"What about the house?"

"That's the good news. No suspicious chemical compounds were identified, but I took the liberty of having my specialists review James' security logs and feeds. Given what we know, you should take every precaution."

"The construction crew?" I'd nearly forgotten Martin remodeled and had the walls repaired. It would have been the perfect opportunity for someone to spray the oxidizing agent all over the place or burn down his house, especially when we'd been staying at the apartment for the last few months. "What about them?"

"It's okay." My boss offered a reassuring smile. "It's a completely different crew than the men Haskell suspects. I ran background checks on each of them and checked the materials they used. It's safe. The arsonist hasn't been there."

"But our apartment. My apartment." I paced Cross's spacious office. "He burned down my apartment building, and he plans to do it again." Images of Tara's burns came to mind, and I fought back the tears. "It can't be a coincidence."

"Property records show your name on the lease. That's probably how he found you. You must have crossed paths with him." Cross steepled his fingers and tapped them against his chin. "How much more convincing do you need before you admit it's Galen Strader or Dante Bisset?"

"It doesn't make sense," I screamed.

"Alex," Cross said calmly, "you confronted both of them. You sat in on their interrogations. They aren't stupid. They know Easton hired you to protect him, and you foiled their break-in and had them arrested. This is about revenge."

"The police haven't let them out of their sight."

"Then maybe they sent someone else to do the dirty work."

"Unless it's Asher York." The chef remained missing. The police figured he skipped town, but maybe he was just good at hiding. "According to building security at Martin's apartment," at the moment, that was the easiest way to refer to it, "York catered an event for the Ellington's. He's the only familiar name I saw on the guest list. Strader and Bisset haven't been anywhere near Martin's apartment."

"York." Lucien nodded several times. "Okay, I'll bite. He's a possibility, but the piece of plastic found in the lock at Sizzle is the same type of polymer Strader uses in his printer."

"It's commercial-grade. Anyone could buy that, just like the frickin' lard."

"I suppose. But how many people do you know with a 3D printer?"

"Don't your techs have one?"

Cross glared at me. "I didn't burn down Sizzle or your apartment."

"I know. You weren't on the list." But come to think of it, Cross had been to my apartment, knew when I'd be returning home, and probably could have altered the investigation from the get-go. Shaking it off, I knew Cross wasn't responsible. Logic like that was dangerous. That's how he arrived at the foregone conclusion Strader was to blame. I wasn't about to make the same mistakes he did. I rubbed my eyes. "Is there any way of determining when the oxidizing agent was sprayed in Martin's apartment building?"

Cross shoved the paperwork across his desk. "It's stable. The mixture of chemicals act like a preservative, preventing it from degrading. It could have been sprayed earlier tonight or years ago."

"I wish the fire inspectors had known to check when they reported to the toaster oven fire a few weeks ago."

"Where was that?"

"Fourteenth floor."

He snatched the file away, even though I was standing over it, reading. "Which apartment?"

"1408."

"Like the movie?"

"That's the only reason I remembered."

Cross's lips moved as he silently read the words on the page. "We found the oxidizing agent concentrated on the fourteenth floor, all around the crown molding and along the baseboards. The techs found smaller quantities on several other floors, but the largest amount was near 1408."

"So that fire wasn't an accident either?" My mind was blown. "But wait, that would mean the arsonist had been inside the apartment right before the fire broke out, or the guy who lives there is the arsonist and nearly cooked himself." Except those theories felt wrong.

Lucien reached for the keyboard and typed in the owner's name. "Does he look familiar? Did he pop up in any of the research you've done for Easton?"

I moved behind Lucien's desk, the first time I ever stepped behind the curtain. "No."

"Okay." He picked up the phone and asked the computer techs to check the footage for the date of the fire.

"How do you have access to that?" The reason I moved to that building was because of the top of the line security, but if Cross could hack it, it couldn't be that secure.

"Would you prefer if I wait for the police to come through with their court order?"

"No, I'd prefer if you answer the question." A photo near

the computer caught my attention, and I looked at the tiny frame. It was a picture of the busty redhead from Vegas. Her hair was shorter than it had been, so the photo couldn't be recent.

"James asked them to provide me with access. They respect my reputation and know whatever I discover will not be fodder for the press."

"I'm surprised they fulfilled his request."

"You'll be hard-pressed to find more than a handful of people in this city unwilling to fulfill James Martin's requests."

I found that hard to believe, but I didn't say anything. Instead, I went back to pacing. Right now, the police were questioning the apartment manager and staff. Professional crews were testing and cleaning the building. One fire nearly took down a building. I wouldn't let it happen again. Staring out the window, I wondered how many other places the arsonist targeted. How was he getting in to deliver the chemical compound?

"Until now, the attacks didn't appear personal, with the exception of Chef Easton. The fires were about damage, not inflicting injury. But with Easton, it could have easily escalated to murder."

"What about tonight?" I swallowed. No one called yet, but Payne said the firefighters performed a search and recovery. They thought the building was clear, but during the second walkthrough, who knew what they would find. And that didn't include the number of victims carted off to the hospitals. I'd seen enough TV shows to know people in fires didn't always make it. Smoke was deadly. Burns were deadly. Honestly, I couldn't imagine a worse way to go. And I'd had some pretty nasty close calls, but fire was different. It might have been the thing that scared me the most. It had to be the most painful, the most devastating, and the most frightening. I shivered. "Why haven't we figured this out yet? We're supposed to be the best fucking investigators in the city. What's wrong with us?"

"We didn't know," Lucien glanced up at me, "and the police aren't helping."

I swear if another disparaging comment came out of his

mouth, I'd slap him. "Who's the woman in the photo? The one I saw you with in Vegas? The one with the tattoo?"

"I don't see how this is the time."

I shook my head. It wasn't, but I needed to shift my focus and give my subconscious a moment to catch up. "I want to know."

"It's not your concern."

"Is she local? Did you take her on vacation?"

"I wasn't on vacation. I was pursuing new partnerships. It was a business trip."

I took a seat across from him and reached for a notepad and pen and began doodling in the corner. "Did you take her with you?"

"No."

"So she lives there?"

"What does it matter?"

"Her tattoo," I pointed at him with the pen, "when I got shot, you told me you could recommend a good tattoo artist to cover up the scar." I stopped. "What happened to her?"

Lucien's look could have killed. "We are not discussing this now."

And that's when brilliance struck. "Shit. The arsonist came to Martin's apartment building after the fire, not before."

"You're sure?"

"It's the only reason the building's still standing."

Despite Cross's sour expression, I knew he agreed. Reaching for the stack of files, I had a hunch. If I was right, this case was about to become even more unsettling. A firefighter set the fires. They were the only people with access and knowhow who knew I was investigating on Easton Lango's behalf.

THIRTY-FIVE

"Alex?" Voletek knocked on my open door. During normal office hours, someone from reception would have escorted him, but it was the middle of the night and Cross Security was operating on a skeleton crew since he had teams and investigators scouring the city for evidence. "I just came from the apartment fire. I'm so sorry. Are you okay?"

"Fine." I remained hunched over my computer screen. Martin stood and stretched, nearly causing Voletek to jump out of his skin. Voletek's hand moved half an inch for his gun before realizing Martin didn't present a threat. I ignored the detective and focused on Martin, who'd only drifted off a few minutes ago. "Go home, handsome. It's late." Earlier, I wasted twenty minutes trying to convince him to stay with Mark Jablonsky or the O'Connells, but he wouldn't budge.

"I'm heading to my office since you have work to do. I'll take a page out of your book and catch a catnap before Luc shows up." Martin rubbed his eyes. Remembering his manners, he held out his hand. "James Martin."

"Jake Voletek, homicide."

"Nice to meet you, Detective."

I slid out from behind the desk, and Martin hugged me.

Normally, he wouldn't kiss me on the mouth in front of people we just met, especially at work, but tonight wasn't a normal night. Or maybe he called Nick, and O'Connell warned Martin to mark his territory.

"Call me at lunch and let me know you're safe," he whispered in my ear. "And get some sleep."

"You got it."

Martin nodded at the detective and left the office.

"Do you guys need a place to stay?" Voletek asked, hovering near the doorway.

I shook my head and scooted my chair to the side to make room behind my desk. "Let me catch you up."

"There's more?"

"Isn't there always?" I patted the empty client chair and told Voletek what I suspected. "Aside from residents and authorized personnel, the only people who've been inside Martin's apartment building were the firefighters responding to the fire."

"And since the entire place didn't go up in a puff of smoke, you're guessing the accelerant wasn't there until after the fire."

"Right."

Voletek picked up the list of names of the managerial staff, building maintenance, cleaning crews, workers, and the list of residents and their approved guests. "What about deliveries?"

"They get left in the lobby."

Voletek ran his finger down one column and up the next, stopping on the name I highlighted. "Asher York? Is it the same Asher York?"

"Yeah, the Ellington's hired the chef for the night to cater their daughter's engagement party. Apparently, they liked his baked Alaska. For the record, it is pretty damn tasty."

Voletek narrowed his eyes at my computer screen. "Is that a live feed?"

"No, it's footage from the night of the toaster oven fire. Evacuations went off without a hitch. No one doubled-back. As far as I can tell, no one ever poured or sprayed anything around the molding or on the floors during the evacuation." We watched men in turnout gear knock on each of the doors. They didn't linger. They performed their duties. I paused the feed from the fourteenth floor hallway when the camera angle suddenly jutted upward. "What the hell?" Someone intentionally tampered with the camera.

Now, we could only see the tops of a few fire helmets, but not much else. I rewound, hoping to figure out what hit the camera. Several of the firefighters carried tools of their trade, but nothing looked high enough to have accidentally bumped it. Writing down the timestamp, I sent a note upstairs and asked the techs to see if they could determine what happened to the feed.

"That fits your theory that a firefighter's responsible for setting the fires," Voletek rubbed a hand over his mouth, "but that's a serious allegation and this is circumstantial."

"Just like everything else." I pushed back, letting the detective have free rein over the mouse and the next three weeks' worth of security footage. I had only scratched the surface. Remaining motionless would cause my brain to combust, so I climbed out of the chair and paced behind the desk, keeping one eye on the monitor. "The arsonist knows I'm on to him. My name's been on tons of request forms that have circulated throughout the BFI and trickled down through the rest of the fire department. Given the givens, I can't shake this thought or rule anyone out."

"But the toaster oven fire occurred prior to you taking Easton's case. Whoever did this must be targeting a ton of buildings in the city, not just yours." Voletek rubbed a hand down his face. "We have to stop this guy." The compromised camera ruined our chances of IDing the culprit when he doused the fourteenth floor, so Voletek gave up and clicked to a different floor. "The accelerant was found in other parts of the building. Let's figure out how it got there."

"We don't know since we have no basis for knowing how long it's been there. Our best bet is the fourteenth floor because we have a useable timeline." Either one of the city's bravest was the arsonist, or the bastard happened to live in the same building I did. Neither option held much appeal, but I didn't see any other alternatives, except our missing chef. "York catered two days after the fire. He could have done it, if he found a way to sneak around the cameras. He had the access, but why did someone knock out this camera that night unless they were dousing the floor with the oxidizing agent and planning a bonfire?"

"When did the camera angle get corrected?" Voletek clicked to the next day, but the angle had returned to normal.

"Security fixed it mid-afternoon." Cross had made a note, though I hadn't watched that far.

"Okay, so based on the facts in evidence, the arsonist has a beef with Chef Easton, and now he's picking a fight with you." Voletek glanced at me. "I have to ask. Do the two of you have anyone or anything in common?"

"I never even heard of Easton Lango prior to the maiden voyage of Easton's Eats." Martin knew the chef by reputation, but Martin knew a lot of people by reputation. That didn't mean a damn thing. "I guess we have Easton's ex in common since she has a connection to Cross Security, but I only met her once."

"After you started investigating?"

"Yes."

"Who else have you confronted on Easton's behalf?"

"Confronted?" I laughed. "Easton's ex and Dante Bisset."

Voletek didn't believe me. "Let me ask this a different way. Who have you spoken to since taking Easton's case?"

I ticked off Bouillon's staff, though the only one I spoke to directly aside from Chef Strader was Bryan the dishwasher. I even offered up the names of the stores, clerks, and city officials we'd spoken to about the fires. My mind circling back around the same conclusion I reached while in Lucien's office. Our arsonist was a firefighter.

"Asher York would have every reason to target you, and given his feud with Easton and his sudden disappearance, he makes the most sense."

"How would York know where I lived or anything about me?"

"He could look it up."

"I don't know. He's not trained to think like that, but

cops, firefighters, private investigators, we think like that. Plus, since he found the apartment I share with my boyfriend, why would he check to see if I had my own place? That's redundant."

"You know what his attorney would say to that?" Voletek asked.

"I'm speculating."

He made a finger pistol and pointed it at me. "Bingo."

"Did you ever confront Strader about the plastic piece you found in the lock?"

"He said he didn't do it. I don't know what to believe, but we checked his computer data and the techs scoured his print history. They didn't find a key, but he had the means, motive, and opportunity. Even the lard in Sizzle's vent matched the exact same brand and consistency as the lard at Bouillon."

"What about Bisset?"

Voletek shook his head.

"Did you question his aunt again?"

"She admitted her nephew has the occasional tantrum. She called him sensitive. It's why he gets depressed and reclusive, according to her. The case against Dante Bisset and Galen Strader is solid for the breaking and entering, stalking, and harassment, but that's it. I have officers sitting on their locations. Neither of them was anywhere near your apartment building when the fire started. Honestly, I wouldn't put it past any of these chefs to have done it, but it doesn't seem likely. We need to find York. We need to question him." Voletek turned back to the footage and picked another location where we found concentrated amounts of the compound on the twenty-seventh floor, set the speed to sixteen times, and stared at the screen as the footage played.

"Whoa, stop right there." I braced myself against the desk and leaned closer.

"Do you recognize him?" the detective asked.

"Isn't that Lt. Payne?"

"Who?"

"Ted Payne, BFI's arson investigator."

Voletek squinted at the screen. "I think you're right."

Payne stood alone in the hallway, his back to the screen. He had something in his hand, though I couldn't tell what it was. Voletek hit resume, setting the speed to half normal, and we watched Payne crouch down, running something along the seam of the door which tested positive for the chemical compound. He moved in a duck-walk, stopping beneath the sealed fire hose box. He stood, unlocking and checking the inside before resetting the box and wiping off the outside with a rag. By the time he turned around, whatever had been in his hand had disappeared into his pocket. "That's definitely Payne. Did he mention anything to you about this?"

"No."

"Okay, let's not jump to conclusions. He's probably just doing his job."

"He's an arson investigator. Why is he doing an inspection?" I ran through our interactions, wondering if there had been any clues I missed. Payne didn't seem the type, but he also told me the fire at Sizzle wasn't arson. He gave me examples of other fires that weren't arson, but in the last two weeks, we'd proven him wrong on nearly half of them. Could he have been using his position to cover his tracks all along?

"I don't know. Short-staffed. Budget cuts. Things happen, Alex."

"Do you really believe that?" I challenged.

We checked the rest of the footage from the other cameras. We saw several white shirts from the fire department performing the inspection and a few still in turnout gear walking the hallways, but Payne was the only man we spotted at several of the locations where the substance was found, with one glaringly obvious exception—the fourteenth floor.

"When I bring him in for questioning," there was no if about it, "I'll ask if he performed a check of the fourteenth floor. We'll take it from there." Voletek went back to the footage from the twenty-seventh floor, but aside from the night of the fire, nothing odd happened in Martin's apartment building. "I'll have to bring in the building's cleaning staff. They routinely vacuum the hallways and spray down the trim in the halls to get rid of dust and prints. Anything could be in those cleaning solutions. Maybe we have it wrong." Voletek pointed to the footage from four days ago, showing a janitor wiping down the baseboards. He flipped to other floors, showing the same man working his way up the building, doing nothing but wiping the baseboards and trim. "He could be our arsonist."

I zoomed in on his name tag and found him on the list. Minimizing the feed, I opened the window where Cross had already saved the background checks. "No criminal record. In decent financial shape. Has only lived in the area for the last two months." I stopped reading. "Explain to me how he set fire to Sizzle from Quebec." I clicked another key, pulling up the man's passport information. "He wasn't in the country, unless you think he snuck across the border."

"Alex, I'm not your enemy. I'm here to help."

"Then help me. Some bastard burned down my apartment." The blood drained from my face as I recalled Payne's words from earlier tonight. "What if it's Payne? He had the audacity to show up at my apartment tonight. He said the BFI was sending investigators to every fire in case the arsonist struck again, but maybe he wanted to watch. He even said it was common for serial arsonists."

"It's common for most criminals to return to the scene of the crime, but with pyromaniacs, they get off on watching the flames. That's why police officers take names and a few wide shots."

"I need to see that list and whatever footage they've taken from the fire."

"It's being compiled. I'll get a call when it's ready to go." Voletek reached for his phone. "But your theory warrants investigating. It might not be Payne, but it could be someone else in the BFI or one of the other firefighters. I'll request a list of the firefighters who responded to the toaster oven fire and the ones who were at your apartment tonight. I'll flag any matches and work backward. We already have the names from those who put the fire out at Sizzle. If the arsonist is one of the city's bravest, we'll identify him. He won't be able to hide from us. He's recognizable. People will have seen him. The men in his chain of command will know where he was. In the meantime," Voletek tugged the folder clear from beneath the drink carrier which contained the coffees he brought for us that remained untouched, "this is all the PD's dug up on Asher York. Maybe you could take a look and work some of your P.I. mojo and find this prick."

"Cross has been trying, but I'll give it a whirl."

THIRTY-SIX

"I heard what happened. Did anyone you know get hurt?" Renner asked. It was just after seven.

"I don't know." I'd been afraid to call the hospital or check the news.

"What can I do to help?" Renner took a seat beside me, glancing back at the cluttered desk and two coffee cups. "Are you double-fisting the caffeine now?"

"No, Voletek's been here since four. We've been going over leads. He just stepped out to take a call."

"Lucien must love that."

"He doesn't care. We need to find Asher York. Where's Easton?"

"He's in my office."

I stood a little unsteadily and blinked. A migraine was coming on. Too much caffeine, not enough sleep, and no food. I needed to eat. "Can you ask him to meet me in the break room?"

"Sure thing."

I opened the pantry and fridge. Cross kept the kitchen stocked with hot beverages, fresh fruit, and various snacks — things we could offer clients or eat when working late. Finding a fresh basket of baked goods from the local café on the counter, I grabbed a croissant and an apple and sat at the table. By the time Easton stepped in, there was nothing left but crumbs.

"Want some breakfast?" I asked, crossing to the basket and grabbing a second croissant before searching the cabinets for hazelnut spread.

Easton looked disgusted and perplexed, but he was polite enough not to voice his opinion as he watched me squeeze the packet onto the croissant and practically swallow it whole. Admittedly, it wasn't my finest hour. "Are you okay?"

Wiping my mouth, I slid my notepad across to him. "We have to find Asher York. After he was released on bail, he fell off the grid." Renner had already questioned Easton about his rival, but it wouldn't hurt to do it again. "He hasn't used his credit card. He hasn't reported to work. His neighbors thought they saw him pack a bag, but most of his belongings are still inside his apartment. You know him. Where would he go? Where does he like to hang out?"

"Did he take his car?" Easton asked.

I shook my head. "It's parked in his reserved space."

"Well, it's Asher." Easton glanced back at Renner. "I said you should check the bars. But since it's been two weeks, maybe the dumpsters or skid row."

"You think he's on a bender?" No one mentioned this as a possibility.

"He's an alcoholic. The only thing he wants more than being inside a kitchen is getting a drink. Most of the time, he finds a way to do both."

"We already checked the bars and clubs he frequents. No one's seen him. The police canvassed all the places that serve liquor near his apartment and Delicious. Nothing. We even checked the liquor stores and quickie marts." Renner grabbed a cherry Danish and took a bite. "We checked with his staff and the few friends and family we could find. No one's seen him, and no one knows where he is."

"Do you think he would hurt himself?" I asked Easton.

"Not intentionally, I don't think." Easton rubbed a hand through the blue and silver, though the dye had dulled since I'd seen him last. "I don't really know. We exchanged barbs. I used to think they were friendly, but y'know, shit happens. People go crazy and burn down other people's restaurants. After that, nothing's very friendly."

"Tell me about it." I gave the basket of pastries another look, deciding going from a sugar crash to a sugar high was a bad move. Where would a drinker go if he wasn't drinking? Rehab. I pushed away from the table. "Have we checked hospitals and rehab centers?"

"Hospitals, yes. Rehab, no." Renner eyed me curiously. "You think he checked himself in?"

"I think we should find out."

It took several phone calls and various creative lies, but by nine a.m., I found Asher York. The day after he was released from police custody, he checked himself in to one of the top rehab facilities in the city. The kind that didn't accept insurance and would never publicize which A-list stars they currently housed. Unfortunately, if they took their patients' privacy a little less seriously, they could have saved my colleagues weeks of searching and speculating.

"I can't discuss a patient's progress with anyone he hasn't personally authorized," the receptionist said.

"I understand that. This is about his court date."

"You said you're his lawyer?"

"No, I work with his law firm. I'm a legal secretary." I mumbled a name. "We just need to verify his whereabouts before we send over the affidavit. The judge will only allow a continuance if it's for documented medical reasons." Let's hope Cross's lawyers could keep me out of prison for this.

"Ma'am, Asher York hasn't left the facility since he checked in."

"Can you prove it?"

"His room is locked at night. The staff would have noticed if he left during the day."

"Do you have security cameras?"

"This isn't a prison."

The problem with lying was it made explaining why you needed answers and the truth that much harder. I exhaled and rubbed the kink in my neck. "Of course it isn't, but addiction is a difficult disease to combat. You must have medications on the premises that have to be locked up, so there are cameras and security systems to guard them, right?"

"Yes," she responded, making the answer sound like a question, "and a few in the hallways."

"Great. Thanks." I hung up before she could inquire about my identity for the fourth time. My cover story and questions didn't pass her sniff test, but when confronted with legal terminology, even if inaccurate, most laypeople tended to err on the side of caution and divulge extra information.

Reaching for the phone, I dialed Cross's extension. He didn't answer, but Justin did. "I'll let him know you located Asher York."

"Tell him I'll let the police know they can call off the search." I hung up and started dialing again.

"What search?" a man asked from the doorway. I jumped, knocking over a stack of files in my haste to grab my nine millimeter. "Whoa, easy." Lt. Payne held up his palms.

"I'm sorry, Ms. Parker," the receptionist said from the corner of the doorway. "Mr. Renner told me to send him in."

I tucked the gun into my holster instead of leaving it in the top drawer, where it had been most of the night. Painting a smile on my face, I said, "That's fine. Can you tell Renner to call Jake?" She nodded. "Thank you."

Payne entered, dropping to his knees to help pick up the fallen papers. He sorted them into a neat stack and placed them back on my desk. "I don't blame you for being jumpy. If now's a bad time, I can make an appointment." He grinned as if it were an inside joke.

"Actually, I was just about to call the police to get an update and then check in with your office."

"No wonder my ears were burning." Payne picked some fuzz off my client chair and took a seat. "How are you holding up? Last night, you looked like you were about to kill someone."

"Jury's still out." I sized him up, wondering if he was fucking with me. "What can you tell me about the fire? Was it arson?" I eyed the folder tightly tucked beneath his arm. "Which apartment did you say was yours?" He already knew. It was a matter of public record.

"None of them. I just moved out."

"So your apartment would have been empty."

I stared at him. This was a man I originally thought of as an ally, but now I wondered if he wasn't just a wolf in sheep's clothing. These questions might be a game. A taunt. Did he know I was on to him? "As far as I know. I haven't taken inventory, but I've been told the movers were thorough. Before you ask, I do have an alibi. I've been out of town for almost two weeks. I just got back last night. I was on my way to the apartment to make sure nothing had been left behind when I saw the fire engines."

"Thank you, but I don't believe you're a suspect."

"So it was arson."

He nodded, opening the folder and pushing it across to me. "It's the same man who's been torching the city. We found trace amounts of what remained of the oxidizing agent sprayed across the hardwood floor. The fire originated in your apartment. Again, it was meant to look like an electrical fire. The point of origin was the wire behind your refrigerator." He removed a photo from the folder and placed it on the desk between us.

I stared, numb. I didn't know if it hurt me to look at it, but I knew I shouldn't hurt for myself. I should hurt for the other people who lived in that building, who lost their homes, their possessions, and maybe even their lives because I pissed off some asshole with a fire fetish. But I didn't feel remorse. I didn't feel anything but anger.

Payne pulled another photograph out, showing an obvious trail across the kitchen floor and into the living room. "Basically, the fire would have been contained to these areas. We didn't find the presence of oxidizing agents anywhere else in the building."

Memories of last night flooded my mind. "The roof collapsed, partially. Twice."

"That was from the venting. It happens a lot in fires."

"Why did it spread? Why didn't it remain here? There was nothing else inside my apartment to feed it. Why did the building burn?"

"It wasn't supposed to." Payne blinked. "It shouldn't have."

Those words sounded like a confession. It took every ounce of restraint not to lunge across the desk and strangle him where he sat. Surreptitiously, I hit the record button on the computer, activating the mic and webcam. Though the camera faced me, Payne's voice would register loud and clear. Now I just needed to get him to incriminate himself further. Either he didn't know we were on to him, or he wanted to gloat, just like last night.

"Why did it?" I asked. "How did the fire spread?"

"It was concentrated in this area. In the center of the room. It probably would have burned itself out, maybe taken out a good chunk of the floor and your downstairs neighbor's ceiling if left unattended, but the smoke detector and fire alarms should have alerted the fire department. Under different circumstances, it would have been extinguished before doing any real damage."

"How did it spread?" I repeated.

"Do you know the woman who lives below you?"

"Tara." I remembered the burns on her legs. The rest of her body had been covered when she was loaded into the ambulance. "She was burned. Is she...did she survive?"

"I'm sorry."

"You son of a bitch," I whispered, covering my mouth with my hand and hoping he didn't hear me. Idly, I wondered if I shot Payne if Cross would cover it up. He didn't like the police. He wouldn't want dozens of them lurking around in the offices. The techs upstairs must know a foolproof way to dispose of the remains. "How did this happen?"

"She was a hoarder. Did you know that?"

I shook my head. I'd never been inside her apartment. She always just seemed like a lonely, old lady. When I first moved into the building, I figured she was the ghost of my Christmas future. Now she was just a ghost. I hid my shaking hands in my lap.

"Newspapers. The *Times* and the *Post*. She must have had decades' worth of newspapers, piled from the floor to the ceiling. Literally. It acted like tinder. The whole place went up, and it spread quickly after that. By the time the fire department arrived, most of your neighbors had evacuated. A few were frozen by fear, hiding in the bathroom or under the bed, but we got them out. From the reports I read, aside from Tara, no one sustained any serious injuries. Only a few minor burns which were treated on scene. Three people were sent to the hospital for smoke inhalation, but their prognosis is good." Payne slipped the disturbing photographs back into the folder, and I wondered if he kept copies as trophies. "Do you have any idea who this bastard is?"

Was I crazy to think I might be looking right at him? "How do you know what kinds of newspapers she had?"

"What?"

"You said she had the *Times* and the *Post*. How do you know that if they burned?"

"We found burned up scraps throughout the fifth floor. We could read a few words here and there. Even some dates. That's when we realized how many thousands of papers must have been saved inside that woman's apartment."

"What about the toaster oven fire?"

He cocked his head to the side as if the question didn't compute. "What toaster oven? The fire started when the power cord on your fridge sparked, igniting what may have been leftover packing materials or a cardboard box, which then fed off the arsonist's custom chemical compound. There was no toaster oven in your apartment, Ms. Parker."

"Not my apartment." I leaned back, giving myself space in case I had to shoot him. With the way the conversation was heading, it seemed like a growing possibility. "How do you know so much about the cause of the fire and what must have been inside when everything's destroyed?"

"This is what I do. Remember, I gave you that crash course a few weeks ago, when we looked through other case files and did a walkthrough at Sizzle." He rocked forward, gazing intently into my eyes. "Are you okay? You weren't inside the apartment last night, were you?"

"No."

"Are you experiencing any headaches or dizziness?"

"Both but that's nothing unusual." He pulled a pen light from his shirt pocket, but I stood before he did something with it that we'd both regret. "The toaster oven I'm referring to was a fire inside a different apartment building three weeks ago."

He blinked a few times. "I'm sorry I don't recall a toaster oven. Do you have a case number?"

Before I could say a word, Renner and Voletek knocked on my door. "Hang on a second." I opened the door to find the homicide detective had come prepared with records from the fires in question.

Voletek jerked his chin into the hallway. "I need to talk to you alone."

"We located York," I said.

"This isn't about him." Voletek's gaze traveled to Payne, and I knew the detective had found something damning on the arson investigator.

I looked at Renner. "Keep an eye on him, and don't let him anywhere near a power outlet."

THIRTY-SEVEN

"Ted Payne isn't listed as responding to any of these fires. He didn't write any reports. He didn't sign any paperwork. There's no record of him reporting to the fire at your apartment last night or the one at your boyfriend's place three weeks ago. Though fire department personnel can place him at both scenes." Voletek stalked the enclosed space of the break room. We had locked the door to make sure we weren't interrupted. "I made some calls, pissed off my captain and half the brass at the fire department, but no one had anything bad to say about the lieutenant. If anything, they applaud the guy for his dedication."

"How do they explain his presence at these fires?"

"They wrote it off, figuring Payne might have popped in to help out. Apparently, he does that."

"How long has he been doing that?"

"Years."

"Don't they realize he could be our arsonist?"

"The man's saving them money and time. The BFI always has a backlog. Since Payne took over for Haskell, he's eliminated almost 75% of their old cases. The turnaround on new cases has gone from months to weeks. Instead of questioning why that is, they give the guy commendations for a job well done. Meanwhile, you and Haskell do some digging, and it turns out half the fires he wrote off as accidents were arson." Voletek swung his arms like he wanted to pop his back or was loosening up for a fight. "Payne could be using his position to cover his tracks or cover for the real arsonist. I think you're right about the plastic we found in the lock. It exonerates Bisset and probably Strader by association. And since York's been voluntarily locked up this entire time, it has to be a first responder or someone else you've pissed off." Voletek glanced out the blinds. "Has Payne said anything odd to you?"

"I just asked him about the toaster oven fire, but he acted like he didn't remember it."

"Let's show him some footage and see if it rings any bells. For the record, whatever you ask and he answers won't require me to notify him of his rights."

"I figured as much. I've been recording our interview. He's been skirting the edge, but it's not enough." I swallowed, images of last night's fire still fresh on my mind. "My downstairs neighbor died."

"I know." Voletek dug his hands into his back pockets, unsure what to do or say. "I'm sorry."

"So am I. The arsonist is the reason she's dead, but I was the catalyst." Damn, this might have been the healthiest I'd ever been. Until recently, I would have blamed myself for Tara's death. Now, I only felt tangentially responsible. Martin's counseling sessions must have been rubbing off on me through osmosis. "I'm going to get this bastard. Since he likes fire so much, I want to see him burn."

Voletek took a step back. "Has anyone ever told you you're scary as hell?"

"You haven't even seen me at my worst."

"I don't want to, but maybe you could pull a little of that out." He opened the door to the break room. "Payne might run into burning buildings for a living, but that's nothing compared to the two of us."

We showed Payne the feed from the twenty-seventh floor. He watched it without blinking an eye. "I remember now. You wouldn't believe how many calls we get in the middle of the night or how many calls we get about toaster ovens. Toaster ovens and curling irons, those are the two most common when it comes to small appliance fires."

"We found the arsonist's special sauce spread strategically throughout the apartment building," I said, failing to disclose it was my apartment building, the only one I had left. "Specifically in the area you're doing whatever it is you're doing."

"I was checking for carbon monoxide emissions," Payne said.

"Why? Shouldn't you have checked a fireplace or furnace, rather than beneath some guy's door?"

"It was an inspection. According to building records, he had a gas fireplace in his apartment. If it was leaking, low levels would have registered on the scanner." Payne looked perplexed.

Voletek took over, flipping to a feed of the fourteenth floor. "Based on the location of the fire and the amount of accelerant we found in the vicinity, we think the arsonist sprayed it after firefighters cleared the building. See this." He pointed to the screen. "Now watch what happens." The camera jolted upward, ruining our visual. "We were hoping you might have seen someone that night who didn't belong there."

"I don't remember much. I passed out orders and picked up the slack." Payne must have realized he was a suspect. "Why the sudden concern?"

"What about last night's fire? What did you do there?" Voletek asked.

"After the fire was out, I checked for signs of arson. The police have the reports, and I updated Ms. Parker."

"Did you see anyone suspicious last night?" Voletek had brought photos and bodycam footage from the uniformed officers on duty. He spread out an array of hard copies. "We looked but didn't notice any familiar faces. Do you? You're a constant at fires, and like you told Alex, since the police have opened an investigation into the arsonist, the BFI's been reporting to every fire. Maybe someone stands out. Maybe you remember crossing paths one too many times."

Payne studied the photos for a long time, longer than any witness ever had. "I don't know. I don't recall any familiar faces in the crowd."

"Look again," I said, "but this time, look at the men who were sent to put out the fires."

The lieutenant's eyes went wide. "You think a firefighter is responsible for this?"

"We've exhausted all other possibilities. The only people left who know about my investigation are firefighters. Whoever did this," I opened the file Payne had left on my desk and stabbed at the photo with my pointer finger, "targeted me. You said it yourself. Someone found my apartment and torched it."

"But you weren't inside. The arsonist probably found an empty apartment to stage the fire. How do you know this is about you? You told me last night you recently moved."

"Yeah, and my new apartment had to be evacuated because the arsonist doused the building in that same chemical cocktail." I glared at Payne. "But at least I can rest assured there are no carbon monoxide leaks."

His Adam's apple bobbed, and a few beads of sweat broke out on his forehead. "I can't imagine a firefighter would risk his life and the lives of his brothers by intentionally setting dangerous structure fires."

"Lives don't matter to this guy, at least not anymore. He broke from his MO," Voletek said. "With the exception of Chef Easton, no one's been present at any of these other fires. No one's ever been hurt until now. Last night, someone died. This isn't just arson. It's murder. He doesn't care. He'll keep killing unless we stop him. Unless you help us stop him."

"The men I work with, the men who run into burning buildings, they save lives. They don't take them. We don't start fires. We stop them. What part of that don't you understand? I don't believe anyone I work with is capable of doing something like this." But his expression said otherwise.

"What about you?" I asked.

Anger thundered into his words. "What about me?"

"What do you drive off duty?"

"A truck." Payne's gaze went from me to Voletek.

"What color?" Voletek asked. "Is it the dark silver SUV I saw parked in the visitor space at the end of the row?" Payne nodded. "Did you ever eat at Sizzle?"

"I'm not answering any more questions. I have work to do. I came here as a courtesy. We," Payne made a wide circle to include the detective and me, "have to work together to stop this guy. I don't know what this is, but I won't be railroaded." He glared at Voletek. "I'll be speaking to your commanding officer. We work for the city. We're on the same fucking team. It would serve you right to remember that, Detective, or you'll find yourself in a world of hurt the next time you need the fire department to clear away an accident or send EMTs to the scene of a shooting. God forbid what would happen if you needed us to put out a fire."

"The chances of that seem slim, unless you're the one who started it," Voletek retorted.

For a moment, I thought the homicide cop was crazy. Then I realized he wanted Payne to hit him. It'd be grounds to arrest him. As it stood, it'd be a tough sell to get an arrest warrant unless Payne crossed the line. It was a good thing Cross Security had no idea where the line even was.

Payne grabbed the file and stormed to the door. He spun, rather dramatically, to face me. "Ms. Parker, last night was traumatic. You're not thinking clearly. When you come to your senses, give me a call. I want to stop this guy as much as you do."

I slumped into the chair, seeing the mistakes we made with perfect twenty-twenty hindsight. Hitting the speaker button, I dialed Renner's extension. "Is Easton with you?"

"Yeah." Mumbling came from Renner's end, and I figured the chef must have been responding to my question too. "He's working on his shopping list for tonight. What do you want?"

"Fuck it." I pressed the button again. It'd be easier to go down the hall and ask in person if Easton recognized Payne.

Voletek collected the photos. "Alex, go home. Go to a

hotel. Go somewhere. Get some sleep. Get something to eat. Do something. Because right now, I'm still a little bit afraid of you."

"I'm not as scary as a fire since Payne didn't quake in his boots." I snorted. "How the hell did you ever become a homicide detective?"

"Nepotism."

"Normally, I'd say that makes you an asshole, but y'know what, good for you." Which meant I was at the point where I didn't give a rat's ass anymore. It was time to do something that mattered. "Show Easton the photos of the firemen you identified at the three different scenes. See if he recognizes any of them. If he does, ask if he knows a good recipe for preparing crow. In the unlikely event we're wrong about Payne, we'll be eating it soon enough." But I didn't think we were wrong. Payne was covering up the fires. I just had to prove it was intentional and not incompetence. The best way to do that would be to prove he had a vendetta against Chef Easton and me.

"Y'know, I might not be the best or the brightest, but I do know how to ask relevant questions," Voletek said as I waved him away.

I ran a background check on Ted Payne. He had an upside down mortgage that he was in the middle of correcting. He didn't have a wife or children. As far as I could tell, he was a bachelor, which meant he wouldn't have to account for his whereabouts to anyone.

After copying down his address, I went to his house, but he wasn't home. The truck Voletek had seen wasn't in the driveway. According to Payne, he had to work, so he shouldn't be back for hours.

I parked down the street and opened the trunk. It was summer, which made it difficult to conceal one's identity without sticking out like a sore thumb, but I'd rather look suspicious than be recognized. I slipped into an oversized hoodie, hid my hair underneath, tied a bandana around the lower portion of my face, and put on a pair of oversized sunglasses and leather gloves.

Payne had one of those stupid doorbell cameras, which was great at deterring thieves and porch pirates but not so great at keeping me out. I spotted it from the sidewalk and slipped around the back of the house. Either he didn't have an alarm system, or he was smart enough not to post the notices in his windows.

Hoping it was the former, I cut the screen, jimmied open the back window, and hoisted myself into his house. I remained completely still, scanning the area for signs of motion sensors or surveillance cameras. A fluffy pillow moved across the living room floor. I blinked, realizing the pillow was a cat, probably a Persian, with silky, snow white fur. It turned to look at me with its sharp green eyes, which reminded me a little of Martin. It let out an annoyed meow, letting me know it didn't appreciate the disturbance, and went into another room. That meant I didn't have to worry about motion sensors.

I looked around the kitchen. Payne kept his house just as neat and orderly as his office and his appearance. The living room and bedroom were clear, except for the occasional catnip mouse shoved under the bed or a few loose strings hanging from the edge of the rug.

Opening the closets, I didn't find any bulk chemical compounds. I closed the door and went across to the spare bedroom. Payne had converted it into an office. I skimmed the files on his desk. He had several copies of the cases I asked him to look into, but that didn't tell us anything. A contraption about the size of a small microwave sat in the middle of the attached workstation. For a moment, I didn't know what it was, and then I saw the name. It was a 3D printer.

I eyed it curiously, resisting the urge to touch anything. I didn't know enough about the technology, but its presence might link him to Sizzle. Maybe he printed the key Voletek found inside the lock.

I turned away from the desk. A card table sat in the corner of the room with little miniatures of the city. I picked up a tiny plastic building. That's why Payne had the printer. He was recreating the city. On a free standing corkboard behind the table were photographs of the skyline. It didn't look sinister, but when I flipped the board around, a pit formed in the center of my stomach.

Photos of each of the fires Cross Security had deemed arson were pinned across the cork. Beneath each one was a copy of the inspection certificate, including Sizzle's. From the printed dates on the copies, Payne had printed these before the two of us ever even crossed paths. It looked like a trophy board, but maybe he'd argue he was conducting his own investigation. This situation was so twisted, I wanted to scream.

I pulled out my phone and photographed the board. I checked beneath each photo and paper for notes or any other piece of evidence. Beneath Sizzle's inspection certificate, I found a receipt. It was dated four days before the fire. I snapped several shots, searching for a name or credit card number. The customer paid cash, but maybe the server would remember the guy. We needed Easton or one of his former staff to ID Payne. It was the only way we'd stop him.

I looked back at the model of the city. From the looks of it, he'd only recently gotten started. I couldn't find any of the burned down buildings. That could be a coincidence or intentional. Pocketing one of the smaller pieces near the end, figuring he might think his cat knocked it over should he realize it was missing, I left the same way I came in.

THIRTY-EIGHT

"He's been lying to our faces this entire time. He knew the fires were arson, and he has a fucking receipt from Sizzle. Don't tell me that's not enough." My emotions were getting the best of me, but I didn't care. "What did Easton say? Did he recognize Payne?"

Voletek shook his head.

"Get out of my way." I pushed past him and banged on Renner's office door. "Bennett?"

"They left," Voletek said. "Easton's prepping for tonight. A security team took him to the store, and then they're going to get his truck. Bennett had another issue to deal with."

"What could be more important than this?" All right, I heard it then. The crazed, sleep-deprived irrationality that had taken over my already abrasive personality. "God, I'm sorry."

"It's okay. We all have bad days." He glanced around, seeing the receptionist and one of the security guards watching from the end of the hallway. "Why do I feel like a known shoplifter walking around in a high-end department store?"

"Welcome to Cross Security."

"There's that smile." His phone buzzed. It had been

doing that a lot while I gave him a breakdown of what I 'suspected' he might find in Payne's possession. "After reviewing the footage from your apartment and listening to the recording you made of your interview with Payne before I arrived, the DA says we have enough for a search warrant. I'm guessing after we search his home office, we might have enough to bring him in for questioning. It'll depend on what we find. I don't know what we should expect." He winked. "I'll call if I need anything else from you or Easton. I suggest you get some sleep. I'll see you tonight at the launch of Easton's Eats."

"You're going?"

"I wouldn't miss it for the world."

I walked the detective to the elevator. When the doors opened, Cross waited on the other side. He stepped out of the car, glowering at the detective. "We gave you copies of the security footage and the recording. What are you still doing here?"

"Just leaving." Voletek stepped into the elevator, unfazed when the security guard stepped in beside him. "Thanks for your help, Lucien."

"Let this be the last time you rope my people into your problems." Cross waited for the doors to close before glancing at the receptionist, who immediately busied herself with answering the phone. "Are you all right, Ms. Parker?"

"Fine."

"Do we need to have a discussion about proper workplace behavior?"

"No, sir." He must have heard or seen my meltdown in the hallway.

"Good," he leaned an elbow against the reception desk, "order a car to take Ms. Parker to lunch and drive her wherever she wants to go."

"I don't need your charity."

"And I don't need you to get into an accident and crash the company car. You're angry, and you're tired. Those are the only two reasons I can see why you're getting this emotional in my hallways. That means you shouldn't be behind the wheel of a company car. I don't need you to sully my reputation more than you already have." For a moment, his cheek twitched and his eyes twinkled. Was Lucien Cross teasing me?

"Whatever."

He reached across the reception desk and pulled a sheet of paper from the printer tray. "Here's a list of Sizzle staff who worked the night in question. Go see what you can find out. The techs will notify you once we determine the type of plastic used in the toy you dropped off."

Despite the months I'd spent at Cross Security, I still couldn't make heads or tails out of Lucien's motives. His actions often contradicted his words. "Great."

He watched me trudge toward the elevator. "We protect our clients. That's what we do here. Don't forget it."

Nodding, I watched Lucien disappear behind the closing metal doors.

*　*　*

By the time five o'clock rolled around, I found my second wind. The catnap I took at Martin Technologies when I dropped off lunch had been enough to sustain me through a dozen interviews. None of Easton's former staff recognized Ted Payne. Easton recognized him, but only in regards to the arson investigation. The chef didn't recall seeing him before, and even when I showed him photos and mock-ups of Payne's truck, he didn't know if that was the vehicle driven by the Molotov cocktail wielding prick.

Cross Security used the limited camera footage to run a comparison, but according to the experts, the results were inconclusive. However, the plastic polymer of the model I stole matched the plastic shard found in the lock. Whenever the police finished their search and ran a test, they'd discover the same thing we already knew. I just didn't know if it would be enough. And since no one from Sizzle recognized Payne, I was starting to have doubts. Actually, I doubted everything at this point, especially my own sanity.

Desperate, I concluded my afternoon at the rehab facility. Asher York agreed to see me, and he apologized for his behavior at Delicious. "Throwing knives at my sous chef made me realize I was already at rock bottom. Actually, getting wrestled to the ground and arrested in my own restaurant was rock bottom."

"Were you drinking that day?"

"I drank every day. A glass of wine at family meal. A few shots when the dinner rush kicked up. More wine later to relax when things slowed." A blissful grin teased the edges of his lips. "And a snifter of brandy to call it a night."

"I'm sorry."

"Don't be. It's my demon to fight. I never thought it was a problem. I didn't think I had a problem. It was part of the lifestyle until it wasn't."

I wasn't sure how committed he was to staying sober once he got out of rehab, but the first step was acknowledging the problem and committing to battling against it. "Take care of yourself, Chef."

Asher looked up at me. "You work with the police. Make sure they know I'm taking steps in the right direction. Maybe you could pass word along to the prosecutor."

I gave him a tight smile. He hadn't told me anything useful about Easton's enemies or why Galen Strader or Dante Bisset threatened Easton and broke into his house. Although, I was sure he'd been told to keep his mouth shut. Facts like that might be worth trading for a reduced sentence. The facts he wanted me to know and share were ones that would paint him in a positive light and show he was already attempting to reform himself. Rehab might have been nothing more than a suggestion by his attorney, but I could be wrong. Cynicism and skepticism were hazards of my job.

Returning to Cross Security, I trudged down the hallway to my office. Easton's Eats planned to relaunch in roughly three hours. It wasn't enough time.

"Parker," Renner called, "how are we doing? Cross said the plastic was a match, but we didn't get a hit on the truck. What did Sizzle's crew say?"

"No love."

"Damn."

I bit my lip, trying to think through the problem. This

shouldn't be so hard. We had plenty of suspects. We identified the source of the threatening messages, but Dante and Galen didn't start the fire. And neither did York. "I don't get it. Payne doesn't seem the type, but after what I found in his house, it's clear he's involved."

"You don't think he's the arsonist?" Renner refilled his mug and poured a second, which I graciously accepted.

"Right now, I am spinning."

"Okay," Renner pulled out a chair, "let's break it down. How much do we even know about Ted Payne?"

In the last twenty-four hours, we learned a lot. His stellar record, personal recommendation letters written by his mentor, and commendations given to him by the city made him look like a hero. But the items on his corkboard said otherwise. He had photos from the fires and copies of the inspection certificates printed weeks before we ever crossed paths.

"When exactly were they printed?" Renner asked.

I scrolled through the photos on my phone, zoomed in, and read the printer's timestamp. "It varies. The oldest dates back a few years."

"What about more recent trophies? Like from last night's apartment fire?"

I shook my head.

"Did you notice any lab equipment or a workstation where he creates his custom fire feeder?"

"Fire feeder? You should trademark that." I rubbed my eyes, searching my memory. "No, he didn't have anything set up like that. His only workstation was a neatly organized desk with files and cases and his 3D printer and play area."

"Play area?"

I showed Renner the photo of the miniature city. "He looks like a hobbyist, but he could be using that to pick his targets."

"That's right. We don't know how the arsonist picks his targets or how he's getting inside the buildings. No one spotted Payne at your apartment prior to the fire. From the footage Lucien found, it doesn't appear Payne visited these other locations prior to the fires either."

"The oxidizing agent doesn't degrade. He could have planted it anytime, maybe while conducting an inspection."

Renner thought for a moment. "If he wore regulation gear, no one would recognize him, and they wouldn't think twice about a firefighter checking out a building."

"It could be any of them. All this asshole needs is access to the gear."

Renner went to the door. "Send me the photos you took. I have a hunch. I'm gonna check on a few things."

"What is it? Did you see something?"

"I don't know yet. You did pass those along to Cross, right?"

"Yeah."

He nodded, the wheels turning, though I wasn't sure why. "Good."

THIRTY-NINE

"You're late," I said.

Detective Voletek looked around the fairgrounds, taking a seat on the bench beside me. "We arrested Lt. Payne on suspicion of arson and attempted murder."

"That sounds serious."

"It must be why he lawyered up. Payne's claiming he's been conducting his own off the books investigation for the last few years, ever since Haskell started researching construction companies and insisting one of the crews played a role in the area fires. Payne said he pulled the inspection certificates and made copies of the photos from the fires as part of his research."

"If that's true, why didn't he say something to me when I approached him about Sizzle being arson?"

"Obviously, he's lying. When I confronted him with the receipt, he said he found it on his desk and held on to it in case it was relevant. As if he expects me to believe evidence just materialized out of thin air. We printed it, but aside from some partials, the only identifiable prints belonged to him. We also found some old turnout gear in his trunk. No name was stenciled on the back, so he could have been one of the unidentified firefighters who conducted the evacuation and inspection at your boyfriend's apartment. He probably concealed the accelerant inside his coat, sprayed down the fourteenth floor and a few other places, ditched the gear, and came back inside to conduct official business. He's probably been doing it for a while. He could have doused every building he inspected or any place where he responded to a call. Either he waits for a fire to accidentally start, or he goes back, like he did at Sizzle, and sets it himself. Officers are still searching for where he keeps the compound and the delivery system, but we'll find it."

"Bastard."

Voletek watched the shutter roll up on the order window of the food truck. "Easton looks nervous, not that I blame him." Voletek glanced around, noticing the earpiece in my ear. "Is that a fashion accessory?"

I shook my head. On Bridget Stockton's orders, Cross pulled out all the stops. Four teams covered the opening. Two men stood guard at either end of the food truck. Another team milled about the fairgrounds, blending into the crowd while assessing potential threats. I jerked my chin at the third team, who were seated throughout the food court pavilion. The rest were monitoring the entrance for strange activity or incoming bogeys.

Easton peered out the window at the waiting crowd. He caught my eye and waved. I pressed the button on the radio. "How's it looking? Are we clear?"

After several affirmatives, I gave Easton a thumbs up. He opened the window and fired up the grill. Easton's Eats was officially open for business.

Voletek saw the clustered people form a line, and he got up from the bench. "Do you want anything to eat?"

"I'm good."

"Suit yourself."

The detective got in line, and I scanned the vicinity again. The crowd outside the club during Easton's Eats' first run was nothing compared to this, and the club had been filled to capacity with screaming music fans, who just happened upon Easton's food truck. Tonight, the screaming fans were here for Easton. Thankfully, none of them were screaming, but the crowd was easily three times larger. The social media blast Easton sent out must have gone viral. Within a minute's time, a line snaked around the pavilion, looping all the way out the front entrance.

"Are the police working crowd control?" I asked.

"Affirmative."

Several patrol cars were parked near the front entrance. A few had even parked inside the fairgrounds. Though, they might have been here to serve and protect actual fair-goers and not just Easton's fans. How did a chef garner such a following? I didn't understand it, but I didn't understand the intricacies of posting images of breakfast, lunch, and dinner online either.

Lucien moved stealthily through the crowd, suddenly appearing beside me like an apparition. He sat down and watched Detective Voletek inch forward as Easton worked at breakneck speed to feed the hundreds of people waiting in line. "The police made another arrest."

"I heard."

"Do you think they arrested the right guy this time?"

"Chef Strader didn't firebomb Easton's house or burn down Sizzle."

"I'm aware."

I gave Cross a sideways glance. "You were wrong."

"You do enjoy pointing that out." He looked behind us before turning back to me. "But you didn't answer my question."

"Payne came to Martin's apartment building the night of the fire. He personally checked the areas where your techs found the chemical compound. And he was outside my apartment last night when the fire broke out."

"When it broke out or after?"

"I don't know." I looked at Cross. "Do you?"

He shook his head. "I spent a good deal of today pulling strings and reviewing nearby CCTV feeds. I didn't see anyone go inside prior to the fire."

"The cameras at my apartment, my old apartment, are shitty."

"I would have installed some of our equipment if you

had asked."

"If I knew this was going to happen, I would have." I stared into the crowd. "I hate this. I approached Payne. I told him it was arson, and I told him I wouldn't let this go. That's why he did it. That's why a bunch of people are homeless, hurt, scared, and," my mind went to Tara, "dead."

"This isn't your fault."

"No, but no matter how many times I say it, the more it feels like it is." A car backfired, and I jumped, reaching for my gun. Cross did the same. Before either of us drew our weapons, the security team told us what happened, and we relaxed. "Easton didn't hear that."

"How do you know?"

"He would be cowering on the floor in a quivering ball if he did."

Cross gave me a funny look. "I've spent quite a bit of time with the chef after I returned from my trip. He's been strutting around my office like a peacock with that ridiculous blue and silver tuft of hair. I thought he'd at least pretend to act more macho than that."

"Fear is fear. It doesn't matter who you are. You can't just will yourself to not be afraid."

"The people who work for me don't act like cowards."

"That doesn't mean we're not scared." I glanced at Cross again. "Have you seen Renner? He said he'd meet me here, but I haven't seen him."

Cross looked around again before keying the radio. "Does anyone have eyes on Bennett Renner?" A chorus of negatives came through the earpiece. "When's the last time you spoke to him?"

"At the office. He said he wanted to check on a hunch."

Cross pulled out his phone and dialed Renner's number. "He told me he was dropping off a retainer contract with Mr. Zedula. He might have gotten held up."

"Again?"

"I didn't mean it like that." The call went to voicemail, and Cross frowned at his phone. "Do you want to give it a shot?"

I texted Renner, asking for his current location and

ETA. A moment later, my phone chimed. I read the message and held it up for Cross to see.

I found something you need to see. It's about the fires. Can you meet me now?

Lucien jerked his chin toward the entrance. "Go. I'll keep an eye on things here."

"Make sure the police don't let things get out of hand," I teased.

"Don't worry, I won't. And I'll make sure they don't get out of hand either."

Rolling my eyes, I sent back a response asking Renner for his location. When he didn't reply immediately, I tried calling, but it went straight to voicemail. Before I had time to wonder if he ignored the call, he texted the address, apologizing for not answering since cell service was spotty.

I programmed the address into the GPS, wondering why he wanted to meet at an old paint factory. Maybe he found where Payne stashed the chemicals. That's what we had been discussing before he left to follow his hunch. According to the navigation system, the drive should take ten minutes. I wouldn't be waiting in suspense for long.

Seven minutes later, my phone rang. I glanced down and hit the speaker button. "Hey, Martin, is everything okay?"

"Where are you?"

"On my way to meet Renner."

"I thought you and the rest of Cross Security were supposed to be working the fairgrounds for Chef Easton's opening."

"Renner had a hunch. I don't know what it is, but Cross has a bunch of guys covering the food truck, and the police are out in force. Easton's safe. Are you okay?"

"Yeah, fine." Martin sounded distracted. "I didn't know where we were sleeping tonight. When you stopped by for lunch, you didn't seem keen on the idea of going home. I assume it's because of the fire and the close call at our apartment."

"Look, Voletek arrested a suspect, the arson investigator I spoke to last night. He's been at both our apartment buildings and has photos and inspection certificates hanging in his house like trophies." And the receipt from Sizzle. Payne had to be our guy. Hopefully, Renner found enough evidence to put Payne behind bars for decades.

"So we can go home?"

"You can go home. My name's not on the property records. You'll be safe. I want to see what Renner's found before I make any hard and fast commitments."

"It's too late. You already did," Martin teased.

"I'm serious."

"I know, but you have to sleep somewhere. Unless you want to explain to Lucien tomorrow morning why he found us spooning on the couch in your office, you might want to consider picking a place with a real bed."

I pulled to a stop in front of the building, spotting Renner's company car and a familiar hunter green 4x4 parked at the side door. "What the hell is Haskell doing here?"

"Alex?"

"Sorry, something's up. I'll call you back."

Haskell was waiting inside his jeep. He waved at me and rolled down his window. "Hey, do you know what this is about?"

"What are you doing here?"

"Mr. Renner called and told me to meet him down here. He said he needed my expertise on something, but he's not picking up his phone." Haskell showed me the list of unanswered calls.

"Did you try texting? He said cell service is spotty." I looked up at the building, an uneasiness creeping into my bones. "The equipment inside could be interfering."

Haskell climbed out of the car. "Should we go inside?"

I peered into Renner's car, but aside from the normal collection of fast food wrappers and fountain drink cups, I didn't see anything indicative of where he was or what he was on to. "I guess so."

The side door was cracked open. The chain that had secured it in place had been cut and was lying in a heap beside the door with a block propping it open. Haskell pulled the door wider. "Ladies first."

I stepped into the dark factory and turned on my

flashlight. "Bennett?" Haskell coughed loudly, and I glanced back at him while he bent forward and continued to hack. "Are you okay, Mr. Haskell?"

"Dust," he choked out. He straightened, wiping the back of his hand over his mouth. "Did you hear that?" I didn't hear anything except his coughing. "Mr. Renner?" He pointed toward a door at the side. "I think I heard something coming from there."

"Bennett?" I tried again, but Haskell beelined for the doorway. My gaze swept the area, and I undid the snap on my holster. The air felt electric. I stayed close to the wall, following the path Haskell took. "Hold up," I said, stopping Haskell at the next door. Reaching for my phone, I dialed Renner's number, but I didn't have a signal. "That's weird."

"What is it?"

"No signal."

Haskell dug out his phone and checked the display. "Mine neither." He looked back at the narrow strip of light coming from the crack in the door. "Do you want to call for backup?"

Renner's car was here, which meant he had to be close, but I knew something wasn't right. "I'll keep looking. Would you mind calling Cross and telling him where we are?"

"I'll make the call, but I'm not comfortable leaving you alone in here, not until we find Mr. Renner. What do you think he wanted to show us?"

"I don't know." I jerked my chin toward the door. "Go make the call. I'll wait here. I'll be fine. I'm a big girl."

"Be careful." Haskell went back to the door, and I pulled my gun and cautiously opened the interior door. "Renner?" I hissed. I didn't hear anything, so I crept forward, letting my flashlight beam lead the way. Finding a light switch on the wall, I flipped it, but it didn't do anything. The power had been turned off. "Renner? Where are you?"

The hallway opened up into a large square room, which squatters had used at some point. Makeshift tents and mattresses lined three of the four walls. Some graffiti covered the dusty, flat surfaces. Two paths broke off from this central room, one going straight back and the other off to the right.

A snuffling noise sounded from behind, followed by more hacking coughs. I turned my flashlight on Haskell, noticing blood in the corner of his mouth. He wiped it away with a tissue which was more red than white.

"How bad is it?" I asked, lowering the beam of light.

"What?"

I jerked my chin at the tissue he hid away. "You don't have a cold or allergies, do you?"

He didn't answer. Instead, he picked a path and pushed his way to the right. "Mr. Renner?"

I followed behind, the familiar twitching nagging at me from the back of my mind. My thoughts flashed back to the green 4x4. It fit the description of the truck the firebomber drove. "After we find Renner and he shows us whatever it is he wants to show us, we should get some soup. Easton makes a wonderful beef and vegetable."

"I don't eat fancy stuff like that."

"Oh, come on, it'll be great. My treat." The hairs at the back of my neck prickled. "Did you have a bad experience at a fancy restaurant?"

"Not me, my granddaughter."

"Food poisoning?" I asked.

"No," Haskell spun to face me, "she waitressed to help pay for college. God knows her parents couldn't afford tuition, and on my salary, neither could I."

"What happened?" I asked, my eyes darting to the single room at the end of the corridor. "Renner?" I called again, but Haskell didn't even wait to see if my colleague would reply before launching into his story.

"The chef took a liking to her. She was young, smart, and entirely out of his league. He was older," he sneered, "a predator really. She was still a baby. My grandbaby. He knocked her up. I don't even think the bastard knew, or he just didn't care. She miscarried, and it destroyed her. She dropped out of school." Haskell squeezed his eyes shut. "She tried to kill herself. She didn't succeed, but you can see it in her eyes now. She doesn't care if she lives or dies."

"Where did she work?"

Haskell didn't answer. He turned his head and coughed

again. This time, blood and spittle painted the wall. "I'd gladly trade places with her, but it looks like I'm the one dying and she wishes she was."

"Cancer?"

He chuckled cynically and rubbed his chest. "Years of fighting fires and this is what's gonna do me in." Bitterness and resentment contorted his face into a hateful mask. "I told the brass the safety inspections were too lax. Too many corners were getting cut. Too many questionable materials were allowed in construction, but they all got kickbacks. None of them cared. We're just grunts working the front line. What do we know? We're expendable and interchangeable. We get a watch and a shitty pension, and they count the seconds until we drop dead, hoping we don't have a surviving spouse so they don't have to pay anymore and we aren't a drain on the budget."

"I'm sorry."

"If they listened, if they made the inspections more stringent, most of the fires I reported to, that other men reported to, never would have happened. We wouldn't have been exposed to as much. We wouldn't be sick now. And the best part is with fewer fires there would be less expense. They still would have benefitted, but they didn't listen." The venom in his voice raised the hairs on the back of my neck, and I lowered the flashlight and reached into my pocket. Turning to the side, I glanced down, seeing one bar. It wasn't much, but I had to be sure. Renner's number was still on my screen, and I pressed dial.

A second later, the phone in Haskell's pocket rang.

FORTY

I aimed at Haskell, a lighter materializing in his hand. He flicked it, holding the flame up. "Where's Renner?"

The arsonist stared at me like I was nothing more than a hindrance. "Look around, Ms. Parker. This corridor is coated in flammable chemicals. One spark and the entire place goes up. You should think twice before shooting me."

I glanced around, seeing piles of discarded towels, crumpled up papers, and other flammable items nearby. "Where's Renner? What did you do to him?"

Haskell pointed to the doorway at the end of the hallway. "He's fine. I just needed him out of the way for a little while. I didn't hurt him. I'm on a crusade to get the city to enact more stringent safety inspections. I was providing a public service. I wanted to make the brass see reason. Last night's fire was supposed to distract you and encourage Cross Security to take up my cause. No one was supposed to get hurt."

I moved backward, never taking my eyes off Haskell. "You killed someone last night. You tried to kill Easton Lango twice. You wanted to hurt him. What changed? What happened to your noble cause?"

Haskell scoffed. "A week after I retired, I was diagnosed,

went through treatment, and was in remission. Eight months ago, I got the bad news. They said I had a year left. If I'm going out, that prick is coming with me. He doesn't deserve to live after what he did to my granddaughter."

"You don't think he deserves a future because you don't have one?"

Haskell held the lighter in front of him, realizing I might still shoot him. "I'm not crazy or evil. I'm doling out justice. Same as you."

"That's what you call what happened to Tara last night? That was justice?"

"That wasn't my fault. If they listened, the safety inspector would have identified the issues inside your building and had them fixed. The fire in your apartment would have left a burn on the floor and that would have been it. That's what was supposed to have happened. If stupid Ted ever did his fucking job right, last night wouldn't have ended in tragedy."

"Is he your accomplice?"

"He's my worst failure."

"Did you have him spray your chemical cocktail inside the buildings?"

"No," Haskell glared at me, the lighter the only thing keeping me from tackling him to the ground and cuffing him, "I told Ted about the lax standards and warned him about the construction crews using shitty materials, but he didn't get it. So I took matters into my own hands. When the fires started, I figured he'd see reason, but he didn't."

"How'd you get access to the buildings?"

"I still have friends in the department. I know what inspections are on the books, so I put on some of my old turnout gear and show up a few weeks early. I spray down the place and wait to see what happens. If the inspectors do their jobs, the buildings will be fine. There won't be any exploitable weaknesses, but if they fail, you know what happens."

"You go back and set the fires."

"No," he screamed. "The fires happened because of electrical weaknesses. I didn't set them. The only fires I set were to that asshole's restaurant, his house, and your apartment. The fire department set the others by failing to raise their standards and identify weaknesses. None of those buildings would have burned if the actual inspectors did their fucking jobs. Those fires weren't my fault. It's the department's fault."

It didn't look that way from where I stood. "What about Sizzle?"

"That was different. That was personal. It took time and planning. I had to sit through an entire meal that asshole prepared and pretend to compliment him, just to get access to his keys. Once I had a copy, I waited every fucking night for him to be alone. Except he's like a cockroach. He just won't die. Tonight, that's gonna change. I just needed to get you and Renner out of the way."

"Parker?" Renner's voice sounded from the room behind me.

"Are you okay?" I yelled.

"It's Haskell," Renner replied.

"I know." I stared at the hero turned villain, wondering if there was any chance he was bluffing. "Are you okay?"

"I'm stuck," Renner said.

"I didn't hurt him. I just locked him inside and took his phone. Now it's your turn. I don't need either of you interfering. The only thing that matters is ridding this world of that prick of a chef. I don't want to hurt you. Once it's done, someone will find you." He jerked his chin at the locked door. "Now get inside."

Reluctantly, I flipped the lock and opened the door. Renner was pinned beneath a heavy shelf. Blood coated the floor. The former detective struggled to get free, and I spun, lunging for Haskell.

He stumbled backward, dropping the lighter. It fell to the ground, igniting a path of chemicals and setting the nearest pile of cloth and papers on fire, separating us by a barrier of flame. I aimed, but Haskell was halfway down the hall.

For a dying man, Haskell moved fast, bolting for the door as the fire lined both sides of the hallway. The flames in the middle burned out, clearing the path, but I couldn't chase after him. I had to get Renner out.

"The next time you have a hunch, you better tell me what it is." I moved to the side, seeing Renner's hip and thigh pinned beneath the corner of the large metal shelf.

"He locked me in here. I tried to break the guard rail off the front of the shelf to use as a pry bar, but the bolt against the wall must have rusted. It snapped, and the whole damn thing came down on top of me."

"All right. Let's find a way to get you out."

Renner looked through the open door at the growing blaze. "He has barrels of that shit just waiting to go up. There's no reason we both need to cook. Get out of here, Parker."

I looked up, realizing we were in a supply room. "Shit." I tried lifting the shelf while Renner attempted to pull himself free, but from the screams that escaped his lips, I knew this wouldn't work. It was solidly constructed, at least ten feet high. Each shelf could probably hold hundreds of pounds. "I need a lever and fulcrum to get this off of you." I looked around the room, but the only things close by were more heavy shelves bolted to the walls. "How did you end up here?"

"I called Haskell. His office purchased large quantities of the chemicals used to make the compound. When you didn't find anything at Payne's apartment, I checked the purchase history of chemical suppliers, but Payne never bought any chemicals. So I asked Haskell if he knew of other suppliers since he had purchased tons of the stuff. I guess that tipped him off. He told me he knew of some abandoned factories that still had chemicals on the premises and thought it might help us identify the arsonist." Renner coughed, his eyes going wide. "Parker, you have to go. Now."

"I won't leave you." I tossed him my phone. "Call for help. Keep trying until you get a connection." The hallway was now a tunnel of fire, the flames licking the ceiling. I didn't spot anything I could use to help me move the shelf. Needing to buy time, I dragged the drums containing the fire-feeding chemical compound as far from the door as possible. "That should buy us a few minutes."

"Parker. Go."

"How's the dialing coming along? Did you try sending a text?"

"It's spinning."

"Fuck." I braced myself on the floor beside Renner, getting low enough to get my hands beneath the edge of the shelf like I was about to do a bench press. "On the count of three. I push, you pull."

When that failed, Renner glared at me, coughing as the smoke grew thicker. "Do you have any idea what Cross will do to me if you die on the job?"

"I hate to break it to you, but we'll both be dead, so it won't matter."

I flipped around to the other side, pushing against the shelf and hoping to knock it off Renner. Since only one of his legs was partially pinned, I thought maybe I could make it teeter, but that didn't work.

Renner let out another sharp gasp. "You know, maybe it won't be so bad. The smoke will probably get us first."

"Not with the way that fire's moving." I looked around the room, but there were no windows. I couldn't tell how deep into the building we were. "Easton's pissed you didn't go to his launch. You better have a great excuse."

"Don't you think this counts?"

"He won't have much sympathy. He's still angry about Sizzle."

"Well, it's his second launch. I was at the first one. That should count."

"Right, you nearly scared him to death." We couldn't keep up the banter as we grew more frantic. Renner begged me to go. "I won't leave you."

"You don't have a choice."

For a moment, I thought I heard Martin's voice. Every near death experience always resulted in a hallucination of him. Maybe that's how you defined true love or justified moving into a padded cell.

"Did you hear that?" Renner asked.

"God, you're hallucinating too? It must be the smoke."

"No." Renner jerked his head at the hallway and yelled, "Help. We're back here."

A minute later, a man I never expected to see burst

through the door. "Martin? What the hell are you doing here?"

"Hey, sweetheart." Martin knelt beside me as I struggled to lift the shelf off Renner. "You know you made me a promise. I'm having doubts about your commitment to keeping it."

"I have every intention of keeping it," I shoved against the shelf, hearing Renner bite back a whimper, "just as soon as I get this off of him."

Martin tried to help me lift it, but it was too heavy. He took a step back, taking a moment to assess the situation. "Can you feel your leg?" Martin asked.

"Yeah, it hurts like hell," Renner said. He moved his foot ever so slightly, but the weight of the shelf was too much for him to be able to wriggle his way out. Renner looked back at the door. "You two need to get the hell out of here. There's no reason we should all die."

"I called the fire department," Martin said. "They're on the way. We'll be fine." But he crouched down, eyeing me. "I'll lift up. You push from that side." He looked down at Renner. "You try to slide out." Martin's hands slipped. "Fuck."

"It's too heavy. We can't move it," I said. "Martin, go. Wait for help to arrive."

"We're already here," Cross said from the doorway. He and two members of his security team positioned themselves at the corner of the shelf while Martin pushed from the side. I crouched down, grabbing Renner beneath the arms. On the count of three they lifted and pushed, and I yanked backward, pulling Renner free. The shelf crashed to the floor, covering the bloody smear left by Renner's hip.

Two more members of Cross's security team remained in the hallway, clearing a path with fire extinguishers. "We have to get out of here. Parker, Martin, go. We're right behind you," Cross said. Cross and one of the men lifted Renner between the two of them, and they carried him out of the burning building.

By the time we got outside, Haskell was long gone. Renner and I briefed Cross and the security team, who notified the police to be on the lookout.

Sirens sounded in the distance, and Cross's mobile medical units pulled into the parking lot. I put my hands on my knees and bent over, coughing while I watched burning embers drift through the air. Once Renner was secured in the back of Cross's private ambulance, Martin returned to my side.

"What are you doing here?" I always knew Martin would walk through fire for me, but this was ridiculous.

He hugged me, squeezing tight. "It doesn't matter. All that matters is you're okay."

I clung to him, feeling him shudder. "How'd you find me? How'd you know I was in trouble?"

"Lucien called when you didn't pick up. He thought you might be in danger."

"Why did he call you?" I pushed away from him, glancing at my boss who busied himself with instructing the security team to get back to the fairgrounds and be on the lookout for Dil Haskell. "Answer me, Martin."

"He said he couldn't get a current location on your phone. He said the signals were jammed. He wanted to verify your last known location before the signal cut out. He didn't want to waste time, if you were no longer in the vicinity."

"That doesn't explain why he called you."

Shame was written all over Martin's face. "I asked Lucien to get me a tracker to put inside the charm on your necklace."

I stepped back. "You what?" Suddenly, he felt like a stranger. "When?"

"In Vegas. I know it was wrong. I abused your trust. I just needed peace of mind. It was driving me crazy not knowing where you were."

I slapped him. "You had no right." I coughed again, the world spinning. Even as the words left my mouth, I knew his betrayal was the only reason Renner was alive, which made the issue complicated because, at the end of the day, I couldn't fault him for taking actions that saved a life, no matter how fucked up and wrong they were. His heart was in the right place even though his brain must have relocated to a paranoid, controlling black hole somewhere up his own ass. "We'll talk about this later."

Martin reached for me and pulled me into his chest. I wheezed, and he released me. "You need to get checked out."

"So do you."

Cross's medics helped me into the second mobile unit. They unbuttoned the first two buttons on my blouse and listened to my lungs. While they were doing that, Cross stepped inside. "Bennett's on the way to the hospital. He'll need x-rays, but it looks like his titanium hip and the metal plate and pins in his leg kept him from getting crushed under that shelf." Cross's gaze dropped to the rings dangling from the chain around my neck and the tiny heart containing the hidden tracker, but he didn't comment. "Any idea why Haskell did this?"

"He's dying. He blames the city for failing him and Easton for fucking up his granddaughter's life. We have to stop him before it's too late."

FORTY-ONE

By the time we arrived at the fairgrounds, Detective Voletek, several uniformed officers, and Cross Security personnel had surrounded Dilbert Haskell, who remained inside his 4x4. The window was cracked open, and several cops had a bead on Haskell.

"Shit." I sprang forward, but Lucien grabbed my arm.

"What are you going to do?"

Honestly, I didn't know. "Talk him down. I need you to make sure Easton's clear. Keep eyes on him. With the way things have been going, more nutjobs are probably waiting to crawl out of the woodwork and kill the chef."

Cross keyed the radio, dispatching another team to guard Easton. I skirted around the edges until I got close enough to Voletek. The detective nodded, and uniforms stepped out of my way as I took up a spot beside him.

"He said he has enough kerosene and propane in the back of his truck to blow us all to kingdom come. The only way he's going to back down is if we bring Easton out. Sharpshooters and the bomb squad are on the way. He won't let us get close enough to see if he's serious."

"He's serious."

"I thought he might be. I called in the negotiator."

"It won't help. Haskell's dying. At most, he has four months." I watched the firebug twitch. He held something in his hand the police believed to be a dead man's switch. "You should evacuate the area."

"Already on it." Voletek gestured, and a few of the officers backed up. He shouted at one of them. "Tell Cross to get his people out of here. That includes you, Alex."

"Here's the difference between what you do and what I do, Detective." I holstered my weapon and stepped closer to the jeep. "I don't have to follow orders." I held my palms up and slowly moved forward. "Dil," I bellowed, "when I was watching my life flash before my eyes, I gained some clarity. I understand. I do."

Haskell didn't believe me. "Stay back."

"Okay. No problem." I took a step back. "You don't want to kill me. As you can see, I'm okay. In fact, you made me realize I don't want to die for some loser prick like Easton Lango. Cross is getting him now. We don't need the headache of protecting him. Do you have any idea how many people want to destroy this guy? That's why it took us so long to figure out it was you."

"I don't blame them."

"Me neither. I'm sorry about your granddaughter."

Haskell didn't respond.

"Liza, right? That's her name." On the way here, Cross had the techs run a profile and brief us. "She's twenty-two. Her entire life is ahead of her. If she's anything like her grandpa, I bet she'll find a way to bounce back. But doing this," I spread my arms wide, encompassing our surroundings, "she won't bounce back from this. No matter where she goes or what she does, this will follow her around forever. She'll always be the girl whose grandpa went nuts and bombed the fair. You'll be labeled a terrorist, and the stupid, ignorant people out there, they won't understand why you did it. Hell, the really bad ones, they'll try to hurt her because they can't take their revenge out on you. Easton Lango ruined her life. But if you blow up your truck, a lot of innocent people are going to get hurt. You're going to ruin their lives and their loved ones' lives. Are you sure you're prepared to do that? It'll only hurt Liza. I know you don't want that."

"It's already too late."

"No, it's not." I hoped that was true. For all I knew, he might have rigged some kind of timer, and we were about to go boom. Damn, I wish I had told Martin I loved him. "Right now, you still have a legacy. People will understand your actions were meant to protect them. They'll understand what the fires were about. They'll remember you as the hero you are." I took another step closer. I had to see what was in his hand.

"Parker," Voletek warned. In the periphery, I saw the police tactical unit surround the area. Uniformed officers worked to clear the crowd as quickly as possible. Snipers were in position. "Step away."

Haskell rubbed his thumb against the item in his hand, and I recognized it as one of the miniature buildings from Payne's display. He didn't have a dead man's switch or a detonator. Though, I had no way of knowing if his vehicle was loaded down with gas or accelerant.

I spun around. "It's not a detonator." I didn't even get the word out before the crack of the rifle sounded. Voletek raced toward me, shoving me away from the car and ushering me to safety in case the vehicle blew. But it didn't.

Eventually, the bomb squad arrived, checked for booby-traps, and opened the jeep. In the back, they found several highly flammable substances. It wasn't a bomb in the traditional sense. Based on the amount of fuel, it probably wasn't meant to destroy anything except Easton and his food truck. Given what we knew about Dil Haskell, he must have thought he'd be able to drive into the food truck and blow them both up in a blaze of righteous glory.

Based on the line surrounding the food truck when it first opened for business, I didn't want to think about the potential number of civilian casualties. I just wanted to go home.

"Are you fucking insane?" Voletek asked. "Were you a professional negotiator?"

"Obviously, you weren't paying attention to our exchange." I felt hollow and exhausted. I pushed through the crowd until I found Cross and Easton. "Cops are probably going to have questions," I said.

"I'll take care of it," Cross said.

Easton swallowed. "I don't know Dilbert Haskell. Why would he want to hurt me?"

"You were almost a dad," I said. "Liza miscarried, and that was the straw that broke the camel's back."

"Liza? My Liza?"

"She's not yours, Easton. She was Dilbert's granddaughter first. Your screwing around cost you your marriage, nearly cost a twenty-year-old kid her life, and nearly cost you yours. Think about that the next time you decide to fuck around."

Cross probably wanted to berate me for speaking to a client like that, but he didn't. "Go home, Ms. Parker. If the police have questions, I'll have them schedule an appointment."

I nodded, turning and bumping into Voletek, who hadn't left my side. He heard the whole thing, though he simply fell into step beside me and made sure I was allowed out of the perimeter. "Guess I torpedoed your chances of a privately catered reward."

"I ordered the special tonight. Easton's not that impressive, but you are."

"I'm taken." I spotted Martin's town car parked across the street, just outside the evacuation area. "Let me know what happens with Lt. Payne because I'm not even sure which way is up anymore. He might have been helping Haskell or he suspected what his mentor was up to."

"Ah, actual police work. It's about damn time I get back to that." He wiped some soot off my face. "You can rest easy tonight, Alex. The city's safe."

*   *   *

"Are you sure you don't want to get a tracking chip implanted in my shoulder, like a dog?"

"Sweetheart," Martin said, "I have anxiety issues."

"It's a good thing you're seeing someone about that." I looked at the tiny heart-shaped charm. It didn't look like much. I thought Martin got it to be sweet since he knew I wouldn't wear the rings on my finger because they ruined my left jab and he wanted to dress up the necklace a little. Instead, he gave me the charm to keep tabs on me. "Why didn't you just ask?"

"I was afraid you'd think I was acting irrationally."

"You are, but you failed to consider one thing."

"What's that?" His fingers traced the tendons in the back of my hand.

"Knowing what you've been going through, I would have said yes."

"Is that why you said yes to the commitment ceremony?"

"Don't make that about this." I put the necklace back on and tucked it into my shirt. "For the record, this is grounds for an annulment."

"We can't get an annulment."

I grinned evilly. "Do you want to bet?" I held out my hand. "Give me your watch."

He took it off his wrist and laid it on the desk. Carefully, I cracked open the back and stuck a tracking chip inside. To be fair, I had considered doing this years ago, but the fear of someone hacking his location overpowered my desire to keep tabs on him. Though he didn't know that and never would. We both had anxiety issues, but I was better at hiding the crazy. At least, that's what I told myself.

"There. Whenever you get rid of yours, I'll get rid of mine. And until then, this," I waved my hand between us, "isn't a healthy relationship."

"You're right. However," the cocky smirk erupted on Martin's face, "one might argue this isn't about cheating or control. It's about safety. I'm not afraid of you stepping out on me. I'm afraid of what might happen if people can't get to you in time."

"Like today?"

He swallowed, cocking his head to the side.

"Renner wouldn't have made it, if it wasn't for you," I said quietly. "So I'm only saying this once and you will forget it immediately, but thank you for being overprotective."

"You're welcome."

I entered the serial number on the connected app, which Cross promised was more secure than the NSA's computer network, and made sure the tracker was active. "You might trust me not to step out on you, but I don't have a history with runway models and actresses. I'll expect you to account for your whereabouts at all times of the day and night. When this says you're at a club at midnight, I'll need to know why."

"That's where the unhealthy part comes in," Martin said, knowing I was teasing him. "Now can we please go home?"

I kissed him and locked up my office. When the elevator opened, Lucien was standing inside. He stepped back, making room for us.

"Did you hear the news?" Lucien asked. "The police let Payne go. It's my understanding Payne suspected someone in the fire department was behind the fires but didn't have any proof and wouldn't drag anyone's name through the mud unless he could prove it. He went to Haskell for help, and Haskell led him on a wild goose chase."

"How did Haskell end up with one of the toy buildings from Payne's display?"

"Haskell used to hang out at Payne's all the time. When the police searched Haskell's apartment, they found a copy of Payne's house keys. Since he had access, the police figure Haskell probably printed a copy of Sizzle's key and broke in to set the fire."

"Why aren't they charging Payne with obstruction?" Martin asked. "If he knew about the fires and failed to disclose, he's responsible for allowing the damage to continue."

"You'd have to take that up with the police department," Cross said bitterly.

"Seriously, what is your deal with hating the police?" I asked, unable to hold my tongue. "Does it have anything to do with the woman with the leopard tattoo?"

"Did you tell her?" Cross asked Martin.

"No."

"Tell me what?"

Cross narrowed his eyes. "You're one hell of an investigator. I'll give you that." The doors to the elevator opened, and we exited into the garage. "James, I'll see you Tuesday."

"Sounds good." Martin shook Cross's hand. "Thanks for reaching out. And thanks for today."

Cross nodded. "Anytime." Martin slung his arm around my shoulders, heading toward the car when Cross cleared his throat. "Alex, I'll speak to legal tomorrow about benefits under your new contract. We'll work something out."

"I'm not holding my breath." I waited until Lucien got into his car before asking, "What haven't you told me?"

"Cross and I are going into business together."

"Why?"

"After the pitch he gave and hearing Jade's story, I couldn't say no."

I didn't understand Martin's sudden change of heart, and I fingered the charm around my neck, knowing the two events were somehow connected. "Jade?"

"When Cross first started out, before this place became this place, a woman came to him. She was in an abusive relationship. Her boyfriend beat her, abused her, isolated her from everyone and everything. She was terrified to leave him and even more terrified to stay." Martin looked uneasy and opened my car door. "He was a cop."

"Shit."

"Lucien promised he'd protect her. He set her up in an apartment, got her a new identity, but he didn't have the resources and network he does now."

"Her boyfriend found her."

Martin nodded. "Lucien tried to shield her, but she was shot four times in the leg Apparently, he was shot several times in the back. It was touch and go for months. Officially, the police said it was an unknown assailant with an automatic rifle. They said Jade's boyfriend intervened and was killed in the line of duty. However, it was a cover-up, and the police department settled with Cross. That's how Cross Security became Cross Security. The settlement came with a gag order, which is why Lucien can't talk about it, but that's the story Jade told me. It's why Lucien wants to develop body armor using biotextiles. He doesn't want history to repeat itself. He doesn't want any of his investigators or clients getting killed."

"And it's why he hates the police." I stared at Martin. "You're afraid that's going to happen to me."

"We practically lived the same story, except our villain wasn't a cop and you would have died trying to save me."

"If I'm remembering correctly, you actually shoved me out of the way. You almost died."

"Alex, I'm doing this. I have to. I have to do something."

"I get it. I just hate that you're compromising so much for me."

"I'm not." He shut my door and slid in beside me. "What new contract was Cross talking about?"

"I'm no longer a Cross Security employee. I'm a private contractor. He'll pass any cases they can't handle my way."

"How is that different from what you do now?"

"It's not," I rubbed the platinum band on his ring finger, "but the new designation allows Lucien to distance himself from the police and frees me to consult and take whatever jobs I want without implicating his firm in any possible legal fallout or conflicts of interest."

"Is this what you want?"

"It means I can walk anytime without penalty. You never know when that might come in handy, especially now that you and Lucien are in bed together. I thought we agreed to no threesomes."

"You can walk, just as long as the only person you're walking away from is Cross."

I laughed. "I can't walk away from you. You're tracking my every move."

"Like you would let that stop you."

I entwined my fingers with his. "I told you I'm sticking around, and I meant it. But you know I'm skittish. Don't push me too hard. And this better be the last time you do something without my consent." I fingered the charm before circling the two rings around my neck. He loved me, even if he had an odd way of showing it.

"It is. I swear."

"So what's Tuesday? Is that when you're implanting the tracking chip in my shoulder?"

"No. After the fire at your apartment, I decided to set up a charity for fire victims. The city has some stuff in place, but it's not enough. After witnessing the destruction firsthand, I wanted to do something. Apparently, Lucien had the same idea and approached me about partnering up. We're meeting Tuesday at the MT building to discuss it and other things."

"You remember the money I tried to pay you?"

"Uh-huh."

"Put it toward that."

Martin kissed my temple. "As our first official donor, you're entitled to certain perks."

"Like what?"

He whispered something highly inappropriate in my ear and gave me his patented devilish smirk. It was going to be a good night.

DON'T MISS THICK FOG, THE NEXT NOVEL
IN THE ALEXIS PARKER SERIES.

SIGN-UP TO BE NOTIFIED ABOUT THE
LATEST RELEASES.

http://www.alexisparkerseries.com/newsletter

ABOUT THE AUTHOR

G.K. Parks is the author of the Alexis Parker series. The first novel, *Likely Suspects,* tells the story of Alexis' first foray into the private sector.

G.K. Parks received a Bachelor of Arts in Political Science and History. After spending some time in law school, G.K. changed paths and earned a Master of Arts in Criminology/Criminal Justice. Now all that education is being put to use creating a fictional world based upon years of study and research.

You can find additional information on G.K. Parks and the Alexis Parker series by visiting our website at
www.alexisparkerseries.com